Hi Olivia!

Eric Wilson

Victoria 2015

Eric Wilson
Canadian Mysteries
VOLUME 3

Books by Eric Wilson

The Tom and Liz Austen Mysteries

1. Murder on The Canadian
2. Vancouver Nightmare
3. The Case of the Golden Boy
4. Disneyland Hostage
5. The Kootenay Kidnapper
6. Vampires of Ottawa
7. Spirit in the Rainforest
8. The Green Gables Detectives
9. Code Red at the Supermall
10. Cold Midnight in Vieux Québec
11. The Ice Diamond Quest
12. The Prairie Dog Conspiracy
13. The St. Andrews Werewolf
14. The Inuk Mountie Adventure
15. Escape from Big Muddy
16. The Emily Carr Mystery
17. The Ghost of Lunenburg Manor
18. Terror in Winnipeg
19. The Lost Treasure of Casa Loma
20. Red River Ransom

Also available by Eric Wilson

Summer of Discovery
The Unmasking of 'Ksan

Eric Wilson
Canadian Mysteries
VOLUME 3

THE EMILY CARR MYSTERY

THE ST ANDREWS WEREWOLF

THE INUK MOUNTIE ADVENTURE

ERIC WILSON

Harper*Trophy*Canada™
An imprint of HarperCollins*PublishersLtd*

As in his other mysteries, Eric Wilson writes here about imaginary people in a real landscape.

Find Eric Wilson at www.ericwilson.com

Eric Wilson Canadian Mysteries, Volume 3
Copyright © 2010 by Eric Wilson Enterprises, Inc.
The Emily Carr Mystery © 2001, 2003 by Eric Wilson Enterprises, Inc.
The St Andrews Werewolf © 1993, 2003 by Eric Wilson Enterprises, Inc.
The Inuk Mountie Adventure © 1995, 2003 by Eric Wilson Enterprises, Inc.

Chapter illustrations by Richard Row.

Published by Harper*Trophy*Canada™, an imprint of
HarperCollins Publishers Ltd

HarperCollins books may be purchased for educational, business, or sales promotional use through our Special Markets Department.

HarperCollins Publishers Ltd
2 Bloor Street East, 20th Floor
Toronto, Ontario, Canada
M4W 1A8

www.harpercollins.ca

The Emily Carr Mystery. First published in paperback by HarperCollins Publishers Ltd: 2001.
The St. Andrews Werewolf. First published in hardcover by HarperCollins Publishers Ltd: 1993. First paperback edition: 1994. Revised paperback edition: 1996.
The Inuk Mountie Adventure. First published in hardcover by HarperCollins Publishers Ltd: 1995.
These three books first published in this omnibus edition: 2010.

Library and Archives Canada Cataloguing in Publication information is available upon request.

ISBN 978-1-55468-824-1

Printed in the United States of America
RRD 9 8 7 6 5 4 3 2 1

Contents

The Emily Carr Mystery

For my dear wife, Flo,
and our friend Sadie

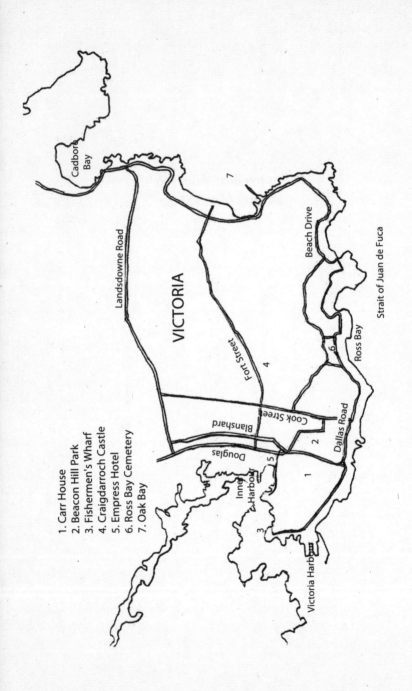

1. Carr House
2. Beacon Hill Park
3. Fishermen's Wharf
4. Craigdarroch Castle
5. Empress Hotel
6. Ross Bay Cemetery
7. Oak Bay

VICTORIA

Cadboro Bay
Landsdowne Road
Fort Street
Beach Drive
Blanshard
Cook Street
Douglas
Inner Harbour
Dallas Road
Ross Bay
Strait of Juan de Fuca
Victoria Harbour

1

Our boat was the greatest—a classic cruiser called the *Amor de Cosmos*.

But I wasn't happy.

I almost screamed as our cruiser heeled over. Cold spray whipped my face as we raced through the night. I grabbed for support, thinking I'd tumble into the dark sea waters.

From above, on the command bridge, came laughter. It was my friend Tiffany, who was feeling good. Tiff was beside the man she soon would marry—Paris deMornay. As I watched, Paris fed more horsepower to the twin turbocharged diesels—our cruiser leapt forward even faster through the waves, making me stagger.

Paris was movie-star handsome. A spotlight shone on his perfect face as he smiled at Tiffany. Paris was 22 and wore shorts, a sweater, and a gold necklace. Apparently his deck shoes had been shipped from an exclusive shop in Hawaii; Paris bought almost everything on the Internet.

The deMornay family was very wealthy, and so was Tiff's. The families were a unit, bonded together by the friendship of the two mothers. Paris was three years old when Tiffany was born; at the time the mothers quipped that eventually Paris and Tiffany should marry.

Then the family joke turned into reality. Tiff fell totally in love with Paris during her teens. It happened so easily—the families spent a lot of time together. Tiff and Paris made a natural couple.

Recently, though, tragedy had struck. Two years ago Paris lost his parents in a terrible car crash. He was especially devastated about his father, and Tiff had spent a lot of time consoling Paris. Then one day I learned that Tiffany had accepted his marriage proposal.

Now I was in Victoria for the wedding. But I was feeling upset—somehow, things didn't seem right. Sighing, I looked at the sky. A silvery moon watched from the glorious heavens; below, whitecaps raced across the waters.

"The lights of Victoria look so pretty from out here," I said to Tiffany, as she climbed down a ladder from the bridge. "Thanks for inviting me to British Columbia for your wedding. Imagine, two full weeks in Victoria—and I love it here."

Tiffany flashed her blue eyes my way. "That's wonderful, Liz." Tiny, blonde and pretty, 19 years old, she'd been raised in the exclusive world of the ultra-wealthy. With her own personal fortune Tiff could have bought and sold some countries, but she was the sweetest and most natural person. We'd met volunteering at a children's hospital in Winnipeg, and our friendship was the best. Tiff was two years older than me, but it didn't matter.

"Tiff," I said, "remember all those times Paris came to Winnipeg to see you? He was such a fun guy, and I was so happy about your wedding. But . . . somehow he's changed."

"Of course he has!" There was an edge to Tiff's voice, and I realized I'd touched a nerve. "How would you feel, Liz? His parents have died, and he's still grieving."

I braced myself against the rolling of the sea. "I guess you're right, Tiff. You know what? You always find the good in people."

"Liz, he needs me. Besides, I want children and a husband. I like the West Coast—I can be happy here." She lovingly touched her engagement ring. "Paris and I are in this together. Through the good times and the bad. We've got so much in common—"

Then Tiffany screamed. "*Look out*," she yelled at Paris. Tiff pointed across the sea. "That's the *Clipper*, and we're going straight at it!"

I stared at the *Clipper* as it raced out of the night. A high-speed catamaran carrying tourists between Seattle and Victoria, the *Clipper* rode above the water on two pontoons with an open space between.

Now I saw what Paris had planned—he was trying a daredevil stunt, aiming our boat directly at the space between the pontoons. "We'll never make it," I yelled into the shrieking wind. "Don't be crazy, Paris!"

Grinning, he fed more power to the diesels. From the *Clipper*, a loud horn split the night air—warning us of the danger. Tiffany and I grabbed the railing, horrified at the vision of the *Clipper* coming swiftly at us.

Suddenly our boat heeled over, changing course. With a laugh, and an arrogant wave of his hand at the other vessel, Paris took the *Amor de Cosmos* safely out of danger.

Grabbing the steel rungs of the ladder, I climbed to the command bridge. It rolled and pitched as Paris hotdogged the cruiser across the sea. Before him, on the control console, blue dials glowed.

"Listen, Paris," I said, "how about cutting back on the throttle."

"Sure, Liz, no problem."

The engines slowed, right down to a low growl. I heard whitecaps crashing against each other in the night.

"I was just having some fun," Paris added.

I didn't want to object once again to one of his stunts, so I said nothing about the *Clipper*. Instead, I commented, "This is a beautiful boat."

"It belonged to my father."

"You miss him, eh?"

"Yeah." Paris sighed.

"Listen," I said, "thanks for letting me stay at your estate while I'm in Victoria. That's generous of you, Paris."

"Hey, Liz, you're my fiancée's closest friend and one of her bridesmaids. I'm only sorry you can't be maid of honour. Why's that, anyway? Tiffany never told me."

"The maid of honour has to be at least 18 to sign the

wedding register. I'm a year too young."

"I'm sorry about that," Paris said with genuine sympathy.

"Robbed of the chance to be maid of honour at my best friend's wedding. Gee, you could have waited a year! But Tiff wants wedding bells, and the pitter-patter of little feet."

Paris grinned. "Tiffany sure loves kids. Me, too. I want a son and heir. We'll name him for my father."

Then Paris opened his cell phone; it had commanded attention by loudly playing "Jingle Bells."

"Yes?" Paris said. He listened for a moment, then replied, "Four K on Bigoted Earl. That's all I can manage. Goodbye, now."

Turning to me, Paris smiled. "I was going to mention, Liz, a lot of smuggling happens here. I thought you'd be interested."

Paris looked across the water at the lights of a distant city, sparkling on the shoreline of the United States. Above, the Olympic Mountains rose into the night sky. White snow glowed on some peaks, even though it was summer.

"That's Port Angeles over there," Paris explained. "It's in the state of Washington." He turned toward Victoria. "I can always spot the smugglers—maybe we'll see one tonight. They come out of Canada, moving fast, with no running lights. They carry drugs, forged credit cards, illegal immigrants. If someone can make a buck smuggling, they'll do it. Personally, I think it's crazy."

Tiffany joined us on the command bridge. As she cuddled against Paris, I took the other seat. From here, the view was beyond awesome. It was a total panorama—not a single tree or building blocked the horizon. I could see every star, even little faint ones. It was so romantic.

Tiffany snuggled closer to Paris. "Remember when you called me 'princess'? When we were kids? I loved that, Paris." She smiled at me. "We used to play wedding, and Paris would be the groom. I was Lady Diana."

Paris kissed her cheek. "Tiff, you'll always be my princess."

I smiled at him. "How'd you come up with your boat's name?"

"Amor de Cosmos was an actual dude, long ago. He arrived in British Columbia in the 19th century and ended up as premier, running the place. He started life as William Smith, then picked a new name—cool idea, eh? *Amor de cosmos* means 'lover of the universe.'"

Tiffany touched his dark hair. "That's a perfect description of you, sweetheart."

"My dad was quite the guy," Paris told me proudly. "A sports champion in his time, and adored by all the cuties. He bought this classic cruiser when he was young. The *Amor* has a cedar-strip hull on oak. I added the twin diesels for real power. They're turbocharged."

Tiffany glanced at her Rolex. "Let's head home, Paris. Daddy will be calling soon."

"Phone him on your cell, and we'll stay out longer."

Tiffany shook her head. "Daddy needs to know I'm safely home from the sea. Otherwise he won't be able to sleep."

"He's staying downtown at the Empress Hotel?" I asked.

Tiffany nodded. "Daddy loves that place."

Before long we approached Oak Bay, Victoria's luxurious neighbour. Through binoculars I studied the Oak Bay Beach Hotel, then the expensive mansions, houses, and condos along the shoreline. Lights glowed from the windows, looking cosy.

"What a sight under a full moon," Tiffany said. "It's like being in a dream."

"*Hey*," Paris exclaimed. Grabbing the binoculars from me, he looked north along the water in the direction of Thirteen Oaks, the estate owned by his family. "I see some boat, stopped abeam of my house. No running lights. Let's check this out."

"Could it be a smuggler?" I asked excitedly.

"Possibly."

"Be careful," Tiffany warned, as Paris fed maximum RPMs to the twin beasts that roared below decks. "This could be dangerous!"

We moved north along the shoreline, feeling the wind on our faces. As we approached the mystery craft, Paris studied it through his state-of-the-art night binoculars. "It's called the *Outlaw*. There's an open deck and a wheelhouse. Some guy's inside—I can see him. He's got blond hair and two gold earrings. Looks maybe 20 years old, 25 max."

Above the cliff stood an ancient mansion. Moonlight glowed on the ivy embracing its walls. The stone building was very large, dominating the enormous estate known as Thirteen Oaks. There were several chimneys; smoke curled from one. From the gardens of the estate, a crooked path led down to a beach. Nearby was a small island with no signs of habitation.

The *Amor de Cosmos* powered forward, moving in

on the mysterious *Outlaw*. Suddenly a spotlight glared across the water. A man's voice yelled, "Clear away."

Paris swore angrily. Veins bulged in his throat as he screamed, "Forget it, jerk. And what exactly are you doing? I live in that house up there." The engines rumbled as Paris moved our craft closer. "Who are you, anyway?" he cried across the water. "Identify yourself."

Silence from the *Outlaw*. I gripped the railing, aware of the painful throbbing of my heart. I was so scared.

Then Tiffany screamed. "A gun! Paris, he's got a gun!"

I stared across the tossing waves. "Holy Hannah." A nickel-plated revolver shone in the spotlight's glow. "That thing looks real. Let's—"

Fire burst from the muzzle. Something hummed past into the night, and then I heard the shot. It was total confusion on our boat as I dove for cover beside Tiffany while Paris grabbed for the throttle, and our cruiser leapt away across the waves.

"That was a real bullet," I yelled.

Paris looked behind. "He's coming after us, but we'll outrun him. This baby can really move."

The other boat fell away into the night as we escaped north. Then, without warning, the mighty roar of our engines turned to a coughing gasp, followed by utter silence. Out in the night, we heard the *Outlaw* coming our way.

2

"We're out of fuel," Paris yelled. "We'll have to swim for it."

Paris hurried forward to drop the anchor. Kicking off his deck shoes, he glanced toward the nearby shoreline. Then he dove into the night. His body describing a perfect arc, Paris sliced down into the sea—then surfaced.

"You next, Tiffany," he cried from the waves. "I'll swim with you, but hurry. I can see the spotlight. He's coming fast!"

Moments later, Tiffany was in the water and swimming toward safety. The other boat was getting close—the spotlight beam swept back and forth, searching. I was freaked out of my mind!

Kicking away from the *Amor*, I sailed out over the

waves. I flinched, then cut deep into the freezing waters of the Pacific.

Surfacing, I gasped for air. Wiping salty water from my eyes, I watched the spotlight play across the command bridge of the *Amor de Cosmos*. The other boat moved closer to the *Amor*; on its deck was a young man.

Whatever he held was on fire. A bottle stuffed with a flaming rag? Then I understood. *A Molotov cocktail*, I thought. *There's gasoline in that bottle*.

The weapon flew through the air, smashing on the deck of our boat. Almost immediately, it began to burn. Flames licked greedily across the hardwood. From the *Outlaw*, a voice called, "Don't mess with me."

As the *Outlaw* powered away, I started swimming toward shore. I was so cold, but I forced myself to keep moving. Seawater was in my eyes and getting down my throat, but finally I stumbled up a rocky beach. Tiffany and Paris were hiding behind a bush. Tiffany waved me over; her teeth were chattering.

"Are you okay?" I asked anxiously.

"Sure, I'm just so cold . . ."

Paris had his arms around Tiffany. "That's one serious dude. We were lucky to get out alive." His sombre eyes gazed across the water. Orange and red flames were eating into the wooden deck and up the deckhouse of the *Amor de Cosmos*. The fire spread quickly; black smoke smeared the stars.

"What would my dad say?" Paris groaned.

Tiffany squeezed his hand.

I looked at Paris. "Do you think that guy was planning a break-in at your estate?"

He nodded. "That's probably it."

On the sea, flames chased each other across the doomed vessel. They were reflected in the eyes of Paris deMornay. "I can't believe what I'm seeing. The *Amor* is finished."

"Honey, we're safe," Tiffany said gently. "That's what matters. The *Amor de Cosmos* was only a boat."

"Sure," Paris said, hanging his head. "But it was my father's boat."

* * *

The next evening, thunder boomed and lightning exploded across the sky. What drama! I was at Thirteen Oaks, sitting with Tiffany, Paris, and Paris's younger brother, Hart, on stone benches in the garden. We were watching an awesome light show illuminate the dark ocean waters. So far, rain had not fallen.

"Thunderstorms are unusual for Victoria," said Hart deMornay, smiling at me. Hart was 20, and there was also a younger teenage sister named Pepper. These were the deMornays; their parents' death had left them a large fortune that was controlled by a family trust.

Hart had luminous grey eyes and chestnut-brown hair; a lock fell across his lightly freckled face. He seemed really West Coast, like he'd been hiking through forests and windsurfing since childhood— which was true. "Wow," Hart exclaimed as a lightning bolt shot down, scattering bright colours across the sea. "What a spectacle."

"Here comes the rain," Paris said, as large drops pattered on the leaves above us. "Let's make a run for the house. Dinner will be served soon."

As we approached the front door, Paris signalled to a servant who stood waiting. Immediately the heavy wooden entrance swung open, and we all rushed inside. I was beside Tiffany, who was beautiful as always. My friend closely resembled Grace Kelly, the movie star who became a famous princess; all Tiff needed was a sparkling diamond tiara on her blonde head—and she'd probably get one as a wedding gift from her wealthy dad.

Tonight Paris was very stylish, wearing a white dress shirt and pleated light wool trousers. "What's the story on your estate?" I asked him. "It's an amazing place."

"This part of Victoria is called the Uplands," he explained. "It's super classy. One of my ancestors built this big old mansion. The deMornays are a famous family in Britain. My great-grandfather came out to Canada and made a fortune."

"Your name sounds French."

"Maybe"—Paris shrugged—"but I'm British aristocracy. If I lived in England, people would call me Lord Paris deMornay. Impressive, eh?"

"I saw the story in today's *Times Colonist* about your boat going down. I hope the police find that guy."

"The chances are slim," Paris replied. "A high-speed boat like the *Outlaw* would be difficult to capture."

We were walking along a wide hallway past old-fashioned furniture and oil portraits of the deMornay ancestors. What a gloomy bunch. Then I heard the opening notes of "Jingle Bells." Paris grabbed his cell phone, and fell back to answer. The others kept walking, but I hesitated. I remembered the phone call to the *Amor*. Some might call me nosy, but it comes with the territory. I was born to be a detective.

"I'll join you later," I whispered to Tiffany.

Pretending to adjust my shoe strap, I glanced at Paris as he listened to the person who had called. A frown creased his face. "I'll call you back," Paris said, snapping shut the phone.

Paris disappeared through a doorway. I counted to 10, then followed. Finding stairs, I climbed up past cold cement walls. In the upper hallway, small yellow lights gleamed above the oil portraits lining the walls.

I heard a voice from behind a door. It was Paris, talking on the phone. I tiptoed closer.

"Don't threaten me," I heard Paris say angrily. "You'll get every dollar, very soon. Yes, plus your exorbitant interest."

I held my breath, listening.

Then I heard a noise from down the hallway. Footsteps—someone was coming my way!

* * *

I was motionless, frozen, as a tall man approached. He wore formal clothing. His cheeks were hollow, his white hair was thin. It was Cambridge, the butler at Thirteen Oaks.

"Good evening, Miss Austen," Cambridge said with a dusty voice as he walked past.

A door opened, and Paris stared at me. The cell phone was in his hand. "Liz? Why aren't you at the dining room?"

"I . . . I'm lost."

"Huh?"

"I can't find my room."

Paris shook his head, looking impatient. "There's a map of Thirteen Oaks. Ask Pepper for a copy."

"Is that your office?" I asked, looking at the room behind Paris. "May I take a look?"

"Sure, I suppose so." Paris closed his cell phone, not bothering to say goodbye to his caller.

Meanwhile I began looking around. A portrait of Paris's father hung above the desk; clearly he'd once been handsome, but in the portrait looked stern and unfriendly.

I liked the large mahogany desk and the electronic gear, but I was highly offended by the sight of real animal heads mounted on the wall. A deer, a mountain goat—even a beautiful polar bear.

"That is so depressing," I exclaimed.

Paris glanced at the heads. "Hart and Pepper don't like them, either. My father bagged those trophies. He was quite the hunter. I inherited this office from him."

"You're getting rid of them, of course."

Paris shook his head. "Not a chance. Those trophies were my dad's pride and joy."

I decided to abandon the subject—Paris could be stubborn. Instead I asked a question. "What's your job, Paris?"

"Spending my share of the family fortune. Believe me, it's a full-time occupation. The deMornay family trust has plenty in the bank. Our ancestors made big money in British Columbia from lumber and coal and fish. Back then, the pickings were easy. Unions were weak or non-existent. We got rich."

I looked at the wastebasket, which contained a bunch of ripped-up lottery tickets. "How's your luck?"

"Not good, but my horoscope predicts a big win soon." Paris looked at me. "Tiffany says you're into arts."

I wondered if he was changing the subject.

Then I nodded. "I've learned some martial arts. Occasionally they come in handy."

"No, I mean stuff like painting. The Group of Seven and other famous artists."

"We studied those guys in school," I replied, "but I can't say I'm an expert."

"Care to see a unique treasure?"

"Sure thing."

At the ground floor we followed a long hallway. "I haven't been in this wing of the house," I told Paris.

He smiled. "It would take days to explore Thirteen Oaks. It's a big place—but my parents were happy here."

"Hey," I exclaimed, "what's with the laser beams?" We stopped at the door of a large library. Red beams, pencil-thin, shone from wall to wall.

"Any intruder steps into here," Paris said, "and the beams trigger alarms everywhere."

"What are you protecting?"

"Can I swear you to secrecy?"

"Of course."

Paris punched numbers on a security panel outside the library door. (I couldn't help noticing the code.) The red beams were instantly gone, although the room still seemed to glisten with their energy.

"You've heard of the acclaimed artist Emily Carr, of course," Paris said, as we stepped into the library. As well as lots of books, there were several leather sofas and mahogany writing desks.

I nodded. "She's really famous. Every Christmas my brother and I give Mom the new Emily Carr calendar. Mom loves her paintings."

"Miss Carr was born in Victoria in 1871," Paris said, "the same year that B.C. became the sixth province of Canada. For many years she travelled British Columbia by horseback and canoe, capturing totem poles and forest scenes and First Nations communities with her artistry. It's beautiful stuff. The way she did some forests, it's like the trees are actually moving—you can feel the power of the wind. Most of those old totem poles were collected by museums, or rotted and fell down, so it's good she recorded them in their original settings."

"In grade 10 we read Emily Carr's book *Klee Wyck*," I said. "Our teacher said that means 'Laughing One.' Klee Wyck was Emily Carr's honorary name, given to her by the First Nations. Mrs. Silsbe told us the people liked Emily Carr."

Paris turned to the fireplace, where no fire burned. Above the mantel was a large oil painting. It showed totems outside wooden longhouses; I could see people chatting, and canoes pulled up on shore. In the foreground, a woman laughed heartily. Beside her was a child with solemn eyes. The woman's face was radiant with life. Printed in a corner was *M. EMILY CARR*, followed by the date *1912*.

"Is that Emily Carr? The woman in the picture?"

"No," Paris replied. "I imagine she was a resident of that village back in 1912, when Miss Carr painted this picture."

"I haven't seen it before," I said. "It's never been in Mom's calendars."

"That's because it's a secret," Paris explained. "You're looking at Emily Carr's unknown masterpiece. It's called *Klee Wyck*."

"Just like her book," I commented.

Paris nodded. "Miss Carr gave the picture to my grandfather, in return for something she wanted from our family store downtown. She was usually broke—a typical artist. Her paintings didn't become really valuable until after her death." A smirk touched his perfect lips. "Emily Carr desperately needed furniture, so Grandfather traded some junky old stuff in return for this painting. Our family did well, and no one got hurt. Thanks to my clever grandfather, we own an Emily Carr original that is unknown to art collectors. Can you imagine its value?"

"Multi gazzilions, at least," I said, shaking my head. "No wonder all the security."

"I promised my father I'd protect this painting," Paris said, "and never sell it." In the hallway he punched in the code, and the red lasers bounced back to life. "It's time to eat."

"Where's the dining room?" I asked.

"I'll lead the way," Paris responded. "This is a big old house, eh, with lots of crooked hallways. I used to explore this place with Hart and Pepper when we were kids."

We turned a corner—and the others were visible in the distance. I could see Tiffany chatting with Hart and Pepper deMornay. The dining room was like something from an old horror movie. Outside tall windows, rain lashed down on a marble statue of a Greek goddess and blew in crooked streams across the glass.

Thunder crackled and lightning split the sky. Around the table were solemn servants wearing white aprons over black dresses, with white caps on their heads. They were serving food to Tiffany and the others, who sat on hard chairs at a long table surrounded by the large, dark spaces of the bleak room.

A gust of wind, smelling of the sea, guttered tall candles along the table. I hurried to join Tiffany, who was giggling with Hart deMornay, who looked *really good* by candlelight.

"Sorry I'm late," I said.

Turning to Pepper, I smiled hello. Pepper deMornay was 17, like me. She was a single parent with an 18-month-old named Amanda. Pepper's eyes were big and brown, and she was very friendly. Pepper's chestnut-coloured hair fell to her shoulders, and was beautifully cut. She wore a nice blouse, jeans, and cowboy boots.

To my right, a face leaned in. It was sad-looking Cambridge, the family butler whom I had seen earlier upstairs. Cambridge was middle-aged, but acted older. He took my order for a glass of chocolate milk, then withdrew.

We were served B.C. salmon for dinner, and it was really toothsome. Tiffany and I talked to Hart about his love of the wilderness, and I could tell that Tiff was impressed by Hart's passion for life.

Then Tiffany accidentally dropped her fork; she looked embarrassed, but I just smiled. "That means a female visitor," I told her. "If you'd dropped a knife, Thirteen Oaks could expect a male visitor."

She grinned. "Oh, Liz. You and your superstitions."

Hart turned to Paris. "There was a call from the Royal Victoria Yacht Club. Your membership payment is way overdue, but I guess that doesn't matter now."

This upset Paris, and the brothers began arguing.

As they bickered, Pepper leaned close to me and murmured, "Did you see *Klee Wyck*?"

I nodded. "How'd you guess?"

"I told Paris to show you," Pepper replied. "I figured you'd be interested. Liz, is the security code still 7-7-6-6?"

When I hesitated, Pepper grinned. "So, it is, eh? I knew you'd notice. It's about time Paris changed the code. It's been used for weeks. All the servants probably know it by now."

She stopped talking as a servant presented us with frosted silver dishes of my favourite dessert, ice cream! "Did you know," Pepper said, "that Emily Carr was profiled on *Biography* in June? They did a week of famous artists." Pepper shook her head. "I bet the value of *Klee Wyck* rises by thousands of dollars every minute."

A deep *boom-boom-boom* came from the grandfather clock in a gloomy corner. Pepper jumped and nervously checked her watch before turning to Tiffany.

"Would you hold Amanda for a while?"

"For sure."

As my friend eagerly accepted the bundle of joy, Pepper picked up her cell phone from the table and left the dining room. I smiled at Tiffany—she seemed totally at peace whenever she cuddled Amanda. Tiff adored babies and was looking forward to starting a family.

When Pepper returned to her chair, she glanced at

Paris. "You still think my idea is stupid?"

"You mean the recording studio you're going to buy? The one that's vastly overpriced?"

"I'm going to become a music producer, Paris, and you can't stop me."

"Pepper, your idea is *so* bad, I've gotta laugh. You're always talking about stuff you're going to do. First it was producing for television, then lamebrain dot-com investments. Get a grip, Pepper. You're an unwed teenaged mother. How are you going to be a successful producer?"

"I'll have the money soon," Pepper declared. "You wait and see."

Hart leaned forward to squeeze her hand. "Personally, sis, I like your idea a lot. You could do anything, you're that smart."

Pepper blushed. "Thanks," she said, smiling shyly.

Tiffany looked at her fiancé. "Please stop arguing with Pepper and Hart, okay? Lately there's so much yelling. My nerves can't take it."

Pepper looked at her brother with hostility. "Ever since Mom and Dad died, you've been different. You're so crabby and jittery. Your friends were always phoning, and now you sit alone. What happened to all your snowboarding pals? When your money dried up, they did, too?"

Paris slammed his hand against the mahogany table. "Mind your own business, Pepper. Just leave me alone, okay?"

Standing up, he hurried from the room. Tiffany immediately went after him, and I followed. I found my friend in a dark hallway, staring moodily at the portraits lit by small lights. "Where'd Paris go?" I asked.

Tiffany shook her head. "He's disappeared. This old mansion is full of secret passages, and the deMornays know them all."

"Secret passages? Really?"

"That's what Pepper was saying."

"Tiff, *is* Paris different these days?"

"Sure, Liz, but he's under tremendous pressure. Cut him some slack, okay?"

"I'll try my best, Tiff," I replied, vowing to refrain from further comment.

We wandered in silence through the gloomy old mansion, and then I grabbed Tiffany by the arm. "Look," I whispered.

In the distance was the library, home to the highly prized painting by Emily Carr. But something was wrong—we couldn't see the lasers that provided security for the artwork.

Then a flashlight beam cut the darkness inside the library. It flickered and flashed—a spooky image. Next we saw a young man step into the hallway. He wore black jeans, a jacket, and a woollen cap. Two golden hoops glittered in his right ear.

He was carrying the painting.

3

Glancing at Tiffany, I put a warning finger to my lips as we shrank back against the wall. My heart was pounding overtime—what if the guy heard us?

Kneeling down in the hallway, he swiftly removed the painting from its frame. He used some kind of staple remover; each *kachunk* was a scary sound, echoing past us. Rolling up the painting, the intruder quickly slipped it inside a large metal tube. Then he was gone, disappearing down a hallway. It was all over in seconds.

Tiff stared at me in horror. "Liz, what should we do? Paris is going to be *freaked*. That painting meant everything to his father."

"Okay, Tiff, take it easy. Let's follow that guy."

Was this crazy? I wasn't sure, but my friend was highly agitated and I wanted to help. "This way," I said, leading Tiffany along the shadowy hallway. From the distance came sounds; we followed for what seemed an eternity. Down one hallway we went, then another.

Eventually we felt fresh air on our faces and smelled the ocean. We reached an open door—outside, the rain was pouring down. A concrete path led to the nearby shore, where I saw an old wharf. On the sea was a boat I recognized. It was the *Outlaw*.

Almost for sure, the stolen painting was on board.

As the vessel raced away into the night, Tiffany stared after it. She looked so sad. "We've lost the Emily Carr. I can't believe this has happened."

* * *

Tiffany and I were silent as we returned to the library. The laser beams remained down, their mission in ruins. The others had discovered the theft and were standing outside the library. Hart, Pepper, Paris, even Cambridge and several servants—they all clustered around us. Everyone kept saying, *What happened . . . What happened*? Paris was so upset; he didn't say a word, but his fists were curled up hard.

The abandoned frame lay in the hallway outside the library. "Don't touch the frame," I warned. "The police will want to dust it for fingerprints. That thief wasn't wearing gloves."

Paris started to speak, then changed his mind.

Everyone was glum as we went into the library. I looked at the large empty space above the mantel, then turned to the circle of watching faces. "This was an inside job," I declared. "Someone helped that thief."

Hart stared at me. Then he asked Cambridge to bring some coffee to the library.

"Have you called the police?" I asked Paris.

He gazed into the empty fireplace. "No."

"But why?" I asked.

"The police weren't called because we don't want publicity. No one knows about our painting—and that's how it stays. This information stays inside the family."

"I know about it."

"Sure, because you're my fiancée's best friend and you're trustworthy. No one else must learn the secret."

I was amazed at such foolishness. Without police help, the family might never recover the *Klee Wyck*. I turned to the others, expecting astonishment equal to mine. But no one cared. Pepper looked bored and Hart was whispering something to Tiffany.

Then Tiff looked at me. "I agree with Paris. We must protect our families—that's what counts the most."

Not impressed, I shook my head at their folly. Paris smiled, obviously pleased that he'd demonstrated who was boss at Thirteen Oaks.

* * *

Tiffany and I left the library, heading for our rooms.

"Paris really should call the police," I commented. "After all—"

"Let's trust him," Tiff snapped. "Paris knows what he's doing."

"Okay," I replied. "I didn't mean to upset you."

"Don't worry about it, Liz. I'm just on edge."

We stood for a moment outside Tiffany's bedroom. "Lock your door," I urged her. Tiff smiled at me with huge angel eyes. She seemed so fragile, like the famous Tiffany glass designs that share her name.

"I like Hart," I said. "He's nice."

She smiled. "That guy has so much energy."

Saying goodnight, I opened the door to my bedroom. The storm was over. Bright moonlight shone through the tall windows, glinting from the crystal angel I'd hung there.

Crossing the large room, I looked at the midnight garden. The radiance of the silver moon filled the sky, spreading a shining lustre over bushes and trees. A driveway curved past rolling lawns toward the estate's main gate. Somewhere in the night a vehicle passed on Beach Drive; I heard its tires on the wet pavement, but tall trees hid it from view.

I yawned hugely—what an evening. Going into the bathroom, I brushed and flossed at the marble sink while thinking about the mansion's strange inhabitants. Wearing my favourite PJs, I crawled into the big four-poster bed, made notes about the case, and then fell sound asleep.

* * *

Up early the next morning, I went outside. The first gentle rays of sunshine lit the garden leaves, green and wet with dew. The grass was so beautiful—it looked like velvet. The garden was filled with honeyed scents.

Surrounded by roses and sweet honeysuckle, I wandered through the gardens of the estate, then approached the ocean. The sea air was delicious—I snuffled the morning breezes like a cat and let sunshine warm my face.

"Hi there."

Turning, I saw Hart deMornay climbing a path from the shoreline below. His face was radiant. Grinning at me, Hart swept back a lock of wavy brown hair. Beyond him, sunshine sparkled on the ocean, where seagulls swooped and played.

"I was out in my kayak," Hart explained. "Hey, Liz, you look all sunshine and happiness."

"Thanks." I was pleased. "Actually, I've been feeling down."

"Because of the robbery?"

"I guess so."

"You're a private eye type, eh? Got any theories?"

I studied Hart's large eyes and pleasant face. He looked so trustworthy, and yet . . .

Then Hart spoke. "Liz, be careful. My brother has a short temper. Don't rattle him."

"Hey! Paris and I are best buddies."

"Maybe once," Hart said with a smile. "But not now."

Opening the door of a small shed, he stowed the kayak's paddle inside. I looked at the scuba gear on the walls. "Look at this stuff!"

"All my family scuba," Hart told me. "Pater taught us."

"Who?"

Hart grinned. "*Pater* means 'father' in Latin. It's a snobby way of saying Daddy, and my father was a snob. Worse, he was a rich snob." Hart glanced suddenly at me. "When the *Amor de Cosmos* was firebombed, did you recognize the person who threw the Molotov cocktail?"

"No," I replied.

"Are you sure?"

"Of course," I said, smiling. "I'm very observant."

"Because—"

A screen door slammed, then Pepper appeared on the porch with her baby. Pretty in pink, Amanda looked so cute in her mother's arms. "Hey, you two," Pepper said, "come for breakfast. Liz, please tell me again about the werewolf in New Brunswick. I like that story."

"Okay." I grinned. "But this will be the third time."

"I'll join you shortly," Hart said. "I've got an important phone call to make."

Pepper and I ate in a pleasant sunroom overlooking both the ocean and the driveway. Just offshore was the small island I'd noticed before, its many trees emerald green in the morning sunshine. "I'd love to explore that island," I said. "Is there a rowboat or something I could use to get there?"

Pepper surprised me with a warning. "Stay away from that island, Liz. During the last war it was used by the army for training exercises. There are unexploded bombs and mines, all over the place."

"Are you certain?"

"Of course. It's called Hidden Island. I know everything about Thirteen Oaks. I'm totally into the past, just like Hart." She paused, thinking. "I guess we're both curious, like our mom. She was always talking history." Pepper sighed. "I wish I'd lived back when Thirteen Oaks was built. All that luxury, and all those parties. Sometimes, these days, I get so bored."

* * *

Arriving at the sunroom, Hart poured us all a glass of organic apple juice. It was some good. As I was downing a second glass, we heard a car stop outside.

"It's Laura," Pepper said, immediately leaving the room.

"What a car," I exclaimed, gazing out the window at a top-of-the-line BMW. Behind the steering wheel was a woman in her 30s; her auburn hair was stylishly swept back from an intelligent face with large, expressive eyes. Her makeup was immaculate. "I told Tiffany there'd be a female guest," I said, smiling at Hart.

"That's our family lawyer," Hart said. "Her name is Laura Singlehurst. Laura is responsible for the family trust. All the expenses at Thirteen Oaks are paid by the trust, and we each receive a large allowance." Hart glanced at me. "I don't need extra money—I own a company that does well in ecotourism. So I donate my allowance to the Hospice Society."

"Laura looks so interesting," I said, as the lawyer stepped from her elegant vehicle. From the colour of her car to her earrings, dress, and shoes, Laura was totally coordinated. Everything was the same lovely shade of green.

"Laura's very pleasant," Hart said. "I like her, and Pepper does, too. Laura's kind of a mother figure—if someone that glamorous can be called Mom." Hart chuckled. "But Paris hates Laura because she refuses to increase his allowance. You've heard that a fool and his money are soon parted—well, Paris is a perfect example."

As I stood up from the kitchen table, I saw Pepper approach Laura. They had a short conversation that left Pepper scowling.

"Laura didn't approve of Pepper dropping out of school because of the baby," Hart explained to me. "Sometimes Laura gets too bossy with Pepper. She can take the mother figure stuff a bit too far, if you know what I mean."

"Why don't you say something to her?"

Hart gave me a rueful smile. He swept back a lock of chestnut-coloured hair. "I guess I'm not very assertive, Liz."

Outside, the summer air was warm. Hart introduced me to Laura, who was kind and charming. We chatted about the wedding, then Laura produced a copy of the Victoria *Times Colonist*. "Look at this, Hart," she said proudly, opening to a report on the city's social scene. "I'm mentioned again today by Jim Gibson." She thrust the newspaper into Hart's hand. "Keep this copy—I've got more."

"You're always in the newspaper, Laura. With all the publicity, you'd be a natural for politics."

"Not a chance." Laura leaned on the car horn. Its sharp sound vibrated off the stone walls of the house, making birds fly up from the garden.

The sleepy face of Paris deMornay looked down from an upstairs window. "What's with the noise?"

"Get down here fast," Laura called to him. "I've got news about your stolen painting."

Paris stared at Laura in amazement, then he disappeared from the window.

Hart's face also registered astonishment. "How'd you know the *Klee Wyck* was stolen? My brother strong-armed us into silence on that one."

The lawyer held up her cell phone. "I just had a call from some guy demanding a ransom."

"Could you identify his voice?" I asked.

Laura shook her head. "Only that he sounded young. Maybe 20 or so."

"Have you got call display?"

Laura nodded. "It said Unknown Caller. He was at a pay phone, I think. I could hear traffic sounds. Then a construction jackhammer started pounding, and he cut the connection."

Paris joined us and heard the details. "We must pay the ransom," he declared. "How much is it?"

Laura produced a pocket notebook. She'd written the ransom demand in ink the same elegant colour as her car.

When Paris saw the ransom, his face turned white. "That's . . . it's so much, I . . ."

"It's a lot," Laura agreed, "but the trust has enough money. However, that's only if you three considerably reduce your allowances for the next two years."

Paris gulped. His skin was pale, and he hadn't shaved. "We'll pay the ransom," he said at last. "That painting was Pater's favourite thing, and I just can't face losing it."

"That's okay with me," Hart said, and Pepper nodded her agreement.

"What happens next?" I asked Laura.

"I was told to expect another phone call, but I don't know when."

Paris looked at us all. "Say nothing about the painting being gone. I don't want the media to get wind of this story."

"What about the police?" I asked. "Have you changed your mind about telling them?"

"No way," Paris replied vehemently.

* * *

Later that day, Tiffany and I left Oak Bay for downtown Victoria. Her father had arrived a week earlier from Winnipeg and was staying at the world-famous Empress Hotel. He was treating us to the hotel's celebrated Afternoon Tea at four o'clock.

Tiffany drove a candy-apple red Jeep, open to the sky. On the radio aerial, a Canadian flag whipped back and forth. The air was sweet as we zoomed along Rockland Avenue, Tiff's favourite route to downtown. Sometimes we'd detour past Craigdarroch Castle so we could gaze at the impressive setting for her forthcoming wedding.

"Victoria has police radar," I warned, noting the 30-kilometre speed limit.

As a gesture to me, Tiffany slowed down. Leafy trees shaded the road, which curved past ancient mansions featuring massive, amazing gardens. Every size of blossom seemed represented in the Rockland neighbourhood.

"Listen, Tiff," I said, "has Paris mentioned someone called Bigoted Earl?"

She nodded. "Paris often goes to Sandown to see the earl."

"What's Sandown?"

Tiffany shrugged. "I've no idea."

She glanced at her diamond—a big, honking solitaire. "The castle is up that street," she said, gesturing past the trees. "But I guess you know that."

"You always talked about a church wedding, Tiff. That was your dream."

She nodded. "Yeah, but Daddy insists on the castle for the wedding. He's showing off, I think—but what can you do?"

"I hate to repeat myself, but isn't 19 kind of young for marriage?"

Tiffany smiled comfortably. "Princess Victoria, daughter of Queen Victoria, was married at 17—"

"You've told me that, but . . ."

"In the upper classes, Liz, many young people are pledged to each other. I've known couples to marry the moment they're of legal age. That way the benefits can get started. Like combining families and fortunes, and maybe titles."

"And how do you feel about Paris? Still happy?"

Tiff produced a smile of sweet innocence. "Paris loves me, Liz. Since I was 12, I knew I really did want to marry him. We're so good together—and we understand each other." Her voice trailed off, and she frowned. Then she seemed to shake off her thoughts. "Anyway," she said brightly, "we've been through the same fires growing up. Both our fathers demanded a lot of us, right from childhood. It turned into a terrible burden for Paris. He could never meet his father's expectations. I understand that, and I help Paris with his feelings. He really needs me."

"What do *you* need, Tiff?"

She shrugged. "To have a family, and to know my parents are okay."

"What about college or university? You're very bright. You could have a career."

"I've got a lifetime supply of money, Liz. I don't need a career. I want my very own babies, a real family, and then I'm going to establish a charitable foundation. I'll help children, especially in war zones."

The Jeep hung a left, and we moved south under leafy boughs. In Cook Street Village the chestnut trees were glorious, shading little shops and wide sidewalks where people read newspapers outside coffee shops and lovers kissed.

As we approached the ocean I began to notice the wind, how it bent trees low. I saw whitecaps out on the sea racing toward shore.

"It's a windstorm," Tiff said. "Let's go watch."

She followed Dallas Road to St. Charles, where we found parking. "Hart brought me here during a storm," Tiffany said, as we left the Jeep. "It was so awesome. The waves were, like, huge."

The white buildings along the seashore reminded me of the Mediterranean, and so did the sea. The breakers were blue and green, tossed and turbulent. Spray flew away as they pounded ashore, noisily rattling stones when the waters ran back into the sea. In the distance, wave after wave crashed on the stony beach and came racing toward us along the shoreline.

I noticed that police had set up a roadblock, preventing vehicles from using this section of Dallas

Road during the storm. Huge waves crashed against the concrete roadway, scattering ocean foam and seawater across the pavement.

I looked at the far side of the roadway. "What's there?"

"Ross Bay Cemetery. Cambridge told me it's the oldest burial ground in the city. Some famous people are in it, like Emily Carr."

"Wow," I suddenly exclaimed, pointing at the ocean pounding the roadway. "Look at that *vision*."

Out of the waves came a blond runner, a tall guy in his late teens. Head down, he plunged through the cascading waves with total determination. He was soaked but he kept moving.

"He's really something," I said, watching as the runner stopped at a small low-rider truck parked nearby on St. Charles. The windows were tinted; I couldn't see the driver. "Maybe that truck's from Seattle."

"How come?"

"It's got a Washington plate."

Tiff smiled. "You're so observant."

"I forgot my camera," I replied, "and I regret my foolishness. I could use a photo of that dreamboat. Maybe he's in movies. Lots of shows get made in B.C."

"Put that guy on the screen and he'll be the next big thing."

A window rolled down. I couldn't see the driver, but it seemed he was speaking to the blond guy. Then the runner was handed a wad of bills. After carefully counting the money, he disappeared up St. Charles. The truck also took off. I never got a look at the driver.

4

Soon after, Tiffany parked the Jeep near downtown on Burdett. This was a pleasant street of apartment buildings and dignified mansions dominated by a massive cathedral. As Tiffany snapped a locking device on the steering wheel, I nodded my approval.

Sunlight filtered down through the leaves. A clergyman riding an old bicycle waved hello, and a young mother pushing a baby carriage smiled at us. "It's a friendly town," I commented to Tiffany, as we walked to Fort Street for some shopping on Antique Row.

Our mission was to purchase gifts for the wedding party, then meet Tiffany's dad for Afternoon Tea at the Empress Hotel. Many of the storefronts made me think of Olde England, back in the days of Scrooge and his creator, Charles Dickens. Displayed in windows along the street were many treasures, from antique jewellery to the finest furniture.

In a jewellery shop, Tiffany studied two large buttons on display. "Objects are different when they're old," she said. "These buttons are so heavy, eh? I bet they're from a soldier's uniform, back in the First World War."

Tiff studied the Latin inscription on the buttons. "You know something, Liz? I have a real emotional affinity for those times. Even when I was very small I was fascinated by images from the days of the British Empire." Tiffany paused. "If ever I lived before," she said, "it was then."

Back outside, we wandered past an upscale auction house. "Look at these classic train sets," I said, stopping at the window. "My brother Tom would love this place—"

"Liz, look!" Tiffany pointed into the auction house. "That painting—it's Lady deMornay. But I saw it at Thirteen Oaks, just days ago. It was in the morning room. That's where Lady deMornay used to sit, watching the sea."

Tiffany snapped open her miniaturized cell phone. "Hello, Paris?" she said, moments later. "Listen, that portrait of your mother has maybe been stolen. Liz and I just spotted it, up for auction."

As she listened to Paris, Tiffany frowned. "But she's your own mother, Paris. How could you auction her portrait? Hart and Pepper will be devastated." Tiffany kept talking, then stared at the phone.

"He hung up on me."

I started to comment, then pointed in the window of the auction house. "Tiffany, look who's in there."

"Oh, gosh—it's Cambridge, the butler."

"See how he's staring at the portrait of Lady deMornay? Like he's going to start crying."

We watched Cambridge for a few minutes, but nothing much happened. I felt impatient to do something— to make progress on this case. Opening a map of Victoria, I located the Maritime Museum. "We could check their records for information about the *Outlaw*. Like who's the owner and where it's registered."

"Sure, let's try that," Tiffany immediately replied. "Anything to find the painting. Paris was in a really bad mood this morning."

* * *

Without highrise towers to block the sun, the downtown streets were bright and attractive. They were crowded with tourists and shoppers and office workers. People looked so fit and healthy!

"Look at that crow," I said, pointing. It had landed on a bicycle that leaned against a lamp standard; in the bicycle basket was a shopping bag containing bagels. The crow took a bagel, then lifted off with it.

"Stop, thief," Tiffany called, laughing.

At Bastion Square we found a lively street market with booths selling artwork and wonderful crafts. I got started on my own gift list by finding something pretty for my mom (earrings made of cobalt-blue glass beads), then we went inside the Maritime Museum.

With luck, we happened to meet the museum's director, a nice woman named Yvonne. "We're looking for information about a boat called the *Outlaw*," I said. "Can you help?"

"Perhaps," Yvonne said. "Let's try the library."

She escorted us into an unusual elevator. "This is the oldest operating birdcage elevator in Canada," Yvonne told us.

The double metal doors clanked closed, and our birdcage began to rise. I grinned. "This is cool."

At the top floor, Yvonne opened the elevator door. "There are some beautiful old buildings in Victoria, many dating back to the gold rush. This one is from the 19th century; it used to be the courthouse. You've heard of Matthew Begbie?"

We both shook our heads.

"They called him the Hanging Judge because of the number of people he sentenced to die. This is the actual building where he presided."

The ceiling of the library was high; above us, portraits of British royalty were displayed beside the Canadian coat of arms. "You know something I like about Victoria?" I said. "All the connections to England. Like those British candy shops we've seen."

The museum's librarian, Lynn, was smart like Yvonne. Diligently searching the archives and photo files, they managed to discover one vessel named the *Outlaw*. "It's listed in *Lloyd's Register* of ships," Yvonne said, studying a thick volume. "But it can't be your *Outlaw*. This one's a freighter, built in 1946 for general cargo and registered in Malta. I'm sorry, I guess you're out of luck. Probably the boat you're seeking has never been registered. It's an *Outlaw*, just like its name implies."

I smiled at them. "Thanks, anyway, for trying."

In the hallway we stopped at an original poster from 1911 showing the *Titanic* and her sister ship, the

Olympic. A shiver went through me, thinking of the iceberg and that horrifying night.

Inside the birdcage elevator again, we descended noisily to the ground floor, where Yvonne introduced us to a bearded man named Richard, who also worked there. Richard wore a tie displaying nautical flags, and he was an expert on matters of the sea.

"My suggestion," he said, after hearing our story, "is to visit Fishermen's Wharf. Ask for Fossilized Pete. If anyone's heard of the *Outlaw*, it'll be Pete." Richard smiled at us. "Tell you what, I'll phone Pete and set up a meeting. He's a friend of mine."

I spoke to Pete, who sounded friendly, and we arranged to meet in the early evening. After thanking Richard, we returned to Bastion Square with Yvonne, who was going on a break. Above our heads, flags fluttered in the summer breeze. A few paces from the museum, Yvonne showed us a row of bricks embedded in the pavement. "The wall of Fort Victoria was here." Yvonne looked toward the city's nearby Inner Harbour. "The fort started at the ocean and ran past us to Government Street. Things were pretty calm in Victoria until the big gold rush of 1858. Twenty thousand prospectors came through here, heading for the goldfields."

Tiffany looked at Yvonne. "We're on Vancouver Island, right? But the city of Vancouver is over on the mainland. That's, like, totally confusing."

"I agree," Yvonne said. "George Vancouver was an English sea captain who mapped the waters of the Pacific Northwest. Adding to the confusion, in Washington state there's another city named Vancouver."

"Wasn't Captain Vancouver eaten by cannibals?"

"No." Yvonne shook hands goodbye. "Look for the statue of Captain James Cook near the Empress Hotel—he once explored these waters. You'll also see Captain Vancouver, high atop the Legislative Building. And good luck in finding the *Outlaw*."

"We'll do our best," I promised her.

* * *

At Government Street a busker was thumping a guitar, while his friend sang with a powerful voice. "They're great," Tiffany exclaimed at the end of the song. She gave them a generous donation.

"Wow, thanks," the boy said, staring at the money.

The singer hugged Tiffany. "You're so cool."

"Where's the food bank?" Tiffany asked.

The singer pointed north. "It's on Queens."

Soon we reached the Mustard Seed Food Bank, which was a busy place. "There are a lot of young families," I said in dismay. "Look at all the kids. It's shocking."

"I know," Tiffany replied sadly. "It's so wrong that a country as wealthy as Canada allows children to live in poverty. It's a national disgrace."

Tiffany asked to meet the manager of the Mustard Seed, then wrote out a cheque. The manager gasped when she saw the amount Tiffany was donating. "Thank you so much. Let me show you around the premises."

As we returned to sunshine, Tiffany consulted her watch. "Time to meet Daddy."

"Will your mother be attending the wedding?" A year earlier there'd been a divorce, and Tiff's mother now lived on Grand Cayman Island.

Tiff shook her head. "For some reason she no longer approves of Paris, and she and Daddy haven't been getting along lately, so it's probably for the best."

Tiffany was looking anxiously along Johnson Street. "Oh, good—there's a Kabuki Kab."

Kabukis are popular with tourists in Victoria. You sit in a cab attached behind a bicycle, and the driver describes why he loves this city while pedalling you to a destination.

Our driver was friendly, and I enjoyed the ride. Soon we arrived at Victoria's Inner Harbour, where the waters of the Pacific reach into the heart of the city. People were posing for pictures; beyond them was the spectacular sight of the provincial Legislative Buildings, where British Columbia's government holds its meetings. Above the imposing stone walls were many green domes, the tallest topped by a golden statue of Captain Vancouver. Many other buildings overlooked the water; some were brick and stone structures still surviving from the gold rush days, but we also saw the latest in luxury condos and upscale hotels.

Plus, of course, there was the fabled Empress.

A favourite of Hollywood stars and the very wealthy, the enormous hotel dominated the scene. Its walls rose high above to a giant Canadian flag that fluttered against the blue sky.

Two friendly doormen in fancy uniforms welcomed us to the Empress; the lobby was filled with huge bouquets of fresh flowers radiating sweet fragrances. Right away I spotted Tiff's dad, Major Wright. His skull shone beneath grey, brushcut hair; the Major was short, resembling a small bulldog in a three-piece suit as he paced back and forth while glancing impatiently at his gold watch. Tiffany's father was proud to have served in the armed forces, and still liked to be called "the Major."

"Daddy," Tiffany cried, running to her father for a hug.

They were obviously pleased to see each other. I shook hands with the Major. "Thank you for inviting us," I said. "I'm looking forward to this."

Major Wright smiled at me. "It's good to see you again, Liz."

People were lined up, waiting their turn to enjoy the ceremony of "taking tea" in the grand hotel's original tea lobby. Portraits of long-ago British monarchs were displayed against elegant wallpaper. We saw many exquisite flowers and even some genuine palm trees. Silver spoons clinked inside china cups. I could smell the delicious tea, and my mouth watered at the sight of the goodies being served.

"Look at the whipped cream," I whispered to Tiffany. "For sure I'm having crumpets with jam and *dollops* of whipped cream."

Major Wright snapped his fingers at a waiter. "We have a table reserved."

Soon we were seated under a portrait of Queen Mary, who wore many diamonds. "This hotel was named in honour of Queen Victoria," the Major told us, as our waiter poured tea from a silver pot. "She was the Empress of India."

"These cucumber sandwiches are so good," I said, then took another bite.

Major Wright beamed at his daughter. "Great news. I've sold our house in Winnipeg. I'm moving to Victoria, to be close when my grandchildren start arriving. My life has changed for the best, Tiffany, all thanks to your forthcoming marriage."

"That's nice, Daddy."

"My own little girl will soon be Lady deMornay, chatelaine of Thirteen Oaks. Liz, isn't that great?"

"Major Wright, you're an expert on titles. Why can't Hart become Lord deMornay?"

Tiffany's blue eyes darted to her father. "That's an interesting idea."

But Major Wright threw cold water on my brainwave. "The title goes automatically to the eldest son." He turned to his daughter. "Wouldn't it be something to meet the Royal Family, Tiffany?" Major Wright's eyes grew bright with excitement. "Maybe when you're Lady deMornay, royalty will visit Thirteen Oaks, and even stay with you. Wouldn't the folks back home in Winnipeg be jealous?"

"I guess so, Daddy."

"Call me a sentimental old fool, but I can't wait for your marriage. Joining together the Wrights and the deMornays is so important for both families. Your marriage to Paris will unite us with Victoria's top society. You'll be living in the Uplands, at the number one address—Thirteen Oaks."

Eventually the Major's enthusiasm ran down, and for a while nothing more was said. We munched the goodies and sipped delicious tea. Then Tiffany took a deep breath. "I've been thinking, Daddy, about the wedding."

"Yes?"

"Maybe I should postpone it? Even just a little bit?" Tiffany spoke rapidly; her voice seemed breathless. "It's just that . . ."

"Tiffany, sweetheart. What's wrong?"

"It's just that Paris, he's changed. I'm not sure . . ."

Major Wright took her hand; his eyes were as blue as Tiff's. "Of course he's different, sweetie pie. He's grieving for his parents. Wouldn't you be?"

"Of course, but—"

"Think about the grandchildren you and Paris will give me. Those kids are the next generation of the Wright and deMornay empire. With parents like you and Paris, they can't fail." He gently touched the side of Tiffany's face. "Think of the babies, honey. You're going to love them so much."

"That's true, but—"

"The invitations have been sent, Tiffany, and beautiful presents have arrived. You can't return those! Besides, calling off the wedding would look bad."

I looked at him. "Other people have cancelled weddings."

"Sure, but—"

Tiffany interrupted his response. "Liz, I understand what Daddy means. What would people think? That's important, you know."

"If you say so," I replied.

As the Major patted Tiffany's hand, his cell phone shrilled. He answered and spoke briefly, then looked at us. "Good news. Paris is joining us for tea. His limousine just arrived outside the Empress."

"That's wonderful," Tiffany exclaimed. She fluffed up her blonde curls and straightened her skirt, but a frown remained on her face.

I watched Paris approach across the hardwood floor, smiling at the women who glanced his way. He wore a suit the colour of vanilla ice cream, with a beautiful shirt and a tie of blue silk. In his ear was a small golden hoop. His dark hair was swept back dramatically.

Paris shook hands warmly with the Major, then sat down beside Tiffany and gazed into her eyes. "Sweetheart, it's so good to see you."

Tiffany smiled happily. "You, too, Paris."

Paris turned to the Major. "Sir, you'll recall I put your name forward for membership in the Union Club. It's very exclusive, but I've got wonderful news. You've been accepted as a member."

"Wonderful." The Major shook hands with Paris. "You're a fine young man." Then he turned to Tiffany with a smile. "My own dear Lady deMornay. I can hardly wait."

* * *

Outside the Empress we said goodbye to Major Wright and Paris. Then, before I could speak, Tiffany raised her hand. "Please, Liz, no advice about my marriage. This is important to Daddy and it's important to me."

"Still, I'm glad you mentioned your doubts, Tiff. Maybe that got your father thinking."

After shopping in Chinatown, Tiff and I enjoyed a tour of the Legislative Buildings. Then we returned outside to the sight of the Inner Harbour as evening came to Victoria. The distant hills were lovely, turning dark and mysterious before our eyes.

The air was warm; many people were out this early evening, strolling arm in arm or passing in horse-drawn carriages. Stopping at a low stone wall, we gazed at the vessels cruising the Inner Harbour. There were luxury yachts and sleek kayaks and noisy seaplanes, plus a large Zodiac full of tourists returning to port from a whale-watching excursion.

The setting sun glowed on a huge sign reading WELCOME TO VICTORIA. The words were made entirely of flowers. "Excuse us, girls," a man said with a drawl, "but how's about taking our picture?"

"Sure."

Through the lens of his camera, I focused on a middle-aged couple dressed in shorts and "Victoria City of Gardens" T-shirts. Beyond them was a statue of Queen Victoria, the famed British monarch who gave the city its name.

"You're from out of town?" I commented, after capturing the couple's self-conscious grins for posterity.

The man's bushy eyebrows rose high. "Now, little lady, how'd you guess?"

"It was easy." I smiled. "You're carrying a copy of *WHERE Victoria*. That's a tourist guide."

"Shucks." The man laughed. "For a moment there, I was impressed."

Tiffany shook her finger at the man, but in a friendly

manner. "Now, listen up. My friend's a successful detective. She's very smart."

"Say," the lady remarked to me, "ever met Nancy Drew?"

"Not so far!"

The man photographed the nearby Royal British Columbia Museum. "We're here on business, hoping to sell this town a hockey arena. But we might just move to Canada. Shucks, the air is so clean—why, you can taste it."

"Some of those big flowers are *amazing*," his wife added, "and folks are so friendly."

The man looked at the Legislative Buildings. "That fellow on top, the gold statue. He's holding something, maybe a hockey stick. Someone said that's the legendary star Wayne Gretzky. Is it true?"

I shook my head. "That's Captain George Vancouver."

After saying goodbye, we descended stone stairs to the Lower Causeway. Here people strolled, licking cones as they watched buskers perform and sidewalk artists paint and sketch. Young kids were blowing rainbow bubbles, which drifted lazily through the warm air. This seemed like a carnival by the sea.

On enormous white yachts, boaters sat chatting in deck chairs or panned their cameras across the enchanting scene. Red and gold sunset colours reflected from the water and I could smell the salty ocean.

I consulted my watch. "It's time for our meeting with Fossilized Pete at Fishermen's Wharf. Richard at the museum suggested getting there by harbour ferry."

"There's one," Tiffany said, pointing.

The ferries were loading passengers at a nearby wooden wharf, which creaked with the movement of the sea. The ferry was so cute—it looked like a tiny tugboat. We stepped down into a small cabin, where other passengers waited for the departure. Surrounded by windows, we could see everything.

"Please let us off at Fishermen's Wharf," I asked the captain, as he took our fares.

"Going for fish and chips?"

I shook my head. "We stuffed our faces at the Empress."

"Will this ride make us seasick?" Tiffany asked.

"Not a chance," our captain replied. "The Inner Harbour is almost totally enclosed by land. It's very calm. We're also protected by the Sooke Hills." He pronounced it *Sook*, with a silent e. "The first inhabitants of those hills were the Tsouke people."

Proudly displaying the flags of B.C. and Canada, the ferry plowed a furrow of small waves as its bow cut through the water. Our relaxing journey ended at Fishermen's Wharf, where various vessels were moored along the wooden wharves. Signs at Barb's seafood stand asked customers to refrain from feeding birds. But one guy totally ignored the warning, holding a juicy morsel aloft to tempt the gulls that wheeled and screamed above.

"He'll lose a finger," I predicted, but I was wrong.

We followed a series of wharves to the home of Fossilized Pete; it resembled a tiny house, floating on the sea. There was even a picket fence.

A porthole overlooked the houseboat's tiny porch. As I leaned close, hoping to see inside, the door opened and Fossilized Pete stood before us.

I had expected a grizzled type, white whiskers and weathered skin, but instead Pete was quite young. He had large eyes like those of a puppy dog, and neatly trimmed black hair turning to grey. He wore deck shoes, faded jeans, and a T-shirt reading "TerrifVic Jazz Party." I asked about the *Outlaw*, showing him a rough drawing I'd made. Then I held my breath. Surely Fossilized Pete could help us.

To our delight, Pete nodded his head. "Yes, I've seen this craft before."

"Wonderful," we both exclaimed.

Pete pointed across the water. "Last night I spotted the *Outlaw* heading toward the West Bay Marina. You can see the marina's lights from here."

I exchanged an excited glance with Tiffany. "How do we get there?" I asked Pete.

He gestured at a small boat moored beside the wharf. "That's my skiff. Hop aboard."

"Wonderful."

Minutes later we were skimming across the water, powered by an outboard in the stern of the skiff. I felt determined, yet nervous. Suppose we found the *Outlaw*—what would happen then?

5

"I'm a volunteer with the Victoria Marine Rescue Society," Pete told us, as our boat sped across the waters. "We're out a lot, helping boaters in trouble, that sort of thing."

"How'd you get your name?" I asked. "Fossilized Pete doesn't really suit you."

"Actually it's a nickname. I don't smoke, I don't drink, I don't do drugs. For that, some people back home called me a fossil—you know, old-fashioned. So I moved to the West Coast, where people are more accepting of differences. I'm not considered a fossil now, but I've kept my nickname, just for the memories."

"What's your T-shirt about?" I asked.

"The Jazz Party is an annual event in Victoria. People come from all over the world. I've danced to some great bands—Zydeco, swing, you name it. And I volunteer at the special Saturday party for kids."

For a time I was silent, thinking.

"Is it dangerous on the open sea?"

"Sure," Pete replied. "Especially for the dunder-heads, the ones with no training. They don't keep a weather eye out. Then suddenly they're overboard into bitterly cold water. People have died out there."

Looking down into the depths, I shivered. Night had closed around us; the breeze chilled my face. Directly ahead was the marina, where lights glowed inside houseboats and cabin cruisers. People on deck talked to each other across the water, and I could hear music and barking dogs. It was like entering a small town, afloat on the sea.

"I'll drop you here," Pete said.

"How do we get back?" I asked.

"Take a harbour ferry. They stop here."

Jumping onto a wharf, we waved goodbye to Fossilized Pete. Then we wandered around, hoping to spot the *Outlaw*. We showed the drawing to lots of people, but the search was doomed. It all seemed a big waste of time.

Until we spotted the thief.

He was on a nearby wharf. I his spiky bleach-blond hair and the two golden hoops in his ear. "That's him for sure."

"What'll we do?"

"Let's get closer."

Then his cell phone beeped. "Jason speaking," he said. His voice came clearly to us. After listening to his caller, Jason nodded. "Thanks for the warning."

Jason dashed to a boathouse, opened the door, and disappeared inside. Moments later, we heard the throaty roar of a powerful engine as a cruiser appeared from the boathouse.

"Look," I cried. "It's the *Outlaw*."

* * *

Jason was inside, alone at the controls. "He's getting away," I said urgently. "Come on, let's stop him." I pointed along the wharf. "There's someone who can help."

We ran toward an open boat with an oversize outboard motor, mounted at its stern. The guy at the wheel had just started the motor when we reached him.

"Help us," I shouted. "We must stop that cruiser."

"O . . . kay," the guy replied. "Throw off the lines . . . and . . . and jump aboard."

The boat was stripped bare of seats and anything else that would slow it down. As we held tightly to a railing at the stern, it roared away from the marina. Many stars shone above. I could see the *Outlaw*, moving fast. I looked at the lights of condo towers, shining on the water, then felt our boat pick up speed. The motor was powerful; spray lashed back, soaking us. Lights blurred past—I shook saltwater out of my eyes, fighting to see.

"Hang on," Tiffany screamed, as the boat heeled to the side. Then I looked at the guy at the wheel—and understood our problem.

He was drinking from a vodka bottle, and it was almost empty.

* * *

The guy leered at us with bloodshot eyes. "Enjoying the ride, girls?" he yelled.

Laughing, he twisted the wheel. We both screamed as the boat almost overturned before the guy managed to right it.

I staggered forward, balancing myself, as the drunk twisted the wheel back and forth. "Keep back," he yelled at me.

"Be careful, Liz," Tiffany called.

We'd left the Inner Harbour behind and reached the open sea. Directly ahead was the massive bulk of the *Coho*, a large ferry carrying vehicles and passengers to Victoria. Its horn sounded a warning, startling the drunk. He weaved back and forth, holding tightly to the wheel, trying to watch the ferry and also watch me.

"Danger," I suddenly cried, pointing over his shoulder. "Right there!"

"*Huh?*" the drunk responded, turning to look.

I leapt for the wheel, determined to take control. But the drunk saw me coming and lashed out with his foot. Avoiding the kick, I hit the deck and rolled. Trying to aim another kick, the drunk accidentally released the wheel—and immediately the boat changed direction, veering sharply to starboard.

The drunk staggered, then fell. His head smacked against the deck, and he went silent. Stumbling forward, I managed to grab the wheel. Somehow I got the boat under control, and we zoomed safely away from the *Coho*.

"Is he breathing?" I yelled back at Tiffany.

"Yes, but he's out cold."

I turned the boat toward the Inner Harbour. A crisis had been averted, but I didn't feel good. Somewhere in the night, the *Outlaw* was getting away.

We'd lost our quarry.

* * *

We left the boat at a wharf near the Empress. When we walked away, the drunk was leaning against the bulkhead, head in his hands. He was groaning.

"When we get home," I said, "I'll phone the police about spotting the *Outlaw*. But I'm guessing Jason will move his boat to another location."

"I wonder who warned him about us," Tiff said.

"Good point."

A lot of young people were hanging out across the street from the Empress. One of them was Pepper. She was comforting a teenager who was crying; I saw tears on the girl's face. Nearby, three well-dressed teenagers were staring with hostility at Pepper.

As we approached, Pepper smiled. "Good to see you," she said. "Laura's arriving any minute now. She's giving me a ride home to Thirteen Oaks."

Laura's shiny BMW pulled smoothly to the curb. At the same moment, a city bus stopped nearby; Pepper escorted the forlorn girl to the bus, then waved good-bye as the bus pulled away.

We all climbed into the BMW. "Brother," Pepper exclaimed. She was in the back; Tiffany was up front with Laura. "I hate gossip—I hate it. Words can cause so much pain."

"What happened?" I asked.

"That girl I was with—some boy started a rumour about her. He wrote lies on a wall, looking for revenge. You saw those three girls? They're treating the rumour like the truth and passing it along. I told them what I thought."

"You did the right thing," Laura said. "You didn't join the finger-pointers. The only way to stop that stuff is not to be one of the sheep. You showed courage, Pepper, giving friendship to an outcast."

"Thanks," Pepper said, looking embarrassed. "Anyway, no one tells me what to think. I make up my own mind about people."

* * *

We soon reached the Jeep. "Liz and I can drive Pepper home," Tiffany suggested to Laura. "It'll save you the trip."

Laura declined the offer. "I feel like a drive. I've worked hard today, and I need to unwind."

"Okay to go with you?" I asked Laura. "I'd like your advice about what happened tonight."

"You bet," Laura replied.

We all said good night to Tiffany, and the BMW purred smoothly away. As I gazed at the charming houses passing by, I told Laura and Pepper about the events at the West Bay Marina. "I feel like I'm getting somewhere on this case," I said.

"How so?" Laura enquired. She was remarkably beautiful.

"Well, Jason is clearly connected to the *Outlaw*, and he also stole the painting. I should tell the police, don't you think?"

As Laura pondered this, Pepper studied her face. Then Laura nodded. "Yes, do tell the police about Jason's link to the *Outlaw*. But you'd better not mention the painting. That would upset Paris."

"Okay," I replied, somewhat reluctantly. "Have you heard anything about the ransom?"

She shook her head. "Nothing so far."

"Do you think the caller was Jason?"

"Probably," Laura said. "You're a good detective, Liz."

I grinned. "Sleuthing's in my blood. My mom's a lawyer, just like you. She loves it."

"I went into law to have a career," said Laura. "That way I'd never be financially dependent on anyone else."

The BMW rolled quietly through the deeply shadowed streets of the Uplands district, until it reached the stone walls of the Thirteen Oaks estate. Stepping out of the luxurious car, I sniffed the fragrant breezes.

Laura waved to us from behind the wheel. "Goodnight, girls."

"Goodnight, Laura," I said. "Thanks for the ride."

The lights of the beemer disappeared into the night, and we entered the quiet gardens of the estate. The moon was lovely, and so were the glorious stars that twinkled across the heavens. "It's so perfect under the moon," I exclaimed to Pepper. "I love this place."

* * *

The next morning, Tiff and I wandered together through the gardens of Thirteen Oaks.

The garage stood at the edge of the estate. Cambridge was shining the chrome on the family limousine. The vehicle sparkled in the morning sunshine. It was a Daimler, manufactured in England. It had right-hand drive and a cream and navy two-tone finish—very nice indeed.

"The Daimler's for sale," Cambridge told us. "Master Paris has ordered me to spiff it up. He's ordered a new limousine from Detroit—it's got bulletproof glass."

"Where's the chauffeur?" Tiffany asked.

"He's quit, miss. A disagreement with Master Paris."

Cambridge then began talking about the Moss Street Paint-In. "Are you going?" he asked. "It's a famous event in Victoria, and very popular."

"What's it about?" Tiffany asked.

"All along Moss Street, local artists set up their easels. You can watch them painting, or ask questions. I go every year." For a moment Cambridge stared at the ground. "When I was young, I dreamed of being an artist. I had real talent—but it didn't work out."

"Do you still paint?" I asked.

"Oh, yes, miss. I have a small studio above the garage."

"May we visit sometime?" I asked.

Cambridge shook his head. "I don't like people to look at my work. It's . . . Well . . . Well, I do it because . . ." His voice faded away, then he straightened up. "You'll see some good work today at the Paint-In. I suggest that you go."

* * *

It was a beautiful Saturday, and sunshine warmed our faces as we headed south in the Jeep on Beach Drive, admiring the view. Yards in the Uplands were big, big, big, and featured beautiful trees and flowering bushes, a lot of them taller than people. The hollyhocks were particularly sensational with their fat blossoms of pink and dark red. The careful landscaping in the Uplands was so elegant—many houses seemed to be set into nests of greenery. Big trees shaded us from the sun; south of Willows Beach we passed Glenlyon-Norfolk School, located beside the ocean. "According to Pepper," Tiffany said, "that place was originally a private home owned by a famous architect named Francis Rattenbury. He ended up murdered."

I stared at the building. "I wonder if there's a ghost."

"Probably not. The murder happened in England."

At Windsor Park we paused to watch a cricket match, then headed for town by way of Oak Bay Village. What a great place. The village totally reminded me of England, with its little shops selling chocolates and flowers and other delights.

One place was called the Blethering Place Tea Room. "What's a blethering place?" I wondered aloud.

"That's a Scottish expression," Tiffany explained. "It's a place where people gather for gossip and good food."

"Hey, we could ask people there if they know anything about the *Outlaw*."

Tiffany smiled. "Instead of always investigating, Liz, you could help me relax. I am getting so nervous. My wedding is exactly one week away."

People on the sidewalk watched us pass in the red Jeep, and then a beautifully dressed white-haired lady waved, and I returned her sweet smile. She was with a younger woman in an elegant outfit.

"This is a very nice area," I said, then turned to Tiffany to discuss something that had been on my mind. "I've been thinking—maybe Cambridge has been stealing artwork from Thirteen Oaks. He's got a background as an artist, so he'd know the value of the stuff."

"But Cambridge has been with the family forever. Why would he do something like that?"

I shrugged. "Could be he needs the money." It was amazing what people would do for money, I'd learned in my years of investigating.

Soon we reached Dallas Road, where a sleek cruise ship moved splendidly past on the sparkly blue ocean. In the distance, the snow-capped Olympic Mountains added grace and majesty to the scene. It was hard to believe that so recently we'd faced danger on those same waters.

Parking spots near Moss Street were at a premium, but Tiffany deftly manoeuvred the Jeep into a tiny place. Jumping out, we gazed at a welcoming scene. Sunshine splattered down through leafy trees—all along the street, artists were at work, while spectators strolled from easel to easel, sculpture to sculpture.

The atmosphere was pleasant. A girl with a French horn played a love song, while young children passed by, their faces painted to resemble clowns and cats. The houses had wonderful gardens—one place reminded me of Snow White. Somehow I could just picture her, looking down from the tiny upstairs window with its leaded-glass panes and little curved roof.

After wandering for a while, we purchased lemonade from some kids and then joined a crowd watching a woman at work on her canvas. "The painting must have movement," she explained to us. "Without movement, art is nothing."

A yellow butterfly drifted past. I watched its serene passage through the warm air—then stared in shock.

"Tiff," I exclaimed. "Look who it is."

* * *

"It's him," Tiffany said. "From the storm."

We'd last seen this guy running through the waves as they crashed ashore on Dallas Road. He was one of the artists, and sat working on a canvas. His work was certainly impressive; several large canvases of B.C. scenery were on display. My personal favourite showed emerald forests sweeping down through a mountain valley. I longed to visit that place.

"How much?" I asked, smiling at the handsome blond artist.

He grinned. "For you, it would cost nothing. But unfortunately, it's from my private collection. This one's not for sale."

"My name is Liz," I said, "and this is my best friend, Tiffany Wright."

"I'm William. It's nice to know you."

"Well," I said reluctantly, "we'd better move along. I'm sure other fans want to talk with you."

"Hey, don't go." William studied me with his large,

green eyes. "You know, my cousin has been showing my art today. I've been at my studio, working on a rush assignment—for real money, I might add. Anyway, I'm just here for an hour while my cousin gets a break. Luckily, it's the hour when you passed by."

I blushed.

"We're from Winnipeg," Tiffany explained to William, "but I'll be living here now. I'm getting married at Craigdarroch Castle."

"That's a cool place for a wedding." William turned to me. "It's totally out of the Victorian age. It's got stained-glass windows and a tower with an unforgettable view of the city. Hollywood producers have used the castle in some movies. The ballroom dancing in *Little Women*, for example."

"With Winona Ryder?"

"That's the one."

I examined William's artistry with admiration. "You're really talented. But you're, like, so young."

He smiled shyly. "My teacher says I have a gift, but I need to work, work, work. It's difficult, you know, trying to be an artist and also earn a living. When I'm not painting I'm on a Kabuki Kab, earning money for art lessons and supplies."

William told us about his admiration for Emily Carr. "My teacher is an expert on her," he explained. "Robert says some of Victoria is essentially unchanged from the days when Emily Carr lived here. You can walk the same streets, paint the same scenes."

I was dying to tell William about the theft of Emily Carr's unknown masterpiece from Thirteen Oaks, but of course I couldn't. Instead I asked, "What's her art worth?"

"Plenty," William replied. "There was an auction recently for one of her pieces called *War Canoes, Alert Bay*. It fetched more than a million dollars."

"Yikes."

"For more than 20 years Emily Carr struggled to earn money, and had little time for her art. She raised sheepdogs and operated a small apartment house."

William told us about Emily Carr's monkey named Woo, and how she'd take Woo for walks in a baby carriage. "Some people called her eccentric—but artists can be difficult to understand. Our challenge is to capture the essence of life, and that's a tall order."

"You're passionate about it," I said.

"Liz, my art is everything." Then William smiled. "Perhaps I'll see you again." He scribbled his phone number on a piece of paper. "Call me sometime, okay?"

"Sure," I replied, feeling amazed and happy.

Walking on, Tiff and I discussed William in detail. "He's going to be famous," I predicted. Then I grabbed Tiffany's arm. "Look, there's Hart. Who's his pretty friend?"

"I don't know." Tiff stared daggers in her direction. "Hart told me there's no one special in his life."

I glanced at Tiff. "You sound miffed."

"I doubt it."

"Methinks the lady doth protest too much."

Spotting us, Hart hurried over. "Tiff and Liz, please meet my cousin, Lorna Taft—she's arrived early for the wedding. Lorna's from Terrace, in northern B.C."

"Your cousin?" Tiff said, sounding relieved.

"Is the north a cool place to live?" I asked.

"You bet," Lorna laughed. "Especially in January."

I noticed a warm smile pass between Hart and Tiff. "We're going to visit Craigdarroch Castle," Hart explained.

Lorna nodded. "I want to see the castle where you're getting married, Tiffany."

"Come with us," Hart suggested. "The castle's a short walk from here."

"We'd love to go with you," Tiffany responded with great enthusiasm.

Chatting together, we walked through the festive Rockland neighbourhood. Every type had come for the Paint-In: grandmas and grandpas, parents and kids, yuppies and hippies, all having fun. Passing by the elegant houses, I daydreamed about being a famous artist who lived in Victoria and was adored by all.

Then the castle appeared, looming high above us. "The castle's Scottish name means 'Rocky Oak Place,'" Hart explained to us. "It was built for a man who got rich operating coal mines. Back then, the castle was surrounded by 28 acres of meadows with many Garry oaks and an artificial lake. It must have been so beautiful."

"The castle's still impressive," I said, staring at the granite walls and tall chimneys. I could just imagine a princess brushing her hair at one of the arched windows, or gazing down at her curly-haired swain from a balcony far above.

"It's like we're in Scotland. I love the red-tiled roof."

We purchased admission tickets, then stepped into the opulent luxury of the Victorian era. Ahead was an enormous sandstone fireplace; a scene was carved inside.

"Those are players in an opera by Wagner," Hart told us. "Much of the castle remains exactly the same as when the Dunsmuirs lived here. Just imagine—this place has 17 fireplaces."

"A life of abundance," his cousin commented.

Hart nodded. "The Victorians lived in a luxurious world of leather-bound books, Tiffany paperweights, stained-glass windows, and pianos by Steinway."

A wooden staircase spiralled above us to an alcove, where I could see a bouquet of flowers on an organ under a stained-glass window. "My father admires James Dunsmuir," Tiffany told us, "because of the power and prestige he commanded. That's why Daddy insists that I get married in Dunsmuir's castle." Her red lips pouted. "I was hoping for a church."

Tiff turned to me. "One of James Dunsmuir's daughters had 30 bridesmaids and flower girls— there's a picture upstairs of her wedding day."

Next we studied the drawing room. It featured a lovely chandelier, its crystals glittering blue like the sea and red like the most exquisite of rubies. In exactly one week Tiffany would be married here; the ceremony was planned for the evening, after the castle had closed to the public. Not for the first time, a wave of uneasiness passed over me as I thought of the wedding.

6

That evening Paris and Tiffany went out for supper. I summoned my courage and phoned William. My heart was beating hard, and I hoped I wouldn't sound too anxious.

To my relief, William was happy to hear from me. "I was just reading the newspaper," I said, my voice trembling. "There's a special lantern ceremony tonight. It starts at eight." I took a deep breath. "Care to go with me?"

"You bet," William replied. "I've been working hard and I could use a break."

"Wonderful."

We arranged to meet at a bus stop on Toronto Street in the James Bay neighbourhood. Stepping from the bus, I saw William waiting. He wore a "Kabuki Kabs"

T-shirt and long khaki shorts, and had a string of small shells around his neck. It felt so good to see him.

We walked south on Government Street, getting to know each other. "I've been worried about my mom," William told me. "Lately her bronchitis is so bad. I want Mom to spend time in Arizona, because of the dry air." William smiled happily. "The project I'm working on will pay for getting her to Arizona for the winter. What a relief."

We were walking past wooden houses that dated back to pioneer days. We admired the gingerbread decorations on Emily Carr's childhood home, then watched tourists pass in a graceful carriage pulled by a big horse.

"What's the story on this lantern ceremony?" William asked.

"It's apparently a tradition that began in Japan," I replied. "People are launching lanterns in paper boats to honour those who died when nuclear weapons ended the last world war."

"Now I remember—I heard about this on the radio. The boats are released on the water, while everyone prays for world peace. Right?"

I nodded. "It sounds very moving."

A lot of people had gathered beside a large, round pond. Many kids were there, carrying paper boats they'd made. A swallow darted past, moving fast in the gathering dusk; beyond the Sooke Hills, wispy clouds turned orange as the sun disappeared for the night.

William and I listened to speeches from a Japanese lady and a man wearing a white beret. Then a street person emerged from the darkness, wrapped in an old blanket, and disrupted the ceremony by making loud comments in a voice slurred by booze. People shifted uneasily, but nothing happened until William left my side and approached the man.

They spoke quietly, then William returned to me. The drunk said nothing more during the remaining speeches and the launching of the paper boats on the pond. Some were beautifully decorated, while others displayed only the single word *Peace* on their sails. Inside each boat, a candle burned; filled with light, the boats drifted together and then apart. Some people wept, while others closed their eyes in prayer.

After the ceremony ended, I looked at William. "That was wonderful. But what happened with that guy? You totally silenced him."

William shrugged. "I explained the importance of the ceremony. He understood."

I looked for the man, but he was gone.

William glanced at his watch. "Liz, I've got to run. I've really got to get back to work."

I was disappointed. I wondered if William was secretly a workaholic, but I didn't say anything.

He smiled with those big, green eyes. "My project must get finished, Liz. I have to deliver within days." He touched my arm. "I shouldn't have come out tonight. But I wanted to see you."

"Well, I understand. Perhaps we'll meet again?"

William nodded. "You'd better believe it."

* * *

Asleep that night, I thought I heard my cell phone ring. "William's calling," I mumbled to myself, stumbling around the room in search of the phone.

But the call was only a dream—I realized the phone had never rung. "Oh, William," I whispered, wandering to the window to gaze at the moon. "Are you thinking of me?"

In the morning I was anxious to tell Tiffany about William, but she'd gone downtown with the maid of honour. "Wedding errands," Pepper explained, as we ate breakfast together. "Tiff gave you the day off."

I yawned, still sleepy. "Maybe I'll phone William for a chat."

"Who's he?"

"This guy I met. Pepper, he's so cool. I hope you'll meet him."

"Feel like going to the park?" Pepper asked. "I'm taking Amanda to visit the Children's Zoo and see the ducks."

"Let's do it," I replied. "It's fun being with you."

I phoned William, but got his machine. *Please leave a message*, his recorded voice requested pleasantly, but I didn't. I knew I shouldn't be bothering William while he worked on his project.

The day was rainy, so the park was almost empty and virtually silent, except for the distant sound of slow-moving traffic. Above us, an eagle soared past. I wandered the pathways with Pepper, who had rain-proofed Amanda in her stroller. The flower beds were beautifully planted with many wonderful flowers. Many trees were *huge*.

"Emily Carr loved this place," Pepper said.

"Look." I pointed up at a huge nest. "There's a heron."

We watched the heron spread an enormous wing for a careful cleaning, then it lifted off from the nest. After a couple of flaps, the heron sailed gracefully down across a small lake to land near an elderly man who was feeding ducks from his park bench.

"Let's get closer," Pepper suggested.

Near a path beside the lake, we took shelter under a weeping willow. "This is more mist than rain," I whispered, watching it collect on leaves to form chubby raindrops that plopped to the ground.

We watched the man tossing birdseed to the noisy ducks crowded all around. His wooden cane was hooked over the park bench. My heart melted at the sweetness of the scene—until the man produced a package of cigarettes and lit up!

Shaking my head, I walked away with Pepper and Amanda. At Fountain Lake we stopped to watch ducks paddling in search of food amongst a carpet of lily pads. The petals of their flowers were pure white; each encircled at its heart a burst of yellow, as though the sun lived there.

"Even on a cloudy day," Pepper said, "that glow can warm your soul."

I watched a white-haired lady pass by, chatting happily with a younger man. Then I smiled fondly at Amanda, who was fascinated by the ducks. "Isn't it difficult, coping with a child? I mean, you're so young."

"Well, the servants help a lot."

"Any regrets?"

Pepper shook her head. "Amanda was born on February 14, and she'll always be my favourite Valentine. But I tell you, Liz, getting dates is tough. Lots of guys don't want a kid around."

At that moment the sun broke through the clouds, and as the day became warmer, steam began rising from the pathways. Drawn by the sound of music, we came upon an outdoor bandstand. A pretty woman with long hair was on the stage with her band, entertaining an appreciative audience seated on benches. *Music for the Trees,* read a banner behind the band. *Send a message of love to B.C.'s trees.*

We stopped to listen. Pepper and I were both impressed by the singer; I loved the idea of music serenading the trees.

"Maybe I could sign her to a contract," Pepper said. "You know, when I'm a music producer. It won't be long now."

After the concert we walked to the Inner Harbour, where Cambridge was waiting with the Daimler outside the Empress. Pepper got into the limo with Amanda, but I decided against returning to Thirteen Oaks. "You see that boat with the big sign?" I said to Pepper. "They offer a three-hour sail. I think I'll get a ticket. What a perfect day for riding the ocean waves."

We said goodbye, then I crossed Government to the Inner Harbour. There was a nice hum of activity, what with the boaters and buskers and lots of tourists. A nice-looking guy approached, smiling. It was Fossilized Pete, who'd taken us to the West Bay Marina.

"How'd that turn out?" Pete asked, after we'd exchanged hellos.

"We found the *Outlaw*."

Pete looked surprised. "Tell me more."

I decided not to mention Jason by name, but did describe his boat escaping into the night. I also told Pete about the drunk. When I finished my story, Pete smiled. "You know Laura Singlehurst, eh? She's a friend of mine. I saw Laura the other night—she was looking for someone named Pepper. She mentioned you."

We chatted for a few minutes, and then I said good-bye to Pete and climbed on board the boat. It was the *Thayne*, a 17-metre gaff-rigged ketch (as the captain told me). About a dozen tourists waited on the deck, and I said hello while searching for somewhere to sit. From below came the smell of fuel; a dinghy with an outboard was attached to the stern.

The captain was young and friendly. "We'll use the sails, once we've left port. This schooner was hand-built from bits of old Victoria houses, so it's got some nice vibes."

As we left port, I waved at people in a harbour ferry, then turned my face to the sun. As always, the water was heavy with vessels; on shore, people watched our passage from an oceanside pathway. I saw joggers and cyclists passing before some large buildings.

"Those are condos and townhouses," our captain explained to me. "It's a nice location, but the seaplanes can get noisy."

"Be careful your captain's cap doesn't blow off," I warned him, as the wind gusted briefly.

"Huh?"

"If your hat blows overboard, you're marked for drowning."

He grinned. "Hey, you're superstitious. Just like my wife."

We glided past a Coast Guard station, then a gigantic cruise ship moored at a wharf where a really big mural welcomed people to Victoria. "Cruise ships visit here every summer," our captain said. "This is a favourite stop on their journey to Alaska."

"I'd love to get on board." I felt smaller than an ant, staring up at the balconies on the many decks.

Out on the open sea, large orange sails were unfurled. Finding them, the breezes sent our vessel running swiftly forward. It was so quiet, with just the wind in our ears. One passenger felt seasick, but our captain told him to keep watching the horizon, and that seemed to help.

"Look," someone cried, pointing to starboard. "There's an orca, right beside us."

What a thrilling sight. For several minutes the whale swam near us, its dorsal fin, white "flash" and immense black body glistening each time it emerged from beneath the surface. "Sometimes this happens once we've turned off the engine," the captain told us. "There's no noise to frighten the orcas, and people say they're naturally friendly."

The captain watched me take some more photos of the beautiful whale. "Are you using colour film?"

"Sure."

"But why?" He grinned. "The orca's in black and white."

I chuckled at his joke. "Okay to use your binoculars?" I asked.

He passed me powerful Zeiss-Ikons. I trained them on the distant Victoria shoreline, hoping to spot the

Outlaw prowling along. I needed a break in the case, something to help crack it wide open. But luck wasn't with me.

The mysterious craft was nowhere to be seen.

* * *

On Monday I went downtown by bus. The sun was hot but the air was pleasantly free of humidity as I walked to the Cyber Station.

Inside its cool depths, I asked to use a computer terminal. There was something about Paris that had been niggling at me. I could have used a computer at Thirteen Oaks, but I needed to work away from prying eyes.

Lots of people sat at the terminals; some were tourists, speaking together in foreign languages as they read e-mail messages or surfed the Net. I read the news from my family and friends, answered everyone, then checked the Tourism Victoria Website for the name Sandown. Sure enough I found something, and soon had tracked down the truth about Bigoted Earl.

* * *

I was feeling pleased with myself as I rode beside Tiffany in the Jeep. We were heading out of Victoria on West Saanich Road, which wandered amid thick stands of trees and past scenic homes and small farms. Our destination was known only to me.

Tiffany glanced my way. "You're certain this mystery trip is necessary, Liz? I'm very busy, you know."

"Yes, yes, I do know. But you're going to see something important. Just follow my directions."

Eventually we approached a parking lot filled with vehicles. Beyond them, a large wooden grandstand rose into the air. We could hear loud cries from the spectators.

"What's this place?" Tiff asked.

"Sandown," I replied triumphantly. "It's a track. Horses race here. One's called Bigoted Earl, and it's running today." Before Tiffany could respond, I punched numbers into my cell phone. When a man answered, I gave him a short message.

"Now let's see what happens," I said to Tiffany. "This should be good."

* * *

A few minutes later, Paris came out of the grandstand. I waved at him, and he hurried forward. Then he saw Tiffany, and his face turned pale.

"Tiffany, why are you here? Liz told me there was an emergency, but she never mentioned your name."

Tiffany's blue eyes stared at Paris; she seemed confused and frightened.

He scowled at me. "I knew you'd betray me to Tiff."

"Well," I said briskly, "why not confess? You've been gambling money at Sandown Raceway. Today you're betting on Bigoted Earl, right?"

Tiffany was totally shocked. "Well, Paris?"

"I guess . . . I guess it's true."

I waited for Tiffany to throw her engagement ring at his feet. Instead, she did nothing—absolutely nothing.

Then Paris said, "Listen, Tiff, how about a loan? I've got inside information on the race. Bigoted Earl can't fail. Let's win this one together."

I was shocked and appalled. Then, to my horror, Tiffany nodded her agreement. "Okay, I guess. But only this time, all right?"

Paris grinned. "You bet. Thanks, sweetheart."

Tiffany handed Paris a bunch of cash. As she did, my heart almost broke. What did the future hold for a girl as sweet and trusting as Tiff?

* * *

As I feared, Bigoted Earl ran out of the money. The horse was a loser, just like Paris. He stayed for more races, but we left the raceway.

"Tiffany," I pleaded, as we walked to the Jeep, "don't lend him more money. He'll just gamble it away."

"Paris needs me, Liz."

"He needs your bank account!"

"Since his father's death, I've been his constant strength."

Once again, I gave up. At Thirteen Oaks we collected Pepper, then headed to the Artful Needle for a dress fitting. After that we continued downtown for more errands. Tiff parked the Jeep at the Eaton Centre, a large mall with a British theme, and we wandered along tourist-thronged Government Street. Then I glanced east and saw that people had gathered at a nearby street.

We hurried to join the crowd. "What's going on?" Tiff asked a bicycle cop who was on traffic duty. "Is this the marathon for charity? I read about it in the newspaper."

She nodded. "A run across Canada is ending today in Victoria. The guy will pass here in a few minutes, heading for Mile Zero at the ocean."

"What charity is the runner supporting?" Pepper asked.

"This guy wants to help abused kids," the officer replied. "He was assaulted himself—by his coach when he played junior hockey. He kept the secret all through his years as an NHL player, but eventually he told and the coach went to prison."

"Telling takes such courage," Tiffany said. "It's so cool that he turned his problem into a way to help others. I like kids—I wish I could help."

She got her chance when we put donations into a can carried by a volunteer. All around us, people were cheering as the runner approached. He was young and handsome, and tears were streaming from his eyes. I started to cry, and so did the others, as everyone applauded the runner and shouted praise.

Then he was gone, trailed by TV cameras and media photographers and kids on bikes. Returning to Government Street, Tiffany talked nonstop about the runner's accomplishments. "Imagine telling on your coach. They're such authority figures, right? I mean, where'd he find the courage?"

"By taking one step at a time," Pepper replied.

7

Tiff dropped me in the Cook Street Village. I'd looked up William's address in the phone book, and decided to walk past. Just in case he was around—you know? But also because I was curious to see his home.

Thick, beautiful chestnut trees sheltered Cook Street. There was a fish and chips shop, a stationer, some food stores, and several of those ubiquitous West Coast coffee shops. I noticed a small low-rider truck pass by, throbbing with music; the driver was hidden behind tinted windows. The truck carried Washington plates.

I remembered William accepting money from someone in a similar truck, perhaps even this one. I wondered who the driver was.

Soon after, I reached William's address. He lived near the park in a three-storey house divided into apartments. Big steps led to the building's front door. William sat on the steps.

He looked exhausted. As I approached, he hardly seemed to recognize me. Then William folded a thick envelope and stuck it away in his jeans pocket. "Hi, Liz," he said, managing a smile. "I'm so beat. I've been working around the clock."

"You got paid?"

"Yeah. Now I can send Mom to Arizona. I tell you . . ."

William stopped speaking. His eyes stared past me, down to the street corner. I followed his gaze, and saw the truck with Washington plates. William watched the truck pass by, but said nothing. When it was gone, he turned to me. "Liz, I'm dead tired. See you another time, okay?"

I was disappointed but not surprised. I'm familiar with workaholics. My dad can get totally absorbed during his police investigations, and Mom's often consumed by her cases.

I said goodnight to William and went home by bus.

* * *

I was feeling sorry for myself, but a surprise invitation soon cheered me up. Laura Singlehurst had phoned Thirteen Oaks, wanting everyone to join her at Butchart Gardens for an evening picnic.

"She especially asked for you, Liz," Pepper said, as we got ready. "There are fireworks tonight. It gets chilly after dark, so bring something warm to wear."

"Why the invitation?" I asked. "What's the occasion?"

Pepper grinned. "Who knows? Who cares?"

Tiffany stayed home with tummy problems. The rest of us piled into the Daimler; with Cambridge at the wheel, we drove north out of Victoria to Butchart Gardens.

Laura met us at the entrance. We all thanked her for the surprise, and she smiled happily. "Have you ever visited Butchart Gardens?" she asked me.

I shook my head.

"For flower lovers," Laura said, "this place is heaven on earth. There are thousands and thousands of blossoms, and they're so fragrant."

"Still nothing heard about the ransom?" Paris asked Laura.

"Not a word. The kid has gone silent. We still don't know exactly what he wants."

"I'm getting nervous," Paris said. "Maybe I should inform the police. I simply can't lose the Emily Carr—Dad treasured it."

"You're a bit late calling 911," I commented disapprovingly. "The painting could be anywhere by now—some crooked collector may have bought it."

Paris glared at me but said nothing. He was in a sulky mood, and I wished he'd stayed home.

Hart knew a lot about Butchart Gardens. "They were created by a remarkable woman named Jennie Butchart," he explained. "She loved adventures, like horseback riding and hot-air ballooning, but mostly she loved her gardens."

Hart pointed at an attractive, old-fashioned house surrounded by flowers. "Long ago, the family lived in that house. All around was the Butchart quarry, where limestone was dug to make cement."

He turned to a nearby vista of flowering plants, shrubs, and evergreens. "Jennie Butchart didn't like her view of the cement works. She planted gardens and trees to hide it, then she filled the abandoned quarries with gardens. She had a great talent for design. Pretty soon she was famous, and everyone came visiting."

Hart smiled. "In 1915 Jennie Butchart served 15,000 cups of tea to visitors. Her gardens became more and more popular, and now there's got to be easily a million visitors every year. It's beautiful here at Christmas, with the lights sparkling everywhere, but personally I love the summertime fireworks concerts. There's one tonight—they are amazing events."

"Concerts?" I said. "You mean, like a band has a concert?"

"Kind of," Hart replied. "We'll be watching fireworks set to music."

Cambridge returned from the gardens' dining room, carrying a picnic basket full of gourmet goodies Laura had ordered especially for the occasion. "We'll be eating soon," Laura promised us.

We posed for a picture with the picnic basket beside a giant boar fashioned from bronze. "Why's his nose so shiny?" I asked.

"People touch the statue for good luck," Laura explained.

"I could use some good luck," Pepper muttered, vigorously rubbing the boar's nose.

The comment caused Laura to glance at Pepper, but she said nothing.

A path beneath cedars and Douglas firs led to a lookout above the Sunken Garden. We leaned over a railing, amazed at the visual splendour spread out below. "This was a quarry," Hart explained. "Limestone from here was used to make cement. See the tall chimney in the distance? It's all that remains of the cement factory. The ivy on the quarry walls was part of Jennie Butchart's vision."

Laura looked at us. "My aunt says that Jennie used to be lowered by rope into the quarry with seeds and tools, then she spent the day creating her gardens."

"Look at that enormous dahlia," I exclaimed. "It's like a soccer ball—it's colossal."

"Wait till you see the Rose Garden," Hart said. "The West Coast has a perfect climate for growing roses. They love it here."

We watched the dancing waters of a pretty fountain located deep within the walls of the former quarry. Then we followed a pathway to grassy lawns where a large crowd was gathering for the fireworks.

"There's got to be three thousand people here," I exclaimed, with a whistle of astonishment. "Are the fireworks that good?"

Hart smiled. "Wait and see. They start at dusk."

Finding our way through the crowd, we located some open grass and spread out blankets. We were totally surrounded by beautiful flowers and many vibrant shades of green. It was a festive scene. I noticed flash cameras popping all over the crowd. People were having a good time together, their buzzing voices making them sound like a convention of gossiping locusts.

The scrumptious picnic was spread out, photographed, and drooled over. Then we dove at the food. My favourite was probably the chilled prawns with pesto mayonnaise, or maybe the teriyaki chicken, but *everything* was a fantastic taste sensation.

Since the fireworks wouldn't start until dusk, we played card games and read books. I was totally involved in a creepy tale when Pepper touched my shoulder, making me jump.

"I'm going to the snack bar, Liz. Come with me, okay?"

"Sure thing," I replied, reluctantly closing the book at an extremely suspenseful scene.

The delicate lights of Japanese lanterns shone close to the forest. The night was closing in, and I crossed my fingers for luck—a frequent habit of mine. We found our way through the chattering crowds, and then, at the snack bar, I got a surprise. A young guy behind the counter said, "You're Liz Austen, right?"

"Sure, but how'd you know?"

"Somebody left an envelope for you, and described your looks. They were right—you're gorgeous."

"Out of three thousand people," I said doubtfully, "you recognized me?"

"Well . . ."

"Come on, Liz," Pepper said impatiently. "Take the envelope, and let's get going. Otherwise we'll miss the fireworks."

"Okay," I replied.

My name was on the envelope; inside was a brief message written in emerald ink. *Liz*, it said, *Meet me at the Japanese Garden at exactly 10 tonight. Please don't be late. Don't tell anyone—this is very important.*

The message was signed with a single letter. My heart skipped a beat when I saw it. It was a W—as in William.

* * *

As we returned to the others, slowly finding our way past the many blankets and lawn chairs, I glanced at Pepper. "You gave that guy at the snack bar a big tip. I guess you liked him."

She shrugged. "He was okay."

Pepper didn't ask about my message, and I didn't volunteer any information. I was confused by what it said, and needed time to think.

Our blankets were on a slope, facing a small lake. Beyond the water, the forest was silhouetted against a pale orange sky. Looking up, I searched for stars. Then I smiled at Laura. "Thanks for treating us all to Butchart Gardens. I'll never forget this—it's so lovely here."

"You're very welcome, Liz."

A starburst lit the pale sky. Thousands of voices went *oooooooh*, then everyone cheered as shooting stars exploded above—purple, white, blue, green, red, everything!

From the trees came beautiful music—violins, and the voice of a singer. More fireworks shot above us, then displays suddenly ignited. Multicoloured fountains arose at the lake, twirling sparkles into the night, while a huge golden hive came to life with artificial bees twirling noisily in the night air. Beyond the lake, a colourful train choo-chooed past, as cameras flashed from the crowd. Amazingly, everything was made of fireworks.

"How have they done this?" I exclaimed. "It's magical."

I looked at my watch. Almost 10 o'clock—time to go! "I'll be back soon," I said to Laura. "I've got someone to meet."

She looked surprised. "What's going on?"

I shrugged, trying to appear nonchalant. "I'm, um, meeting someone. I won't be long."

"I'm not so sure . . ."

"Please, Laura. This is important."

"Well, okay, but take my cell phone." Laura handed me a tiny ruby-coloured phone. Then she turned to Paris. "Got your cell here?"

"Yes," he replied.

"If you need us," Laura told me, "push Memory-1 on my cell. Paris will answer."

"Where should we meet?" I asked.

"At the parking lot, following the fireworks. You remember where the Daimler is parked?"

I nodded.

"We'll see you there."

Slowly I found a path through the throng while *ooooooohs* and *ahhhhhhhs* sounded from open mouths, cameras flashed, and deep *booms* echoed from the hills. Leaving the show behind, I was soon alone in the vast central gardens. I looked up at the fireworks and saw whirling colours and fireballs trailing diamonds in their wake, and even a comet burning across the sky.

"Totally cool," I whispered to myself.

The evening smelled of summer; all around, flowers slumbered in their beds. As I followed signposts along a cinder pathway, I discovered places where invisible pools of warm air had gathered, filled with sweet fragrances. Half expecting to meet the ghost of Jennie Butchart wandering her earthly paradise, I finally reached the Japanese Garden. Lights shone on delicate plants, and water trickled between ponds where small statues represented pagodas.

Where was William? I felt very alone, and was glad that Laura had provided her cell phone. Was this some kind of hoax? As I hesitated, wondering what to do, I heard my name.

Liz, a voice called from the trees. *Liz! Liz!*

* * *

I squinted, looking for movement. Light flashed— once, twice, three times. I was confused for a moment, then realized I was looking at reflectors on the heels of someone's joggers.

Someone who was running down a path, away from me.

I quickly followed. The path sloped down, following a zigzag pattern lower and lower through the trees. I became aware of the ocean's salty smell, and I could hear waves slapping against the shore.

The roar of an engine split the night. I was startled by the noise, but pressed on. Moments later, I reached the ocean. The path ended at a wooden dock. Out on the water I saw a boat zooming away under the stars; no name was visible. At the controls was a figure, impossible to identify.

A surprise awaited me—lying on the dock was a metal tube. "Wait a minute," I exclaimed to myself.

"The thief at Thirteen Oaks put *Klee Wyck* inside a tube just like this."

I opened the tube at one end. Something was in there. Working quickly, I soon was able to remove a painting and unroll it. To my utter astonishment, I found myself gazing at a picture of a woman with a laughing face.

"Wow," I exclaimed. "This is the missing painting! This is *Klee Wyck*."

* * *

Seconds later I punched Memory-1 on the cell phone. When Paris answered, I immediately asked for Laura. "Guess what?" I exclaimed, and quickly told the news.

"We'll be right there," Laura said. "Guard that painting."

I heard Paris yelp, "What painting?" followed by dead air. Switching off the phone, I contemplated the laughing face of *Klee Wyck*. How wonderful that she'd been found!

Voices soon approached through the trees, then I saw Hart and the others. Pushing Laura aside, Paris hurried forward to grab the painting from my hands. "Amazing," he exclaimed. "This is marvellous. *Klee Wyck* has actually been returned."

"But why give back the painting?" Laura demanded. "It doesn't make sense."

"I guess that kid got cold feet and decided to abandon the thing." Paris kissed the painting. "I'm so happy. This ranks with the time I hit the jackpot at Vegas. No—it's even better."

Laura turned to me. "Liz, what happened?"

They listened to my story, then Laura smiled. "You deserve a reward. Don't you agree, Paris?"

"I guess you're right, Laura. Liz did find the painting."

"But why me?" I said. "Why the voice calling my name, and why the message in the envelope? What's going on? Nothing makes sense."

"Who cares," Paris exclaimed happily. "I've got my painting back. That's what matters."

Hart looked at him. "It's *our* painting, Paris. It belongs to the family."

"Okay, sure." Paris looked around at us. "Remember, you're sworn to secrecy. Keep a tight lid on this, okay?"

* * *

On Tuesday evening, Paris summoned a family gathering in the library at Thirteen Oaks. He wanted everyone to see the *Klee Wyck*, safely returned to its place above the fireplace.

Laura Singlehurst was there, looking glorious in a spectacular fashion creation. Major Wright also attended, which was a surprise. Somehow he'd learned the truth about the brief disappearance of *Klee Wyck*.

I stood beside Tiff, admiring Emily Carr's painting; the totems and the longhouses were captured with such artistry. I smiled, looking at the spirited face of the Laughing One, then I snapped out of my revery when Paris began shouting at Hart.

"I told you—*no way*." I stared at Paris—a vein bulged at his temple.

"We do not involve the police. Not now, not ever."

"But things don't add up, Paris. Why steal the painting, then return it?"

"It would be hard to make money with a stolen painting," Laura suggested. "Maybe the thief gave up trying."

Paris nodded. "I agree with Laura. Jason stole the wrong thing."

"If so," Hart responded, "he'll be back, looking for the right thing. I agree with Liz—something is rotten in the state of Denmark."

"Huh?" Paris said. "What's that mean?"

"It's nothing," Hart replied disdainfully. "Forget it."

Paris laughed. "Hart, you are such a fool."

Laura looked at the deMornay brothers. "In my opinion, don't involve the police. What are your thoughts, Major Wright?"

The Major focused his attention on the family circle. "I agree with Miss Singlehurst and Paris. We can't risk informing the police. Liz Austen's got a hyperactive imagination. Everyone in Winnipeg knows that."

Tiffany turned to the Major, annoyed. "Liz and her brother are famous crime-busters, Daddy."

"Tiffany, this is not a crime. The painting is hanging on the wall, in front of our eyes. Let's stay focused— we can't let anything spoil my daughter's romantic wedding."

Glancing into the dark hallway, I saw the butler. Cambridge lurked in the shadows, listening to every word. Noticing my stare, however, he hastily entered the library with refreshments on a wheeled trolley.

* * *

The gathering broke up soon afterward, with Paris ordering us to remain silent about anything involving Emily Carr's unknown masterpiece.

"Let's keep this in the family," he said, repeating one of his favourite arguments.

Later that evening, Tiff and I were still in the library. The security lasers were off; Hart had promised to return later to enter the code. (After the theft Paris had changed the code from 7-7-6-6, a classic example of closing the barn door too late.) Hart and the others had scattered to distant corners of the moody old mansion, leaving us alone with *Klee Wyck*.

"It's good Emily Carr went to those villages," I said, studying the painting, "so we've got her take on British Columbia long ago. I wish I could have met her."

Tiff shivered. "I'd be scared the monkey would bite."

I wandered around the bookshelves, studying the titles. The deMornay family liked to read; recent best-sellers shared the shelves with some really old books.

"This is a history of Thirteen Oaks," I told Tiff, selecting a mouldy oldy from the shelf. "Hey, look. There's a map of the estate in here. Maybe we could learn something."

I settled down on a leather sofa to read. But moments later, Pepper rushed into the library. "Liz, Tiff. Put down that book and come quickly!"

Tossing it down, I jumped to my feet. The three of us hurried into the dark hallway.

"I've looked everywhere for you," Pepper said.

"There's been a message from that guy Jason. From the *Outlaw*."

"That's amazing," I exclaimed.

We hurried through the old mansion. "We're going to the family office," Pepper explained. "Jason said to wait at the office, and he'd call back. It's you he's calling, Liz."

* * *

A long time passed while I paced back and forth in the office. I kept thinking about Jason's call—what could it mean?

"I'll make some lemonade," Pepper eventually offered, leaving for the kitchen.

When she returned, we glugged down the delicious, cold beverage. Then I stood up. "Forget Jason—he was pulling a hoax. It's time for bed."

"Are you sure?" Pepper asked.

"Yes—I'm sick of this. I'm going to the library to get that history of the estate. I need some bedtime reading."

The laser beams were still down at the library. I was looking forward to reading about Thirteen Oaks, but instead I got a surprise.

The book was gone.

8

I searched the library, but found nothing. The next day I returned with Pepper, and we both tried, again without success.

"This is so weird," I said, as we sat with glasses of lemonade. "First the painting disappears, and now a book. What gives?"

Pepper shook her head. "It beats me."

Later, driving downtown in the Jeep, I debated telling Tiffany about the Curious Incident of the Book in the Night. Only three days remained until her wedding, and Tiff was sometimes very agitated. Finally I decided against mentioning the book. Tiff looked tense, and I didn't want anything else to bother her.

We met Paris downtown at Ming's for a delicious Chinese meal with friends of theirs. I was the fifth wheel, but I didn't mind—I liked the other couple and, anyway, William had called, and I'd be seeing him later that evening. Nothing could bother me.

I have to admit that Paris was good for Tiff when she was moody. He whispered sweet nothings in her ear, and soon she was cheerful again. Leaving them at the table, I went to the washroom with their friend, Jennifer Scriver.

"Have you known Paris long?" I asked, as we combed our hair in front of the mirror.

Jennifer nodded. "I went to Shawnigan Lake School, same as Paris and Tiffany. He was a fun guy, but something's gone wrong."

"Meaning what?"

Jennifer looked at me in the mirror. "Paris went from grief about his dad to reckless behaviour. Now he's unstable, and looking for security. Someone to cling to."

"And Tiff is rock solid."

"You bet," Jennifer said. "Tiffany knows exactly what she wants—marriage and a family. She's also got a bank account. For Paris, it's the perfect package."

* * *

As we left the restaurant, Paris took Tiffany aside. I could see her shaking her head, then finally she frowned and handed him some money. Paris waved goodbye to me, and walked away with the other couple.

"They're heading for Sandown Raceway," Tiff said glumly. "I refused to go."

"I'm visiting William," I said. "Come with me. You need cheering up."

"You're sure William won't mind?"

"I doubt it."

I was right—William welcomed us warmly. His funky place was filled with objects and art that hinted at a unique personality. As I roamed the walls, studying everything, Tiff and William chatted in the tiny kitchen.

Heading downstairs, we met William's neighbour in the lobby; Sadie was the singer who'd been at the park, performing a concert for the trees. We enjoyed a friendly chat with her, then went outside.

"Sadie's multi-talented," William told us. "She paints miniatures—very beautiful. You should see the flowers with their tiny petals. Victoria is full of incredible artists."

Behind the house was a garage that William had converted into a studio. Inside, we saw his landscapes—he really loved British Columbia's forests, mountains and oceans. William concentrated on big vistas and filled his scenes with light.

"I love your art," I said. "It's so like Emily Carr."

"I certainly admire her work," William said, "and her courage. She didn't do things the easy way. She got into her canoe, and went out into nature. She went in pursuit of truth—to show the totems in their natural setting, in the forest and the villages, how they really looked. Emily Carr went through tremendous difficulties in pursuit of her art—you can imagine the social pressures against her. That's so admirable for a woman of her time, being brave enough to chase such a beautiful dream."

"I love listening to you," I said.

"That's good, Liz, because—"

A shrill *brrring* shattered the moment. I looked in annoyance at the phone, a paint-smeared relic with a rotary dial.

William picked it up and said, "William speaking."

Frowning, he listened to the caller. "You can have it back," he said angrily. "It's dirty."

Then William stared at the phone. "He hung up."

"Who was it?" I asked.

"No one important," William replied, avoiding my eyes. "Listen, I need a sweater. Wait here, okay? I'll get one from my apartment in the big house."

Tiff and I wandered around the studio, looking at canvases stacked against the walls. Then I stopped at a wooden desk in the corner; scattered across it were some photos, face down.

"I wonder what these are?" I reached toward the nearest photo. "Maybe preliminary studies for William's next project."

Then I heard William's voice. "Don't touch those."

Startled, I turned toward the sound. William stood in the doorway, pointing at me. "Liz, please don't touch those pictures."

"Sure," I replied, raising my hands. "No problem."

William scooped up the photos, dropped them into a drawer, and turned the key. "It's just," he said, pocketing the key, "that I'm . . . very superstitious."

"Me, too," I replied.

"Letting anyone see my next project would be really bad luck. You understand, Liz?"

"Of course." I studied William's handsome face. His eyes flicked from me to the desk, then back to me.

Was I making a mistake here?

"My uncle works on the pilot boat," William told us. "It's going out tonight and he's invited us along. Care to go?"

We both happily agreed.

"What's a pilot boat?" I asked later from the Jeep's back seat, as Tiff reached Cook Street.

William turned to her. "Let's stop at the Chateau Victoria, and I'll explain."

At the upscale hotel we took an elevator to the 18th floor, where seagulls winged past large windows enclosing a restaurant high above the city streets. It was early evening, and the descending sun made every colour intense. Beyond an assortment of roofs, we saw the green trees of Beacon Hill Park and a big freighter on the beautiful waters of the ocean strait. Visible beneath the mountains on the strait's far side was the city of Port Angeles, Washington.

"Lots of oceangoing vessels pass along this strait," William said. "In these narrow waters they need a nautical pilot on the ship to guide the captain safely through. The pilot is taken out to the vessel from Victoria on board the pilot boat. Uncle Joe is the boat's captain. We're going out as his guests."

"Cool," Tiffany exclaimed. "I need a distraction from all the wedding talk."

"Thanks so much," I said, smiling at William. This time I thought to myself, *He's so nice*.

* * *

Soon we reached Ogden Point, home to the pilot boat. The small vessel was sheltered from storms by a large breakwater, where people strolled as darkness arrived. Scuba divers explored the waters near the breakwater; some had neon glow ropes, which looked eerie shining beneath the surface. Nearby were large wharves; at one was a U.S. navy vessel, in town for a visit.

On board the pilot boat we were introduced to its captain, William's friendly uncle Joe. "A cruise ship named the *Galaxy* is passing by tonight," he explained, "bound for Alaska. We're taking a pilot to board the *Galaxy*, out on the strait."

"Why doesn't it stop in Victoria and collect the pilot before it sails?"

"Not all cruise ships visit here. Some passengers prefer a bigger city like Vancouver, but others find our town very friendly. Some locals even dress up in old-fashioned garb and hand out flowers at the cruise ship wharf. The passengers love that."

"Is your work dangerous?" I asked.

"It can be, especially in a storm. Our boat is mighty small alongside some of those cruise ships."

The pilot boat was indeed small, with an open deck and an enclosed cabin where the pilot was working on some papers. As Uncle Joe started the engine, he pointed at a blue heron standing near the shore. It looked so regal, totally focused on the water as it hungrily awaited a passing meal. "We call that heron Doug," Uncle Joe explained. "Doug's lived in this basin for 23 years."

Reaching open waters, Uncle Joe opened the throttle. A powerful roar sounded from below decks as the boat gathered speed, leaving a plume of spray in its wake. The boat had a solid hull and lots of power, so it moved smoothly through the waves.

Wearing fluorescent life preservers, we stood beside William's uncle on the deck. He was at the wheel, controlling the boat with an effortless grace. Behind us, the lights of Victoria glowed along the shoreline. It was a warm night; stars lit the dark sky as surf rushed away across the restless depths.

I pointed at the Dallas Road cliffs. "I guess that's Beacon Hill Park, up on top. What's the other dark area, farther down Dallas Road? Is that Ross Bay Cemetery, where Emily Carr is buried?"

"Yup," William replied.

"Maybe I'll go visit her grave."

I asked Uncle Joe if he'd seen the *Outlaw*. "The name sounds familiar," he said, looking at my drawing of the mystery boat. He promised to watch for it, then answered more questions about his work. "The worst thing is the fog," he told us. "You can imagine—buried in swirling mists while you're rocking and rolling on heavy seas, trying to park this small craft beside a huge elephant like the *Galaxy*. That can get pretty hair-raising."

"Ever had a man overboard?" William asked.

He nodded. "Pilots have to jump between vessels—sometimes one lands in the drink. But we're quick to save them. We have a safety procedure which we practise frequently."

The cruise ship approached out of the night, glittering with lights. It looked like a birthday cake with every candle glowing, and it was soooo big. My heart pounded with excitement; this was an amazing experience.

We moved in close to the *Galaxy*. It was impossible to see the upper decks, so far above; down at the water level, a large open door awaited the pilot. He wore a shirt and tie, plus a corduroy jacket and tan trousers. As we moved in on the cruise ship, the pilot tensed, ready to leap across the cold waters.

"Now," William exclaimed, as the vessels met. Immediately the pilot sailed through the air, landing nimbly inside the cruise ship. We three cheered and applauded; the grinning pilot bowed deeply, as Uncle Joe powered our vessel away from the *Galaxy*.

"Gosh," I said dreamily, watching the cruise ship's radiant lights twinkle away into the night. "That is such a vision."

* * *

The next morning I awoke long before dawn. Unable to sleep, I went to the kitchen. Cambridge was already there, moodily preparing coffee. Outside the window, birdsong heralded the coming day. "They're up early," I commented, glancing into the garden. "What a sweet sound they make."

A grunt was the butler's only reply. I pressed on, determined to remain cheerful. "Do local buses run this early?"

He glanced at the clock. "Yes, Miss Austen."

"How would I catch a bus to Dallas Road? I'm thinking of walking the cliffs, then visiting Emily Carr's grave."

The butler's shaggy eyebrows rose. "Why Emily Carr?"

I shrugged. "I'm a fan."

Cambridge disappeared from the room, then returned with a well-thumbed paperback. "This is the John Adams guide to Ross Bay Cemetery," he told me. "Take it with you—there are lots of fascinating stories about the people in that cemetery. It dates back to 1873, so you'll find the graves of many famous types. The quirky ones usually have the best stories. Like Emily Carr, for example."

"Thanks, Cambridge. You're very kind."

"It's no problem," he replied. "You see—"

Cambridge was interrupted by a plaintive *meow*. Opening the outside door, he looked down at a scrawny cat with ragged fur. "This stray's been coming by for food," Cambridge said, preparing a dish of leftovers, as the waif rubbed around his ankles, purring. "My brother owns a pet store in the Fairfield Plaza. He's always pleading with people—don't give pets as Christmas presents, because they can get abandoned once the festivities are over."

Cambridge watched the cat hungrily devour its feast. "Buy a pet in January, once you're certain it's not just a holiday whim."

What a nice man, I thought a little later, while hurrying through the quiet Uplands to the nearest bus stop. After a pleasant journey, I stepped from the bus in the quiet James Bay neighbourhood. At Dallas Road a sign pointed the way to a beach named for marathon runner Steve Fonyo. I photographed the sign, then moved on.

A paved walkway wandered along the clifftop, with the occasional path or stairs providing access to the ocean far below. In the pale sky, swallows flitted past, appearing to play, but probably chasing McInsects for breakfast. Over at the western hills the newborn sun reflected from the windows of homes, transforming the glass into sparkling jewels.

I wandered along the pathway, pausing to watch the pilot boat heading toward a large freighter. The tide was out, exposing wet seaweed on the rocks below; in the distance were the mountains, pale blue under the pink sky of early morning.

The path led to Beacon Hill Park, where a large sign announced this as Mile Zero of the Trans-Canada Highway. Inside the park, thick bushes and trees grew along the pathway. I studied a tugboat on the water; it looked motionless, straining against the mighty weight of the logs it towed. I watched birds winging across the water on important business, and heard pleasant whistling cries from within the trees. Yellow broom was scattered everywhere, lending its sweet fragrance to the morning air.

I then spotted the world's tallest totem pole, which I remembered from researching Victoria on the Net. Nearby was the hill that probably gave this park its name; in the days before lighthouses, a beacon up there would have warned boats away from the cliffs.

Before long I left Beacon Hill Park behind, but continued walking above the cliff. The early morning sun was on the ocean, shining a golden path for my pleasure. Beside me was a large green space, then a road and some small houses. White and purple wildflowers scattered their colours along the cliff. A kayaker was out, enjoying the good life, B.C. style. Seagulls called across the water, and waves lapped softly against the rocky beaches below. A blue heron lifted away from the water, circled, and was slowly airborne on impressive wings.

Finally I reached Ross Bay Cemetery, an oasis of shady trees beside the blue ocean. I opened my pack-sack, looking for water and more film, then leaned against a marble tombstone while I flipped through the cemetery guidebook. It was loaded with interesting stories.

At Emily Carr's grave, I was touched by the inscription, *Artist and author, lover of nature*. I took a photo, then wandered on. I stayed on the paved walkways, wanting to avoid crossing an unmarked grave (as many people know, doing so can cause your body to develop a serious rash). I studied a holly tree and then a monkey puzzle tree, its curved branches so like the tails of playful monkeys. One tombstone was called Pooley's marble angel; it was said to cry on nights with a full moon, according to the guidebook.

"I should check this out with William," I murmured to myself. "Too bad we missed the full moon."

In the guidebook, Cambridge had underlined several notes in green ink. Walking west, I studied the notes, trying to find a pattern. One note referred to a teenager who'd drowned in the Gorge waterway, so perhaps Cambridge—

Somewhere in the cemetery, a stick cracked loudly. I lifted my head and looked around—there were a lot of big tombstones. Bushes and trees also provided hiding places.

I could feel my heart thumping. For moments I waited. Nothing stirred but the occasional leaf drifting to earth.

I stared at a cobweb, shining on a stone cross—it was beautiful, but I felt frightened. I decided to go home; closing the guidebook, I lowered my packsack to stuff the book away. But my camera accidentally fell, smacking hard against the paved walkway. Annoyed, I picked up the camera—had it been damaged?

He came out of nowhere, a blur of motion.

Energy pumped through my body. I rolled swiftly aside to avoid the attack, then sprang into the ready position I knew from martial arts. Behind me, a hill fell down to Dallas Road. I breathed deeply, centring my energy and power in my torso.

The attacker wore a ski mask—all I could see were his eyes. For a moment he stared, then he lunged at me. Stepping swiftly aside and bringing up my foot, I kicked out at his leg. He yelled in pain and surprise, then went over the side. As he disappeared, I heard branches breaking and rocks pouring down the slope.

Running to the edge, I looked down. The guy stood up, painfully and slowly, and gave me a malignant stare before limping quickly away. Then he was gone from sight.

I knew what I had to do. I was going straight to the police.

9

I called Laura from a pay phone at the nearby Fairfield Plaza. She answered on the first ring and promised to join me ASAP. While waiting for Laura, I kept an eye on Fairfield Road; a car passed with Paris at the wheel, and that surprised me. He didn't seem the early-morning type.

Nervously I paced, watching shopkeepers opening their premises for the day. They were a relaxed crowd, exchanging greetings in the sunshine as they got ready, and I felt slightly better.

I saw Laura's BMW pull into the lot. As she stepped from the car, tall and elegant and so in control, I ran quickly to her. I guess I needed a hug more than I'd realized.

"I was so scared," I told Laura, as we headed for police headquarters in her car.

She patted my hand. "I know how you feel, Liz. I went through a similar experience."

After parking, we walked to the ultramodern police station on Caledonia Street. A detective took us into her office, where she poured coffee for Laura and bottled water for me. She listened carefully to all the details, then told us she'd be in touch if anything came up.

Back outside, I walked with Laura to her car. She'd offered to take me to the Inner Harbour. "I probably won't mention the attack to anyone," I said. "Tiffany would be really upset."

"That's a good idea," Laura agreed.

"Do you think this wedding makes sense?"

Laura smiled. "I've got an opinion, Liz, but I won't comment publicly."

* * *

At the Inner Harbour all kinds of people were out strolling, enjoying the musicians and artists. Boats of every type lined the wharves near the Empress Hotel, which glowed in the warmth of the sun. Some people were having their picture taken in front of the hotel, and other tourists were boarding red double-decker buses for tours of the city.

As arranged, I met Pepper at the statue of Captain Cook. We leaned against a stone wall, checking out the yachts and people below. The happy scene made me feel better. Four young men were singing "The Lion Sleeps Tonight." They harmonized without musical instruments, and received loud applause when the song ended. Everyone's mood seemed good—this was a beautiful place to be sharing.

I looked at the Empress. "Tiffany's in there right now, meeting with Major Wright. Tiff told me she's got news for her father, but she wouldn't tell me what it is."

Descending stone stairs, Pepper and I joined the crowd strolling the Lower Causeway. "I can't believe all the languages I'm hearing," I commented. "People must visit Victoria from the entire globe."

We paused to watch musicians from Peru performing on the causeway against the backdrop of the Legislative Buildings. Two men played panpipes—the music sweet and haunting—while another thumped a drum. The musicians were having fun, occasionally dancing in a circle around an open instrument case that awaited donations from onlookers.

We moved on. "I was interested in the band members' shoes," I said. "They seemed to fit each guy's personality, except for the tall one. He was heavy-set, but he wore paper-thin dancing shoes."

"You're quite the detective," Pepper said. Then she glanced at me. "How do you think the painting was stolen from Thirteen Oaks, Liz? Got any theories?"

"Someone inside the house must have been involved. Otherwise, how did the thief get past the security codes at the library?"

"Who do you think it was?"

I shook my head. "I can't say. There are too many suspects, and there's no real evidence."

As we continued our short walk, Pepper hummed a cheerful tune. A number of tents had been set up for a FolkFest, not far from the Empress. Arts and crafts were on display from all over the province. Pottery, jewellery, sweet-smelling soaps—even a First Nations raven mask with copper eyes.

A feature of the FolkFest was free entertainment on a large stage. Sitting on aluminum stands, we watched young Ukrainian dancers high-kick in bright costumes, while tiny girls from the audience joined in the fun, bouncing around in front of the stage to the rousing music, their parents watching from close by.

"I'm so lucky the servants help with Amanda," Pepper said. "Kids are so much work."

"What about her father helping?"

"He left town," Pepper replied. "You know, Liz, I can't imagine being a teenager alone with a baby, carrying diaper bags everywhere. I never realized the work involved—and the worry. I'm always freaked about Amanda—like, is she safe?"

"You mean from kidnappers?"

"I guess so," Pepper replied. "But I never thought about kidnappers before now. I just meant being safe from falling down. That kind of thing."

"Sorry," I said, feeling foolish.

"Don't worry, Liz," Pepper replied. "You're nice, and so is Tiffany. I wish she wouldn't marry Paris."

"Why?"

"For starters, he's a control freak. He's lucky that Tiffany is so sweet-natured—other women would tell Paris to take a hike." Pepper sighed. "Everything changed for Paris when our parents died. Pater's will contained a large cash payment for each kid. Hart made a smart investment with his legacy, but I lost mine buying into a dot-com company that failed."

"That's too bad."

Tiffany shrugged. "Anyway, Paris totally went stupid with his legacy. My brother's lifestyle was wild—you can't imagine the parties at Thirteen Oaks. The clothes he bought—incredible. Plus crazy stunts, very expensive stuff. Like flying his friends in chartered helicopters to Whistler for snowboarding and more parties. I've seen him burn through so much, so fast."

"Does Tiffany know about this?"

Pepper nodded. "Anyway, I guess Paris blew all Pater's money. Now he's back to his allowance from the family trust. For me the allowance is plenty to live on, but Paris is a different breed of cat."

"Tiffany is so trusting," I said. "She always looks for the good side in people. Major Wright is a pretty nice guy, but basically an emotional manipulator. He's decided this marriage makes sense for Tiffany, and he thinks her doubts are just pre-wedding jitters."

"She's bought into that?"

"So far," I replied. "Tiff really loves and respects her dad. She values his opinion." Lost in thought, I absent-mindedly ran my fingers through my hair. Then I turned to Pepper. "You know what Tiff believes? If she gives Paris enough love, he'll get over his problems. And I'm just not certain it's possible."

* * *

We visited the food stands, where the goodies looked scrumptious and the smells were so delicious. I settled on a vegetarian pita from the Mediterranean stand, perogies from the Polish White Eagle Association, and

Rose's "Awesome" chocolate cake from the Jewish Community Centre.

People were eating at outdoor tables. "I'll tell you the problem with Paris," Pepper commented, as we looked for vacant chairs. "Too much money, and no Pater to control him. Our father ruled by fear, and Paris always toed the line. He wasn't a rebel until Pater died. Then my brother went crazy, doing all the things that would have scandalized Pater." She paused. "Of course, I'm not perfect, either. Pater was *so* upset when I got pregnant." Pepper shook her head. "What a crazy family I was born into, Liz, but I love them anyway. They're my kin."

"It's fun to know you, Pepper."

She smiled. "You, too."

At a sunny table we sat down next to a mother and her kids; when a ladybug landed on our table, the eldest girl said, "Now we'll all have good luck."

That superstition was new to me, and I thanked the girl for it. "We need some luck," I said, thinking of Tiffany. "I'll be watching for more ladybugs."

Pepper looked into the distance. "Wow," she murmured. "Who is this?"

Turning, I saw William walking toward our table. He was tall and so blond in the sunshine, and people noticed him. Seeing me, William's face broke into a beautiful smile.

"Liz, you're here. And you're safe."

"Sure, I'm fine," I replied, and introduced Pepper. "Why are you surprised?"

"I heard something happened at the cemetery," William said. "Is it true?"

"Yes, but how'd you find out?"

For a moment, William looked confused. "It was . . . well, from someone I know."

"Someone in the police?"

William shook his head. "No. You see—"

The ringing of my cell phone interrupted William. When I answered, I heard Tiffany's voice. "Liz," she exclaimed, "it was horrible."

Walking away from Pepper and William, I covered my ear against the noisy crowd. "Tiff, what's wrong?"

"I told Daddy I couldn't marry Paris, and he got so upset. Liz, he was crying. In the Empress, in front of everyone. People were staring."

"But . . ."

"It was just a mess, Liz. I can't hurt Daddy's feelings, ever again. I'm going ahead with the wedding."

"Tiff, where are you? I'll come to you—we'll talk."

"Not now. Daddy's so upset, he needs me. I'll stay a while with him, okay? Then I'll go home to Thirteen Oaks. I'll see you there."

"Sure, but—"

"Liz, I gotta go. Talk to you later."

The call upset me greatly, but I said nothing to William or Pepper. Leaving the FolkFest, we walked together to a transit stop where Pepper caught a bus. She was heading home to Thirteen Oaks, to see her darling Amanda. We waved goodbye, then William turned to me. "There's something I've wanted to mention. You see . . ."

Silently, I waited for him to continue.

Then William shook his head. "Maybe later, Liz." He paused, thinking. "There's a special event tonight at Carr House, which is the birthplace of Emily Carr. They're holding a Victorian salon, with refreshments and singing around the piano. Care to go with me?"

"Certainly."

William and I lingered at the Inner Harbour until evening came to the city. He seemed worried, but said nothing about his thoughts. He was very quiet as we strolled south on Government Street.

Carr House reminded me of an old-fashioned doll-house with its little windows and gingerbread decorations. In the garden, small signs carried passages from Emily Carr's writings. Reading them, William cheered up. "Emily Carr was also a prolific author," he told me. "Ever read her *Book of Small*? It describes her child-hood here. When Emily was a girl, she'd come outside and sing to the family cow!"

I laughed. "It's nice to see you smile again," I told William.

At the side door we were welcomed by Jan, the cheerful woman in charge of Carr House. She knew William well because of his interest in the famous artist; after the introductions, she beamed at William. "It's about time you found someone special."

He grinned and shrugged and shuffled his feet, while Jan and I exchanged a smile.

Inside the house I met Jan's friendly daughters. She explained that the "marbled" wallpaper was hand-painted, and the elaborate outfits hanging on pegs were similar to the clothes worn by Emily and other members of the Carr family.

"People come to Victoria from all over the world," Jan told me, "just to visit the scenes of Emily Carr's life. Many are like pilgrims—they can relate to her struggles. She was an artist ahead of her time, and quite misunderstood. Much of the fame happened after her death. Do you know, only 50 people attended her funeral. Sad, eh?"

"Personally," William said, "I love this place. Imagine, Emily Carr's spirit may still linger here, within these very walls."

The parlour was exquisitely furnished in the Victorian manner. Above the fireplace was a large oval mirror supported by two fish carved from wood; I also noticed a framed portrait of the famous monkey, Woo, wearing a dress with a big yellow bow. "When Emily Carr lay dying," Jan told us, "that portrait of Woo was near her bed. She really must have loved her little friend."

Several seniors sat on velvet chairs, singing along as a lady made enthusiastic music at the piano. We joined in for "A Bicycle Built for Two," our voices loud. Then I glanced out the window. Into this perfect scene came a white horse pulling a white carriage, its big wheels slowly turning. A couple sat in the carriage, enjoying an outing through the yesteryear streets of the James Bay heritage neighbourhood.

But I got a surprise. The man in the carriage was Tiffany's father, Major Wright. Who was the woman?

* * *

Outside Carr House, William and I speculated about the woman's identity. Then I lowered my head, feeling shy. "I've got an idea."

"What's that?"

"Feel like going to the Ross Bay Cemetery?"

"Sure, but why?"

Now it was my turn to shuffle my feet. "You see, in the cemetery there's a stone angel. She's said to cry during a full moon. Maybe it's true."

William glanced up at the quarter moon. "But . . ."

"I don't really care about the angel, William. I just thought it would be a nice quiet place . . ." My voice trailed off. To be truthful, being with William had made me forget about the attack, but now I wasn't too sure about going back there.

But before I could say anything more, William nodded. "Next stop, Ross Bay Cemetery."

We walked east along Dallas Road. Above the ocean the sky glowed with stars and moonlight; we saw a ship passing by, its lights shining in the night. The tree-shaded streets of the city were quiet as people settled in; I saw a man walking two Scottie pups, but otherwise nothing stirred.

At the cemetery I paused, feeling nervous. I remembered the attack, but I overcame my fear. "Let's keep moving," I said to William. All around were the dim outlines of really old monuments to people who had once lived and loved in the homes of Victoria. Now they slumbered here; I somehow felt that their spirits accepted our presence on this beautiful night.

William looked at me. "Liz . . ."

My heart was beating in triple time. What would happen next? "William . . ."

I saw a movement in the dark trees. "Someone's there."

William laughed nervously. "You're joking, right?"

I shook my head. "I saw something."

"What are you saying—a ghost?"

"I doubt it." I looked at William. "I'm going to investigate."

"I'll go with you."

"Thanks," I said gratefully.

Out on the ocean a seabird cried, breaking the silence. Cautiously we moved through the cemetery, then finally took shelter behind a large tombstone. Close by was a monument, very wide and very tall. Carved into the marble were names and dates; at the top was a cross, and the name *deMornay*. A single red rose lay on the monument.

Standing nearby was Cambridge, the butler from Thirteen Oaks.

As we approached, Cambridge turned in surprise. "Miss Austen?" he said, wiping tears from his eyes. "Why are you here?"

"We're, um . . . out for a walk. Are you okay, sir? I mean, you've been crying."

"It's just the blues, Miss Austen. Occasionally I come here with a rose for Lady deMornay. She's the person who hired me to work at Thirteen Oaks. She was a fine, fine woman."

I nodded. "Hart and Pepper both miss her a lot. I'm not so sure how Paris feels."

Cambridge shook his head. "Master Paris just sold her painting at auction. Can you imagine? His own mother, and he sells her portrait for money."

Suddenly I slapped my forehead. "Listen, I'm being so rude. Please, let me introduce my friend."

To my pleasure, Cambridge knew William's name. "I follow the local art scene," he explained, "and people call you a rising star."

"Wow." William looked astonished. "That is so amazing."

"Your work is influenced by Emily Carr, I understand. In time you'll find your own, unique voice, but for now she's an excellent role model."

"That is just so nice," William enthused, shaking Cambridge's hand. "Thank you very much!"

I smiled, happy for William.

10

Early the next morning I talked to Tiffany, who was feeling slightly better. "It'll be a good marriage," she promised me. "Besides, I simply can't upset Daddy. What if his heart fails? Our family doctor warned me that Daddy has high blood pressure."

Tiffany left in the Jeep, heading for downtown and breakfast with her father at the Empress. I was in the sunroom reading Danda Humphreys' history of Victoria street names when Hart appeared. He was wearing a white shirt and black trousers.

"Hey, Liz—remember saying you'd like to get aboard a cruise ship? Well, close that book, because your chance has come."

"Excellent."

We hurried outside. "Cruise ships dock at Ogden Point," Hart explained. "We're invited aboard the *Crystal Paradise*."

At the estate's 10-car garage, Cambridge waited beside the Daimler. "Normally I'd ride my bicycle to Ogden Point," Hart said, as we settled back on the limo's luxurious leather seats, "but we're running very late. I slept in. It was a busy night."

"For me, too," I responded.

"Quickly, please," Hart said to Cambridge, who was at the wheel. "We're late."

Hart turned to me. "I belong to a service club called Victoria A.M. We promote local tourism—for example, by welcoming cruise ship passengers to Victoria."

"Why belong to a service club, when you're so wealthy?"

"It's important to give back to the community, Liz. Besides, I've got my own ecotourism business. I like talking shop with other members of Vic A.M."

"Pepper mentioned something about you greeting the cruise ships. Exactly what happens?"

"We give each lady a flower and each gentleman a handshake as they leave the ship."

"That sounds like fun."

"I've got permission for you to join us. I just made arrangements with Rachel and Bob, who organize our Meet and Greet Program. They've been married for 57 years. Mary Helmcken also may be there. Her family goes back to Sir James Douglas, the first governor of British Columbia."

"Cool—I'd love to meet her."

"You ladies will wear splendid dresses from the Edwardian period, and the gentlemen will be in top hats and evening suits. We'll get photographed a lot—wait and see."

"Has Tiffany ever done this? I bet she'd look gorgeous in one of those dresses."

"I've thought about inviting Tiff," Hart replied. "But she's engaged to Paris. It wouldn't be proper."

"I'll tell you something, Hart. I don't think Paris is right for Tiffany."

He turned to me, startled. "Really? Why's that?"

"Where do I begin? There are a million reasons. Haven't you noticed?"

"Sure, but . . ." A blush spread slowly across Hart's face. "But what would happen to Tiff? If she didn't marry Paris? What would she do? Where would she go?"

I smiled. "She'd think of something, I'm sure."

When the Daimler reached the Dallas Road cliffs, I looked for the *Outlaw*, but without success. Then I was distracted by the sight of the cruise ship docked at Ogden Point. Even from this distance it looked massive, looming over the dock and the red double-decker buses parked alongside many taxis and limousines for hire.

"Cruise ships stay in port all day," Hart explained, "so most passengers come ashore to sightsee."

At a small building near the wharf we changed into our costumes. The members of "Vic A.M." were a cheerful lot; I chatted with Rachel and Mary while their friend Flo helped adjust my elaborate hat and gown of crimson satin.

Hart and the other men walked with us to the ship; each of the ladies carried a basket of brightly coloured flowers. The cruise ship's bow shimmered with sunlight that reflected from the ocean waters, an impressive backdrop as we took photos of each other.

Cruise passengers waved to us from the many decks above. One of Victoria's famous hanging flower baskets was placed beside the gangplank for photo opportunities, and then the passengers descended.

At first I was timid, but the people were very friendly. "You look real English," said a man with a southern twang to his voice. "How about letting me get a photograph of you?"

I was impressed, listening to Flo speak in French to people from Québec and Europe. The others also kept busy, giving advice on what Victoria attractions to visit, plus constantly posing for photographs.

Then it was time to board the cruise ship!

We climbed the gangplank behind Tommy Mayne, a retired high school teacher who'd been energetically clanging a brass bell in his role as Victoria's town crier. Our identification was checked by a crew member at the top of the gangplank, and then we entered the ship's central atrium.

I looked up, surprised at the open and airy spaces above. In this large gathering place, passengers strolled or chatted with crew members; along one side, glass-enclosed elevators rose to the many upper decks. Bright waters streamed down a wall, framing a statue of a dancing couple. Nearby was a crystal piano—an amazing sight.

We began handing out flowers while answering questions from people curious about our outfits. The passengers came from many countries—and everyone said they'd like to live in Victoria. After posing for more pictures, we ascended a grand staircase that swept up to a collection of shops displaying expensive gowns, jewellery and perfumes.

Flo's husband, Eric, smiled at me. "Did you bring your platinum credit cards, Liz?"

"Unfortunately not," I laughed.

We chanced upon the ship's movie theatre, where a man slumbered alone amidst the empty seats. Flo took a picture and the flash woke the man, who looked around blearily. Giggling together, we scurried away.

The others were waiting for an elevator. When it arrived, we crowded inside. We adjusted our hats in front of the mirrors, while the elevator swiftly rose an amazing 11 stories to the Lido Deck.

Through a glass door I could see some people lounging beside a large swimming pool. We entered a restaurant where others were enjoying breakfast; when Tommy clanged the brass bell, they all jumped. Then everyone relaxed and smiled as we rushed around dispensing the last of our flowers. "Welcome to Canada's best bloomin' city," I kept saying—an expression I'd heard the others using.

Our duties complete, we received our treat—a late breakfast, courtesy of the cruise ship. The selection of delicacies was mind-boggling; we were offered 10 different juices, omelettes loaded with smoked salmon, fruit, link sausages, bacon—you name it.

Carrying trays laden with food, we went outside to the open deck. I took Flo and Eric's photograph beside a statue of a mermaid, then joined Hart, Les Chan, and Tommy at a round table. The others sat close by.

Munching our delicious breakfast, we enjoyed Rachel's description of the deer she'd seen in her yard that morning. "Their coats were as sleek as this table-top," she said. "We even had a mom and two little spotted babies—they were so cute. I put out carrot peelings for them."

"We've had deer in our garden, too," Tommy said, "eating the tender leaves of the hydrangeas."

After finishing my meal I strolled to the railing, where I looked at the blue waters far below. A number of small boats had assembled, their occupants staring up at our mighty vessel.

Then my cell phone rang. It was William, sounding agitated.

"Liz," he exclaimed. "Can you meet me? I've made a decision—we must talk."

"Of course," I replied.

"Be outside the Royal B.C. Museum in one hour. I've got something really important to tell you."

* * *

Forty minutes later, Cambridge stopped the Daimler outside the museum, which was located near the Inner Harbour. "What a mob scene," I said, surprised at the number of people gathered on the large lawns outside the Legislative Buildings. They sat on rugs and aluminum chairs facing the water, where a barge had been anchored. "What's going on?"

"Later tonight," Hart explained, "the Victoria Symphony Orchestra will be on that barge, playing classical tunes. It's an annual event called the Symphony

Splash. These people have arrived early, to get the best spots."

"I wouldn't mind attending," I said wistfully.

"Didn't anyone tell you? Major Wright has invited us all to watch the Splash from his suite at the Empress. We'll have a choice view."

"Excellent!"

After waving goodbye to Hart and watching the Daimler drive off, I studied the museum. It was a large, handsome building of white stone. Through big windows I saw ancient totem poles that had been gathered long ago, perhaps from the very villages that Emily Carr captured in her books and paintings.

Then my heart lurched.

At the Inner Harbour I saw William—with someone else.

The two of them strolled arm in arm along Belleville; she looked pert and summery in a yellow dress and sun hat. Then, to my horror, I saw William hug the girl. As she hurried away, she turned to blow him a kiss.

I watched William walk toward the museum. I was horrified—frozen by indecision. I thought, *maybe she was in those photos that William scooped into hiding in his studio*. Pain stabbed me. I remembered seeing Hart with that pretty Lorna, who turned out to be family. Maybe this had the same explanation? Not likely, I thought bitterly.

William saw me and smiled. In the distance beyond him, I could still see that girl in her yellow dress. I really wished I'd never seen them together—I felt so down about it. I wanted to run, to escape the jealousy. It hurt so much.

As William approached, I produced a totally phony smile. He looked surprised, but I didn't care. Bad vibrations ruled my heart.

"What's wrong?" William asked, looking at me with those wonderful eyes.

I refused to melt. "Nothing," I replied, giving him another frosty smile.

"Something's bothering you, Liz. Please, tell me what's wrong."

"Hey," I said, looking for a diversion, "this museum could be interesting. Let's take a look, okay?"

"Sure, but what's wrong?"

"Nothing much."

"Liz, there's something I need to tell you. That's why I asked to meet."

"Later, maybe," I replied. I was so sulky.

I felt terrible, especially when William fell into silence. I was quiet, too, lost in misery. We stepped onto an escalator; at the top, William turned to me. "Let's go see the woolly mammoth. It's my favourite exhibit."

"You go, William." I looked at my map of the museum. "I'm going to check out the First Peoples Gallery. It interests me more." I was lying—what I really needed was time alone, time to think. I'd never felt this way before. It was horrible.

"Okay," William said. "I'll meet you in the gallery. Wait for me, okay? I know you're angry, Liz, but don't walk out."

I watched William disappear around a corner. Instantly I felt alone, and awful. What monster of jealousy had seized my heart? I felt so guilty, and I badly needed to apologize.

Hurry back, *William*, I whispered anxiously.

I entered the First Peoples Gallery, where the lighting was dim. I was in a room designed to resemble a longhouse from the days when Native villages dominated the B.C. coast. I looked at the four totem poles supporting a wooden roof, trying to picture Emily Carr visiting a longhouse like this.

The gallery continued into a second large room containing many huge totems. Indirect lighting glowed discreetly, as did a red *Exit* sign over an emergency door. I studied a replica of a seaside village, complete with miniature canoes on a beach. The village looked perfect in every detail.

Then I saw William, reflected in the glass of the display case. He'd just entered the room.

William looked grim, but I wasn't surprised. I'd been really spiteful, and I couldn't wait to apologize. What to say? I stared at the miniature village, trying to find the right words. Then a loud buzzing distracted me, and a door slammed shut. Turning from the display, I looked for William.

But he wasn't there.

I searched the gallery, then walked quickly to the outside corridor. Tourists passed by, chattering happily. I couldn't see William—what was going on? Now I felt really bad about my sulky mood.

After rushing back inside the First Peoples Gallery, I hurried to the Modern History Gallery. I searched the face of every tall boy, unable to believe this was happening. I felt as if I'd entered a dream state, and I wanted to cry.

Entering a town from the Old West, I tried to decide my next move. Happy people surrounded me, laughing and exclaiming as they wandered past the Grand Hotel and an old railway station and other exhibits.

At last I made a decision. After looking for William at the woolly mammoth, I left the museum. As enthused people hurried past, I took out my cell phone and called Laura Singlehurst.

"Please be home," I whispered, as her line rang and rang. "Don't let a machine answer."

Then Laura was there, her voice breathless. "I was outside, talking to the moving van guys. I ran to catch the phone—I thought it could be important."

"It is important," I cried, as tears rolled from my eyes. "Oh, Laura, please come get me. I'm at the Royal B.C. Museum, and I'm so frightened. Please drive me home, so I can talk to you."

"I'll be right there."

True to her word, Laura soon pulled up in a bright red Cadillac. "This is a rental," she explained, opening the door for me. "I've sold the BMW."

I told Laura everything. "I was so sulky," I moaned. "What if I never see William again? I was horrible to him!"

Laura patted my hand sympathetically. "There must be a simple explanation. What about the emergency exit at the gallery? You heard the door slam shut."

"You mean, William left that way?"

"He could have," Laura replied. "I think maybe his feelings are hurt, but he'll come back. Wait and see."

"I should contact the police."

"Not yet," Laura said. "Wait at least 24 hours, in case William shows up."

Soon Thirteen Oaks appeared ahead. At the front door of the mansion, I quickly thanked Laura, then ran inside. I was longing for a message from William.

But there was nothing. Alone in my room, I broke down and cried and cried.

* * *

Two hours later, Tiff returned home. In her room, I confessed my foolishness.

She listened sympathetically.

"What are your instincts saying?" she asked.

"To trust William."

"There's your answer. He'll return, don't you worry." Tiffany sighed. "I'm getting married tomorrow," she moaned, "and meanwhile Paris insists that we attend the Symphony Splash this evening after the rehearsal. But I just don't want to."

"Then, don't go, Tiffany."

"Paris doesn't want to upset my father. Daddy has invited us to his suite at the Empress overlooking the Splash activities. Everyone has to attend."

"I'm not going," I declared. "I'm too upset about William."

"Maybe he'll be at the Splash," Tiffany suggested.

"That's a thought. But what if he's with that girl?"

"Then the truth will set you free."

"I don't want freedom," I murmured sadly. "I want William."

Late in the day we attended the wedding rehearsal at the castle. The Major kept checking his watch, probably feeling impatient about the 24 hours still remaining until his daughter became Lady deMornay.

After the rehearsal Pepper returned home with her baby, who was fussy and maybe coming down with something. Major Wright left early in a taxi for the Empress Hotel. When the rehearsal ended, the rest of us crowded into the Daimler. I was squeezed in beside Kate Partridge, maid of honour to Tiffany. Kate lived in Victoria, and told some funny stories about the city as we drove downtown. The classic limousine attracted a lot of stares. Crowds of people were on the sidewalks, carrying lawn chairs and blankets toward the Inner Harbour.

"They'll never find a place to sit," Cambridge predicted from the wheel. "Forty thousand are expected for the Symphony Splash. According to CBC Radio, people started arriving at dawn to pick a good location."

We stepped from the limousine on Douglas Street. "Please, wait for me," Tiffany said to Cambridge. "I'll be back in a few minutes, and I'd appreciate a ride home."

Cambridge touched his chauffeur's cap. "Very good, miss."

Hart looked disappointed. "What's wrong, Tiffany?"

"Too many things to do," she replied. "Hey, tomorrow night I'm getting married."

Paris smiled at her. "Your father's going to be upset. I bet he'll have other guests, all anxious to chat with his perfect daughter."

"Well," Tiff replied, "that's just too bad."

A security guard checked our identification, then admitted us to the Victoria Convention Centre, which adjoins the Empress Hotel. We hurried past a magnificent indoor totem pole and climbed a few stairs to the hotel, where the reception would be held after the wedding.

I looked at Tiffany. "You're missing the Splash? Won't your father mind?"

"Maybe," Tiffany replied. She looked scared; she was breathing deeply as we entered an elevator and rode up. We stepped out into a hallway—it was very wide, with portraits of British royalty on the walls. Major Wright waited at the door of his suite; at his side was a woman I recognized. She'd been on the carriage ride with the Major.

"This is Marjorie," the Major said. "We met last week—we were both taking tea in the lobby. Marjorie's in Victoria on holiday from Texas." He beamed at Tiffany. "Marjorie's my date for this century's most romantic event."

"I enjoy high-society weddings," Marjorie told me. Stepping closer, she lowered her voice. "The deMornay family is, of course, *very* high society."

Tiffany looked at her father. "Daddy, I'm not staying for the Splash. I'm going home."

"Nonsense," the Major replied. "Come into the suite."

"But, Daddy, I'm getting married tomorrow."

"Please, honey. This is important to me."

"Daddy, I'm sorry. I can't stay."

Tiff quickly told me and Kate goodbye, then rushed toward the elevators. The Major took a step in her direction, then stopped. Glancing at Marjorie, he faked a jolly grin. "Kids these days."

Paris looked at him. "It's just pre-wedding jitters, Major Wright. Nothing to worry about."

"Let's hope so," the Major replied.

His large suite overlooked the Inner Harbour. Laura was there, along with several of the Major's Winnipeg friends, in town for the wedding. We exchanged handshakes and small talk, then I finally rushed into the adjoining room. I'd brought binoculars from Thirteen Oaks and was anxious to scan the crowd for William. With forty thousand in attendance my chances were slim, but I had to try.

From the window I saw an enchanting scene—the evening sun was a golden sphere that reflected from the blue waters of the harbour and threw long shadows behind the people who crowded the lawns below.

Laura joined me, carrying a platter of food. "The crab sandwiches are delicious," she said. "Or try the *paté de foie gras*. The taste is heavenly."

"Thanks, Laura, but I'm not hungry."

"No news about William?"

I shook my head mournfully. "Nothing."

"I'm so sorry, Liz."

The harbour was dominated by the barge where the symphony would play. On the water, music lovers had assembled to listen in canoes and motorboats, kayaks and cruisers. The shore was dense with people, and they covered every available spot as far as the distant steps of the Legislative Buildings.

"This is hopeless," I said, training the binoculars on the crowd. "William could be anywhere."

In the distance a helicopter lifted off from Ogden Point and moved slowly toward the Inner Harbour, sunlight glinting from its whirling blades. "Sight-seers," Laura said. "They've paid a lot of money for a bird's-eye view of this scene. A friend of Hart's owns that helicopter company."

On the barge, the members of the Victoria Symphony Orchestra warmed up their instruments. Then these sounds stopped, and we heard the opening notes of "O Canada." Immediately the spectators stood up, on the lawns and the streets and out on the bigger boats, to sing the national anthem.

The concert began with a rousing selection that received a huge cheer from the enthusiastic crowd. Then people nodded along to Bizet's "Carmen Suite" and Gershwin's "Fascinating Rhythm." But the big hit was a solo performance of a Mozart piano concerto by Victoria's 12-year-old Samuel Seong, who exhibited great self-confidence.

During the intermission we watched the Canadian Scottish Regiment march proudly past to the rattle of drums and the skirl of bagpipes. Glow ropes had appeared in the crowd, their neon colours beautiful in the gathering darkness; I saw a young Splash volunteer and another boy having a mock sword fight with lime green glow ropes.

With the binoculars I scanned the crowd, hoping, always hoping. Laura returned from the other room, auburn hair swinging. "There'll be some great music after the intermission," she said, "followed by the grand finale. It's the '1812 Overture,' Tchaikovsky's celebration of a famous Russian military victory over Napoleon's armies. It was written to be performed outside, with the loud ringing of church bells and the sound of cannons adding to the victorious music. The music went immediately to number one on the classical charts, and it's been popular ever since. It's rousing, cheerful stuff." She smiled at me. "We'll hear bells and cannons tonight, followed by fireworks."

"It sounds wonderful, Laura. I just wish William was here."

"Don't worry about that other girl, Liz."

"Thanks, Laura. I'll try not to."

Laura went to visit with Kate and Marjorie, the Major's friend from the United States, and I scanned the crowd with the binoculars. Hart joined me for a talk, and then Paris appeared. He dropped into a nearby chair and flipped through the pages of a magazine.

I tried the crowd again with the binoculars. "Oh, my goodness, there he is!"

11

Hart leaned close to the window. "William?"

"No, that kid Jason. The one from the *Outlaw*. He's beside the statue of Captain Cook—I'd know him anywhere."

I handed the binoculars to Hart. "I'm going down there. First that guy took a shot at us. After that, he firebombed the *Amor*, then he stole the painting and returned it. I want to know what's going on."

"Let me go with you."

I shook my head. "No thanks, Hart. I've got my cell phone, and I'll be perfectly safe in that big crowd. I work best on my own."

"How can I reach you?"

I gave Hart my cell number, then thanked Major Wright for his hospitality. After explaining my mission to Laura, I hurried to the elevator, took it down, and left the Empress. Jason was across the crowded street, holding a cell phone against his ear; suddenly he snapped it shut, and surveyed the crowd with suspicious eyes.

Then he was gone, down the stone stairs beside Cook's statue. Shouting for him to stop, I hurried forward through the crowd.

At the statue I groaned in dismay. On the causeway below was a solid wall of humanity; using brute strength, Jason was forcing a path through the crowd. People shook their fists after him, as parents comforted wailing toddlers and others expressed disgust in loud voices, but Jason just kept moving. Only once did he pause, when he turned to wave up at someone in the Empress.

All around were the rich sounds of powerful music. Without my noticing, the concert had resumed. I looked up at the hotel, searching for the Major's suite. All vehicles had been banned from the immediate vicinity, so the wide expanse of Government Street was filled with strolling people, many speaking foreign languages.

I walked south through the throng, envying people their happiness. Seeing the Royal B.C. Museum, I remembered my last moments with William. He'd have loved this scene—the night air was festive and the musicians on the brightly lit barge looked so spectacular, all of them wearing white.

People were clapping in time, while others bopped around to a Sousa march, a favourite of my dad's. I smiled sadly, wishing my family were here. I could have used my brother's help with this investigation, but he was on summer holidays with his pal, the odious Dietmar Oban.

My cell phone went *ta-ta-tring-tring*. It was Hart calling. "Are you okay, Liz?"

"Yes."

"That's good. Any sign of Jason?"

"I lost him in the crowd."

"Too bad. Listen," Hart continued, abruptly changing the subject, "I've got news you'll like. A friend just called, offering you a free seat on tonight's final helicopter tour. Cambridge is waiting with the Daimler outside the Crystal Garden. He'll take you there, but hurry."

Immediately I took off running toward the corner of Douglas and Belleville. "What's with the chopper?" I asked Hart as I ran with my phone.

"My friend owns it. Someone cancelled their trip, and he offered me seats."

"I hope you're coming along," I shouted into the phone, running hard toward the Daimler. I saw Cambridge waiting, the door already open.

"No thanks," Hart replied. "There isn't enough time."

"Thanks for the opportunity!"

The drive didn't take long. The helicopter waited near the wharf where we'd visited the cruise ship; it resembled a large insect with its giant blades and large windows. For a moment I imagined spotting William from the chopper, but even with binoculars he'd be impossible to see from up that high.

To my surprise, Cambridge asked for permission to join the trip. "Sure thing," the pilot replied. "There's enough space."

When the helicopter lifted off, I was unexpectedly reminded of what happened when I was a hostage at Disneyland. Closing my eyes, I pictured hot-tempered Serena Hernandez, and how she behaved. It was a horrible memory.

When I opened my eyes a few moments later, I saw people below in their yards and on apartment balconies, watching the sky for the coming fireworks. I sat in the best seat, beside the pilot. She smiled at me.

"We'll reach the Empress exactly as the '1812 Overture' concludes. Watch for the cannons to fire."

Far below we saw the fairy lights that decorated the Legislative Buildings, and the streets twinkling all the way to the ocean at Oak Bay. On the water, the orchestra's bandshell shone brightly.

Beside the Inner Harbour, orange flames exploded from cannons. "Those guns are fired by sailors from HMCS *Quadra*," the pilot told us. "They're antique cannons, brought to Victoria each summer for the Symphony Splash. They're firing blanks, of course."

A sudden explosion burst in the sky, scattering colours. "The fireworks," the pilot exclaimed, looking at the bright jewels exploding in the night. "Oh, aren't they beautiful!" It was thrilling to watch the eruptions of fire and light from here, and I kept wishing William could see this incredible scene.

Then, too soon, it was over, and numerous headlights sprang to life all around the Inner Harbour.

"There'll be a traffic jam tonight," Cambridge predicted gloomily. "Just the thing to set off Master Paris's bad temper."

Our helicopter headed south over the slumbering trees of Beacon Hill Park. In the distance I saw the outline of the Olympic Mountains; close by, the Dallas Road cliffs overlooked the shoreline.

"Wait a minute," I said, sitting up straight. "Look at that boat—it could be the *Outlaw*. Can we get closer?"

The pilot glanced at her watch. "There's time, if—"

"No," Cambridge said sharply. "We must return immediately to Ogden Point."

"But," I pleaded, "surely . . ."

"My name is not Shirley," Cambridge replied crossly, "and I haven't got time to waste on a wild-goose chase. Master Paris will expect the limousine back at the Empress Hotel. He'll be furious if we're late."

It was hopeless to argue, and I watched sadly as the boat disappeared in the direction of Oak Bay. It could have been the *Outlaw*, but how would I ever know?

* * *

The next day was terrible.

I tried and tried to reach William by phone, without success. As for Tiffany, she sat at her window, gazing out to sea. I couldn't get her to talk, and she looked a misery.

At seven p.m., the wedding party gathered in the drawing room at Craigdarroch Castle. A marriage commissioner was there to perform the ceremony. Paris deMornay looked so smug; he wore a white tuxedo, and so did Hart, who was best man. They stood with us in front of the white fireplace, awaiting the arrival of the bride. A couple of dozen guests sat in chairs, glancing expectantly toward the door. When would Tiffany arrive?

From outside the panelled oak doors, we heard an organ play the opening bars of "Here Comes the Bride." Laura and the other guests stood up. The bride appeared, and my heart just about stood still; her downcast eyes were puffy from tears.

Beside Tiffany was the Major. Wearing an expensive suit and shiny shoes, he bristled with nervous energy. His eyebrows twitched as his blue eyes flicked from face to face. Father and daughter walked slowly forward, with Tiffany's eyes still on the floor.

I glanced at Paris; he grinned in satisfaction, his white teeth gleaming. Hart looked extremely unhappy, but he was a gentleman and would never dream of stopping the ceremony.

For a wild moment I thought I should do something—maybe yell, *Tiffany, don't,* and just see what happened. But I remained silent as the commissioner asked, "Who gives this woman?" and the Major presented Tiffany as a gift to Paris.

The ceremony commenced. Blood drummed in my ears throughout the long and terrible time; at moments I feared I'd fall on the floor in a dead faint. Paris promised his bride he'd love, honour, and respect (what a lie), and then the commissioner turned to Tiffany for her pledge.

Taking a deep breath, my friend looked at Paris. "I can't do this," she said quietly.

He frowned. "What?"

Tiffany swallowed. "I always loved you, Paris. But I can't go down this road with you."

Paris continued to frown but said nothing.

"You're doing stuff that is so damaging. Money is your god—and before, it never was." Now Tiffany's voice was clear; everyone could hear the words. "You're being so reckless, Paris, taking such chances."

"I doubt it," Paris said, but his voice lacked conviction.

"You know what's the worst thing, Paris? Other people get hurt by your shady deals, and you don't care. In fact, you don't even notice. Even when it's family like Hart and Pepper, and me."

"Okay, Tiffany, okay. Message received. Now let's get married, eh? The commissioner's waiting, and so's everyone else."

Paris took Tiffany by the arm, but she pulled free. "It's not going to happen, Paris. Wedding bells aren't ringing for us."

Fear crept into his eyes. "Tiffany, please." Paris pleadingly reached out a hand. "We both need this marriage."

Major Wright was staring at Tiffany from his seat in the front row. "What's going on?" he demanded. His friend Marjorie patted the Major's arm, trying to keep him calm, but he ignored her. "What's going on?" he repeated.

"Daddy, I can't. I don't love Paris anymore."

The Major stood up. He looked broken-hearted. "Tiffany, honey, what's the matter? Of course you're going to marry Paris. He's a great guy. Now listen, you're just having an attack of nerves. Don't worry, just—"

Tiffany put her roses into my hands. "I was going to throw you this bouquet, Liz, so you'd be the next one married. Now I can't."

I felt radiant with joy. Hugging Tiffany close, I whispered, "I'm so proud of you, Tiff. Now get out of here—before you change your mind!"

Paris grabbed Tiffany's arm. "Please," he begged, "don't leave me. I'm sorry for the times I hurt you. It'll never happen again, Tiffany. Don't leave—I love you."

"You liar." Tiffany shook off his hand. She looked wonderful—so defiant and proud. "You love money, Paris. You won't get mine now."

Then my friend was gone, out the door to freedom. Major Wright's jaw hung open, and Paris looked totally astonished, but the room hummed with excitement. The guests hadn't expected this!

Pepper rushed to me. "Wasn't Tiffany *wonderful*? That took such bravery—my brother is a first-class power tripper."

"I'm so glad she found the courage," I said.

Pepper beamed with happiness. "Hey, what about the cruise? What'll happen now?"

"You're right," I said. "I'd completely forgotten."

Major Wright had booked a luxury suite on a cruise ship to Alaska. That was his wedding gift—Paris and Tiffany were supposed to sail tonight at midnight. Now the Major was stuck with the suite—but I figured he could afford it.

* * *

Outside the castle, the wedding guests were still murmuring excitedly. I watched Major Wright speaking urgently to Paris as they climbed into the Daimler.

Hart and Marjorie joined them, and the limo zoomed away.

"They've forgotten us," I said to Pepper.

"Too much on their minds."

After talking a while with the other guests, we took a taxi together to Thirteen Oaks. Pepper went in search of Amanda, and I changed out of my bridesmaid's dress. Then I looked for Tiffany.

I found her in a chair, looking out at the sea. "Hey," I said, "I bet you're the talk of Victoria."

"I'm worried about Daddy," Tiff replied. "The wedding meant so much to him."

"He'll get over it," I said, sitting down beside her. "Why'd you change your mind?"

"Laura told me to ask my angels to give me direction. So I spent today thinking about Paris. He's been clinging to me like a weight, hoping I'd solve his problems. I need an equal partner to help raise a family, not some guy who acts like he's drowning. He's an okay guy, Liz, but the wrong guy for me." Tiffany sighed. "Paris slipped into some bad habits after losing his dad. I tried to help—it's my nature, I guess. But I felt like his mother or something, getting him through crisis after crisis."

"You put more money into his gambling?"

Tiffany nodded. "Paris used up all his financial resources trying to maintain his reputation as a party-on dude. He borrowed big-time from all his friends. Then he turned to gambling to fix things. Now everything's dried up, and Paris will hit the wall."

"He'll survive," I predicted. "You wait and see."

* * *

Later that night, Tiffany was summoned by her father to the cruise ship. She asked me to go along for support, and we drove downtown in the Daimler, with Cambridge at the wheel.

The cruise ship looked beautiful, its sleek white lines dominating the busy night at Ogden Point. Taxis and limos and tour buses were delivering passengers for the midnight sailing of the *Romance of the Seas*. From the many decks above, faces looked down at the bustling scene.

After the Daimler pulled away, we climbed the gangplank. I felt worried about Tiffany, wondering if she'd still cave in. The Major was skilled at using emotional power to control his daughter.

"What's going on?" I asked Tiffany, as our identification was checked at the top of the gangplank. "Why has your dad summoned you here?"

She shook her blonde curls. "I don't know, Liz."

A young ship's officer was waiting for us with a personal welcome, and escorted us into a glass-enclosed elevator. We rose rapidly, looking down at clusters of passengers below. From the elevator we entered the Royal Deck, where the corridor was wide and deep purple carpeting pampered our feet. Each cabin had a name; at one called Suite of Dreams, the officer knocked discreetly.

"Major Wright," he called. "Your daughter has arrived."

The door opened. The Major's blue eyes stared at us, then he turned to the officer. "Thank you."

The officer saluted.

"Come inside," the Major snapped. "Marjorie's here. She's going to be a witness."

"To what?" Tiffany asked.

The Major didn't reply. I goggled at the size and luxury of the suite; there was even a large outdoor balcony with a panoramic view of the ocean and mountains. Marjorie sat on a luxurious sofa; in her hand was a fizzy drink.

"Good evening, girls," she said brightly, nervous eyes on Major Wright.

Hands on hips, he stared at Tiffany. She held his gaze without flinching. "Well, young lady?" the Major demanded. "Where is your apology?"

"Daddy, I—"

"Because," the Major continued, "tonight I am the laughing stock of Victoria society, and it is your fault, young lady."

"No, Daddy. If you hadn't—"

Again the Major interrupted his daughter. "Never mind," he barked. "There will be no further discussion."

Opening his cell phone, the Major punched some numbers. "What's your ETA?" he said into the phone. "Remember—this ship sails at midnight." Snapping shut the phone, the Major gestured at Tiffany. "Go sit with Marjorie and have a chat."

My friend did as ordered. I stepped out on the balcony and sniffed the salty air. Far below, the scene was active; I watched the scurrying ant-like figures, then saw a taxi pull to a stop.

Paris stepped out and hurried toward the ship; with him was Hart deMornay—and the marriage commissioner.

12

Quickly I returned inside. The deMornay brothers entered the suite, and Paris soon stood waiting to resume the marriage ceremony. The Major turned to Tiffany. "Sweetie, please, do this for your dear old pop. Call me a sentimental old fool, but just think what this marriage means."

"Daddy, I—"

Major Wright stopped her with a gesture. "I have this wonderful vision of my little girl marrying into the aristocracy. Surely that's not asking too much."

Tiffany smiled fondly at her father. "I know, Daddy, but face up to it. I will not marry Paris. That's my decision, and I won't change it."

Paris walked slowly toward Tiffany. I saw tears in his eyes. "Sweetheart, is there no way we can work this out?"

Tiffany shook her head. "No, Paris. My mind's made up."

"But . . ."

Tiffany turned to me. "Come on, Liz, let's get going."

Outside in the corridor, we walked rapidly toward the elevators. From behind, Paris called Tiff's name. "I'll take this cruise to Alaska alone," he threatened.

"I guess that's up to Daddy," Tiffany replied.

"I'll meet someone better than you."

"Good luck to her," Tiffany muttered, jabbing at the elevator button. "As for me, I'm out of here."

The elevator door opened, and I saw a young guy wearing a FedEx messenger's uniform. In his hands was a large metal tube. As we entered the elevator, I saw the messenger knock on the door of a suite.

* * *

Back at the estate we found Pepper in the library reading R.S.S. Wilson's *Undercover for the RCMP*. The baby was asleep upstairs. When Pepper heard about the events on board the cruise ship, her eyes glowed.

"You're something else, Tiff."

"Thanks, Pepper."

Looking exhausted, Tiffany left for bed. I stood at the library window, staring out at the ocean. Then, feeling weary and starting to cry, I dropped down on the sofa beside Pepper. "I'm so tired," I said, wiping away my tears. "Everything's just so horrible."

"What's wrong, Liz? What's happened?"

I was surprised. "You haven't heard?"

"About what?"

"I can't believe no one has told you, Pepper. I just assumed . . ."

"Told me what?" Pepper demanded impatiently.

"That my friend William has disappeared."

"*What?*"

Pepper was terribly upset by the news. She stared at me in horror as I described everything, starting from when I spotted William and the girl outside the museum.

Then Pepper leaned toward me. "Liz, I may know where William is."

"What do you mean?"

Pepper looked out the window. "William could be on Hidden Island."

"But why?"

Jumping up from the sofa, Pepper paced the library. There were tears in her eyes. "Liz, you've been so kind. Most people see a kid with a baby and turn up their noses. You and Tiff—that's not your style. You're good people."

"Thanks, Pepper, but what's this all about?"

She took a deep breath. "I helped steal the painting, Liz. I was the inside person. I gave the code to Jason."

"But, Pepper!"

"Liz, I had no idea that William was missing. It was strange to see him with Jason, but I didn't think anything more about it."

"What are you talking about?"

She stared at me with solemn eyes. "Jason's been hiding out in an abandoned boathouse on Hidden Island. Yesterday I saw his boat heading there— William was with him. You know my story about the unexploded bombs? It's not true—I made that up. I wanted to keep people off the island. That way, it's my private property."

"But, Pepper, why'd you give the code to Jason?"

"I was promised enough money to start my recording studio, so I agreed to help."

"Jason was going to pay you?"

Pepper shook her head. "No. We're both working for someone else."

"Who?"

"I can't tell you, Liz."

"But why steal the *Klee Wyck* and then return it?"

Pepper looked at the painting over the fireplace. The colours were so pleasing, the Laughing One so happy. "Because that's not the real *Klee Wyck*," she replied at last. "That's a forgery, a fake."

I was astonished. "But it looks so real!"

"You see, Liz, I told Jason the security code, and unlocked an outside door for him to get into the house. Jason escaped with the *Klee Wyck*. Then some forger made an expert copy, which you were lured into finding at Butchart Gardens. That was so everyone would relax, thinking the painting was safe."

I shook my head. "Why make a copy?"

"So the original can be sold, for major money."

"But where's the original?"

"Until tonight," Pepper replied, "it's been right here at Thirteen Oaks. After you found the forged copy at Butchart Gardens, Jason gave the original to me. I've kept it hidden here until now."

"So you think William's on that island? Then we must go there immediately."

"No problem," Pepper said. "There's an underground tunnel from the library to Hidden Island. Nobody knows about the tunnel, including Jason. I didn't want him getting into our house."

"You didn't mind him stealing the *Klee Wyck*?"

Pepper shrugged. "Who cares, it's just some old painting. Besides, no one noticed the forgery. Paris, Hart—everyone was fooled. Remember the family meeting with Laura? Major Wright and the others— they all said how beautiful it looked." She shook her head, looking amused. "They were all fooled, every one."

"Including me," I said ruefully. "But that painting was so special to your father, Tiff. Didn't that bother you?"

Pepper snapped her fingers disdainfully. "Not even this much," she declared. "You know, when my father crashed the car and killed my wonderful mother, he was driving drunk. I'll never forgive him." Pepper gazed defiantly at me with those beautiful deMornay eyes. "No, Liz, I don't have any trouble about the painting being forged."

"You've been paid for helping?"

Pepper shook her head. "Not until the original is sold."

"Who's paying you, Pepper? Who's your boss?"

She shook her head. "I can't tell you, Liz. Please, don't ask."

I thought of another question. This one made me feel sick, but I had to ask. "What's William got to do with Jason?"

"I have no idea, Liz."

I decided not to press the issue. I had to find William, and this was the closest I'd come so far. "Okay, then," I said. "How can we reach that tunnel?"

Moments later Pepper opened the library's secret panel; I smelled wetness and dirt. We stepped into a tunnel. As the false bookcase closed behind us, Pepper switched on a flashlight. "This tunnel's where I hid the painting," she said, "inside a metal tube. Then tonight a FedEx driver collected the tube from me. I was glad to see it go."

I remembered seeing the FedEx messenger delivering a metal tube. "Did he take it to the *Romance of the Seas*?"

"Yes."

"Pepper, tell me something. Tiff and I were reading a book in the library, then the book disappeared. Did you take it?"

She nodded. Her flashlight beam crawled through the black air to land on the book called *History of Thirteen Oaks*. "It describes this tunnel," Pepper explained, "and how to open the secret panel. I didn't want you discovering the tunnel, Liz. You're a detective—things could've gone wrong. I heard you and Tiff from the hallway, talking about the book. I tricked you out of the library, with a fib about Jason phoning."

I nodded.

"Remember when I made lemonade?" Pepper asked. "Before I did, I raced to the library, opened the secret panel, and hid the book inside the tunnel."

"I thought maybe Jason had stolen the book, while I waited for his call at the office." I paused, thinking. "I remember at FolkFest you asked if I had any suspects."

"I was so glad you hadn't figured it out."

Our voices echoed in the shadowy darkness. I put a finger to my lips, warning Pepper against speaking; I was worried that Jason might hear. My heart thumped noisily and blood rushed inside my ears, but I refused to stop—I was determined to find William.

The tunnel was scary. Enclosed by wet and dripping stone, we stumbled over loose rocks, hearing the noise magnified a thousand times. I kept thinking we'd step on a rat, and I was so thankful when our underground journey finally ended.

I could smell the ocean as we exited the tunnel, stepping onto a grassy slope. "I disguised the tunnel mouth," Pepper told me proudly.

"You did a good job," I commented. "No one would ever figure there's a tunnel here."

In the moonlight I saw the boathouse below; it was overgrown with weeds, and part of the roof had collapsed. "What's in that shack?" I asked Pepper. "The one beside the boathouse."

"Junk. Abandoned outboard motors and oars, that kind of stuff."

"Switch off the flashlight," I cautioned, "in case Jason's around."

Cautiously we descended the slope toward the boathouse. Nothing moved except the waves, thumping against the island's rocky shoreline. A bird cried a warning over the ocean, then the night fell silent.

At the boathouse we peered through a filthy window. The big double doors were open to the sea: the *Outlaw* wasn't there. "I've watched Jason's boat from my room," Pepper said. "He usually goes out around this time, for about an hour. He painted out the name, but I know it's the *Outlaw*. I figure Jason gets bored and goes for a ride."

At the shack we found the lock wedged shut with a chunk of wood. Carefully I worked it loose, then reached for the handle. As the door squealed open on rusty hinges, moonlight flowed into the shack.

William lay on the floor, his arms and legs bound with rope.

I rushed to him, very worried. His eyes were open, but he seemed weak and confused; I cradled him gently in my arms, as Pepper released the ropes.

William tried to stand—he seemed very shaky. "Liz," he whispered, "it's so good to see you. But how did you find me?"

"It's not important right now," I replied. "Let's get you out of here."

"Wait. I've got a confession to make. I'm so ashamed."

"What do you mean?"

"Remember I asked you to meet me at the museum? When I had something to tell you?"

"Of course I remember. I behaved so badly."

"Well," William said, his voice only a whisper. "I . . . I'm a forger. I copied the *Klee Wyck*."

* * *

I was shocked. Since Pepper had broken the news, I'd never considered who the forger might be. I guess I was too intent on finding William. "You were partners with Jason?" I asked, dreading the answer. Had I been so wrong about William?

"Nothing like that," he replied, shaking his head. He was slowly coming around. "I was paid for doing a job. Jason offered good money for an Emily Carr forgery, no questions asked. When I copied the original *Klee Wyck,* I had no idea who owned it. I only learned the truth after Jason kidnapped me."

"At the Dallas Road seawall, someone in a low-rider truck gave you money. Was that Jason?"

William nodded.

"How'd you get hooked up with him?"

"He'd been hired by some local who wanted to steal an Emily Carr and get it forged by me. Jason offered a lot of cash. I figured, why not? I desperately needed the money."

I turned to Pepper. "Did you know any of this?"

"No, and I can't believe it," she responded. "I had no idea William made the forgery."

"But the fake note at Butchart Gardens was signed with a W, as in William." I looked closely at Pepper. "Did you write the note?"

She shook her head. "My boss did. My job was to get the note delivered to you at Butchart Gardens. But I might have mentioned William to my boss. I honestly can't remember."

I was getting worried that Jason might show up, but I needed more answers.

I turned back to William. "Jason paid up?"

He nodded. "After the original was stolen, I received my first payment. Jason later delivered the *Klee Wyck* to my studio so I could produce the forgery. When he collected the finished product, I got the remaining money."

"Why'd you need it, William? To finance getting your mom to Arizona?"

William nodded. "But she turned me down. When I told Mom about the forgery, she called it dirty money. So I phoned Jason. I said I planned to go to the police. He laughed and said I was a criminal myself, a forger. I hesitated about the police, for just a moment too long. Jason grabbed me."

"Jason phoned when Tiff and I visited your studio?" William nodded.

"What were those—" I stopped myself. "No, forget it. I don't want to even think about it."

"You know," William said, "it was so horrible when Jason said he'd attacked you in the cemetery. He—"

"Jason?" I exclaimed. "He's the guy who attacked me?"

William nodded. "I'm just so glad you didn't get hurt. Jason told me later about the attack—he was trying to scare you off, stop your investigation."

"Did you know where Jason hid out? Did you know Pepper was involved?"

"No to both," William replied. "I didn't even know why the forgery." Lifting his head, William looked shyly at me. "Liz, will you forgive me?"

There was no question. William wasn't a criminal, out for personal gain. He'd exercised bad judgement, but anyone might. "Of course I understand, William. Besides, you should forgive me! I was such a shrew. I was jealous because I saw you hugging someone."

"At the Inner Harbour? Before I met you at the museum?"

I nodded.

"That was my sister, Lucille. We'd had a visit, and she was going to work. Lucille was late, or I'd have introduced you."

"I'm sorry," I said glumly. "What a jerk I was."

I turned to Pepper. "Let's get William back to the house, then call for an ambulance and the police."

We left the shack, and William moved slowly up the slope. When we reached the tunnel, I looked at Pepper. "Help William to the mansion, okay? I'll join you there."

"But—" William protested.

"No arguments," I said, gently kissing him. "I'll be okay."

The moment they disappeared into the tunnel, I hurried to the boathouse. After the *Outlaw* returned, I planned to sabotage the engine so Jason couldn't escape from the island.

Inside the boathouse I smelled engine fuel. A sleeping bag lay on the small wharf; nearby was a jumbled heap of clothes and junk food wrappers. Empty cans of pop and beer were scattered around.

Raising my head, I listened to the night. Was that an engine I heard? I looked out the open doors of the boathouse, wondering if Jason was returning. Moonlight lay across the waters, where nothing moved but sea birds on the wing.

Then I saw the lights of a boat, heading my way.

I slipped into hiding behind a big oil drum; the wharf was slippery, the wood stained by oil from the drum. Safely concealed, I watched the boat approach. Jason was at the controls at the open stern, guiding the boat's passage toward the boathouse.

Jason secured the *Outlaw* and hurried from the boathouse. He carried food, perhaps for William. My time was short. Scuttling out of hiding, I climbed down a wooden ladder to the deck of the *Outlaw*. For a moment I watched the door, fearing Jason's return, and then I hurried inside the deckhouse. Looking around, I saw a table, a small galley with basic cooking supplies, and steps leading down to the engine. Fortunately it wasn't covered, making my task that much easier.

As I reached for the engine's distributor cap, though, my luck ran out. I felt a gun in my back and heard Jason's chuckle. "Turn around slowly, you little fool."

* * *

Jason's nose seemed once to have been broken, and his tiny eyes glittered. He licked his lips. "Yum, yum. You're cute up close."

"You're not," I declared defiantly. "William has escaped, and you're finished. The cops are on their way."

"Then, let's be gone. Go out on deck. William was my hostage, but you'll do as a replacement."

I did as ordered. Keeping his nickel-plated revolver pointed at me, Jason released the mooring lines and started the boat's engine. I looked for a way to escape, but it was hopeless; I figured Jason wouldn't hesitate to use the gun on me. Now I wished I'd returned to the house with Pepper and William instead of playing the hero—but it was too late for regrets.

"I know all about the forgery," I said, hoping to rattle Jason. "I even know where the original is."

"So do I—it's on board the *Romance of the Seas*.

My boss plans to take it to some crooked collector in Alaska. The collector's ready to pay top dollar for Emily Carr's unknown masterpiece."

The *Outlaw* rumbled out of the boathouse, turned into the wind, and picked up speed. Above the shore-line I saw the Thirteen Oaks mansion; I prayed that William and Pepper had reached safety.

"My boss made me hang around," Jason said, "waiting for my payoff. Then I figured, why not get all the money, not just my payment but every single penny. That painting's got to be worth at least a million bucks."

"You're not only dangerous," I said. "You're greedy, too."

Jason laughed. He stood at the outdoor wheel; I sat on a wooden bench, huddled in my jacket against the cold wind. "The *Romance of the Seas* left port at midnight," Jason said. "We're going to board it and grab that painting. I'll take it to Alaska and get the money myself."

"Are you some kind of hired gun?"

"That's right," Jason replied proudly.

He cranked up the RPMs, and the shoreline rapidly grew smaller. I could no longer see the mansion at Thirteen Oaks. Shivering, I hugged myself tightly.

"I was hired," Jason said, "to get the *Klee Wyck* forged. Your friend William did a great job, then he developed cold feet. He wanted to return the money. I got to thinking, what if he went to the cops?"

Jason looked at me. "I saw you once with William. You took a bus home to the Uplands, and I followed in my truck. Then I kept an eye on Thirteen Oaks, waiting my chance. I figured I'd hurt you, as a warning to William."

"I notice you're limping," I commented.

"Yeah, thanks to you," Jason muttered. "I decided to kidnap William, in case I needed a hostage. I followed him into the First Peoples Gallery at the museum, and said a bomb was strapped around my waist. I threatened to blow up the place unless he left with me." Jason's laugh was unpleasant. "William figured I was crazy enough to be a suicide bomber, so he obeyed. We stepped through the emergency exit, escaped from the museum, and went straight to the *Outlaw* at the Inner Harbour. William came along quiet and peaceful, because he was afraid people would get hurt."

Jason sighed. "It was boring at Hidden Island, so I went to the Splash for something to do. That's when you spotted me, but I got a warning from my boss and escaped in time."

"Just exactly who is this boss of yours?"

"Fat chance I'd tell you that."

"I bet your boss called you at the marina, when Tiff and I were searching for the *Outlaw*."

Jason nodded. "I thought the marina was a secure hiding place, until you came along. So I moved the *Outlaw* into hiding on Hidden Island and painted out the name. I probably should have done that earlier, right after I firebombed the *Amor de Cosmos*."

"How'd you know there was an abandoned boathouse on the island?" I asked.

"Pepper told me."

"And where'd you keep your truck?"

"On different side streets in Oak Bay."

"You never got your money, eh? What a shame."

Jason ignored my sarcasm. "My boss kept saying, *Wait, wait, wait*. Well, I'm sick of waiting." He looked across the water. I could see the pilot boat approaching the beautifully illuminated *Romance of the Seas*.

"Tonight," Jason said, "we're boarding that ship. I'll waste my boss and take control of the painting. I'll be the one who sells it for big money."

Jason looked at me. There was evil in his eyes. "And when I don't need a hostage anymore, you'll die, too."

13

At low throttle, the *Outlaw* wallowed in the ocean swells. We watched the pilot boat slide alongside the cruise ship, then the pilot jumped onto the cruise ship through the open door in its side. Immediately the boat turned away and began its journey home to port.

Jason cranked up the throttle; with a throaty roar, our boat closed quickly on the cruise ship. "When we reach that door," Jason yelled, "you jump in first. I'll be right behind. If you try to escape, I'll start killing people."

The *Romance of the Seas* loomed over us, so huge. I could hear its engines, and the slap of waves against the luxury vessel's massive steel hull. As the big door came closer, I got ready to jump. I was so tense I could hardly breathe.

"Don't betray me," Jason warned, "or everyone dies."

Suddenly we were beside the open door, and I leapt across. Landing safely, I turned to see Jason jump. The empty *Outlaw* began drifting away and was quickly lost in the night.

Nearby were some crewmen, their backs to us. They were shouting advice and encouragement at a television screen, where two teams chased a soccer ball across a green field. Jason gestured at a nearby corridor. "Let's get moving, before they see us."

We hurried through the sleeping ship; Jason's gun was hidden inside his black jacket. I could hear the muffled vibration of the engines—a constant thrumming somewhere far below. "You saw Paris here earlier?" Jason abruptly asked.

I nodded.

"Where?"

"On the Royal Deck, in the Suite of Dreams."

"You think he's on board now?"

"Maybe," I replied. "He was talking that way."

"Take me to the suite."

Quite a few people wandered the ship at this late hour. In the Grand Atrium four seniors were enjoying a game of cards, while a couple waltzed dreamily on a corner dance floor. No one paid the slightest attention as I boarded a glass-enclosed elevator with Jason and pushed the button for the Royal Deck.

"Why do you want Paris?" I demanded. "Is he your boss?"

"Shut up."

After a quick journey to the heights of the vessel, the elevator doors hissed open. I saw the deep purple carpeting, the wide corridor, and the creamy doors of the suites with elaborate names. One door stood slightly open, and I looked inside. Room service was delivering a late-night snack. It was going to the suite where I'd seen the metal tube being delivered.

The waiter walked quickly to the elevator. Watching him go, I said nothing and didn't cry for help. I was afraid I'd get the waiter shot, because Jason had sneaked his gun out of hiding.

We continued walking along the corridor in the direction of the Suite of Dreams. As we did, I struggled to deal with a new shock—I had recognized the person who received the room service delivery.

* * *

From behind, I heard a sound. I turned to look, so did Jason—gripped in his hand was the shiny revolver. Something was tossed from a suite onto the carpet, and landed with a soft *thump*. I saw the Laughing One, her village and its totems.

"Hey," Jason said. "That's the painting!"

Hurrying forward, he picked it up. "Yes, this is *Klee Wyck*. But how . . ."

At that moment, someone stepped swiftly from the suite. Someone in a floppy hat and sunglasses, someone in an expensive blouse and designer jeans. The metal tube was raised high.

It came down hard across Jason's hand.

With a cry of pain, he dropped the revolver. I leapt for it, but the other person was quicker than me. Seizing the gun from the floor, she levelled the scary weapon at Jason, who was rubbing away the pain in his hand.

"Don't move," the woman warned. Turning to me, she gestured at the painting. "Roll it up, Liz. Put it inside the tube."

As I rolled up the painting, tears were streaming down my face. I felt so betrayed, because I had been tricked by someone I trusted.

The woman removed the sunglasses, and I saw her large, dark eyes. Then she tossed away the hat. Auburn hair tumbled down her back. I was looking at Laura Singlehurst.

* * *

"Pick up the mailing tube," Laura ordered me.

"Laura, how could you? I respected you, and—"

"*No talking.*"

Laura turned quickly to Jason. He stood beside the wall, still rubbing his hand. "Jason," she demanded, "what are you, crazy?"

"I do all your dirty work, boss, then you skip town with the painting."

"You'd have got your money, once I sold *Klee Wyck*."

"I doubt it," Jason scoffed. He stared daggers at Laura. "I was hoping I'd find you through Paris, but this was better. Why'd you come out of hiding?"

"Liz saw me. I figured she'd tell you, and I'd be trapped. I saw your gun and decided to get it. That's why I threw the painting into the corridor—to distract you."

"Are Paris and the Major on board now?" I asked.

"No. I saw them leave the ship before it departed from Victoria."

Jason took a step toward Laura, but her finger tightened on the trigger. He paused, looking apprehensive. "Take it easy, Laura. That thing is dangerous."

Laura pointed at the outside door. "We're going on deck. You two go first, I'll follow behind. If I need to, I'll use this gun."

"Laura," I said, "don't be foolish. Give yourself up, please."

"I already qualify for hard time in prison, Liz. That's not for me—I'll find a way to escape. Now pick up that tube, and let's get moving."

Outside on deck, the night was beautiful. Millions of stars were radiant over the sea, where I saw the lights of other vessels. From far below I heard waves rushing away from the hull.

"We're going to the bridge," Laura said. "Get moving."

I tried to think of a plan. Could I somehow use the metal tube against Laura? How would Jason react? Would Laura start shooting?

"Laura," I said, stalling for time, "why did you do it?"

"I needed money to start a new life. A new identity, a new country. No more maxed-out credit cards, no more unpleasant guys pounding on my door demanding I repay their loans. I was frightened, Liz, I was desperate. Stealing *Klee Wyck* was a great idea."

"You didn't earn plenty as a lawyer?"

"There's never enough money."

"When I first met you, Laura, you said someone had called your cell phone, and a ransom was being demanded. I should have wondered how the criminal knew your cell number—I guess it was Jason who called."

"That's right."

"You set me up to recover the forged painting at Butchart Gardens?"

"Yes," Laura replied.

"Come to think of it, you almost gave yourself away. The note at Butchart Gardens was written in emerald ink. When I first met you, I noticed the ink in your pen was the colour of your green car." I shook my head, disappointed with myself. "I bet Fossilized Pete told you about taking Tiff and me to West Bay Marina. You must have called Jason and warned him to escape."

"That's right."

I looked closely at her. "Did you know Jason attacked me in the cemetery?"

Laura was shocked. "I had no idea." She turned to him. "You fool!"

Jason laughed angrily. "You're the fool, Laura. If you'd paid me, I'd be home in Seattle right now and you'd be sailing happily to Alaska with the Emily Carr masterpiece. Instead we're in bad shape."

"I agree *you're* in bad shape," Laura retorted. "But I'll get out of this—just watch me. I'm very resourceful."

"Laura," I said, "why'd you keep the original *Klee Wyck* in hiding at Thirteen Oaks, instead of somewhere else?"

"If the forgery was ever detected and a search started for the original, Thirteen Oaks was the perfect hiding place. Who'd ever look there?"

"You had the original—why didn't you skip town immediately?"

"The collector in Alaska made that a condition. He wanted the *Klee Wyck* replaced with a forgery, so there'd be no uproar about the theft. He told me to stay in Victoria, to see if anyone noticed the forgery. I decided to wait until after the wedding, then leave town."

"You're planning to start a new life in Alaska?"

Laura shook her head. "No, I'm heading for Hawaii. I love those glorious flowers down there. I'll get my money from that collector, then fly south pronto."

Central command for the *Romance of the Seas* was the bridge, the place where the officers and pilot safely guided the massive ship. A sign warned *No Passengers Allowed*, but it didn't stop us. The door was unlocked; Laura opened it and we entered the bridge, to the surprise of the people inside. An officer in a white uniform turned to us, saying, "What the . . ." Someone else shouted, "She's got a gun."

Stepping swiftly behind me, Laura pinned my neck with her arm. With her other hand, she pointed the revolver at my head. "No false moves," she warned, "or this girl dies."

The officer looked at Laura. "What do you want?" she asked in a calm voice.

"Contact the Coast Guard and order a medical evacuation. Tell them to send a helicopter immediately."

The officer picked up a radio microphone. "*Romance of the Seas* calling Canadian Forces, 19-Wing Comox. Come in, please. We are requesting evacuation of a heart attack victim."

"No fake messages," Laura warned her. "Don't get smart."

"Stay calm," the officer replied. "Think about surrendering that gun to me. It's the smart thing to do."

"Forget it," Laura snapped. "I'm not going to prison."

Laura released my neck, but held me close with a firm grip. She looked at the officer. "This ship has a prison cell?"

"A brig? Yes."

Laura pointed at Jason with the revolver. "Put this kid under arrest. Police in Victoria want him for numerous crimes."

"Including abduction," I said, "and sinking the *Amor de Cosmos.*"

The officer gave an order, and Jason was quickly hustled away. He gave me a dirty look, but went silently. I breathed a sigh of relief, even though the situation remained volatile.

I looked at the pilot, who hadn't spoken since we entered the bridge. "Why did the pilot boat take you to the cruise ship?" I asked. "You could have walked on board."

"My wife is in hospital, so I was delayed. The ship sailed without me, knowing I could board from the pilot boat."

"Is your wife okay?"

"You bet," he replied. "We have a little girl, Mary." He smiled briefly.

Long minutes passed while we awaited the helicopter. Various screens and radars glowed inside the dimly lit bridge; through the big windows I saw the first

traces of dawn's light, bringing the promise of a beautiful day. As pale colours slowly came to the eastern
skies, the jagged outline of a mountain range appeared.

"Here they come," said the officer. Through binoculars, she studied the approaching helicopter, which was
large. "They'll drop a stretcher down for the victim,
then winch it back up."

"I'll be in the stretcher," Laura said, "with the gun
and the *Klee Wyck*. When I reach the helicopter I'll
take control. They can fly me to land, and I'll escape
with the painting."

"Give up," I pleaded. "You'll never reach safety,
Laura. Someone could get hurt on that helicopter—
maybe you."

"No more chatter, Liz. Bring the metal tube with
you, and keep quiet."

Laura looked around at the others. "All of you, listen
up. I'm going outside with this girl and the officer. If you
radio a warning to the helicopter, they will both die. Then
I'll shoot myself—I'd rather be dead than in prison."

Outside, Laura turned to the officer. "Where will the
stretcher be lowered?"

"Aft, at the tennis courts."

Hovering over the *Romance of the Seas*, the rescue
helicopter made an enormous racket, its rotors pounding against the air. A door opened in the belly, then
someone waved to the officer. A stretcher appeared
and dropped swiftly down.

"It's not too late," the officer told Laura. "Give
yourself up."

"Laura," I suddenly exclaimed. "The tube is
empty—the painting is gone."

She turned to me, confused. "What?"

I held out the tube. "Look inside—the *Klee Wyck* is missing!"

As Laura leaned toward the mailing tube, I snapped it sideways, catching Laura's wrist a solid blow. The revolver flew up high; leaping forward, the officer grabbed the gun in midair. Quickly she turned and faced Laura with the revolver.

"It's all over now," she said quietly. "You're under arrest."

Laura burst into tears.

14

One year later, I attended Tiffany's wedding to Hart deMornay. She had requested a spiritual service, so Hart arranged for a ceremony at Victoria's Christ Church Cathedral, one of the largest churches in the nation.

Paris did not attend the ceremony. An audit of the deMornay trust had revealed crooked dealings by Paris, who had secretly drained a lot of money from the trust to finance his shameful ways. Paris left Victoria in disgrace, and now lived in Britain on a small remittance provided by his brother and sister.

Hart had quickly declared his devotion to Tiffany. She shared his feelings, but was determined to be certain of their love. Consequently they had spent much of the year hanging out and getting to know each other, making sure they would be equals in their relationship. They did all kinds of neat things—windsurfing, hiking the West Coast Trail, and even exploring the crystal-clear ocean depths at Powell River in matching scuba outfits.

As for me, I'd stayed in close touch with William. We'd exchanged e-mails and letters, and talked on the phone. At Christmas, William flew to Winnipeg for a wonderful reunion. When I arrived for Tiff and Hart's wedding, I was thrilled to see him waiting at the Victoria airport with pink roses for me.

Tiff's mother had come from Grand Cayman Island for the ceremony and was seated inside the cathedral in a place of honour close to the Major. The vaulted ceiling rose overhead, and the stained-glass windows glowed with the glory of love. The blues were so blue, the greens so green, the reds so pure and rich.

Now, at 18, I was the maid of honour. Kate Partridge had graciously allowed me the privilege. She was now Tiff's principal attendant, and stood with the other attendants to the left of the bride. To the right of the groom were the best man and the ushers. One was William, looking so handsome in a beautifully tailored tuxedo.

William caught me staring, and we exchanged a smile. Then I returned my focus to the service, which was moving and splendid. When Tiffany and Hart exchanged their first married kiss, everyone cheered and the bishop grinned. We all knew this marriage was made in heaven.

Flower girls scattered rose petals down the aisle for the newlyweds, and the cathedral bells pealed in celebration as we gathered outside in the sunshine. As I talked to William, a ladybug landed on my arm, a lucky sign of more happiness to come. There were hugs and kisses and photo opportunities, and waves from passing tourists, then the wedding party piled into white stretch limousines and we took off through Victoria, yelling from the open windows. It was such a relief that the wedding had gone perfectly!

The reception was held at the Crystal Garden, just behind the Empress Hotel. Long ago this had been a famous swimming pool; now it contained tropical vegetation and was home to flamingoes, lemurs, and even the Golden Lion Tamarin monkey (looking at its bright eyes, I was reminded of Emily Carr's Woo).

At the south end of the Crystal Garden was a hardwood dance floor and many large tables; here everyone gathered for delicious food followed by dancing. The Major had brought in two bands for the occasion. One was Victoria's own Big Band Trio, which played great rock, and the other treat was Gator Beat, with authentic Cajun music from deep in the American southlands. Everyone was into it, from kids to grandparents, dancing and singing. What a celebration.

I danced mostly with William. He'd given evidence against Jason, who was in prison. So, sadly, was Laura. William had been sentenced to community service for his misdeeds, and was conducting art classes for seniors.

"They're wonderful students," William said, as we danced together. He was so handsome. "Now I'm hoping to combine my art with teaching."

"William, there's something I've been wanting to ask. For a year, actually."

His eyebrows rose. "What's that?"

"Remember at your studio, you swept some photos into a desk drawer and locked it?"

"Sure."

"Well, I've been wondering . . . Well . . ."

"Go ahead, Liz. You can ask me."

"Were they pictures of some girl?"

William roared with laughter. "Not a chance. I took those Polaroids for reference, as I worked on the forgery of *Klee Wyck*."

"That's all they were?" I said, greatly relieved.

"You're the only girl for me, Liz."

What good news! Now I felt quite chatty. "It's so nice your mom's health is better," I commented brightly. William had sold a painting for a large amount of money and used it to finance getting his mother to Arizona.

"Yes," William said. "Things are going well for my mom."

Things were also good for Tiffany's dad, who was with Marjorie. She'd introduced him to high society in Austin, Texas, where they now lived. "I'm very happy," the Major told me later, as we waltzed together. "You know, I almost sacrificed Tiffany to my romantic imagination. I honestly thought she'd be happy married to Paris. All that stuff about gambling really shocked me. Liz, what a fool I was."

"Tiffany's certainly happy now," I tactfully replied.

"I just hope Paris learned something, and is happy in Britain." A whimsical smile crossed the Major's face. "I remember Paris as a boy—he was such a nice kid."

"I guess people can change," I said. "Tiff was smart enough to recognize that."

"You're a good friend to Tiffany, Liz. I apologize for my sarcasm about your hyperactive imagination. That was rude of me."

"No problem," I said lightly. "I've been called worse."

"What about you, Liz? Any wedding bells in the future? Can I hope to attend another wedding soon?"

"William and I are taking it easy on that one, Major Wright." Then my face split into a big smile. "But so far, so good!"

"Wonderful," the Major exclaimed. "You deserve nothing but the best."

Next I danced with the happy groom. "Guess what," Hart said. "Tiff and I have given the estate a new name—Two Oaks." He smiled. "When our first baby arrives, the estate will become Three Oaks."

"I like it. The old name never appealed to me, perhaps because of my slightly superstitious nature."

"We've recovered the portrait of my mother, and it's back on display at the mansion. Pepper decided to live on Hidden Island with Amanda so we built them a nice cottage. Tiff and I have also invested some money in Pepper's dream to have her own recording studio."

"That's wonderful," I said.

After the dance, we joined Tiffany. She was so happy. I hugged her, then Hart. "Why aren't you Lord deMornay? You're the right type—kinda regal, you know?"

"The title belongs to Paris as the oldest child, but I don't care." Hart brushed Tiff's forehead with a kiss. "What matters is that I found my Lady, and we'll always be together."

I wished Tiff and Hart great happiness (later, she threw me her bouquet of trumpet-shaped calla lilies) and then I joined Pepper at a mouth-watering display of desserts.

"I was so worried," she told me, "about facing criminal charges for helping Jason steal the painting. But instead I got community service. I've been helping street people."

Pepper's eyes travelled to a table where her little girl sat with Caleb, the best man. Amanda was laughing happily as Caleb performed a trick of magic. "Amanda's the light of my life," she said, smiling fondly at her daughter.

"How's the music business?"

"I've signed my first artist. We saw her at Beacon Hill Park, giving a concert for the trees."

"I remember. Her songs were so good."

"Liz, thanks for all the e-mails. You've been a pal."

We joined William at a table. He was talking to his teacher—the noted Victoria artist Robert Amos, who was a great friend of Hart deMornay. Robert, of course, hadn't known about William's actions, but had some interesting insights about the technical aspects of his forgery.

"Emily Carr painted on both canvas and paper," Robert explained. "William used acrylic paint, which dries immediately and is very flexible if a canvas is rolled up—but William was smart enough to make it look like oil. With scientific instruments, the forgery could have been detected, but to the people at Thirteen Oaks it looked exactly like the original."

"Two Oaks," I corrected him, laughing. "And hopefully by next summer it'll be Three Oaks."

One last surprise remained, the perfect ending to a perfect wedding. Glancing at his watch, William jumped up from the table. "Liz, we must hurry."

Together we rushed outside—the night was warm. People wandered along Douglas Street; some were window-shopping, while others gazed at a beautiful horse and carriage waiting outside the Crystal Garden. The driver wore a top hat and tuxedo.

"Please step inside our carriage," William said, smiling at me. "We're leaving for a mystery destination."

"Really? Wow."

What a luxury it was, riding through downtown Victoria in that splendid carriage. In my beautiful dress I felt like a character in a fairy tale, especially when we passed the Inner Harbour and I looked up at the towers of the Empress Hotel. Enjoying the slow *clip clop* of our horse's hooves, I sighed at the sight of the exquisite lights outlining the Legislative Buildings.

Passing Carr House, with its gingerbread decorations, I thought of Emily Carr as a young girl and wondered if she could have anticipated the many twists and turns of a life that would bring such fame. Her genius and determination had inspired William to become an artist, and I felt certain that great success also awaited him.

"Happy?" William asked.

"Mmm," I whispered, cuddling close. "We're living a dream."

Along Dallas Road we followed the cliffs, watching lights on the distant shoreline. In the sky was a quarter moon—such a romantic sight. The minutes passed quickly, and finally we arrived at Ross Bay Cemetery, where our carriage stopped.

As we stepped from the carriage, I looked at the cemetery, feeling confused but trusting William. Above us, the silhouettes of trees moved gently in a light wind. Holding hands, we walked into the cemetery and soon reached our destination.

"We're at Emily Carr's grave," I said.

William nodded. "This is a special place, Liz. That's why I wanted to visit here tonight. I'm praying that Emily Carr will bless us both."

I hugged William and kissed him. "William," I whispered, "I think she already has."

The St. Andrews Werewolf

This book is for "de la",
and it's for every Emily and Wallace.

Acknowledgments

The author would like to thank the following specialists in the field of child sexual abuse who so generously found time to comment on this story:

John Betts, counsellor, Victoria, B.C.

Carol Ann Probert, Victoria Child Sexual Abuse Society

Catherine Hudek, Winnipeg Child and Family Services

Donna Harris, Outreach Abuse Prevention, Oshawa

Jacquelyn Jay, Toronto Hospital for Sick Children

Adeena Lungen and Lynne Parisien, Vancouver Incest and Sexual Abuse Centre

Peter Balcom, The Nova Scotia Hospital, Dartmouth

Brenda M. Knight, psychologist, private practice, Vancouver

Eveline de Koning, Mental Health Centre, Port Hardy, B.C.

Dayle Raine, Royal Ottawa Health Care Group

Correna Carter, counsellor, Sooke, B.C.

Peter Ringrose, Public Legal Information Association of Newfoundland

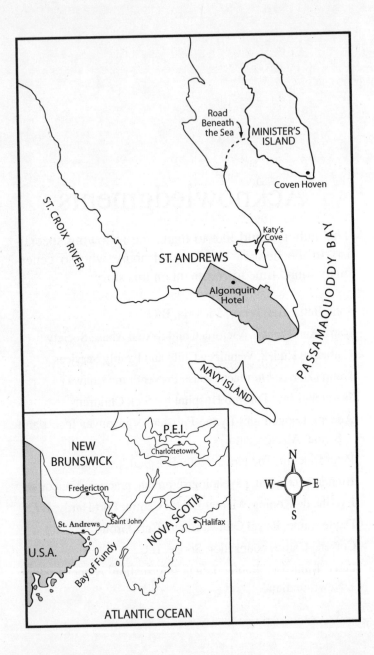

1

"Beware the moon."

I looked at it glowing above, vivid in the starry night. I spun three times on my heel and touched my right ear. "Graveyard monsters roam on nights like this," I said to the woman beside me.

Her name was Fran, and I was her guest for the summer in St. Andrews, New Brunswick. She was a childhood friend of my Mom's. Fran owned some seaside cabins that she rented to tourists. With real generosity, she had helped me get a role in the local stage production of the musical *Annie* and offered me the free use of a cabin.

"You're afraid of monsters?" Fran asked. "But you seem brave, and, I understand, you are a very good detective, too."

"Some things just give me the creeps, Fran. I can't help it! Besides, I am *slightly* superstitious."

"But *you* suggested this walk just to see the Burying Ground. It doesn't add up."

"I can't resist, Fran. I love mysteries and mysterious places. You told me the town cemetery is hundreds of years old, right? It's called the Loyalist Burying Ground, right? Which means it's ancient, and full of old tombstones and maybe some ghosts. I've got to see it, just to satisfy my curiosity."

"You know what they say. Curiosity killed . . ."

I raised my hand. "I've heard that one before."

She chuckled. "I'm glad you're here, Liz."

I'd liked Fran from the moment we met at the airport in nearby Saint John. She's fifty, with big eyes, and hair that's beginning to streak with white. I like her style and the confidence she has in herself.

Driving to St. Andrews, Fran told some amazing stories. Like the one about last winter in New Zealand, when she was in a chopper that power-dove into the mouth of a volcano. Next summer, she's going north to search for artifacts with a team from the University of New Brunswick.

I fell in love with St. Andrews immediately. Only a few thousand people live in the town, which is sometimes called St. Andrews-by-the-Sea. The first settlers arrived when the War of Independence broke out south of the border. They didn't want to be part of the American revolution. Some brought their houses on barges, and a few actually had slaves. They were called Loyalists, and they were so loyal to the English monarch that they named thirteen of their streets after the kids of King George III and Queen Charlotte.

As we walked through town, I glanced at some of the lovely old houses and churches that lined the sixty perfect blocks laid out by the Loyalists. I felt as if I was starring in *Gone With the Wind*.

"Fran," I said, "what are the signs in people's yards? Some say YES: MALL and some MALL: NO WAY. So far, I've counted seven YES and five NO WAY."

"There's a big argument happening here, Liz. You see all the heritage houses? Well, some people don't want anything changed. They're fighting to protect the charm of our town."

"From what?"

"A company wants to build a big mall at the north end of town. We're talking about a huge place, with hundreds of stores and an indoor amusement park like at the West Edmonton Mall. The mall would have a Loyalist period theme. I heard that they plan to call the triple-loop roller coaster the Paul Revere Rocket."

"Sounds great! Tourists would probably come a long way."

"That's the idea, Liz. There'd be a hotel, and a marina for yachts. Money would pour into town. There'd be lots of jobs for the locals."

"Then why the NO WAY signs?"

"Our postcard-perfect town could become an eyesore. In Maine, some towns like this have become a tourist haven, with Kandy Korner shops, mini-golf, traffic jams, polluted water—the whole bit."

"I see what you mean. The charm of this place would be ruined!"

"Not just the charm, but a whole quiet way of life. A new bylaw has been proposed that would allow the mall to be built."

"I figure you're against the mall, Fran. Correct?"

She nodded. "Absolutely! But only the members of the Civic Trust get to vote. The Trust is a small group of citizens with the task of protecting our town's heritage values. They'll vote next week."

"How's it likely to come out?" I asked. "Have any polls been done?"

"It seemed at first that the bylaw might be defeated, but now it seems that the vote'll be close. Some people on the Civic Trust are in a terrible dilemma. They're against the mall, but have family members who desperately need work."

"That's going to be some difficult decision. I'm glad to be here for the drama!" I smiled at Fran. "It's great talking to you."

"To you, too. I always enjoy a good conversation," Fran replied with a wink as we strolled, enjoying the warm summer night.

"Look," I exclaimed. "That's got to be the Burying Ground!"

Trees grew high above the old graveyard, throwing dark shadows across the tombstones that leaned in every direction, like teeth in a dentist's nightmare. There was moss and tangled grass, and a spiked fence.

A feeling of fear washed over me. "I've seen it," I said. "Let's go home."

"Sounds good to me," Fran replied, turning around. "I'll fix us hot chocolate."

"Yikes!" I stared at the old cemetery. "I just saw some kind of monster!" I pointed at a patch of moonlight among the trees. Something bolted through it. In the darkness it looked like some kind of large animal, but it ran on two legs, not four. "Come on," I whispered, "let's find out what it is."

We opened the metal gate of the cemetery and moved cautiously down a path between the graves. My heart was doing triple time. I strained my eyes against the darkness. Among the trees, I sensed a presence, something that was alive.

"Maybe . . ." My voice trembled. "Maybe . . ."

Then I heard it. An unearthly sound. Starting as a low cry, it rose to a long, low sound like a terrible moaning. It made my hair stand on end.

Fran and I stared at each other.

"What was *that*?" we both cried.

The moaning died down. For a brief moment, all was quiet.

"Fran, look! Across the cemetery!"

I could see the creature watching us from the dark cover of the trees. All I could make out was its hulking shape.

"It's some sort of creature, half-man, half-animal," I screamed. "I'm sure of it!"

"It can't be, Liz." Fran took a few paces forward, trying to see into the shadows.

"Didn't you hear the sound it made?"

Before Fran could reply, the creature sprang into the deep shadows and was gone. "Come on, Fran," I cried. "Let's follow it!"

Racing past tombstones and bushes, we crossed the Burying Ground and reached the shadowed trees.

There was no sign of the creature. Beyond the grave-yard, I could see moonlight on a street of homes with big yards. Lights glowed softly in all the houses but one. It stood close to us, beside the Burying Ground.

"Is that an abandoned house?" I asked Fran.

She nodded.

"Maybe the creature's hiding inside," I suggested.

We dashed toward the door of the abandoned house. Suddenly, a ball of fire exploded out of a window, sending us fleeing to the road for safety. Flames began licking up the wall.

"We've got to call 911!" Fran exclaimed. "The arsonist has struck again."

"Arsonist?"

"Yes . . . I haven't had a chance to . . ."

Just then, we heard an engine start and saw an old van pull out from behind the burning house and disappear. Behind it was a small trailer. The left tail-light was out.

Fran raced to the nearest house. I waited on the street, watching the fire take hold on one side of the house. In the upper window, I noticed a cat trapped inside.

I ran swiftly to the house. The door was slightly ajar and opened easily. Smoke was spreading in clouds across the entire ceiling. Covering my nose with my jacket, I ran up the stairs fast and searched for the cat. It was sticking its nose out a crack in the window for air, meowing.

Grabbing it up, I opened the window. Smoke rushed past me into the night. As sirens wailed in the distance, I climbed down a sturdy rose-trellis to the ground. People were running to watch the fire, some of them in dressing gowns.

The cat squirmed out of my arms and ran into the night.

"Thank you for rescuing that kitty," a woman said to me. She had a soft voice and a gentle face. Standing next to her was a dark-haired young girl.

"Emily and I were out walking when the fire started. We saw the kitty, but we didn't know what to do. We felt so helpless. We both love cats." She touched her daughter's hair.

"You're in the musical with me, aren't you?" I asked the girl. "I saw you at the cast meeting today."

Emily nodded and moved closer to her mother.

"I heard you singing. You are truly excellent." I grinned at her.

Emily smiled shyly. Her large eyes looked at me, but she didn't say anything.

Her mother stared at her watch. "Oh goodness, look at the time! We'll be in trouble at home with my husband. We're late. Come, Emily."

"Good night," Emily said quietly. "Thank you for rescuing the poor little kitty."

"It's safe now," I said.

I watched Emily hurry away with her mother. I felt an ache inside my stomach. There seemed to be a real sadness in Emily.

By now, a big crowd had gathered to watch the fire. I searched through the mass of people, looking for Fran, and found her talking to a man with a kind face, horn-rimmed glasses and thinning brown hair. He smiled at me. I recognized him from the big meeting we had at the theatre for all the cast and crew.

"You're acting in *Annie*, aren't you?" I asked.

"That's right. I play FDR. That's short for Franklin Delano Roosevelt, the thirty-second president of the United States. He often summered near here." He extended his hand. "My name is Arthur Dodge, but you can call me FDR. It helps me stay in character."

"Thanks," I said. "I'm kind of nervous. This is my first big show."

FDR smiled. "I'm sure you'll do just fine." He turned to Fran. "As I was saying, you have a point. But I wouldn't be so quick to jump to conclusions."

"This is the third fire in two weeks. It's horrendous."

"I'm sure the police are investigating it. If you'll excuse me, I have things to do."

Fran watched as FDR wandered away from the crowd. I was about to ask her to tell me more about the arsonist when something caught my eye.

"Talk about lifestyles of the rich and famous!"

A black limousine came out of the night and glided toward the fire. Police officers saluted the limo as it purred to a stop. I went closer, watching as a smoky glass window slid down. Inside was a distinguished-looking man about sixty. What little hair he had on his head was grey and neatly trimmed. On his upper lip, he had a bristly, grey moustache. His eyes were large and intelligent. He studied the fire for a moment, then ordered his driver to move on.

The long, black car disappeared into the night.

2

We told the police everything we knew. While we
watched the fire fighters at work, Fran told me that
there had been a series of arsons in St. Andrews recently, and some people believed they were tied somehow to the mall controversy. Then I asked Fran about
the man in the limousine.

"Lots of rich people live in St. Andrews," Fran explained. "In the old days, they came from cities like
Montreal to escape the humidity and relax in the summer breezes. They built some huge mansions."

"I've seen a few!"

"Of course, they had servants in those days. Butlers,
maids, just like in the old movies. Some of them spent
the entire summer in residence at the Algonquin Hotel,
complete with butlers and maids. Even Sir John A.
Macdonald stayed there."

"Speaking of movies," I whispered to Fran, "Colby Keaton is certain to become a star. See him talking to the guys at that fire truck? He's really something."

"He's an actor in your play?"

I nodded happily. Colby turned our way. I waved to him, just to be friendly. He waved back.

"When did the theatre bug get to you, Liz?" Fran asked.

"Over in Charlottetown, I watched *Anne of Green Gables* from backstage. It was great! I auditioned for our school's musical last winter and got to be second lead. My mom thinks I might have enough talent to succeed."

Fran nodded. "So do I, which is why I suggested you to the director of *Annie*."

"I'm glad you did. I've always loved the story of Annie, an orphan, who meets a rich man from New York City. She's so charming with her singing and dancing that she wins him over and he wants to adopt her. But first he advertises everywhere to find her parents, and some crooks try to get the reward money he offers."

Fran nodded. "It's one of my favourite musicals, too."

"Hi," a voice sounded from behind.

I turned to see Colby standing behind me. Man, he was gorgeous. He had black wavy hair and beautiful blue eyes. We chatted about the fire for a few minutes, and then he turned to Fran. "How's business this summer?"

"Pretty good, thanks. My cabins are solidly booked for all of July, and August is looking good."

"If there was a mall, you'd be sold out summer and winter."

"I guess that's true," Fran said with a frown.

Colby smiled at me. "Feeling hungry, Liz? We could have a late-night snack at the Smuggler's Wharf."

"Sounds great." I looked at Fran. "Okay with you?" She shook her head. "It's far too late."

"Okay," Colby said. "How about tomorrow night?"

When Fran gave her permission, I grinned with pleasure. What an added treat to an already exciting summer.

* * *

The next evening, I walked to the harbour with Colby. A pier extended out from shore; laughter and voices came across the water. The moon shone above.

Not far in the distance was the outline of Maine. The hillside twinkled with lights. I wondered if people would come across the border to see our show.

Time passed quickly with Colby. We had a window table, with a view of the moonlit boats in the harbour. We ate chowder and lobster rolls. The restaurant was decorated with hanging lamps and an ancient Union Jack flag. There was a waterwheel in the corner. It was a cosy place to be, and I felt good.

The outside door opened. "There's FDR," I said. "I think he's lonely."

We watched as FDR walked across the restaurant to a table near us. His spectacles glittered in the lamplight. He gave his order to the waitress, waved at us, then opened a novel. I noticed that the cuffs of his trousers were frayed, and there were splits in the leather of his shoes.

"Heard the story on FDR?" Colby said, his voice low. "He lives by himself in an old house. His parents were singers who entertained the wealthy visitors every summer at the hotel. When they retired, the hotel presented them with an honourary key to the front door. Strange gift, eh? Why not a gold Rolex? Anyway, when FDR's parents died, they left him a crumbly old house. People say it's a strange place. It's full of his parents' mementoes, photographs and stuff like that."

"What does he do?"

"Nothing. He lost his job as a teacher and can't get another one."

"How is he able to live?"

"Probably on the last of the family bank account. When that's gone, he's in deep trouble."

My hand brushed the salt cellar, which toppled over. Fortunately, Colby was looking out the window, allowing me to toss a pinch over my shoulder. I didn't know what he might think of my superstitious nature.

Our young waitress, Bridget, arrived with more chowder for Colby. "You're from Winnipeg, right? Someone said so. How do you like St. Andrews?"

"It's great! Full of excitement so far."

Bridget laughed. "For a small town, we have our share. When the summer people aren't here to make it lively, we have our own collection of eccentrics and ghosts to keep the town talking. We even have our own werewolf."

"Werewolf?" My heart started to pound as I remembered the creature I saw the night before.

"It's just an old legend. Something the kids like to scare themselves with," Bridget scoffed.

"They say a werewolf haunts Minister's Island," Colby said, "but no one's ever seen it. I'll show you the island someday."

"I think I saw something in the cemetery last night."

Bridget stared at me. "You actually saw the thing?"

"I don't know what I saw. Some kind of creature. I saw it just before the fire."

"Was it a werewolf?"

"I'm not . . ."

"Wow—I can't believe it's true!" Bridget raced to the kitchen, where we heard her going on about a werewolf in the Burying Ground. Then the door popped open, and the chef stared at me.

Colby smiled. "You're a star attraction tonight, Liz. Do you think what you saw was related to the fire?"

"I don't know. I'm not even sure of what I saw. I sure would like to get to the bottom of this."

"I heard you had a talent for sleuthing." Colby grinned and winked. "What a combo, beauty and brains."

I could feel my face turning a thousand shades of red. I turned away. I didn't particularly want Colby to see me do my neon light imitation.

Across the room, a couple was engaged in a heated debate. One wore a *Yes Mall* button, the other, a button that read *No Way*.

"I can see the mall is a hot topic here. How will the vote go, Colby? Any theories?"

"Funny you should ask," Colby said, producing some handwritten notes. "I've been following the debate and it's going to be close. At the beginning, it looked like the No's would take it. But, recently, several members have changed their minds. The Yes's are gaining support."

"What happens if it is a tie?"

"Then it is up to the chair, Mrs. O'Neal. If it's a tie, she casts the deciding vote. The fate of the mall could easily rest with her."

"I wouldn't want to be in her shoes."

On our table was an electric candle. It threw a soft light on Colby's face. "It's nice being with you, Liz. You've got that beautiful long hair and those ebony eyes."

"Thanks," I said, blushing. "Have you ever acted before, or is *Annie* your first time?"

"In high school I was in some plays, stuff like that." Colby put down his spoon. His blue eyes were thoughtful. "I really enjoy acting. You can be anything you want when you act." Colby looked at the sailboats riding at anchor on the dark water. "When I was a kid, I wanted to pitch in the majors. I'm a southpaw, and pretty good. But few players make it that far so I quit. But acting is something I can do."

"How old are you, Colby?"

"I'm nineteen—been out of high school a couple of years. And you?"

"I'm sixteen, soon to be driving!" I grinned.

Bridget brought us dessert. "Rhubarb and strawberry pie," she said. "Our chef is famous for this."

Leaving the restaurant, we stopped at FDR's table. He was still reading his book, but he put it down to shake hands hello. "It's good to see you," he said.

"Likewise," I replied. "Colby says your parents were entertainers."

"That's correct," FDR beamed. The smile cheered up his face. "Come by my house some time, Liz, and I'll show you a few mementoes of their career."

"Thanks," I said. "I'd like that."

Outside the restaurant, Colby and I stood together in the warm night air, talking. I could smell the nearby sea. There were a few kids hanging around, and occasionally a car rolled slowly past. It was peaceful in St. Andrews, and the street looked pretty with its hanging flower baskets and old-fashioned streetlamps.

"My family owns a great old boat," Colby said. "It's a twenty-four-foot sloop-rigged Shark. Let's go sailing some time."

"Sounds great!"

He smiled. "How about tomorrow, before rehearsal?"

"I can't. My friend Makiko arrives. She lives in Japan. Her father's company imports tuna from Prince Edward Island, where we met. Makiko and her father are in PEI again this summer, so she's coming here for a visit."

"Well, maybe some other time. I'll walk you home."

We saw few people as we walked through town. Then a black limousine came out of the night, moving slowly. A man leaned out the window, holding a leash. At its end, a poodle trotted beside the limo.

I laughed. "I saw that man at the fire. I guess he's walking the family dog."

"He's in the play, too. He plays Drake, the butler. Isn't that weird? In real life he's *got* a butler! Drake has a reputation for being a bit eccentric. Every year he likes to play a role in the local play."

"I saw him the other night. I'm looking forward to meeting him."

"Drake owns a lot of land around here," Colby said. "If the mall gets built, he'll be worth mega money. Real estate will be red hot. The mall's a great deal for this town. I think the Civic Trust should pass the bylaw."

"I don't envy the people on the Civic Trust," I said. "It'll be a tough decision to make."

Before I knew it, we had reached the Burying Ground. A shiver ran up my spine as I recalled the creature I saw.

"How about we check out that werewolf of yours?"

"I'm not sure it was a werewolf."

"There's only one way to find out."

I hesitated for a moment. I looked through the iron rails of the fence.

"Hey, Colby!" I grabbed his arm. "Something's in there!"

"Is it your creature?"

"I think so."

Within no time, we were under the trees, moving cautiously past the old graves. I checked the time on my watch. My nerves were strung tight. Ahead, we could see the figure kneeling on all fours at a grave, searching for something. Beside him was an old-fashioned lantern. A candle glowed inside it.

"Can you see what it is?" Colby whispered.

"I . . ."

At that moment, Colby stepped on a dead branch. The wood snapped loudly. The figure at the grave turned, looking our way. We both gasped aloud.

"Oh no," Colby exclaimed. "I don't believe my eyes!"

The figure's face seemed to be made of two different halves. On one side, its skin was bright red, thick and scarred. The features were distorted, almost completely gone. There was an eye, but no eyebrow, no hair on its head, not even an ear. The long dark hair on the other side of its head hung thick and tangled, like moss hanging from a tree.

The creature rose from its knees. Its eyes stared into the darkness, seeking us. As it turned to escape, one foot caught the lantern, knocking it over. The candle went out.

For a moment, I saw nothing. Then I detected the creature in the moonlight, fleeing across the cemetery.

"Come on, Colby," I yelled. We raced past the tombstones in pursuit.

"That's not a disguise," Colby cried as we ran. "That face is real. It's some kind of werewolf mutation."

In the shadow of the trees, I saw a white horse, tethered to the iron fence that surrounded the Burying Ground. The creature leapt to the top of the fence and, within moments, was galloping away into the night.

"The werewolf's escaping," Colby shouted. "We've got to capture it!"

We chased out of the Burying Ground, but the horse, with its rider, soon disappeared into the night.

"They're heading toward the sea," I said. "We'll never catch them."

Colby snapped his fingers. "I bet the werewolf has something to do with the fires."

"What makes you so sure?"

"Just a hunch."

"I'd like a bit more evidence before I come to any conclusions."

He shrugged. "You're the detective."

Colby escorted me home. The warm night air smelled deliciously of the sea. At my cabin we said goodnight. When Colby was gone, I walked across the lawn to the water. The moon was huge in the velvet night. Stars were scattered everywhere. I could see a satellite passing through space. I wondered where it came from, and what it meant.

Mostly, though, I wondered about the creature.

As I pondered, I heard the squeak of oars. In the path of moonlight, I saw a rowboat near the shoreline. FDR was at the oars, rowing intently. The moon glinted off his glasses and a few wisps of brown hair fell into his eyes.

I waved, and called hello, but FDR didn't seem to notice. The rowboat just kept moving along the shore. I watched until it disappeared into the night.

"That's odd," I whispered to myself, and quickly returned to my cabin. Safely inside, I locked the door.

3

I didn't sleep well that night. Werewolf nightmares disturbed me. In the morning, I dragged myself outside. Birds twittered in the trees, as cheerful as the blue sky. I shook my head, trying to wake up.

The ocean was silver. I saw a sailboat running before the wind, and I wondered if Colby was out in his family's boat. Walking to the beach, I looked at the red sand. The wind had shaped it into ridges. Gulls perched on big rocks, taking the rays. "Makiko arrives today," I exclaimed to myself. "Finally, I get to see my friend again!"

At the Seaside Cabins office, I went inside. Fran was busy on the phone, but she waved. "Grab some orange juice."

In the kitchen, I sipped cold orange juice while looking at the pictures on the fridge of Fran's nephews and nieces and the children of her friends. As I helped her prepare breakfast, I told her about Colby's view of the mall vote. We also talked about the creature. We were both still puzzled. "Maybe it's a mutation," I suggested. "Do they test nuclear fuel around here?"

"Not that I know of."

Outside in the morning sunlight, we walked along Water Street. People sat on their porches. They waved as we passed by. The houses were colorful and solid; they'd been built to last.

Only the occasional car was on the streets of the quiet town. A breeze touched the hanging flower baskets, and stirred the flags over shop doors. The town hall had two cannons in front, and the Shiretown Inn advertised that it had been in business since 1881. I knew Makiko would be taking lots of pictures.

"You know," Fran said, "St. Andrews must have looked exactly like this when the wealthy tourists first arrived. 'No hayfever and a railway' is how they advertised this town. It must have been nice at night, hearing the train's lonely whistle and the clackety-clack of the wheels."

She sighed. "St. Andrews is such a beautiful place—we'd be destroyed by a mall. I've been thinking about Colby's assessment of the members of the Civic Trust. He's right—the vote will be close. Greta O'Neal may indeed cast the decider."

"Was it always so close?"

"When the bylaw first became an issue, more members of the Civic Trust were against the mall. It seems in the last few weeks, somebody's been doing some pretty strong persuading."

"Why are they changing their minds?"

"Don't quote me on this, but two of the houses that burned belonged to people who were against the mall."

"But the third house is abandoned and doesn't belong to anybody."

Fran grinned. "It was just a theory. I didn't say it was a good one."

"If it's a tie, how will Mrs. O'Neal vote?"

Fran sighed. "I've been Greta O'Neal's friend for years. She's hugely proud of this town. She knows the risks of a mall, but she also knows jobs are important. It's a dilemma for her."

"Have you mentioned your feelings to her?" I asked.

"You bet. Me and everyone else in the town. She doesn't want to lose the way of life St. Andrews has to offer. But, then again, there are a lot of people in this town who need work, including Greta's son."

As we talked, we looked in shop windows, killing time while waiting for Makiko to arrive from the airport. I kept looking at my watch. "Makiko's parents know Mrs. O'Neal, so that's why she's staying there. But I already told you that, didn't I?"

Fran smiled. "Makiko and *Annie* are your favorite topics of conversation. By the way, I love your gift for Makiko."

"I bought the beaver and made the rest myself." I looked proudly at the furry little beaver in a Mountie uniform. He held the flags of Canada and Japan.

"How long until Makiko joins her dad in PEI?"

"Two weeks is all we've got," I said sadly. "But it'll be a great time, and she'll be in the audience when our musical opens."

"Let's head for Greta O'Neal's house," Fran said. "They'll be arriving soon."

We hurried through the leafy streets. The green yards were shaded and looked cool in the brightness of the morning sun. A man swung in a hammock, listening to a baseball game on the radio. Kids smiled at us as they rode past on bikes. Everyone was taking it easy. It was a quiet, peaceful town.

Ahead, I could see Mrs. O'Neal's house. It was brick with three chimneys and a carved arch over the door. Fran told me that it was built well over a hundred years ago.

I saw a car coming in our direction. Makiko was in the passenger seat, grinning at me. She waved, and I waved. The car stopped, and Makiko jumped out. I started running, so did she, and then we were hugging each other in the middle of the street. It was really great to see her again. Her eyes were shining, and her black hair glowed in the sunlight.

We babbled away, covering a dozen different subjects as we walked to the house, arm in arm. Makiko gave me a Japanese fan decorated with delicate flowers in gold and red, and I presented the little beaver. Fran and Mrs. O'Neal watched our exchange of gifts. Mrs. O'Neal, whose neatly trimmed grey hair and elegant suit gave her a businesslike air, beamed with pleasure.

"Well!" She smiled. "You girls are so thrilled to see each other! It does my heart good."

We all went inside. "Let me show you around," Mrs. O'Neal said. "This house was built early in the nineteenth century. Back then it was called Chestnut Hall."

The house was filled with antiques. Mahogany, polished oak, crystal, grandfather clocks, silver cutlery, everything.

"You've got the whole nine yards," I exclaimed to Mrs. O'Neal. "This place is a museum! People must have had a great life back then."

"Actually," she said, "people lived mostly in the dark and cold. Just imagine—they wore the same things all winter, day and night. They *slept* in their clothes."

Makiko's black eyes grew larger. "Is that true?"

Mrs. O'Neal nodded. "Oh yes. They were trying not to catch a cold, because people died easily. They didn't have the benefit of our modern medicines." She shook her head. "The women wore enormous hairdos that they rarely took down or washed. I don't know how they slept."

Mrs. O'Neal led us up a curved staircase. "This was designed for protection against attack in the night. A robber was forced to use his gun-hand to follow the curving handrail."

"Ah!" Makiko's eyes lit up. "The robber cannot also hold his gun. The owner gains extra moments for defence."

"Exactly."

Mrs. O'Neal gave us a tour of the upper floor. We saw more antiques, as well as her personal office, which was equipped with all the modern technology. My favorite room was Makiko's, with its four-poster bed. The bed was so high off the ground that steps were needed to climb into it.

Mrs. O'Neal took a pair of white satin wedding shoes from a cupboard. "These have been passed down for generations. Notice the mark of the Paris shoe-maker? I show these to all my guests."

* * *

With the tour over, Mrs. O'Neal led us back downstairs.

"Who's for a snack?" she asked, rubbing her stomach. "I've made some pound cake. The recipe's from a cookbook published over a century and a half ago. The cake uses nine eggs and a pound of butter. Nobody knew about cholesterol in 1839!"

The pound cake was fabulous. We sat in the kitchen, surrounded by the past, stuffing our faces and talking to Mrs. O'Neal about the town. She'd lived here her whole life—sixty-five years.

"You'll like St. Andrews," she said to us, "there's lots to do. My daughter's two mountain bikes are outside in the garage. You're welcome to use them. She moved away last year, to Boston. She teaches at one of the universities there."

"Look," I said, pointing out the window. We all looked out at the street where a small girl was zooming in circles on a pink bike. "That's Emily. She was at the fire the other night, with her mother."

"They're my new neighbours," Mrs. O'Neal said. "I don't know much about them. The mother seems very nice. The stepfather keeps to himself."

"Who owned the empty house that was torched the other night?" I asked.

Mrs. O'Neal hesitated. "The town, but I was going to buy it. The town had accepted my offer. We were just drawing up the papers."

Fran and I exchanged a worried look. It seemed that Fran's theory might be correct. The arson *was* related to the vote.

"Would that property be worth more if the mall gets built?" I asked.

"I suppose it would," Mrs. O'Neal replied. "But the land with real potential is north of town, where the mall would be. Imagine the value of that real estate."

"Any idea why the arson happened, Mrs. O'Neal?"

She shook her head. "Not unless it's connected somehow to my vote on the mall. But . . ."

Just then a phone beeped at her side. Mrs. O'Neal picked it up. As she listened to the caller, her face slowly went white. Her hand rose to her throat. Hanging up the phone, she stared at us.

"I've just been threatened."

"What happened?" we all exclaimed.

She stared at the phone. "It was some man. His voice was disguised. He said, 'Support the mall or the werewolf strikes again.' Those were his exact words."

Fran picked up the phone. "I'm calling the cops."

"I'm so frightened of fire," Mrs. O'Neal said. "I've been receiving calls for the last few days, but usually the caller doesn't say anything, and just hangs up. This is the first time I've been threatened."

Fran patted her hand. "Please, Greta, don't let it rattle you. And don't let it affect your vote."

Mrs. O'Neal's teacup trembled as she raised it. "I won't, don't worry. I plan to make up my own mind, although I'm torn how to choose."

"You know what the mall will mean to the future of our town," Fran said quietly.

"You know as well as I, Fran, how much I love St. Andrews and its way of life," Mrs. O'Neal replied, "but what future do we have if everyone leaves because there is no work?"

"Who's against building the mall?" I asked.

"A lot of people oppose it, including most of the summer people. They own exquisite old houses and have lots of money. They live here during the good weather, and they want things peaceful."

"A mall could change all that," I said. "This town is so beautiful, Mrs. O'Neal. Every house is a postcard scene. It would be ruined!"

"I agree with you and must consider the interests of the people who oppose the mall. But what about the jobs? I have to consider that, too."

I shook my head. "I don't know. It just seems sad." Through the window, I watched Emily playing on her bike. "Think about the kids, Mrs. O'Neal. Maybe they want a peaceful town when they're older. You should ask them! It's their future you're deciding."

"You're right. They are another group whose interests I should consider." Mrs. O'Neal sighed. "It's all so very complicated."

The back door opened. In came Mrs. O'Neal's son and his wife and three little kids. They swarmed around their grandmother, collecting kisses and cookies, then the family presented Makiko with sweet-smelling flowers for her room.

Mrs. O'Neal's son sent the kids outside. He looked at his mother. "I think we've made a decision."

Her eyes filled with tears. "I've been dreading this. You're leaving town, aren't you?"

He nodded. "Please don't cry, Mom. There's no work here."

"Where are you going?" Mrs. O'Neal asked.

"Out west. I heard about a job in Lethbridge, Alberta."

"That's so far away."

Fran signalled to us, and we slipped out the door. "Let's leave them be," Fran said. Her voice was tight with emotion.

Makiko wiped away a tear. "My heart is sad."

We walked through town, talking about Mrs. O'Neal's dilemma. After saying goodbye to Fran, I headed for the theatre with Makiko. "I can't wait to show you the Burying Ground," I said, "and tell you what happened. It was creepy for sure." I looked at my watch. "After rehearsal, we can check the graveyard for clues."

Makiko smiled. "Our first adventure began in a cemetery, on beloved Prince Edward Island."

* * *

The theatre where we were rehearsing *Annie* was on a tree-shaded street. Inside, we walked down the aisle past rows of empty seats. Makiko was nervous about being introduced.

There was all kinds of action on stage. Colby was talking to Drake, the Rockettes were warming up at the *barre,* and the orphans were singing "Tomorrow" led by Margaret, the music director.

Finished with their song, the orphans swarmed around Makiko as I performed introductions. Emily held back, so I brought Makiko over to her. Emily's enormous brown eyes gazed at Makiko as she managed a small hello. One of the other orphans turned to me. Her name was Ashlee. "Is it true you actually *saw* the St. Andrews werewolf? Everyone says so."

All their eyes stared at me.

"Well," I said, "I don't know if it was a werewolf, but I saw something unusual, that's for sure."

"Then it's true!" Ashlee stared at the other orphans. "The werewolf is for real!"

"Hold on," I said, "I didn't say there was a werewolf."

But it was useless. The girls chattered excitedly to each other. "We know where the werewolf comes from," a girl named Tegan said to me. "It haunts the old mansion, over on Minister's Island."

"That's right," another orphan exclaimed. "Long ago, the island was owned by Sir William Van Horne, the guy who built the Canadian Pacific Railway across Canada. It was his summer place—he came down from Montreal in his private railway car and lived there. He built a mansion—it's huge. They had lots of parties, then Sir William died. Now a weird woman and her servant live over there. Nobody's allowed on the island. If you go over, you'll get chased with an axe."

"Not an axe," Tegan said. "A shotgun."

"Why do you think the mansion is haunted?" I asked.

"There's all kinds of stories," Ashlee replied. "Some kids snuck onto the island last year. It was nighttime. They saw something *creepy* run through the moonlight. It had a weird face and long hair—it looked like fur, they said. They were lucky to get away alive! Nobody's been back since."

"So," another girl added, "don't you get it? The werewolf haunts the island. That's what those kids saw in the moonlight. It was the werewolf! Now it's come over to town, to get *us*."

As the orphans buzzed with excitement, we were joined by Colin Skinner, the director of *Annie*. He had lots of curly hair and a nice smile. Colin was really talented and nice. He made everyone feel at ease. In the first act, I'd be a hobo living under a bridge, then later a chorus dancer with the Rockettes, and then a singer on a New York street.

I introduced Makiko to Colin and then to Nicholas and Barbara, a brother and sister team of singers. Then FDR rolled over in the old-fashioned wheelchair he used in the play; it was just like the wooden wheelchair once used by the real-life president.

Drake was there. He wore a gold watch chain and a black coat with dress-tails hanging down. I thought he looked like a real snob. "Do you disapprove of how I walk my poodle? You and Colby seemed quite amused last night."

I shrugged my shoulders. "Using a limousine to walk your dog isn't good for the environment. It pollutes the air."

Drake sniffed loudly, gave me a beady-eyed look, then walked away. A couple of girls smiled and gave me a thumb's up.

I noticed Emily looking at me from one of the old-fashioned dormitory beds used in the show. Her eyes seemed to call me.

I walked over. "Okay to join you? I saw you riding your bike earlier." I sat on the bed. The frame was made of iron and the creak of the springs bothered my teeth. "How old are you, Emily?"

"Nine."

"Wow—I'm impressed you're on the stage already."

She looked toward the other orphans. "The youngest one," she whispered, "is only seven, and *totally* talented."

"Aren't you friends with them?"

She shrugged. "I like to be alone."

Emily was wearing a sweatshirt over unitards with leg warmers and jazz shoes. She looked well-groomed, except for her fingernails. They were grubby and bitten down.

Seeing my stare, Emily hastily closed her hands. "That was brave, Liz, the way you saved the kitty from the fire. I'm not brave at all."

"What are you talking about? You're brave enough to go on stage. What's it like playing an orphan?"

"Kind of fun." For the first time, her brown eyes looked happy. "Acting's good for me," she whispered. "At home, I stay in my room with the door locked, and I act out stories."

"Why do you lock the door?"

Emily stared at me. Something happened inside her eyes. She looked frightened.

Then Colin Skinner called for attention. "Let's get to work. Orphans and Drake, I'll need you, please."

Like a summer storm, Emily's fear quickly passed away. She got up and stood at the front of the stage with the rest of the orphans.

Emily was loaded with talent. Besides being an orphan, she'd been chosen as Annie's understudy. That meant Emily would take over the main role if Annie got sick or was unable to perform. Emily had to rehearse the part so she knew it perfectly.

"Okay, Emily," Colin said, "let's try Annie's first number."

Emily nodded and took her place on the stage. When Emily sang her song, she was exuberant, bubbling with energy and charm.

I stood beside FDR, watching her rehearse. "Emily is transformed into another person on stage," FDR said. "I guess she's happiest as an entertainer. My parents were the same."

"They must have had an interesting life."

"They did. You've seen the tower at the hotel? The room at the top is called the Eagle's Nest. It's reached by circular stairs. My parents were singers in the Nest. Once a week, I sit there drinking a Perrier, looking at the lights below, watching the moonlight on the sea, reliving my parents' glory days." He sighed. "The Eagle's Nest remains exactly how they left it. The same piano, the same furniture. It's a shrine, I guess."

* * *

After rehearsal I stayed on stage, talking to Colby. He wanted me to go sailing, but I'd planned to spend time with Makiko.

"Makiko's anxious to explore the Burying Ground so we're going together."

"Too bad," Colby said. "I brought my camera to get some pictures of you out on the ocean."

Something fluttered in my stomach whenever he smiled. I admit it—I was disappointed. "I promised Makiko," I said. "But maybe another time."

As I packed up my gear to leave the theatre, I saw Emily in the orphans' dressing room. She sat on a bench, looking at me. At her feet was a bouquet of wilted wildflowers. The other orphans had left things in a jumble, but Emily's rehearsal outfit and shoes were neatly put away.

"Why haven't you gone home, Emily?" I asked, going into the room.

Her huge eyes watched me. On her forehead were tiny droplets of sweat. "My stomach hurts."

"I'm sorry," I said, taking her hand. "How can I help?"

"Maybe walk me home?"

"Sure thing."

Outside the theatre, Makiko was talking to Miss Hannigan. In the play, she's a tyrant who rules the orphanage with an iron fist, but offstage she was very nice. Miss Hannigan was a local teacher. In real life, her name was Mrs. Smith. She had a super-nice husband and two adorable little kids.

"I'm in a show every summer," Miss Hannigan told Makiko. "I've loved acting since I was very young."

I walked up Prince of Wales Drive with Makiko and Emily. The street was thick with trees; the thousands of leaves were green in the sunshine. Outside one of the pretty houses, a man pushed a mower across a big yard while a woman took in laundry and a child played in a sandbox.

"It's a beautiful town, Emily. Do you like it here?"

She didn't reply. Ahead of us was the blackened shell of the house torched the night before last. It smelled of fire. "Feel like investigating?" I asked Makiko.

She grinned and nodded. "The game's afoot, in words of most admired Sherlock Holmes."

We searched around the house, looking for signs of the van I had seen the night of the fire.

"Darn," I said, studying the hard-packed ground beside the road. "No chance of tire tracks."

Makiko picked up a tiny chunk of dried mud. "This is red, like island home of beloved Anne. Earth here is brown. Perhaps mud fell from van."

Emily said, "There are fields with red soil outside town. There's a carnival playing there."

"Excellent information," I said. "Thanks, Emily!"

A grin split her face, then she became solemn again. "You're welcome, Liz."

I looked at Makiko. "We should go to see that carnival together. Maybe we can learn something. Carnivals play all over Canada, every summer. They're bizarre."

"I would love to go, Liz," my friend replied. "But first, let us see the Burying Ground."

The Burying Ground looked scary, even in daylight. Makiko's eyes were solemn as she studied the enormously tall trees shading the old tombstones. The iron fence was like a row of spears, spikes up.

The iron gate squealed rustily as we entered the cemetery. I watched a leaf tumble down and caught it. "That's for luck," I said. "A falling leaf is a nice talisman." I swallowed, and looked around the gloomy cemetery. "But it's no guarantee."

We found the grave where I'd seen the creature. "Look," Makiko said, examining the ground. "Knees of some person have pressed into soft soil."

"You're right, and here's the lantern. It got kicked under this shrub." I held it up. The glass was that old-fashioned bumpy kind, and the iron was heavy. "There's a name stamped in the iron. *Coven Hoven*." I picked up some roses from the grave. "The creature may have left these, too."

"Coven Hoven is the name of the mansion on Minister's Island!" Emily exclaimed.

"Thanks, Emily, that really helps." I smiled at her. But inside, I shivered. Maybe what the orphans said about the werewolf on the island was correct.

We left the lantern in the cemetery, in case the creature came looking for it. The thought of it looking through the town for its lantern gave me the shivers.

I have to admit, I felt a lot better once we had left the dusky cemetery and stood in the brightness of the streets. The change had an effect on Emily, too, for suddenly she burst out, "Would you come riding with me sometime? Please, Liz. Please, Makiko. I've got a horse. His name is Midnight. You'll love him."

I stared at Emily, amazed at the sudden torrent of words. Then I smiled. "Sure, Emily, that's a great idea."

"Thank you!" She looked at her watch and grew solemn again. "I'm really late getting home. I can't stay any longer. I wish I could."

"Shall I walk you the rest of the way?"

"No, thanks, Liz. I'll be okay."

With great reluctance, Emily trudged away. Makiko watched her go. "Such a melancholy child," she said. "My heart is deeply touched."

4

"Do you think the creature is setting fires, Liz?"
Makiko asked as we walked through town.

"I don't know. But I think whoever or whatever
started the fire got away in that van I saw."

At the edge of town, we ran into Colby. "How's the
sleuthing business?" he asked. I told him about the
lantern we'd found. Then Makiko explained our theory
about the mud being linked to the carnival outside town.
"We're going there now," I said, "to check for a van.
Maybe this mud fell from the one I saw the other night."

"The carnival doesn't open until dusk," Colby said.
"Want to go sailing until then?"

Makiko's eyes lit up. "Oh, yes. Yes, please, Keaton-
san."

"Keaton-san? What's that mean?"

I smiled. "It's the Japanese way of honouring a person they've met, Colby. Makiko used to call me Austen-san."

On our way through town, Colby stopped to buy a picnic basket filled with goodies. "Maybe we'll get marooned on a desert island," he smiled. "We'll need provisions."

We walked out along the long wooden pier together. It was busy. Makiko took so many pictures her camera was practically smoking. But I had to admit that it was a lovely scene with the white sailboats at anchor and the gulls floating among sparkling diamonds of sunlight.

We bought ice cream from a little refreshment booth and discussed the other tourists as we ate. Then, while Colby made a call from a pay phone, Makiko and I talked to a couple of university students who'd cycled all the way from Québec. They were really sunburned, but cheerful.

"What is that?" one asked, pointing at a huge building on a hill, high above St. Andrews.

"That's the Algonquin Hotel," I replied. "Impressive, eh? In the old days, wealthy people came to the Algonquin with butlers and maids."

"The original hotel caught fire one day in 1914," Colby said, joining us. "There was a wind, so it burned like a torch. The flames must have been spectacular. I wish I could have seen it."

Soon, the sailboat was running before the wind. I wasn't nervous—Colby was a good sailor. We skimmed along the shoreline, splattered by flecks of spray from the bow.

"There's Fran!"

She was out in a kayak, not far from her cabins.

"Fran," I yelled. "This is the life!"

She called back, but I couldn't hear. I waved, then smiled at Colby. Holding the tiller, I felt the strength of the wind in the sail. "The sea's so vast," I said to Makiko. She was studying the shoreline through miniaturized binoculars. "We could sail together to foreign shores, discovering the world."

Makiko nodded, lowering her binoculars. "We are kindred spirits, Liz."

Colby pointed toward shore. "That's where the mall's going to be built," he said. "The land's worth a fortune, if the vote goes through."

"Somebody is willing to do anything to make sure it's a yes vote. Even destroy property," I said.

"What's your theory, Liz?"

"Several Civic Trust members have changed their votes to yes since the arson began. Now some flea-brain is pressuring Mrs. O'Neal because it looks as if the vote will be a tie. They're threatening to burn her house if she doesn't vote for the mall."

Colby looked at me. "What do you mean?"

"It's a stupid strategy, Colby. It's horrible and destructive. Mrs. O'Neal seems like a courageous woman. Threats won't make her back down." I studied the shoreline through Makiko's binoculars. "Does Drake own all that land?"

"Who knows?" Colby replied. "I've heard different stories."

"We'd better check it out, Makiko. The town archives might have some information."

"Detectives at work," Colby grinned. "I love it." He put his arm around me, and Makiko took another picture of us. The wind swept through my hair, and the sun warmed my face. The ocean was beautiful. Waves leapt around us, almost as if they were dancing. After a while, Colby trained his binoculars on an island. It was very large and green and appeared empty except for a big house standing alone above the sea. A shiver passed through me, as though somehow I'd been drawn by destiny to this place.

"You're looking at Minister's Island," Colby said. "That mansion is Coven Hoven."

Makiko nodded. "Famous home of famous man, Sir William Van Horne of the Canadian Pacific Railway. In school, I have studied his story."

"Van Horne was quite a character. He bought that entire island. It's huge. You could spend hours exploring, if you were allowed. Van Horne had the servants cut a pool into the rocks. Every day it filled with sea water, and he went swimming. He didn't build a house, he built a mansion. It's got eleven bathrooms!"

"Why won't the new owners allow anyone on the island?" I asked.

Colby shrugged. "Who knows? Hey, have you heard about the Road Beneath the Sea?"

We shook our heads.

"Minister's Island is connected to the mainland by a neck of land. At low tide it's exposed, so people can reach the island. Not that anyone is welcome there. At high tide, covered by water, it becomes the Road Beneath the Sea."

I looked at Makiko. "That road could be dangerous."

"In Van Horne's day, some people got trapped out there in a horse-and-buggy," Colby said. "The tide came on too fast for them to reach land. The horse got spooked. It froze in fear as the water rose. One person left the buggy and made it to shore, but two others drowned."

Colby dropped anchor, and we were floating on the water, far from shore. We sat on deck, eating the picnic and watching the patterns change on the water. It was so peaceful that we stayed until after the yellow sun had burned down into the sea.

The moment it was gone, the air grew cold. We put on extra gear and listened to the birds call across the darkening water. A few clouds drifted above us. For a long time no one spoke. Then Colby said, "Feel like exploring Minister's Island?"

"Will we cross the Road Beneath the Sea?" I asked. "The sailboat might run aground."

Colby shook his head. "The road's on the other side of the island."

I looked at Minister's Island. Steep bluffs rose above us. Trees were silhouetted against the dark sky. No lights were visible. I looked at Makiko. "If we can prove there's no werewolf here, we might be closer to solving the mystery. Want to check it out? We could go to the carnival tomorrow evening."

She studied the grim island, then swallowed bravely. "Yes," she said. "Let us be brave."

"We'll lower the sail and row ashore near Van Horne's bathhouse," Colby said. "It's a tower in the cliffside, with stairs inside. That's how Van Horne reached his luxurious seawater swimming pool. Man, that guy could live."

* * *

The bathhouse was creepy inside. Every sound echoed as we climbed the stairs. I tried not to touch the cold walls. Makiko's black eyes were enormous. "*Gan-batte*," she whispered in Japanese. "We must press on."

At the top of the cliff, the light of the moon was cold, shining down on Coven Hoven. The mansion was an ominous sight, dark and silent. I saw power lines strung along sagging poles, but not a light was visible. A wind swept around the mansion and stirred the trees, making a rustling noise.

"I keep feeling like someone's watching us," I said.

"Want to leave?" Colby asked.

In the moonlight, he was so good-looking. No way was I wimping out. "Let's explore," I said. "That's why we're here."

Something screeched in the woods.

I gulped. "An owl . . . I think."

Staying together, we moved along a path. The lawn was a jungle, and the flower beds had no flowers. I looked at the woods, where the moonlight slanted down. Something ran through the shadows.

I grabbed Makiko's arm. "Did you see that?"

She nodded.

I pointed into the woods. "Look!"

Visible among the trees was a face, almost hidden behind tangled, thick hair. Around one of the eyes, the skin was shiny red and puckered. The lips were twisted open.

Then, suddenly, the face was gone.

"It's the creature," I whispered, my voice disappearing with fear.

Colby's voice trembled. "It's true! There *is* a werewolf!" He looked at us. "We'd better get moving."

"You're right," I said, and Makiko nodded.

We ran as quickly as we could to the boat.

When we reached the bathhouse, I stopped and looked back at the dark shape of Coven Hoven, still certain we were being watched. What was the mansion's secret? I wanted to know more.

5

In the morning, I did some research. Most communities save old books, newspapers and other information as part of their history; in St. Andrews, these archives are stored at the Old Gaol.

Conditions were rough for prisoners back when the Old Gaol was a jail. I studied a couple of the cells, picturing people crowded together inside the thick walls, miserable and cold. Then, shivering, I headed for one of the cosy research rooms.

Digging around in the archive files, I found some notes written in the southpaw slant of a left-handed writer. The notes were about local land ownership. I started to read about the ownership history of the potentially valuable property north of town. Part of the land was held for a long time by a family named Dodge.

"That's FDR's family," I said aloud.

I turned the page, hoping to discover more, but the page I wanted was missing.

Curious, I decided to try some cross-referencing with back issues of the local newspaper on microfiche. After a lot of looking, I found the article I wanted. I looked at a photograph of Drake, the butler in our play. He was much younger then, with more hair. He had just bought the land at the north end of town. The deal gave him total control of the area. He'd purchased the land from the estate of FDR's parents. An editorial in the same issue questioned the whole deal. The writer of the piece didn't like the way the transaction was handled. The article made some interesting points, so I jotted down a few of them in my notebook.

Later on, I checked the index for Minister's Island—there was a lot to study. I read about the days of Van Horne, how his servants strung nets in the orchard so the peaches wouldn't bruise falling from the trees, and how he built a huge barn to raise expensive cattle. Van Horne was a painter. He also liked to pamper his grandson with every kind of toy. He accomplished all this, *and* he built a railroad that spanned Canada from sea to sea.

After Van Horne's death, the island passed through several owners until it was purchased by Lady Chandler and her husband. There was another article that caught my eye. I made some hasty notes. Finding nothing else of interest, I took what I had written and hurried through town to Mrs. O'Neal's house.

* * *

I was anxious to discuss my findings with Makiko. She was in the kitchen, sipping tea with Mrs. O'Neal and Fran. On the table, Makiko had some articles about overdevelopment and the bad effects it has on a town.

Mrs. O'Neal smiled. "Have you come to convince me to vote no, too, Liz?"

"I think Makiko and Fran are probably doing a good enough job," I replied.

"We're talking about a way of life, Greta," Fran said. "A way you believe in, a way you'll lose."

"I know," Mrs. O'Neal sighed.

"It would be unfortunate if St. Andrews became polluted. It has happened in my country." Makiko added, "It is a very sad thing."

"There are good arguments for the mall," Mrs. O'Neal replied, "and good arguments against it."

I asked if she'd talked to any kids.

Mrs. O'Neal looked down at her teacup. "No, I haven't."

Fran leaned toward her. "Give it a try, Greta. You're deciding their future."

"Everybody's future is at stake," Mrs. O'Neal replied quietly. "But will we have a future if there are no jobs?"

Fran reached across the table and took Mrs. O'Neal's hand in hers. She squeezed it gently. "I think I've pressured you enough for one day. Do you have any of that pound cake left?"

As we ate our cake, I told the others what I'd learned about Coven Hoven. "There must be a good reason for all the secrecy," Fran said. "There's a servant who comes into town for supplies and he's not friendly at all."

I left the house with Makiko. As we walked toward the theatre, I told her about my discoveries at the archives.

"Fifteen years ago, a man and woman died on Minister's Island in a car crash. September 9th was the date of the crash."

"Why is date important?" Makiko asked.

"At the Burying Ground, the creature was kneeling at a grave. It had two names on it, but only a single date for when they died. That means they died together. On the tombstone was a year, followed by 9-9. I remember it."

"9-9?"

"That means the ninth day of the ninth month. That couple died on Minister's Island on September 9th, fifteen years ago. That same date was on the grave."

"Very interesting, Liz, but what does it mean?"

"I'm not sure, but it may have something to do with all of the secrecy at Coven Hoven."

Then I told her all I had discovered about the land on the north end of town.

"So, FDR may have a claim to the land for mall," Makiko concluded after hearing all the facts.

"If he can prove that Drake acquired the land illegally from his parents' estate."

"Why doesn't he do so now?"

"I don't know. Maybe he's waiting until the mall is built. The land would be worth lots more then."

"Maybe FDR-san not know he may have claim," Makiko suggested.

"Could be. It all happened a long time ago."

* * *

Makiko and I entered the theatre. I went on stage and she sat in the audience. Some dancers were warming up, Colby was rehearsing one of his numbers and the orphans were braiding each other's hair as they waited their turn. Emily sat apart from them.

Her eyes looked tired as I dropped down on the floor to say hello.

"How are you?" I asked.

"Fine!" She pasted on a smile. "How are you, Liz?"

Wondering if she was lonely, I got a brainwave. "Emily, I've got a surprise for you."

"What is it?"

"Tell you later." I smiled at her. "It'll be fun."

Colby came over and joined me. My heart fluttered a little as he sat down beside me. I got a whiff of his cologne. It had a nice, clean scent.

"Being on the island was nervous work," he said. "That thing in the woods scared me!"

Ashlee, who was walking by, stopped and stared at him, then me. "You saw something on the island? Was it the werewolf?"

"I don't know," I replied. "But . . ."

Before I could continue, I was surrounded by a pack of orphans, every one of them eager to discuss the werewolf. All of them had a lot of information about werewolves that they were eager to share. Each of them seemed to enjoy scaring the rest of the group with what she knew.

"Werewolves come out only when there's a full moon."

"Some werewolves are werewolves all the time."

"That's not true," Colby said, lowering his voice. The orphans became silent, waiting to hear what he might say next. "When people are turned into werewolves, they become vicious beasts. They can't control themselves and are capable of any kind of destruction. But, during the day, when they are not werewolves, they look like ordinary, nice people. In fact, usually the quietest, meekest person by day is a werewolf by night."

The girls screamed and laughed, delighted to be so frightened.

"I know who the werewolf is, then," Ashlee said solemnly. "He's here in the theatre." Her eyes darted across the stage to Colin, who was talking to Drake, Miss Hannigan and FDR.

"Who?" the orphans all asked at once, anxious to know.

"It's FDR. He's quiet and meek." Several orphans nodded in agreement.

"That's not proof," I argued.

"There's something else," Tegan said. "Werewolves are afraid of dogs." She pointed at Sandy, the collie who had a "walk-on" role in our musical. "She's the world's friendliest collie, but FDR is really scared of her."

"Lots of people are scared of dogs."

Ashlee touched my arm. "FDR is one of the undead. He carries the curse of the werewolf."

"How do you know that?"

"He's weird—he lives alone."

"So does Fran. She's not a werewolf."

"Hey," Molly exclaimed, "maybe she is!"

"Oh, good grief." I slapped my forehead. "Fran is not a werewolf, and neither is FDR."

"But FDR's always going over to Minister's Island and nobody knows why. So that proves it," Ashlee said, with a nod of her head.

I didn't believe that FDR was the werewolf, but that

didn't mean he wasn't linked to the arson. Later, when the orphans were rehearsing, I told Colby all I had learned about FDR and the land slated for the mall.

"FDR could make a lot of money if the mall were built and he claimed the land," Colby concluded. "And FDR sure needs money."

"Drake could make money, too. Maybe he's behind the arson."

Colby's face twitched. "That's too obvious. I think it's FDR. He looks like a nice guy on the surface, but you never know what's going on underneath. Kind of like a werewolf."

It wasn't a nice thought. But I had other things I wanted to discuss.

"Colby, I've got an idea. Emily seems sad today, so I thought a surprise might cheer her up. But I need your help."

I whispered my plan, and he liked the idea. We made arrangements. Then we chatted with Judge Brandeis and FDR, who rolled over in his wooden chair.

"One of the boys was popping wheelies in this chair," FDR grinned. "But I'm no good at it." He gave me a slip of paper. "Please come for a visit tonight. Here's my address. Bring your pal, Makiko. You can see my parents' mementoes. Later this summer, we'll visit the Eagle's Nest, where they performed. The hotel's closed now for renovations, but we'll see the Nest before you leave town. It's part of local history."

"That's a nice invitation," I said, smiling.

The moment rehearsal ended, Emily hurried to me. Her eyes were shining. "What's the surprise, Liz? Is it an adventure?"

"You'll know soon, Emily."

Feeling delighted with my brainwave, I finalized the secret arrangements with Colby. Then Emily and I found Makiko in the lobby, and we went outside into the warm sunshine.

As we walked through town, Makiko praised Emily's singing and she beamed with pleasure. "I think Colby's in love with Liz. Right, Makiko?"

Makiko's eyes sparkled. "Emily-san has strong powers of observation."

I blushed. "Give me a break, guys."

"He's cute," Emily said.

Laughing, I gave Emily a hug. It was good to see her so happy.

But then it ended.

The moment we reached the pier I felt Emily tense up. "Why are we here, Liz? I don't want ice cream."

"We didn't come for cones, Emily. This is your surprise."

Her dark eyes stared at me. Already big, they grew bigger. "Here?"

"Yes! Colby went ahead—he's waiting for us."

As we walked along the pier, Makiko took pictures. I had to force my smiles for the camera because Emily was suddenly so anxious. Her eyes darted back to Water Street. She was taking deep breaths.

Colby waited in his sailboat beside a lower dock. A long, steep ramp led to it. Emily took one step down, then froze.

"I can't," she whispered.

"It's okay, Emily," I said. "I've got another idea. How about if I meet your horse?"

She nodded her head vigorously.

I looked at Colby. Sunshine touched his hair. "We'll try another time. Okay with you?"

"Sure!" Colby winked at Makiko. "How about you, Makiko-san? Care for a sail?"

"Gracious thanks," she replied, "but, please, may I accept a check of the rain?"

He grinned. "I think you mean a rain check, Makiko. You've got it, for sure."

So, in the end, Colby sailed alone. As we walked along the pier, we saw his Shark leave the harbour. The sail dipped low, caught by the wind as it headed for the open seas.

Makiko decided to spend the afternoon at home. "I shall correspond with my family. Many postcards remain to be sent. A pleasant time awaits me. Perhaps O'Neal-san will offer tea with chocolate pound cake as I write my cards."

"What'll you tell your family about St. Andrews?" Emily asked.

"It is paradise."

I grinned. "Tell them for me, too." I turned to Emily. "I bet I can guess the colour of your horse. It's black."

"Wow! I'm impressed."

"It wasn't difficult," I admitted. "After all, you named him Midnight."

"Sorry you missed your sailboat ride, Liz."

"I don't mind, Emily. But I'm curious. What bothered you?"

"Well . . ." She took a deep breath. "Well, it's the ocean." Her eyes stared down. "I . . . I'm scared of water."

"That's okay, Emily," I said. "I'm scared of heights. That's why I go on rides at carnivals—I won't give in to the fear."

"Does it work?"

"There'll always be some goosebumps. But fear doesn't keep me from having fun."

Makiko took our picture together. "Emily-san," she said gently, "each person has strength. It is waiting inside you, like a treasure. When you find your courage, it never leaves again. It will give you peace."

I confess I was lost, but Emily wasn't. She stared at Makiko. "Yes," she said. "I understand."

* * *

We dropped Makiko off at Mrs. O'Neal's and continued to a barn outside town. Inside, Emily fed Midnight a carrot and he rubbed his face against her shoulder. She busied herself brushing his coat. "Be careful," she warned, when I came close. "Midnight is head shy."

I like horses but not when they bite, so I kept clear of Midnight's stall. Wandering around the barn, I breathed the rich smells of hay and oats. I ran my hand over a bridle's chain, which tinkled softly, and listened to the pleasant sounds of the horses munching their food.

Emily's mother came into the barn. She asked if I was enjoying St. Andrews, then smiled tenderly at her daughter. She looked at her watch. "This is my day off work and I'd hoped to ride, but it's later than I thought. Liz, would you care to take my horse, Lightning, today? I'm sure Emily would enjoy your company."

When I said yes, Emily's eyes lit up.

"It's nice to see Emily smile," her mother said. Her eyes were solemn as she stroked Emily's hair. "She's always been a quiet child."

Soon I was up in the saddle, sniffing the air as Lightning and Midnight walked placidly along a pleasant wooded trail. Lightning blew softly through her nose as I patted her warm neck and listened to her tail switching away flies.

"You're a good rider," I told Emily.

"I love to ride."

"So do I. Which do you like better, acting or riding?"

Emily scrunched up her eyes and thought a moment. "I like both the best, but maybe I like acting more."

I laughed. "Me too. The more we rehearse, the more I enjoy it. I think I'm hooked."

Emily was silent for a while. Then she said, "My Mom doesn't like me rehearsing in my room. Dumb, huh?"

I didn't say anything.

"Probably it's 'cause I lock the door. Sometimes I just stay in there."

"Don't you get lonely?"

"Nope." Emily gave her thick brown hair a brave toss. She looked back at me. "Know what, Liz? I'm going to be a star. That's why I rehearse all the time. Then I can live in Hollywood, not dumb old here. Promise you'll come visit?"

"Sure, Emily. But I'd rather go riding with you in St. Andrews."

I heard her sigh.

"I guess living here might be fun. If he went away."

"Who?"

Emily wouldn't answer. Leaning forward, she urged Midnight into a trot, then a gallop. Lightning joined in the fun, and soon the horses were running side by side across an open field. The air was warm and sweet; wildflowers danced in the wind. Lightning tossed her head and snorted happily while her mane blew about my face. I could hear the rhythm of her hooves, pounding against the earth.

"This is fun," I yelled at Emily.

She grinned and waved.

During the ride, we saw the Road Beneath the Sea. "I'd never ride out there," Emily said. "What if the tide came in? Midnight would be trapped." Soon after, we reached a place where the sea came inland into a cove. "I've always wondered what's on the other side," Emily said, stopping Midnight at the water's edge.

"It's not too deep. The horses can walk across easily. Let's go explore," I urged.

As Lightning waded in, I looked back at Emily. She was gazing at the water.

"You'll be safe, Emily. You can do it."

She gazed thoughtfully at me. Then, lifting the reins, she took Midnight into the water. We started forward together. Midnight moved slowly, sensing Emily's anxiety. After several moments she stopped him.

"Liz, I . . ."

Before I could speak, Emily made Midnight back up. Turning back on Lightning, I joined them on shore.

Emily's eyes were huge. "The water, Liz. I . . ."

"Emily, you tried. That took courage."

She didn't say anything.

"I'm proud of you, Emily. I bet your Mom would be, too."

* * *

That evening, Makiko and I rode on Mrs. O'Neal's mountain bikes to the carnival outside of town. We wanted to follow up on our one good clue—the chunk of dried red mud we found at the scene of the abandoned house fire.

When we reached the carnival, we locked up our bikes and checked the earth around the entrance.

"The mud here is brown," Makiko said, holding the piece of red earth for comparison. "Van may not have come from here."

"Let's check inside."

"*Hey, hey, step right up,*" chanted a carny from his booth. "*Prizes here, prizes here,*" shouted another. The carnival was alive with people and noise and music from many different rides.

Everyone was eating junk food. I decided to get some cotton candy. "It always sticks to my face," I said to Makiko. "But I buy it every year."

She was busily eating onion rings. "These remind me of tempura," she said. "My parents have promised wonderful meals for your visit to Kyoto, Liz. Soon, I hope."

We searched the carnival, looking for the van, but had no luck. Walking through the midway, we checked the mud sample we'd brought along, but unfortunately the colours didn't match. "Let's try some rides," I said to Makiko. "At least the trip won't be a total waste."

As we headed toward the ferris wheel, I saw Drake. He was walking fast and looked troubled. "Let's follow him," I said. We moved quickly through the crowd in pursuit. Drake squeezed between two big trailers. We followed. He didn't seem to notice. He approached a semi with a large trailer attached. Painted in big letters on the side of the trailer were the words *Gizmo's Freak Show—Special Effects for All Occasions.*

Drake stepped with dignity over cables and dirty puddles, then knocked on the door of the trailer. The guy who answered had to be Gizmo. Ink from leaky pens had stained his shirt; his trousers stopped above his ankles. Gizmo's hair, thick as a wheat field, stuck straight out. "He's put his fingers in too many sockets," I whispered to Makiko. "But he's no fool—those are shrewd eyes."

At that moment, a large, black motorcycle pulled up and roared to a stop. The rider looked mean in his Harley cap and shades. He had a thick moustache and a long braid of hair down his back. He wore torn jeans and his dusty boots were hung with chains.

"Hello, Rocky," Gizmo sneered at the biker. "Glad you could make it."

Rocky snorted in reply, then joined Drake and Gizmo at the door of the trailer. The men stood in a small circle, talking in whispers.

"Let's sneak closer," I whispered to Makiko.

We crept forward from trailer to trailer. My heart was thumping. The men were motioning wildly as they spoke. Without warning, the sunglasses shifted our way. Rocky's mouth opened in surprise. He pulled his Harley cap lower and turned his head, raising the collar of his leather jacket.

Drake and Gizmo stared at us. "Hey, you kids, go away," Drake ordered. "This is business."

"I wonder what Drake is up to?" I asked once we were back in the noisy crowd.

"Let us stay a while. Perhaps we shall see more," Makiko suggested. "In the meantime, let us try some of these rides."

On the midway, over-amplified rock music boomed from every side. While riders screamed above us on the Ring of Fire, we got tickets for the Gravitron. It spun us like a flying saucer; we were pressed against the wall by gravitational force. I was relieved when the ride ended.

Then we walked through the midway, and worked on some fries. They were thick and greasy. "Even with ketchup they're disgusting," I muttered. There were people all around us. Some wandered, staring, while others stood under awnings, playing the games. I tried to win a couple of giant neon-coloured poodles by tossing baseballs into peach baskets, but I failed. "I never win anything," I complained. "Everything's rigged." But Makiko was awesome with a baseball, depositing one ball after another into the baskets. "You never told me," I said as she collected her pink poodle.

Smiling, she gave the prize to one of the watching kids. "Baseball is my favourite game. Father also. We avidly cheer the Hanshin Tigers."

Nibbling on popcorn, we watched the Bingo players, then talked to one of the orphans from *Annie*. "It's getting late," I said. "Shouldn't you be home?"

"I guess so," she replied, walking away. "I've been here since noon. I've eaten everything I can find, and I've been on every ride twice. See you."

Makiko and I went up on the ferris wheel. The view was breathtaking. The moon made a silver path across the ocean, and the stars dreamed in the night sky. I could have stayed forever.

"Liz, look!" Makiko pointed. "Perhaps this is what we were waiting for."

I followed Makiko's finger and saw Gizmo at the door of his trailer. He seemed nervous. He checked his watch, then looked around. I lost sight of him as the ferris wheel dipped down toward earth.

"We should investigate?" Makiko's eyes sparkled with pleasure.

Once the ferris wheel dropped us back on the ground, we hurried over to Gizmo's trailer. We watched Gizmo from the shadows as he secured the trailer for the night. Smoking a cigarette, he talked to some carnival workers. We heard swearing and noisy laughter. Beyond them, women and men played cards beside fires that burned inside trash barrels. Music continued to pound from the rides.

Then Gizmo left the others. He picked up a large sack and walked past the trailers and converted buses where the workers lived. We followed, hearing voices through open windows. As we turned a corner, Makiko stopped me. "Where is that man?"

I could see nothing but dark trailers. We tiptoed forward. Gizmo was gone; there was no sign of him. I saw empty fields beyond the carnival. Had he gone that way?

Then Gizmo leapt at us from hiding.

I screamed, and so did Makiko.

"You girls," Gizmo shouted into our faces. "Why are you watching me? You beat it, hear me? Get out of here!"

Makiko and I walked quickly away. I didn't look back until I felt safe. When I did, I saw Gizmo hurrying across a field.

"Let's see where he goes."

Makiko nodded. "But this time, let us stay farther back."

Gizmo climbed a stone fence into another empty field. We saw a shed that looked abandoned. Gizmo shoved the door open and disappeared inside. A light went on, glowing through a broken window.

We raced to the shed, then pressed close to the wall. In the light of the windows, Makiko compared some earth to our sample of red mud. "Same colour," she whispered.

Gizmo's voice came through the broken window. "Yeah, yeah, I got the stuff."

A muffled grunt answered him.

"If you ask me, your whole scheme is crazy," Gizmo said. "But your boss is paying big bucks. You want my services, you got 'em."

I heard a door slam. An engine started with some difficulty, then a van towing a small trailer came out of the shed. The left tail-light was broken.

The van bumped away across the field. I looked at Makiko. "That was the van I saw at the fire!"

6

We watched until the headlights disappeared.

"Look at the time," I exclaimed. "FDR's expecting us."

We raced across the fields back to the carnival, where we pushed through the crowd. At the entrance, we found our bikes and were soon peddling through the night.

"Do you think we should tell police, Liz?"

"I told them about the van the night of the fire."

"But now we know it is van of Gizmo."

"We know Gizmo is in the van, but we don't know if he owns it. I wonder who was with him."

We found our way to FDR's house. It looked cosy, with its curtained windows and wide porch, but no lights shone.

"It's odd the house is dark, when FDR is expecting us."

"*Ganbatte*," Makiko whispered.

"You're right." I gave her a weak smile. "We must press on." We opened a gate in the picket fence. Moonlight lay across the garden. We called FDR's name.

Nothing.

The front door was open.

"That's odd."

The hallway was in total darkness. I switched on a lamp. The wallpaper was patterned velvet; I saw a sofa and faded chairs in the living room. The furniture looked comfortable, and well used.

"Hello," I called. "FDR, we've come to visit."

Silence.

We glanced at each other. "I wish we'd brought a loaf of bread," I said. "That would show any spirits we mean no harm."

Then I heard a sound. *Tap. Tap. Tap.* My stomach tightened. I forced myself to move forward. What if FDR was in danger? I saw a library filled with books. Then a dining room with a wooden table and candles in glass holders. The table had a lot of books on it.

Tap. Tap. Tap. The sound became louder. In the kitchen, the shelves had glass doors with porcelain handles. I saw big containers marked *flour* and *sugar*.

Makiko turned off a dripping faucet and the tapping sound ended. "Let's find the stairs," I said. "Something's wrong, but I don't know what."

There was one large room above. It was dominated by a grand piano. On the walls were autographed photos in elegant frames. I recognized some faces from the black-and-white Hollywood classics my parents love to watch on TV.

In front of a bay window was a large desk. It was scattered with papers and textbooks, and had a Canadian flag beside a paperweight filled with bubbles. I turned to Makiko. "Where's FDR?"

On a small coffee table was a tray with glasses of juice and pieces of cake and a teapot. "It is warm," Makiko said. "FDR-san here recently."

"Why did he leave?"

I found a note sitting on the tray. "Look at this! It says, *Liz and Makiko, I'm at the Eagle's Nest.*" I studied the purple ink. "A lefty did this. See how the writing slopes?"

I looked at the Algonquin Hotel. Its large, black shape brooded above the town. "It's creepy without any lights," I said. "The hotel's empty because they're putting in new carpets and kitchens."

"Why would FDR go there?"

"I don't know, but I think we'd better go find out. He could be in danger."

Outside, clouds drifted across the moon. "Let's hope there isn't a fire," I said to Makiko. We looked at the night, seeking signs of smoke. Nothing moved but the trees, swaying softly in the wind.

As we walked toward the hotel, I thought of FDR and what Colby said about him at the theatre. He seemed to be a nice man on the surface, but could he really be dangerous underneath?

"Know what a werewolf does?" I whispered. "It hypnotizes you, to make you believe it's your friend." I shuddered. "They roam at night, looking for victims."

Makiko touched her lips. "Please, Liz, no more of werewolf."

"You're right." I understood what she meant. I pointed into the night. "Look, Makiko! *What's that?*"

* * *

Up by the entrance of the hotel, the moonlight showed a creature. Its face had scary red eyes, a snout and jagged teeth. It looked like some kind of animal, covered in black fur, but it stood on its hind legs. We heard a fearful howling, then the thing rushed away.

Makiko stared at me. "Werewolf!"

"No," I said. "It's a disguise, I'm sure of it." I grabbed her arm. "It ran toward the hotel. Come on, let's follow it."

We hurried across a wide lawn toward a two-storey building on the grounds of the hotel. The creature had disappeared into the shadows of the building. I switched on my pocket flashlight. We found an open door and stepped into a hallway. To our right, we saw another open door which led to a set of dark stairs.

We followed the stairs down to a tunnel. "This must connect to the hotel," I said. "Let's follow it."

Our footsteps made the only noise as we crept through the dark tunnel. But our steps echoed, making the hair on my neck stand on end. I swept my flashlight across the darkness. My light showed nothing. "Come on," I whispered.

We moved along the tunnel cautiously. Water dripped around us. When we emerged, we found ourselves in a hallway that had large doors on both sides.

"There's the kitchen." I flashed my light into the enormous work space. Gigantic jars of mustard, pickles and relish stood in rows and the shelves were full of pots and pans.

Something moved in the darkness. I flashed my light in time to see a jar tilting on a shelf. It hung for a moment, then fell. The glass smashed on the floor with a terrible sound. Makiko and I grabbed each other and screamed.

Another jar fell. This time, I saw the creature pushing it. Snarling, the creature dashed out through a door at the far end of the kitchen. We raced after it into a hallway. At the end of the hall, we saw the thing reach a spiral staircase.

Up it ran, up into the darkness of the tower. We both took a breath, murmured *Ganbatte* and went after it. The tower stairs were very old. They creaked as we climbed carefully. I probed the murky air with my flashlight.

At the end of our climb was the Eagle's Nest. Moonlight poured through the windows. The creature watched us, hunched in the corner. Beside him, a candle burned in an old-fashioned lantern. The creature took the candle out and lit a small pile of papers.

"No!" I screamed.

The flames leaped up quickly, licking at the dry wooden wall.

With a low growl, the creature rushed through a door on the opposite side and down the stairs. I started in pursuit, then realized we had to put out the fire. The flames were hot on my face as I looked for something to smother them with.

"Stand back." Makiko had a fire extinguisher in her hand. "It was on wall outside." She directed the spray onto the flames. The fire was out in no time.

* * *

The climb down those creaking wooden stairs was scary. I kept expecting the creature to leap out at us, but nothing happened. We wandered through the hallways, seeking an exit. In the lower hallway, we saw furniture covered with large sheets, stacks of lumber and many containers of paint.

"What do you think, Makiko? If that was a disguise, who was inside?"

"I do not know, but this was not creature we saw on island."

"No, but that looked like its lantern."

We went outside. The wind felt good on my face. We had just started walking along Prince of Wales Drive when we ran into FDR. He was staggering along the road. "My head," he moaned, clutching it. "I feel so horrible."

"What happened?" I exclaimed.

"I was at home, waiting for your arrival. The phone rang. A man said to meet him at the Algonquin Hotel. I left immediately after I hung up."

"You didn't stop for anything?"

"No." FDR seemed quite surprised. "He made it sound so urgent."

"Who was the man?"

"I didn't recognize the voice. It was muffled, as if he was trying to disguise it. He threatened my house with arson unless I met him at the hotel's pavilion. I was waiting beside it in the darkness when, all of a sudden, stars exploded inside my skull. I woke up a few minutes ago, with a terrible headache."

I studied FDR's face. His pain seemed real, but he did come from a family of actors.

From out of nowhere, Colby came jogging up. "I see everyone is out enjoying the evening," he said, winking at me.

When we told him about the attack on FDR, Colby pulled out a cellular phone and called the police. When they arrived, I heard FDR's story again. It remained consistent.

The police left, taking FDR along for further questioning. Colby volunteered to walk us home.

"It's odd," I said. "FDR told me he left immediately for the hotel after he received the phone call. I wonder why he didn't mention writing the note?"

"Perhaps FDR-san seeks to deceive?" Makiko suggested. "Attack faked by himself?"

"Be very cautious around FDR," Colby warned. "Sure, he seems meek and mild with his glasses and his books. But I've heard rumours he's dangerous."

"Weird, isn't it?" I said. "I'd better ask FDR some questions. I'd like to know what he knows about Gizmo."

"Gizmo?" Colby asked. "Who is Gizmo?"

I told him about what we had seen at the carnival. Colby listened carefully. "But you don't really know whether the person in the van started the fire. It could just be a coincidence that the van was there when the fire broke out that night," he said thoughtfully.

"That's true," I said. I looked back at the shadow-washed Algonquin Hotel. There were so many missing pieces to the puzzle.

That night, as I lay in bed, many thoughts went through my mind. I had a lot of questions to ask tomorrow, and a few things to find out.

* * *

The next morning, I went back to the Old Gaol. I wanted to check the birth records for the last twenty years. I found the entry I was looking for. I made a note of it. I needed to check something else out, but it would have to wait until later.

On our way to the theatre, Makiko and I passed a *Yes Mall* rally. Drake was there, giving a speech. There was a band, and free hot dogs and soft drinks.

"Boy, Drake's really gone all out," I said, as I watched a hundred red and white helium balloons fly up into the sky. "He really wants the mall to happen. I guess he'd do anything to see it built."

"Is that not Gizmo?" Makiko asked. I looked into the crowd. There was no mistaking that hair.

"He sure seems interested in the mall."

"Maybe he just wants free hot dog," Makiko giggled.

"Hey, Liz," someone called. I turned and saw Colby—brilliant blue eyes, gorgeous smile and all. He joined us. "The support for the mall is growing. It looks like it may end up a tie vote."

* * *

The orphans were rehearsing their opening number when we entered the theatre. There was a woman backstage watching from the wings. I recognized her as Emily's mom.

Emily ran over to me as soon as the song was over. Her face was all aglow. I had never seen her so excited.

"Guess what, Liz? I crossed the cove today on Midnight. I did it!"

"Wow, Emily. That's marvellous."

Emily's mother laughed with pleasure. "She couldn't wait to tell you. You're very nice to Emily. Every day she can't wait to go to the theatre." She smiled fondly at her child.

"She's a really excellent actor," I said. "She seems to come alive when she's on stage."

"I was wondering if you and Makiko would like to come over to our house after rehearsal today. I made cho . . ."

"Chocolate cake!" I exclaimed.

Her face fell. "No, I made chopped liver."

As I stared at her in dismay, she smiled. "Fooled you. Emily said you and Makiko like chocolate cake, so I made one."

"We'd love to come," I said. "Thanks, Emily."

Emily had become quiet and withdrawn. "It was my mother's idea."

Just then, Colin called the Rockettes to take their places on the stage. I hastened over and joined the rest of the dancers. The music started. I took my stance and all my energy went into performing.

The rehearsal went quickly. I was so busy with my various roles that I hardly noticed anything else. But I did note that FDR didn't show up for rehearsal. There were a lot of rumours being whispered about him on the stage.

After rehearsal, Makiko and I walked with Emily to her home. Emily wanted to show us her room and all her things. "I've built a really cool home for my dolls," she said. "I made it all by myself."

As we approached the house, we were greeted by the sound of yapping and barking. Emily halted. "That's our new dog."

"What's his name?"

"Max," she said, "but I don't like him."

Emily's mother met us at the door. She held the dog by the collar so he wouldn't jump. Emily seemed afraid of the dog. She kept her distance from him as she entered the house.

The chocolate cake was delicious. Emily's mom could really bake. When we had finished eating, Emily showed us her doll house, her model horse collection and all her books. "Do you want to play Chinese jump rope?" she asked.

"Sure," we both said.

"Don't be too late," her mother told us as we went out the door. "Your father will be home soon."

Emily became quiet all of a sudden. Her face went pale. "Stepfather," she corrected.

Makiko, Emily, and I played Chinese jump rope in the backyard. Emily was winning. Her face was flushed and happy.

"Emily," a man's voice called.

Emily looked up. She turned suddenly afraid.

Her stepfather stood in the back doorway. He had Max with him. The short-haired mongrel was pulling hard against the leash.

"Emily! Isn't it one of your chores to walk Max?"

She didn't say anything. Her eyes were on the ground, and her hands trembled.

"Emily, we've got this new dog. You must take your turn walking it." He held out the leash. "Trust me, you won't get hurt."

"I'm afraid," she whispered.

"You must do as I tell you, Emily." His eyes were very blue. "It's your duty to walk the dog."

"I never wanted to get it. I'm scared of dogs." She looked up at the man. "Last time, it ran away from me and chased someone. You got mad."

"I won't be angry ever again," he replied. "I promise."

"What if it hurts me?"

"It won't, Emily. I'll never let you get hurt."

Slowly, she held out her hand for the leash. The dog was straining forward, anxious for its walk. The man put Emily's hand into the loop on the leash and then let go.

Right away, the dog sprang forward. Emily was caught off balance and fell hard. The cement ripped her knees, and I saw blood. Emily dropped the leash, crying. The dog immediately took off running.

The man swore angrily at Emily, then ran after the dog. It was already in the neighbour's garden, happily digging up flowers. The man looked guiltily in the window of the house, then grabbed the dog and ran back to Emily.

"More trouble," he said, glancing anxiously about. "Come on, Emily, let's go inside. Any more problems with this dog and I'll get sued." He helped Emily to her feet and brushed the pebbles from her torn knees. "Listen, it's our secret about the garden getting dug up, okay? Don't tell, or everything will be terrible. Emily has to go inside now," her stepfather informed us. "Thank you for dropping by."

Emily threw us a look of grief as she was led inside.

7

I was nervous about attending the first dress rehearsal for *Annie*. But I felt better when I saw the spectacular costumes. Dancing as a Rockette, I'd be wearing a top hat and a sequined tuxedo that shimmered under the bright spotlights.

Colin called Makiko up on stage to present her with an *Annie* souvenir sweatshirt. While everyone applauded, Makiko wriggled into the sweatshirt and bowed her thanks.

Colby used spirit gum to attach Elvis sideburns to his face, then sang "Heartbreak Hotel" to Makiko and the orphans. Everyone adored him. After that, Margaret, the music director, warmed up our voices with the show's hit song, "Tomorrow." I felt wonderful. We were like a family.

Then we heard wheels rolling onto the stage. Everyone turned to see FDR in the wooden wheelchair. Light flashed from his spectacles.

"I couldn't miss rehearsal again," he said. "I hope I'm welcome."

"Of course," Colin exclaimed.

Before long, we were under the lights, in full costume. The girl who played Annie was home with the flu, so Emily took the role. She was terrific.

Eventually, we took a break. At the pop machine, the orphans all talked at once about the hotel fire, FDR and the werewolf. People were beginning to think that the legend of the St. Andrews werewolf might be true after all.

"I told you FDR was the werewolf," Tegan said to me.

"You don't have any proof."

"Yes, we do. He started the fire at the hotel. Everyone knows the werewolf is the arsonist."

"That's right," Ashlee added. "And he goes to Minister's Island, dresses as a werewolf, then comes over and burns our houses."

"Why would he do that?" I asked.

The orphans couldn't agree on an answer to my question.

"I'd like a little more proof. There are a few things I want to check out before I jump to any conclusions."

Emily kept avoiding me. After she had finished practicing her big number, I took her aside. "Please thank your Mom again for the chocolate cake, okay?"

"Sure." Her brown eyes stared at the floor.

"It's great you crossed the cove on Midnight, Emily. You're getting really courageous."

A smile flitted across her face. "It was easier than I thought."

"You were dynamite on stage today."

Colin stopped beside us. "We see more of your talent every rehearsal, Emily. You're like a flower, slowly blossoming."

She scuffed her foot against the stage. "Thank you, Colin."

"Thinking of a career in show biz?"

She nodded shyly. "But how do I get ready?"

"Read about theatre at the library. Always believe in yourself, because you won't get every role you audition for. Rejection can hurt."

"Colin," I asked, "how did you get your start? Was it difficult?"

He smiled. "I started as a beginner, just like everyone else. I was scared but determined. I learned my craft, and I was curious. Understanding people sharpens the actor." Colin paused. "It also helps with real-life problems. Sometimes my feelings get hurt. I always ask myself why it happened. Was the other person having a bad day, or maybe feeling jealous? That way, I don't always think it's my fault."

As Emily asked a question, I was almost run over by FDR. "I'm still having trouble with this wheelchair," he apologized.

"No problem. FDR, may I ask you a question?"

"Fire away."

"What would you do if you had a lot of money?"

FDR smiled. "I'd live out my dream."

"What's your dream?"

He smiled shyly. "A charitable foundation with a difference—a panel of kids would decide how to spend the money. Anyone could suggest a project to receive funds. For example, someone in St. Andrews might ask the foundation to buy land for a park. Or maybe scholarships for needy kids to go to university. So much could be done!"

"I like it," I said as Colin called for the rehearsal to continue. "Oh, could you write down your address again? I've lost it."

"Sure thing." FDR fished out a fountain pen. "This was presented to my parents by Irving Berlin. Dad always claimed that Mr. Berlin used it to compose his big hit, 'White Christmas.'"

Using his right hand, FDR wrote down his address.

"Thanks," I said. I studied his writing. The elegant script slanted evenly to the right. I folded the paper and slipped it into my pocket.

* * *

"All this talk about werewolf makes me worry." Makiko's pretty face was pulled into a frown. "The creature we saw at Eagle's Nest was not creature we saw on island. But now people think werewolf on island is arsonist."

"What's your theory?"

"I think someone is trying to make a frame," she concluded.

I agreed. "But who is framing whom?" I asked.

"Perhaps FDR-san is using creature to scare people."

"Somebody is, but I still don't know for sure if it's

FDR." I showed her the sample of FDR's writing and compared it to the note we found at his house. The handwriting was different.

"He could have disguised it." Makiko said.

Although I was pretty sure FDR was not the arsonist, I couldn't rule him out altogether. I knew the only place we could clear up most of this mystery was at Coven Hoven. What was its secret? I told Makiko what I had discovered about the old Van Horne mansion in my last visit to the archives.

"We must go back to the island," Makiko urged.

"I know," I shuddered. I wasn't exactly looking forward to the trip.

* * *

That afternoon, we borrowed a couple of kayaks from Fran. After a little practice, we set out toward the island.

The wind was from the north. The air was cold and fresh on my skin. Far above, black clouds were driven across the sky as if by unseen forces. It felt as if a storm was coming. I hoped it would hold off until we returned.

Gliding swiftly through the ocean waters, we approached Minister's Island. "Let's beach the kayaks near the Road Beneath the Sea," I called to Makiko.

Mustard-coloured moss covered the big rocks along the shore. Enormous signs shouted *Private Property* and *Keep Out*. "I don't feel very welcome," I said to Makiko.

I looked for the Road Beneath the Sea, but the tide was in and it was covered by water. Powerful currents swirled through the narrow strait. We found a place to beach our kayaks. We stumbled across a rocky beach, then climbed a slope to rolling fields that were brilliantly green. The air was sweet, and wildflowers danced in the wind.

"Regard barn," Makiko said. "So excellent!"

It was the biggest I'd ever seen. The walls were high, topped by an enormous roof. On top was a weather vane shaped like a cow. High on the barn, a row of windows looked down like frowning eyes.

My heart beat fast as we entered the barn through a huge doorway. Swallows darted past us into the sunshine.

The barn was almost empty. Beside a wall was some rusty farm equipment and an ancient fire engine designed to be pulled by horses. Above us was a wooden loft.

"I think I just heard footsteps." I studied the ceiling, wondering how to get up there. I listened carefully, then shook my head. "Maybe I'm wrong. I could have heard raccoons in the walls."

"Let us investigate."

We studied the loft above us. "There's got to be a way up to that part of the barn," I said. "But I can't see it."

"I see stairs." Makiko pointed into a dusty corner. "But they go down."

We followed the stairs to the barn's lower floor. The stalls were all empty, but something caught my eye. "Hey, Makiko, there's some fresh oats." I recalled the figure escaping from the Burying Ground. "Remember, the creature had a white stallion."

"I am afraid for this creature," Makiko said as we returned upstairs. I grabbed Makiko's arm and squeezed a warning. Someone stood in the shadows near the old fire engine.

8

A man stepped out of the shadows. His head was totally bald. A ratty little grey beard grew from his chin. He had small, shifty eyes. His face was creased by lines. He wore a long white coat, gloves and boots. He looked at least seventy, maybe older.

"My name is Smart." His voice was thin. He studied me, then Makiko. "You are trespassing on private property. Shall I notify the police? Or shall I imprison you both in a basement dungeon?"

"We've come with a warning," I said urgently. "Do you work for Lady Chandler? Someone is trying to frame the creature who lives on this island. They are blaming it for all the arson. He or she might be in danger."

Smart sniffed. "Absolute rubbish." He pointed to the door. "Get off this island immediately. Never return."

"We were only trying to help," I protested. "You're not being fair."

A voice spoke from the shadows. "The young lady is correct. Apologize to her, Smart."

A very elegant older woman walked toward us. "I'm Lady Chandler." Her voice was deep and rich. Her clothes were eccentric and out-of-date. Her snow-white hair was piled in a bun. Her eyes were black and intelligent. They studied us.

"I appreciate the warning, young ladies. Smart has been very rude. He will now apologize."

His little eyes gave her a look I couldn't read. "Sorry," he mumbled insincerely.

We introduced ourselves to Lady Chandler as we left the barn. Waiting outside was a beautiful horse hitched to a shiny carriage. "Climb up," Lady Chandler ordered. "We're going to Coven Hoven for tea. I haven't had company for years."

Smart glanced at us, then grabbed the reins. Soon we were flying past the tall grass. All around were daisies, clover, and Queen Anne's lace. "The clover makes the hay more sweet for the cows," Lady Chandler said. "In the days of Sir William Van Horne, there were eighty head of Clydesdale cattle in the barn. Sir William didn't want his workers daydreaming, so he put the windows too high to look out. Every night, they traced Van Horne's coat-of-arms in sawdust freshly spread on the barn floor. The workers wore overalls and lab coats—Smart deliberately copies the outfit. We both love this island, and we know its entire history. Did you know that Van Horne wanted to live for five hundred years?"

"Did he make it?" I asked.

Lady Chandler laughed at the joke. "He tried, but unfortunately not. He could be quite a quack, though. He sometimes kept a potato in his pocket to ward off rheumatism."

"How did Minister's Island get its name?" I asked.

"The first person to own the island was a clergyman."

"In school, I have studied about Van Horne-san. Famous man for building famous railway," Makiko said.

"He knew how to get things done, and he had a zest for life. Sir William expected nothing but perfection." Lady Chandler smiled. "I'm afraid I'm talking too much. It's just so nice to have company."

"You should do it more often, Lady Chandler."

She stiffened. "Unfortunately, it is not possible. I invited you girls for tea because you're strangers. You'll leave St. Andrews by summer's end. You won't pester me for visits, and then snoop around. Others have tried that. It hurt me deeply. I told Smart to seal off this island. He has been very successful."

"You're right," I said. "The kids in town are terrified of this place. It seems a shame, when it's such a beautiful island. Couldn't you open it up, maybe just for kids?"

"They wouldn't understand."

"But what's the problem, Lady Chandler? Is a treasure buried here?"

"A treasure, yes, but not one anyone would want. This island is private property, and will remain so. I cherish my privacy."

"Well, we're sure honoured to be invited for tea."

Makiko bowed her head. "Such a delight."

Ahead of us loomed the mansion, Coven Hoven. It was tremendous, stretching in many directions. There were many chimneys and countless windows. "It has eleven bathrooms, and two hundred and fourteen doorknobs," Lady Chandler said. "I've counted them."

Smart stopped the carriage at the front door. Climbing down, I sniffed some pretty roses that grew by the house. "The creature left roses like these on the grave."

"What creature?"

"The one we saw on this island, Lady Chandler."

"You must never use that word again. How horrid!"

When we entered the mansion, we stepped back in time. The place was filled with chandeliers, oil portraits and mahogany furniture. Candlelight glowed in mirrors that filled entire walls. A gold clock ticked on the mantel of a huge fireplace.

"It's like being in another time," I exclaimed.

A ghost of a smile crossed Lady Chandler's lips. She tapped a beautiful rug with her cane. "This was years in the making, entirely by hand. It's irreplaceable." She pointed at two curious chairs. "Those are camel chairs. My husband was independently wealthy. He became a doctor and served the people of Egypt. We retired to Canada twenty years ago, purchased Coven Hoven and restored its glories to the days of Van Horne."

Lady Chandler led us toward a staircase. "Let me show you the upper floor."

It was like a maze upstairs. Hallways zigged and zagged in all directions. "Is your bedroom up here, Lady Chandler?"

"No, I sleep downstairs. This is too gloomy for me."

"Are there ghosts?"

"One night, I thought I heard footsteps up here. Smart and I investigated. The footsteps came close to us, then vanished. The air became extremely cold." For several moments, she said nothing. "I've never heard them again."

"Wow," I said. "Creepy."

I noticed all the bedroom doors were open except for one. "What's in here?" I asked.

"Don't," Lady Chandler exclaimed. She grabbed my hand before I could open the door.

"Sorry," I said.

Downstairs, I saw a comfortable-looking room with a big TV set. Pretty flowers stood in big vases. Two big sofas faced a wall of electronic equipment. I looked at the CDs and laser discs. "This is really great music you listen to, Lady Chandler. You're really into rock music, eh?"

She didn't reply.

We followed Lady Chandler through Coven Hoven, eventually reaching the living room. It was the size of a small air terminal. We sat on a velvety chesterfield, surrounded by soft pillows. Smart appeared from a distant kitchen carrying a silver tray. On it was a tea service that looked like Royal Doulton.

"The tea smells delicious," I said.

"Huh," Smart muttered.

When he was gone, Lady Chandler passed us plates of buttered bread. "Bread for friendship," she said. I nibbled some but saved my appetite for the carrot cake with super-thick icing waiting for us on the tray.

"This is fantastic, Lady Chandler. Your friends must love staying here."

"I have no friends. I have no guests."

"But you live here with your husband, don't you?"

"He died recently, God rest his soul."

Sighing, Lady Chandler lowered herself into a sofa by the fireplace. She picked up a leather-bound book. "Do you know about Mary Shelley? Long ago, she was married to a famous poet. While still a teenager, she wrote this book called *Frankenstein.*"

"I've seen the movie," I said. "Boris Karloff was excellent."

Lady Chandler looked at us. The firelight deepened the lines around her eyes. "The agony of that unhappy brute," she said, "shunned by the world. The cruelty of people!"

"Frankenstein was just a story, Lady Chandler. Besides, these are modern times. My friends don't think it's fun to cause pain."

Her eyes flashed at me. "But it could happen! What then? Frightened people can be so cruel."

There was a loud crash of thunder.

"It's a storm," Makiko said, looking out the window at the tossing ocean. "How will we get back home?"

"I'm afraid you'll have to stay the night," Lady Chandler said. "I'll tell Smart to set two more places for dinner."

I phoned Fran to let her know we were all right and that we had been invited to stay at Coven Hoven. "Take notes," she said. "I'd give anything to visit that place."

* * *

When I came downstairs for dinner, I was still wearing my jeans. I wish I had worn something nicer, but then,

I hadn't expected this invitation. In the big hallway, Smart sat alone at an organ, playing mournful sounds. He glared at me.

"Don't ever come back to Coven Hoven," he hissed, continuing to play the depressing music.

I tried to smile, pretending Smart didn't make me nervous.

Makiko came downstairs, looking beautiful even in jeans. Lady Chandler waited in the dining room. The candlelight was soft, casting an eerie glow on the many paintings.

Lady Chandler sat at the head of the table. I sat on one side of her, Makiko on the other. The rest of the table was empty, although twenty more people could have comfortably joined us.

"I once had happy times at this table," Lady Chandler said. "My son and his wife lived here. The house rang with their laughter."

"What happened, Lady Chandler?" I asked softly.

"They died. In a motor crash here on the island. There was a bad storm. My son drove too fast and crashed into a tree. There was a terrible fire." Lady Chandler looked up at an oil portrait. It showed a handsome young man, his wife and a little boy. "Since their deaths, I have forbidden motor cars on Minister's Island."

"What happened to the little boy?"

A spasm of pain contorted Lady Chandler's face. "He died, too. I adored him."

"Wallace," I said.

Lady Chandler looked surprised. "How do you know?"

"I ran across an article in the town archives about your family."

"Please, don't mention his name again. Let the dead lie in peace."

Makiko gently touched Lady Chandler's hand. "I have great feeling for you, Chandler-san."

She smiled gratefully. "Thank you, my dear. It's good to have you visiting Coven Hoven. Your generation has strength and optimism. My generation has wisdom. If only the young and old could combine forces, we'd make a better world." She opened her napkin. "Now, we must eat."

Smart produced a salmon that was absolutely delicious. We worked on it while talking. Lady Chandler kept us entertained with stories of her life in Egypt. She also told us about how she and her late husband worked to restore Coven Hoven.

"This place is like a living museum," Makiko said.

"Yes," Lady Chandler mused, lost in thought. "But what will happen when I die? That's my greatest worry."

"You're concerned about the future of the island, Lady Chandler?"

"No, about . . ."

She was interrupted by Smart, who arrived with dessert. I tried to encourage her to say more, but she grew silent. "I am tired," she said. "Having company has been exhilarating, and exhausting. I must go to my bed."

Upstairs later, I sat at my window brushing my hair and looking at the moonlight on the sea. The storm had died down and the night was quiet.

I crawled into bed and tried unsuccessfully to sleep. Around midnight, the silence was broken by the sound of distant music. Somebody was playing the guitar. I heard it clearly. Going into the hallway, I met Makiko.

Cautiously, we followed the music along the hallway. We reached the door that had been closed during our tour with Lady Chandler. As I opened the door, it squealed on its hinges.

The sound was a warning to someone inside. I heard the scramble of feet on the roof. I rushed to the open window but could see nothing.

"Let us go to another window," Makiko suggested.

Quickly, we raced back to my room. We scanned the dark night, hoping to get a glimpse of something. A figure emerged out of the darkness, carrying a heavy lantern. It was just like the one the werewolf had at the Eagle's Nest.

"Can you see who it is, Liz?"

"Yes." My heart filled with dismay. "It's FDR."

Smart stepped outside and stood talking to FDR. We couldn't hear their words. Smart handed FDR an envelope. FDR took it and left. Suddenly Smart looked up and caught us watching. He shook his fist and went inside.

I tried to sleep again, but my thoughts kept me awake. Over and over I asked myself the same question—was FDR really the arsonist?

9

The next morning, Lady Chandler stayed in her room. Smart gave us breakfast, but wouldn't let us say goodbye to Lady Chandler. I wanted to ask her about FDR. I started to question Smart, but that was a lost cause.

Smart drove us in the carriage to the gate. "Don't ever come back," he said.

I straightened my spine. "Goodbye, Smart. It's been a slice."

Makiko giggled.

It was a great trip home in the kayaks. Morning mist lay across the ocean waters. The waves moved gently, turning blue, then green. Birds chased each other, crying out in delight.

Fran was waiting for me when I got back. I told her everything I had learned about Coven Hoven as we sat drinking cups of herbal tea.

"It's a shame she keeps that place hidden," Fran sighed.

Just then, Makiko arrived to accompany me to the theatre.

"I have had a long telephone conversation with my family. Each sends affectionate regards to you, Liz."

"Thanks!"

Before we left, Fran had some news for us. "Drake has just offered Greta O'Neal's son a job as manager at the mall. He wouldn't have to leave town. I don't think we could say anything now that would make her vote against the mall."

"Would Mrs. O'Neal let herself be bribed like that?"

"I don't know. I thought I knew her pretty well. But this is a tough decision."

I gave Fran a hug.

"Don't forget," Fran said. "The fireworks start at sunset."

"How could I forget? I love Canada Day celebrations."

* * *

Makiko and I walked through town on our way to the theatre. Canadian flags were everywhere waving in the breeze. Red and white streamers festooned lamp posts. "It is so festive," Makiko laughed.

Colby joined us, carrying hot dogs. "Your favourite," he said to Makiko. Colby looked at his watch. "Another dress rehearsal today."

We bought ice cream cones, and ate them on our way. The salty sea air mingled with the fragrance of freshly mowed grass. I waved at Mrs. O'Neal. She was on her porch, listening to someone who was talking and gesturing wildly.

"That person must be talking about the mall," I said. "Poor Mrs. O'Neal. Everyone's trying to influence her."

"She'll vote yes," Colby predicted.

"Mrs. O'Neal will vote for what is best for the town," I replied strongly.

We arrived at the theatre and Colby went straight toward his dressing room with a quick, "See you."

Backstage, the theatre people discussed the vote as they got into costume and applied their makeup. "I don't like the mall," Miss Hannigan said, leaning toward the mirror with a stick of greasepaint. Bright lightbulbs surrounded her face. "If I owned that land, I'd donate it for a park. Who wants some giant mall in our backyard?"

"I do," one of the singers, Barbara, said. "This place needs jobs—I don't want my boyfriend leaving town."

"Somebody is using some pretty strong methods to force Greta O'Neal to vote for the mall," Miss Hannigan said. "If you know what I mean."

I wandered out to the stage, where Emily found me. "Guess what?" she exclaimed. "Mom and I went riding at night, all the way to the Road Beneath the Sea. Next I'm going to try it alone."

I gave her a hug. "You're getting really courageous."

Drake approached in his butler outfit. He wore a gold watch chain across his stomach, and little pince-nez glasses over his snobby eyes. "Have you seen Colby?" he asked.

"Not since I arrived," I answered.

"I have to find him," Drake muttered gruffly and then stomped away. Emily scurried across stage to join Miss Hannigan and the other orphans for notes from Colin.

I sat by myself on stage. FDR rolled toward me in his wooden chair. "Hi, Liz. Found anything more on the arsonist?"

I shook my head. "Makiko and I have some clues."

"I hope they catch him. He's destroying the town."

"I agree," I said. "FDR, what were you doing at Coven Hoven last night?"

"What?! I wasn't there."

"I saw you."

FDR's smile disappeared and his face became stern. "I think you are mistaken," he said and rolled away.

I was upset. Why was FDR lying to me?

But once I was on stage, I felt better. I finally stopped worrying about when to say my lines—they had become second nature to me. So I relaxed. I forgot about everything that was troubling me. All I thought about was the play. After the opening number, I suddenly believed that *Annie* was real life instead of a make-believe story. It was a magic moment. The rehearsal became really fun. I did a great solo tap in the radio scene.

After the performance, Colin gathered us in the empty seats of the theatre for cast notes. Colby came up and seemed to be in a better mood than before. We sat together during the notes, holding hands.

Colby offered to go with me to the Canada Day fireworks at the Point. "Great," I said, "but I'm going to Fran's after for hot chocolate."

"Maybe I'll convince you otherwise," he said with a wink. "Give me a minute—I've got a message for Drake."

I waited in the lobby with Makiko. Time passed slowly. Colby was gone for about ten minutes, and seemed jittery when he returned. "Drake is in a terrible mood," he said, as we left the theatre. "He's totally stressed about the vote."

* * *

A big crowd of townspeople and tourists had gathered at an outdoor concert stage at the Point. We sang "O Canada" as pink clouds drifted above Passamaquoddy Bay. We were like a family together, a community in harmony with nature. I looked around, wanting the best for everyone. Emily was in the crowd with her mother. They both gave me timid smiles.

After the anthem, the ceremonies and entertainment began. A wild Maritimes band played jigs and reels while everyone danced and clapped along. "It's getting dark," Colby said, spinning me in a dance. "At last."

"You really like fireworks, don't you?" I asked.

He grinned. "You could say that."

The night turned crimson as the first firebomb exploded above us. The crowd went *ooooh* as silver stars burst in bright patterns, then *aaaah* as pinwheels spun in rainbows of colours.

Makiko grinned at me. "Such a happy evening, Liz."

Just then I felt a small hand in mine. I looked down at Emily. "I don't want to go home," she said. "I want to stay with you."

Her mother came out of the crowd. "Emily, we have to go."

"I don't want to." Emily's hand squeezed tighter. "Let me stay with you. Please."

I looked at her mother. "Fran's invited some friends for a girls' night at her place. Maybe Emily could join us for hot chocolate, then Fran could drive her home."

Emily's eyes glowed. "Yes!"

Her mother smiled. "Very well, sweetheart. But straight home after."

"Okay, Mom."

I turned to Colby. "Maybe I'll see you tomorrow."

"You're going to this hot chocolate thing instead of being with me? Skip it, okay? Stay with me."

"This is important to Emily," I said, "and to me."

Colby shook his head. "Okay, Liz. I'll see you later." He walked away, shoulders slumped. Emily's hand was still in mine, and I knew I'd done the right thing, but I was a bit glum anyway.

* * *

"Cheer up," Fran said as the crowd walked back to town from the Point. We were with two other friends of Fran's. One was Miss Hannigan from our musical. "You've got to look below the surface," Fran said. "Handsome is as handsome does."

"What do you mean?" I asked.

"Judge a person by who they are on the inside, not how they look on the outside."

"I know that," I sighed. "But I guess I fell for a pretty face."

"It may all work out." Fran patted my shoulder.

"I don't know. I really don't like his attitude."

At Seaside Cabins, I went to my little place—"Sandpiper"—with Emily for sweaters. She studied every detail of the one room with its tiny attached bathroom. "Did you bring this little jade elephant from Winnipeg?"

I nodded. "It's a present from my uncle and aunt. It goes everywhere with me. I keep it facing the door for protection. It's kind of a superstition, I guess."

"I should get one," Emily said. "Sometimes when I'm falling asleep, I picture a fairy princess going room to room with her wand, making things better." She sighed. "Last night I had a weird dream. I was holding a flower. It was so pretty and fragile, and I was trying to protect it."

"From what?"

Emily shrugged. "I forget."

Her eyes looked scared, so I gave her a hug. "Let's go get some hot chocolate."

We walked together toward the sea. A bonfire glowed on the faces of Fran, Makiko and the others. *Fire's burning, fire's burning*, they sang, *draw nearer, draw nearer*.

The singing was led by Savanna, a friend of Fran's. After a few of my favourite songs, Fran told a ghost story. We roasted marshmallows, then Fran poured refills of hot chocolate. "Such a peaceful night," she said, looking up at the stars.

Savanna began talking about her niece. "She says that things have been happening to her. I know who the man is, and I don't like him. But I think she's making too much of it."

Miss Hannigan looked at her. "Are you talking about sexual abuse?"

"Yes."

"What's she said?"

Savanna told her the details. Miss Hannigan listened carefully, then said, "That girl means it."

"You sound so certain."

"I *am* certain." Miss Hannigan looked at the flames, then at Savanna. "You see, it happened to me."

Emily's hand clutched mine more tightly. I looked at her, wondering if she should be listening to the conversation. I got up to leave, intent on taking her away from the gathering.

"No," Miss Hannigan said. "Let Emily stay." She looked around at the circle of faces. "I felt guilty not trusting someone who said he loved me. My mother loved me, and I trusted her. My father said he loved me and he'd never hurt me, but he *was* hurting me. In my heart, I knew I couldn't trust him."

Fran took Miss Hannigan's hand, and held it.

"I had to get over feeling guilty about this," Miss Hannigan said, "and do something to save myself. So I told. It wasn't easy, but I did it. My Mom wasn't angry. She cried, and she hugged me, and she got us help."

Miss Hannigan stirred the flames with a stick. Glowing sparks danced up into the night. "My counsellors were good people. I'd thought everyone knew about it, but people don't have x-ray vision. They can't see inside your head. That's why my Mom never guessed. It was right to tell the secret because my father was lying. The secret hurt me, and it protected him."

Miss Hannigan looked at us. "After I told, I felt safer. I knew it wasn't my fault it happened." She patted Fran's hand. "Things slowly got better, and today I'm so happy that little girl told the secret. She gave a precious gift to the woman I am. She gave me pride. No one has power over me."

Everyone was silent for a moment. Fran put an arm around Miss Hannigan, who quickly wiped a tear from her eye. "Thanks for listening to me, everyone." Miss Hannigan smiled.

"Thank *you*," Savanna said. "I'm going to pay attention to my niece."

Nobody said much as the party ended. Emily and I helped cover the fire's burning embers, then she climbed into Fran's 4x4 to go home. "Thanks, Liz," Emily said quietly from the window. "You're my best friend."

10

The next evening, I was at the pier with Makiko. After a long day at rehearsal, we were celebrating with an ice cream cone before attending the vote on the mall. "Let's get there soon," I said, consulting my watch. "The place will be packed."

On a wall inside the Charlotte County Courthouse were the portraits of the king and queen, and their thirteen kids, who'd been honored when St. Andrews was founded. "This place has been in use since 1840," I read out from a tourist brochure.

Lots of people were arriving early. The whole town was anxious to know if the mall would be given the green light for construction. People were crowded around us as we searched for a seat. It was hot under the glare of TV-camera lights. The air was electric with tension.

There was a green-topped table where the Civic Trust members sat. Mrs. O'Neal had already taken her place at the table. She studied some notes, then glanced nervously at the crowd. Makiko and I smiled at her, and she lifted her hand in greeting.

Drake had entered and taken a seat in the audience. Colby walked in and searched the room. He waved at me, then went over and whispered something to Drake. Drake shook his head. The two seemed to argue about something. Colby's face twisted into a sneer. As I watched him, I realized I was seeing the real Colby. Even with those blue eyes, what I saw wasn't handsome.

The crowd was restless until Mrs. O'Neal called the meeting to order.

"We all know why we are here," she said. "I suggest we move directly to a vote. Mr. Walker, your vote, please."

A man rose to speak. He wore a three-piece suit and gold-rimmed spectacles. "Tonight we will decide the fate of this town," he said. "I vote yes. I'm aware of what development has done south of the border, but we need the employment. Let's build the mall and hope for the best."

He sat down. A few people in the crowd applauded. Most watched quietly with their arms crossed. "Mrs. Ross, your vote, please."

A woman stood up from the table. She spoke bitterly against the mall. "I vote no," she said. The applause for her was loud.

The next member of the Civic Trust stood up. "I vote against." A ripple of excitement ran through the crowd. The vote continued down the table. The audience grew tense as they awaited the outcome. There were three votes remaining. There was another "yes." Then another member stood. "I vote no." The crowd burst into thunderous applause. Only one more "no" vote was needed to defeat the mall. The next person stood up. "I vote yes." The crowd groaned in disappointment.

It was a tie.

It would be up to Mrs. O'Neal to decide the vote. Every eye was on her. She stood up. There was sweat on her forehead, perhaps due to the heat of the packed room. She wore a beautiful dress of emerald green. Her hair was freshly permed. She looked at her son and his wife, then at others in the crowd.

"Those of you who know me know that this is not an easy decision for me. I've tried to be fair, to consider everyone's interest. I've listened to the arguments for both sides. Many have tried to persuade me, some with threats. But there was one group whose interest I overlooked—the young people of this town. Two remarkable young women made me aware of my oversight." She looked at me and Makiko. "The girls are here this evening."

Everyone stared at us.

Mrs. O'Neal continued. "Deciding to follow the girls' suggestion, I questioned the young people of St. Andrews. After all, we're deciding their future."

She looked at her notes.

"There are some really wonderful young people in this town. As I talked to them, I was impressed by their intelligence and their caring. I was also amazed. I expected them to demand a mall. Instead, most wanted the Civic Trust to preserve the beauty of St. Andrews."

Mrs. O'Neal looked at her son and his wife. "I don't want you moving to Alberta with my grandchildren. Everyone knows that. But I have to listen to my heart. I vote against the mall."

For a moment, there was a shocked silence. Then people cheered and hugged each other. It was like a New Year's Eve party! Whooping and hollering, I grabbed Makiko in a bear hug. People crowded around, shaking our hands and saying thanks for talking to Mrs. O'Neal. But not everyone was happy. Some whispered angrily to each other, and Drake stared at Mrs. O'Neal with stormy eyes. Colby ran out as soon as the vote was decided.

We managed to get through the crowd to Mrs. O'Neal, and shared a big hug. "Guess what?" she said. "I'm invited to Lethbridge for Christmas with my grandchildren. Won't that be nice? I'll see them again in only six months."

"You'll have a wonderful time," I said, hugging her again. "I really admire your courage, Mrs. O'Neal."

Makiko and I took big gulps of the cool night air once we stepped outside the courthouse. Then I stared in wonder at the sky. Hanging over the town was the moon. It was huge and glowing.

At that moment, a terrible howl filled the night. My hair stood on end. Makiko and I stared at each other, eyes huge.

"It came from the direction of Mrs. O'Neal's place," I shouted. "Come on, let's run!"

Makiko and I tore over to Mrs. O'Neal's house. We arrived in time to see flames burning near the wall of the garage. A shape lurked in the shadows near the house. In the flickering orange light, I saw a face and body thick with fur. The thing raised its head and howled. Its fangs glistened in the moonlight.

At a nearby house, someone ran onto the porch, screaming. At another house, a man yelled, "Call the cops. It's the werewolf!"

The creature ran swiftly. It crossed the lawn and ran behind a house to the nearest street. A van came from out of the darkness, turned a corner, and followed the werewolf down the same street. "It's the same van we saw at the carnival," I said.

"We should visit carnival again," Makiko replied. "And soon."

The fire was licking at the garage, moving close to the house. People were running toward Mrs. O'Neal's, carrying fire extinguishers and buckets of water. A siren sounded, moving our way fast. The fire department arrived and quickly extinguished the flames.

Makiko and I grabbed our mountain bikes and rode with all our might to the carnival.

* * *

The carnival lights flashed and twirled, the air boomed with music and kids screamed on the rides whirling above our heads. We hurried past the people who crowded the carnival grounds. Finding Gizmo's trailer, we slipped into the dark shadows behind it.

Cigarette smoke drifted out the open window. Creeping closer, we looked inside. Gizmo was sprawled on a kitchen chair, drinking beer. Rocky leaned against the refrigerator. He was wearing the same motorcycle gear and dusty boots, and held out a container for kerosene. "I'll get rid of this now," he said. "We won't be starting any more fires. I wouldn't want anyone finding this container."

"Don't worry," Gizmo replied. "Everyone in town thinks a werewolf caused the fires."

"And," Rocky added, "they think the werewolf lives on the island." He wiped the beer off his mouth. His moustache slipped. He fixed it, then said, "I'm going to burn the werewolf disguise." He picked it up from a heap on the floor. It had fake fur and plastic fangs.

A man hurried up to Gizmo's trailer and went inside. "Drake," I whispered. "I bet those are his goons. They tried to pressure everyone into voting yes."

Drake's voice reached us through the night. "You fools," he shouted at Gizmo and Rocky. "What are you doing? You're completely out of control."

Gizmo took a puff of his cigarette. "That fool O'Neal ignored our threats," he said. "We had to teach her a lesson."

Drake stared at him. "Who decided on the arson? I'm horrified by your actions!"

Rocky laughed. "I care this much for you," he said, snapping his fingers in Drake's face.

Gizmo slapped his hand on the table. "Give us our money. Now."

"I hired you to make sure the Civic Trust voted for the mall. I asked you to twist some arms, but I didn't expect a terror campaign! I didn't expect arson!"

Rocky's laugh was harsh. "You could have made us stop. But you were afraid the people of St. Andrews would learn the truth—that you don't have a legal claim to all the land. So, you kept quiet."

"Yes, and now I face prison." The light glowed on Drake's face. "I did a stupid thing. I was greedy, so I hired a pair of criminals to help get the mall through. Tonight, I'm going to the police. Tomorrow, when I awake, my world will be in ruins. My honour will be gone, and so will my land."

"I'd think twice about going to the police," Gizmo warned.

Drake looked at him defiantly and headed toward the door. But Rocky wasted no time. He grabbed the kerosene container and hit Drake on the head. Drake dropped to the floor.

"Tie him up. We'll deal with him later," Rocky ordered. "We have a little business to take care of on Minister's Island."

"Our chariot awaits." Gizmo gestured toward the door.

Makiko and I quickly ducked behind the trailer.

"They're heading for the van," I whispered as I watched the two men make their way through the carnival trailers in the direction of the open fields.

"We've got to move fast."

11

We entered the trailer. Drake lay on the floor, moaning. I knelt down beside him to see if he was fully conscious. His eyes looked startled.

"Liz Austen! What are you doing here?"

"Makiko and I have been working on the mystery of the St. Andrews werewolf, which led us here."

"Please untie me," Drake urged.

"Why should I? You're dangerous. You hired two thugs to pressure innocent people, burning down homes!"

"That wasn't my plan, Liz. Things were out of my control."

"Were you being blackmailed?" I asked.

"Yes. Someone in town discovered something I had thought was long forgotten."

"That you don't have a legal claim to all of the land slated for the mall. Right?"

He sighed, and slowly nodded his head. "When I made the deal, I paid off some people so the deal was never questioned."

"But the estate you bought the land from still has a claim?"

"If people found out and someone decided to force the issue, I would probably lose all the land."

"The heir, FDR, is still alive. He could make a claim but he doesn't know that, does he?"

"No. And the person blackmailing me was threatening to tell FDR and the entire town unless I paid him off. And the only way I could afford to pay him off was to have the mall vote go through. He was the one who forced me into hiring those two goons."

"Who *is* threatening you?"

"Colby Keaton," Drake said clearly. My heart sank. I began to tremble.

"And those guys you hired?" I managed.

Drake shrugged. "Colby's contacts. Gizmo works at the carnival, and Rocky is some friend of his. I've never seen him before."

"Maybe you know Rocky better than you think," I said.

"I don't know what you mean." Drake looked terrible, huddled on the floor.

"Just a hunch," I said. "We've got some things to take care of first, but we'll send the police to pick you up."

Makiko and I raced outside and jumped on our bikes. We both knew where we had to go next.

* * *

The kayaks were waiting for us. We jumped into them and paddled over to Minister's Island. The tide was out. The Road Beneath the Sea looked like a white ribbon on the water.

Moonlight glowed on Coven Hoven. We beached our kayaks and ran to the mansion. Gizmo's van was parked near the trees. The house was dark as we approached. "Where's everyone gone?" I whispered.

"The door is open." Makiko entered and I followed. Our footsteps echoed in the empty house. I swept the beam of my flashlight around the dark entry way. Nothing.

"Nobody's here," I said.

"What is that noise?" Makiko touched my arm. We listened for a moment. It was faint, but I could hear it—a steady *knock, knock, knock* coming from a lower bedroom.

Cautiously, we approached the closed door. The constant knocking continued. It sounded as if someone was kicking the door over and over.

Makiko stood on one side of the door, and I on the other. Quickly, I reached over and turned the knob. The door flew open. The knocking stopped. I shone my flashlight into the room.

Inside, we saw FDR, seated on the floor. He was tied up, with a gag over his mouth. Then I saw *him*. He was also tied and gagged. Now that I could see him clearly, I could tell he was no creature. But he had no ear or eyebrow, and his skin was a shiny red. His eyes were bright and intelligent. I helped him out of his ropes and extended my hand. "I'm Liz Austen. You're Lady Chandler's grandson, Wallace."

"Yes." His voice was gentle.

"You survived that terrible car crash that killed your parents."

He nodded.

"What are you doing here, FDR-san?" Makiko asked as she loosened his gag.

"I'm Wallace's tutor. I've been teaching him for years." FDR rubbed his wrists.

"That explains why I saw you here the other night," I said. "But what was in the envelope that Smart handed you?"

"My pay," FDR sighed.

"But why did you deny knowing anything about Coven Hoven?"

"I'm sorry, Liz. I was just trying to protect Wallace."

Wallace turned to us with worried eyes. "My grandmother is in trouble. Two men have taken her to the barn where we have a safe. They want to rob her. We have to help."

The night was clear as we left the mansion. The moon shone in a cloudless sky.

"I know a shortcut to the barn. This way." Wallace climbed over a fence. Makiko, FDR and I followed him as he raced across the estate toward the barn.

The barn was enormous, rising high above us. The fields all around were silver under the perfect sky. The weather vane swayed gently, as if to warn *stay away, stay away*.

I shone my flashlight on the door. The big key was in the lock, and the door was open.

We slipped in through the door. Slowly, my eyes adjusted to the darkness. I became aware of the curved roof, far above. Thick beams criss-crossed the dark air. I could smell dust—a lot of it. In the gloom, I could see piles of brittle hay, an abandoned tractor and empty stalls.

A light was on in the small office at the back of the barn. We crept over. Through the open door, we could see Rocky holding Lady Chandler. Gizmo stood in the corner, picking his teeth.

"You'll just have to be more patient. I'm an old woman." Lady Chandler was fiercely defiant. "My memory isn't as good as it used to be. I'm having trouble remembering the combination."

Rocky pulled out a knife. "Maybe this will help you remember a little better."

"You can bully all you want. I'm not afraid of your threats."

"Let's just see about that." Rocky gave a harsh laugh and brought the knife closer to her cheek. The blade glinted in the light. Lady Chandler didn't flinch.

"Leave my granny alone." Wallace left the darkness and stood in the light of the doorway. "I know the combination."

Rocky turned around, but sunglasses hid his eyes. His mouth was curled into a sneer. "If it isn't the werewolf here to save his poor granny. Welcome to the party." Rocky pointed the knife at Wallace. "Why don't you come in and open the safe?" He grabbed at Wallace as he entered the office, and pushed him roughly toward the safe.

"Run, Grandma," Wallace shouted. Rocky knocked him down. "You little liar. You don't know the combination."

Rocky raised his foot to kick Wallace.

"Stop it, Colby! Stop it right now," I shouted as I rushed into the office.

"Huh? Liz! How'd you know it was me?"

"I recognized your cologne. Besides, 'Rocky,' you almost lost your fake moustache when you were at Gizmo's."

"I told you those kids were trouble," Gizmo snarled.

"Shut up," Colby snapped at him.

"You were blackmailing Drake. You found out about the questionable land deal at the town archives and ripped out the page, thinking you were the only one with proof. But you left enough information to make me think something was fishy." I narrowed my eyes. "You also put Drake in touch with your 'friends,' Rocky and Gizmo, so they could create a scare campaign to change the minds of the Civic Trust to vote yes."

"They needed a little persuading," Colby chuckled.

"But why did you pretend to be Rocky?" I asked.

"I like acting, and I wanted to have a little fun." Colby grinned. I was seeing the true Colby and it frightened me.

"You and Gizmo used the legend of the St. Andrews werewolf to your own ends. You brought it alive with a costume."

"It looked pretty convincing, don't you think?"

"Then you tried to put the blame on FDR. You wanted people to think he was the arsonist, so you called him and told him to go to the Algonquin Hotel. Then you broke into his house and left a fake note for us."

"Yes. And I got you to arrive at the hotel in time to see the werewolf setting the fire. I wanted you to suspect FDR."

"Well, you forgot one thing," I said evenly.

"What's that, Sherlock Holmes?" Colby taunted.

"FDR is right-handed. The note I found was written by a southpaw. The writing slanted to the back. You're a lefty, aren't you, Colby?"

"Very clever."

"You also told me the carnival opened at dusk, but it opens at noon. You invited us sailing so we wouldn't search for the van. And I just bet you phoned Gizmo from the pier to tell him to hide the van."

"You're a smart girl, Liz. You figured everything out. But what are you going to do about it?"

"Tell the police."

"Do you think I'm going to let you leave here?" Colby asked as he moved toward me.

"Stop right there, Colby. You're outnumbered." FDR and Makiko came into the office.

Colby laughed, more like a snort. "By what? A werewolf, an old lady, a wimp and two girls? Give me a break!"

"Why don't you add an old man with a shotgun."

We all turned around to see Smart standing in the doorway, pointing a gun. "Drop the knife."

Gizmo raised his hands in the air. Before anyone could do anything, Colby grabbed me and placed the knife at my throat. "Don't anybody move, or she's toast."

Keeping the knife at my throat, Colby edged me toward the door. "Stay where you are, and she doesn't get hurt. Liz and I are getting out of here."

"What about me?" Gizmo cried.

"Every man for himself." Colby pushed me out of the office, through the barn and outside into the evening air.

"You won't get away with this, Colby. Drake will tell the police everything."

"Well, they'll have to chase both of us, then, won't they?" Colby dragged me across the estate until we came to Gizmo's van. Inside was Colby's motorcycle.

"Get on in front," Colby ordered once the bike was out of the van. I climbed on. Colby sat behind me. He put the knife in his pocket. His arms went around me as he reached for the handle bars. With one big kick, he started the motorcycle. The Harley raced off, heading for the Road Beneath the Sea.

We soon reached the water's edge. The Road Beneath the Sea was still visible, but the tide was beginning to rise. I heard it gurgling and *shlooping* around the rocks. "We'll never make it!" I screamed.

"We'll have to try." Colby turned his powerful bike onto the road and headed off toward the mainland. He leaned forward, causing me to bend. He was trying to outrace the tide.

Halfway out on the road, the bike stopped. The headlights glittered on the water covering the road ahead of us. I looked behind us and saw only darkness. We were a long way from shore.

"We're trapped," I cried. "The water's surrounding us."

Colby and I jumped off the bike and the water swirled around our knees. "We're going to die," Colby blubbered. He was paralyzed with fear.

"You're pathetic," I snorted. I tried to think fast. How could we get to shore?

I heard the sound of something coming up behind us. I turned around. Coming through the night on his white stallion was Wallace.

"Jump on, Liz," Wallace called as he rode up. I pulled myself up behind him.

"What about me?" Colby cried.

"Give me your knife first," I called down to him.

When it was in my hand, Colby scrambled onto the horse. He was shaking in terror.

Wallace turned the horse around and urged him toward Minister's Island. We went as fast as we could along the roadway. We were getting closer to the island, but the stallion was having difficulty. The water was deeper, the currents stronger and we were heavy.

The stallion stopped moving. It nervously examined the water rushing past. I was getting scared. Wallace nudged the horse with his heels, and it cautiously moved forward.

The water pressed against the horse's chest. I could see the shoreline ahead. Wallace urged the stallion, "You can do it! You're a beautiful horse, you're a champion."

The stallion whinnied. He struggled forward. Colby cried out in horror as the horse stumbled. The water roared around us, pulling at the stallion, but somehow he battled forward. At last he stumbled free of the currents, and stepped onto the island.

Lady Chandler and the others were waiting for us. Smart was there with his shotgun. He took control of Colby. I gave Makiko a hug of relief.

The police came in motor boats and arrested Gizmo and Colby. They took us home, too, and I told them where to find Drake.

It had been a long night.

* * *

The next morning, Fran had some important news for me. "I've heard from Emily's mother. She phoned to thank you, Liz."

"For what?"

"Emily was being abused by her stepfather, and she broke her silence yesterday. The person she told went straight to the authorities."

I was shocked. "Emily has so much courage."

"I'm sure it was difficult for her. But you know what?" Fran put her arm around my shoulder.

"What?" I said, looking up at her.

"Emily's mom says that you and Makiko have been such good friends to Emily. So supportive. That kind of positive feeling made Emily feel good about herself. Good enough to make her realize she didn't deserve the treatment she was getting. I'm proud of you girls."

"What's going to happen now?" I asked quietly.

"I'm not sure, but she's going to need some really good friends."

I nodded my head. Emily could count on me.

"And how do *you* feel this morning, Liz?" Fran looked concerned.

"I'm glad that everything is working out and that St. Andrews is back to normal. But I've realized you were right about something."

"What's that?"

"Remember, after the Canada Day celebrations, you told me to look beneath the surface—get to know people by what's inside?"

"Yes."

"Well, Colby Keaton really fooled me. I thought he was a good person, and it frightens me that it took so long to find out the truth."

"You have to trust your instincts, Liz. Your inner voice will guide you." Fran hugged me close.

* * *

We had only one more dress rehearsal before the opening night. That afternoon, I hurried to the theatre. Makiko was already in her usual place in the audience. I waved to her from the stage. She gave me the thumbs up sign.

I hurried toward my dressing room. On my way, I saw Emily sitting by herself. I went over and put my arms around her. "I'm so proud of you, Emily. You were really brave."

Emily nodded. Her face was sad. "I'm not going to be in the play," she said.

"Why? You've worked so hard. You love this play."

Emily nodded. "But people will know I'm bad."

"No, Emily," I said gently. "People know that he's bad. Nobody thinks you're bad."

"I can't go on stage."

"He hurt you. Don't let him destroy what you love."

Emily sat quietly. I gave her a hug. "It must be so hard for you. It took courage to do what you did. I'm so proud of you." Emily nodded. A tear trickled down her cheek.

"I can understand that you don't want to go on stage. But it makes me sad," I said, "because I know you have the courage."

Emily smiled. "Thanks, Liz," she said quietly.

* * *

The next day, I was *exceptionally* nervous. It was opening night for our musical. I kept taking deep breaths as I applied makeup. Stuck to the mirror was a telegram from my family. I'd also received flowers.

There were flowers in all the dressing rooms, and the doors were covered with cards that said *break a leg*.

"Enjoy the show," Colin smiled, handing envelopes to Barbara and me. He'd written everyone a personal note. We'd all worked really hard in extra rehearsals with the understudies who'd stepped in to replace Colby and Drake, who were both in custody, along with Gizmo.

Miss Hannigan was applying number 5 greasepaint. "I hear Lady Chandler has asked FDR to help turn Coven Hoven into a kids' centre."

"That's right," I said. "Kids from all over the world will have fun together on Minister's Island, and experts will attend conferences to discuss issues involving children. Mrs. O'Neal's son will be working on the project, so her grandchildren won't be leaving town. And FDR will start a claim for the right to his property. He wants to fulfil his dream and donate the land to St. Andrews for use as a park."

Above us in the dressing room was a black-and-white TV set. The TV showed the theatre curtain. We could hear coughs from the audience as the orchestra warmed up. My stomach was clenched tight.

After the overture, the curtain rose. On the TV, we could see the iron beds where the orphans were sleeping. One of them was Emily—I knew she'd do the show! The tiniest girl, Molly, clutched a teddy with ragged ears as she looked into the spotlight and began the show's opening song, "Maybe."

It was a hit! The audience cheered the orphans, then they cheered the next songs and the dancing and the sets. They loved it all. On stage, I basked in the laughter and the waves of applause rolling out of the crowd.

During intermission, everyone stood around together in the dressing rooms, talking excitedly. Some parents came from the audience, bringing rave reviews. I saw Emily hugging her mother, and went to say hello.

"Isn't it exciting?" Emily exclaimed. "I love being in this show."

"I'm so proud of Emily," her mother said. "We're living on our own now, Liz. We're getting help from support agencies and there's been a court order—my husband has to stay away from us."

"I get sad sometimes," Emily said, "but it seems a bit better every day. I'm joining a counselling group in September. My social worker arranged it. I like her." She put her arms around me. "But you're my best friend, Liz. Always."

Her mother smiled. "We're doing lots of hugging these days. I need them, too."

* * *

The second act of *Annie* passed far too quickly. I was swept up in the adventure, and wished it would last forever. Our curtain calls were wonderful—the crowd was on its feet cheering as once again we sang the hit song, "Tomorrow." *This is great*, I thought, waving at Makiko in the audience.

Wallace was there with his grandmother and Smart. After the play, they came backstage. Wallace handed me a bouquet of flowers. "You were wonderful," he smiled.

"Thanks," I blushed.

Lady Chandler shook my hand. "I was so wrong about keeping Wallace away from the world. You made me see my mistakes. I was afraid, you see. Afraid that people would be cruel. I just wanted to protect him."

"You were trying your best, grandma." Wallace looked at her. "I was afraid, too. Afraid of what people might see. I didn't want them laughing at me. But people have been nice."

"Well, I hope my plans for a children's centre at Coven Hoven can help me make it up to the people of St. Andrews and to Wallace."

At that moment, Emily rushed toward me and gave me a huge hug.

"See, you *do* have courage," I said, smiling proudly. "Know what's the best? You've set yourself free."

The Inuk Mountie Adventure

Dedicated with love to
Flo Connolly,
angel by my side

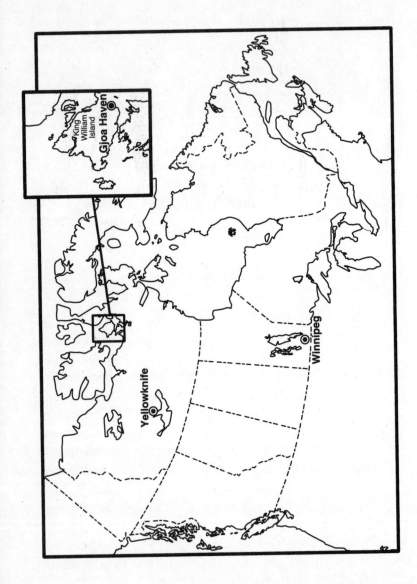

1

"I believe in U-SAC!"

The words boomed from mighty speakers, high above the crowd. At a microphone stood the Prime Minister of Canada, James Dunbar. As he spoke, his handsome face was visible on large television screens around the walls of the Winnipeg Convention Centre.

Tom Austen was watching the Prime Minister's speech from the doorway to the kitchen. He had landed a part-time job as a dishwasher, and it was a busy evening—a lot of people would be hungry after listening to the speech.

Tom had slipped away from his duties to check out the security. It was easy to spot the PM's bodyguards, who had short hair and restless eyes.

Tom's own eyes studied the scene for signs of trouble. Above the crowd, huge balloons were labelled *Vote YES for U-SAC!* Could the balloons secretly contain a deadly nerve gas, waiting to be spilled on the unsuspecting throngs? No—Tom shook his head at that theory.

But what if one of those TV cameras was a fake and had a gun concealed inside, ready to be fired at the PM? Dunbar would be a sitting duck, centre stage in the glare of spotlights.

"Yes," the Prime Minister cried, "the future prosperity of Canada is guaranteed. Once U-SAC is a reality, our financial problems will be easy to solve. I can assure you . . ."

Tom's eyes continued to sweep the scene. What if an assassin with an assault rifle lurked behind a spotlight? What if . . .

"Hey, kid!"

One of the junior chefs gestured angrily at Tom. "Get back to work! You want to get fired, your first night on the job?"

"I wouldn't mind," Tom murmured. Back at his sink, he plunged his hands into deep water; potato peels and scum floated on the gray surface. "Disgusting," he muttered to himself, beginning to scrub a grease-encrusted pan, "absolutely disgusting."

"Hi."

A dark-eyed little girl, aged about six, stood beside the sink. She was clutching some pretty flowers. "These are for the Prime Minister," she told Tom. "But Mommy says I can't meet him."

The girl's mother smiled. She was rolling pastry at a marble-topped table; like the other workers, she wore an apron over her white uniform. "Rosie adores Prime Minister Dunbar. I can understand why—those blue eyes are amazing. At her school, they showed a movie about his life. Rosie insisted I bring her to work tonight, even though she can't meet the Prime Minister."

Drying his hands, Tom smiled at the girl. "You want to see him, in person?"

Rosie nodded.

Tom glanced around—there was no sign of the junior chef. Taking Rosie's hand, he quickly led her around a corner to the doorway that led to the convention floor. "There he is," Tom said, pointing. Rosie's eyes glowed.

"What's he speeching about?" she asked.

"Pretty soon, Canadians are going to have a special vote."

"Do I get one?"

"No," Tom replied. "Only adults get to vote. There is a referendum being held. People get to vote yes or no to joining Canada and the United States together into a single country."

Rosie waited silently for more information.

"People call the proposed new country U-SAC," Tom explained. "That's short for the official name— The United States of America plus Canada. There'd be a new flag, and no border. The Prime Minister thinks it's a good idea, so he's travelling across the country giving speeches. That's why he's in Winnipeg."

"Are you voting for a new country?"

"I'm only 15," Tom replied, "too young to vote. But I kind of like the country we've got."

The Prime Minister's speech ended, and a brass band began performing a happy song called "The Yellow

Rose of Texas." Cheering and applauding, the crowd pressed toward the Prime Minister, straining to touch his hand. More balloons were released, and they soared up to the ceiling far above; each said *YES!* in large letters.

Leaving the stage, the PM and his bodyguards began moving through the crowd. Dunbar was enormously popular, and everyone was happy to see him. Flash cameras popped constantly in the Prime Minister's face, but he never stopped smiling.

"He's coming our way, Rosie. Maybe you can give him those flowers."

But Rosie's mother beckoned to them. "Tom, come back to the kitchen and bring Rosie. Right now! I'm nervous, with that big crowd. What if there's a stampede?" She glanced back at the kitchen. "If that crabby junior chef finds me gone, I'll be fired. Come this instant, Tom—please!" She hurried away.

Tom smiled, knowing a stampede was unlikely. Taking Rosie by the hand, he began walking along the hallway in the direction of the kitchen.

At that moment, a loud BANG! sounded from the convention floor, followed by screams.

* * *

Startled, Tom looked back. Incredible noise filled the hallway—yells of horror, shouted warnings, hysterical shrieks of terror.

Prime Minister Dunbar was racing down the hallway from the convention floor; behind him came the bodyguards. Seeing the Prime Minister, Rosie ran forward with the flowers.

"Out of my way," the man cried, sweeping the child aside with a big hand.

The Prime Minister's eyes were filled with panic. Then he was gone, hustled away to safety by the shouting bodyguards.

Quickly, Tom turned to Rosie. "Are you okay?"

"Yes." She stood by the wall, wide-eyed. The flowers lay on the floor. Tom grabbed Rosie's hand, and ran to the kitchen, where she was safely gathered up in her mother's arms.

All work had stopped in the kitchen. People were shouting questions and staring down the hallway. Then someone came running in with the news: "False alarm! One of those huge balloons exploded. People are calming down—they all thought it was a gunshot."

"Well," someone laughed, "the pep rally is over. The Prime Minister has left the building."

"Where'd he go?"

"Those bodyguards rushed him through the kitchen to a limousine outside. It took off fast with an escort of motorcycle cops."

"Those Mounties weren't taking any chances," Rosie's mother said. "They sure got the PM out fast."

"Dunbar panicked," Tom said. "He was really scared."

"I doubt it," scoffed one of the bakery chefs. "Dunbar isn't afraid of anything. He was a college football star."

"That's right," said Rosie's mother. "Then he was offered a contract to play pro ball—Dallas wanted him." She smacked her fist into a fat roll of dough. "But he went into politics instead. The man is gorgeous—a natural. Everyone thinks he's number one."

"My Mom doesn't," Tom replied. "She says . . . "

"Hey!" The junior chef snapped his fingers at Tom. "You with the red hair—get back to work. You're too fond of talking."

Tom reluctantly lowered his hands into the greasy water. "I don't care what anyone thinks," he said to himself. "The Prime Minister is a coward."

An hour later, the bodyguards returned for Tom.

2

The bodyguards showed their RCMP photo ID cards, explained their reasons, and then hurried Tom outside. It was March, and the air was cold. A black limousine was waiting at the curb. The engine purred.

Inside the limo, a man in his thirties sat on the back seat. His overcoat looked expensive; his circular eyeglasses were the latest style. "I'm Blake Decker," he said to Tom. "Mr. Decker to you. I'm chief adviser to the Prime Minister."

He gestured at Tom to sit beside him. A Mountie climbed in and sat nearby on a folding seat. The limousine pulled smoothly away from the curb and gathered speed.

Tom looked at Blake Decker. "These officers said the Prime Minister wants to see me."

The man's lips curled in a thin smile. "For some reason, the PM told me to find out the name of the kid with the red hair. You were in the hallway when the bodyguards rushed him out, right?"

Tom nodded.

"Well," Decker shrugged, "it's something about that."

Tom looked through the smoky windows at passing lights. He remembered riding in a limousine through Québec City with a girl he'd met in Baie St-Paul. He missed Michelle.

The Mountie said, "Your father's Inspector Ted Austen of the Winnipeg City Police?"

Tom nodded, still thinking about Michelle.

"He's a nice guy. I'm working with him on security for the Prime Minister's visit."

"I'm thinking of joining the Canadian Security Intelligence Service," Tom said. "When I'm older."

"CSIS, eh? That could be exciting."

"It's like being a spy, right?" Tom's sky-blue eyes shone. "I read a book by an ex-CSIS agent. She travelled to all kinds of places, investigating threats to Canadian security. What a life!"

Soon after, the limousine stopped at the canopied entrance of an exclusive Winnipeg hotel. In the lobby, chandeliers sparkled far above the marble floor. People turned to stare at Tom and the bodyguards as Blake Decker led the way to a bank of elevators.

As they rose toward the upper floors, Tom checked his hair in a mirror. "Will the media be present when I meet the Prime Minister?"

"No—this is strictly private." Decker looked at Tom. "Your generation is so lucky, kid. U-SAC will change your lives. I should show you the flag I've designed for the new country."

Tom said nothing.

"Listen, kid, your parents are voting yes to U-SAC. Correct?"

Tom shook his head. "They're against it."

Blake Decker snorted angrily. "Every opinion poll indicates that U-SAC has huge support among the population—huge. Your parents are being foolish."

The elevator doors hissed open. A long hallway, carpeted in red, led to a cream-coloured door. On it, brass letters read, *The Louis Riel Suite*. Two Mounties guarded the door. One held up a hand as Tom approached. "I'll have to frisk you, sonny."

The search was quick and professional. "The kid's clean," the Mountie said to Decker. "You can go inside."

Prime Minister James Dunbar was pacing the floor of the suite's very large living room. He was in shirtsleeves, with his silk tie pulled open at the throat. Tiny halogen beams gleamed on expensive paintings, and large windows displayed the city's twinkling lights. High in the black sky, a plane moved past.

The Prime Minister crossed the room to Tom. Close up, his eyes were a startling blue. "Hi there, Tom!" His voice was a deep baritone; his smile revealed perfect teeth. A powerful handshake made Tom wince. "I'm your Prime Minister. But I guess you know that!"

Tom nodded.

"It's nice of you to visit, Tom. What'll you drink— Coke? Pepsi?"

"Canada Dry, if you've got it. Thanks."

Prime Minister Dunbar glanced at Blake Decker. "Get the kid a drink."

The aide disappeared into the suite's kitchen. "So," the Prime Minister said to Tom, "that was pretty exciting today, right? We all thought someone was shooting." He laughed heartily. "We were wrong about that!"

Tom said nothing. Decker returned with his drink; it bubbled and fizzed in a crystal glass.

"That little girl wasn't hurt," the Prime Minister said. "I had someone find out." He paused, thinking. Blake Decker watched him intently. "So, Tom," the Prime Minister continued, "I'm wondering what you remember about that moment."

"Moment?"

"When someone tripped me, and I fell forward. Don't you remember, Tom? I accidentally knocked that little girl aside. That's how you remember it, Tom. Correct?"

"I . . . "

"I've learned some information about your family, Tom. Your mother is a Winnipeg lawyer, right? I can arrange for her to get some government contracts. The money's very good." Again, the Prime Minister displayed his perfect teeth in a large smile. "It was an accident. Right, Tom?"

The telephone rang. Decker picked it up and began a conversation. "It's good to hear your voice, Ashley," he said. "You've arrived in town safely? Where are you staying?" Decker jotted a note. "JBI-306, correct? Okay, I'll see you soon." He hung up the phone.

Almost immediately, it rang again. "It's a call from the lobby," Decker reported to the Prime Minister.

"Your father just arrived at the hotel. He's coming up to see you."

The Prime Minister groaned. "My father! That's all I need." He looked at Blake Decker. "I had dinner with him last night—that was enough. Get rid of him, Decker."

"Yes, sir."

"I can't take another evening of his complaints." Kicking off his Guccis, the Prime Minister sprawled on the sofa and stared moodily at the night sky. "I made it to the top—all the way to Prime Minister— and Father still doesn't respect me. Tell me, Decker, why should I waste any more time hearing about my failings? The man never approved of me—never!"

"I'll take care of him, sir."

As Blake Decker walked to the door, Tom quickly followed.

"Good night," he said over his shoulder.

"Remember one thing," the Prime Minister called to Tom. "If you sell your story to the media, your mother won't get any government contracts."

Tom didn't reply.

In the hallway, Blake Decker studied Tom's face as they walked toward the elevators. "So, Tom, what actually happened in that hallway? Did the PM slap the kid, or something like that?"

Tom remained silent. He pushed the elevator button, impatient to leave.

"Don't go yet," Decker said. "I could move a bit of cash your way." He touched his pocket. "I've got a few bills in my wallet. Just tell me, Tom, what happened in that hallway?"

The elevator doors opened. Tom saw a sad-eyed older man in a motorized wheelchair. He was terribly thin, and his fingers were yellow with nicotine. His beard and hair were grey.

Blake Decker spread his arms wide. "Professor Dunbar! What a pleasure to see you, sir."

The professor's wheelchair rolled out of the elevator. The doors closed. "I'm here to see my son," Professor Dunbar said. "The matter is urgent." Suddenly, he bent forward, coughing and hacking.

Blake Decker watched him suffer, then said, "Sir, I have bad news. Today at the convention centre there was a serious incident."

"Someone tried to kill my son?"

"Something like that," Decker replied. "So he's taken a pill and gone to bed early. Doctor's orders. I know you'll understand."

"But this is a serious matter!" Again Professor Dunbar was shaken by terrible coughing. When the fit was over, he leaned back in his wheelchair and whispered, "I'd give anything for a cigarette right now."

"An urgent matter, professor? What's it about?"

Decker led the professor down the hallway. They began speaking in heated whispers. Tom moved a few paces closer, straining to hear. Shaking his finger in Decker's face, the professor said something about *CanSell* and *disgraceful* and *media outrage*.

Blake Decker's face revealed nothing as the men returned to the elevators. "I'll arrange a breakfast meeting tomorrow," Decker said politely to Professor Dunbar. "7:00 A.M., sharp. The PM will make you feel better, I'm sure. What you've heard about him is an ugly rumour, nothing more."

Tom and the professor entered the elevator. As the doors slipped together, Tom had a final look at Blake Decker. He was lost in thought, with a worried frown on his face.

* * *

As the elevator descended, Professor Dunbar introduced himself. "I teach anthropology at the University of Manitoba," the man said. "I have a special interest in the Arctic regions."

"That's a coincidence," Tom replied. "Next week, some kids from the Arctic are visiting here. It's a school exchange. We'll be doing lots of great things together. We've booked the James Bay Inn for the farewell banquet."

"Bring them to see the university." The professor coughed badly. "Come to a lecture—it's a bit like a class in school, but with lots more students. My topic this month is Arctic explorers. Some died horrible deaths." For a moment he was lost in thought. Then he looked up at Tom. "So—what do you think of U-SAC?"

"I . . ."

"I don't like it," the professor declared. "U-SAC is not for the good of Canadians—it will only benefit special interest groups. To them, U-SAC is a great way to make big money." He stared moodily at his yellow fingertips. "My son knows it's true."

"Maybe the U-SAC referendum will be defeated, Professor Dunbar."

"Only by a miracle," the professor said, as the doors opened onto the lobby. "And I don't believe in miracles."

3

The next morning, Tom was drinking orange juice at the kitchen counter. His mother came into the room, yawning. She was in her dressing gown, and her long red hair wasn't yet combed.

"I was in court all day yesterday," she said to Tom, "then I worked on legal briefs at the office until midnight. How was your dishwashing job?"

"Disgusting!"

Mrs. Austen chuckled. "Welcome to the real world."

"But something happened, Mom." Tom described in detail the events of the evening. "The Prime Minister offered me a bribe to keep quiet! Isn't that against the law?"

"No. Prime Minister Dunbar was inside the law, but only just. Clearly, he's frightened of looking bad. I'm not surprised. The media will make a sensation out of anything—scandals sell big-time. No wonder some people won't go into politics."

"By the way, Mom, I won't be selling my story."

"Thanks for telling me," she said with a smile, "but I already knew that."

Mrs. Austen switched on the television. "This country has had some great prime ministers, and we'll have more of them. But James Dunbar is a disaster. He wants U-SAC to succeed so he can make a personal fortune. I've heard some scary rumours."

On the news, the Prime Minister was seen boarding a flight to Regina. Blake Decker was beside him, looking unhappy. His sallow face was no match for the Prime Minister's movie star looks.

"The pre-dawn flight was a change in plans," the announcer said. "Although the Prime Minister left Winnipeg earlier than scheduled, he'll stop here briefly next week for a visit with his father. Then he heads to the Maritime provinces, where he'll speak in support of U-SAC."

Mrs. Austen turned down the volume. "We need leaders who are loyal to the country and the people. Not Dunbar with his greed."

She sweetened her coffee with honey. "I heard the Prime Minister has a secret deal with a hush-hush consortium code-named CanSell. This company wants to build huge dams to change the direction of some Canadian rivers so that they'll flow through canals to the southern United States. I understand a few states are getting desperate for new sources of water."

"The professor mentioned the name CanSell when he was talking to Blake Decker."

"Without a border, CanSell's diversion project has a much stronger chance of getting government approval." Mrs. Austen sipped her coffee. "Anyway, that's what people are saying. But there's no proof."

Liz joined them. She was dressed for school, and had her materials neatly organized. "I made you a lunch, Tom."

"Great—thanks!"

As Liz helped herself to oat bran from the stove, Inspector Austen phoned from police headquarters to say hello. He'd worked long hours on the security for the Prime Minister's visit. "Are you looking forward to your guests from up north?" he asked Tom.

"Sure, Dad. We're taking them to Chinatown tonight, then we're going bowling. Know what? Someone said they've never seen trees before."

"You've never seen an igloo, son. So it's a shame you're not going to the Arctic with your class. It's a once-in-a-lifetime chance."

"I know, Dad, but I already told you the reason. My team's got a major tournament the same time as the trip north. The coach says I've got to play. Otherwise, he'll bench me for the playoffs."

"Why's this particular tournament so important?"

"The coach's son is our goalie. He's excellent. NHL scouts will be at the tournament. The coach wants his strongest possible team on the ice, to help his son's chances."

"Well, it's a shame."

"I know, Dad, but that's life."

* * *

A few days later, the Winnipeg airport buzzed with conversation. Tom's friends from his Grade Nine class were waiting to greet the visitors from Gjoa Haven in the Arctic. Among the waiting students was Dietmar Oban, whose name was pronounced Deetmar. Hands in his pockets, he was staring gloomily at the floor.

"More trouble at home?" Tom asked.

Dietmar nodded slowly. "Sometimes, I want to smash every bottle in the house. Maybe then my Dad would quit with the booze."

"Here they are," cried an excited voice. The class pressed forward to greet the northern teenagers. Huddled together in parkas with colourful fringes, the visitors gazed shyly at the waiting crowd.

Dietmar shook hands with twins—a boy and girl. They had raven-black hair. "Welcome to Winnipeg," Dietmar said, introducing himself and Tom. "You'll be staying at my house."

"I'm Rachel," the girl said shyly. "This is my brother, Moses." She handed Dietmar a pin with an image of an Inuk out fishing on a frozen day. It read, *The Hamlet of Gjoa Haven.*

"The lucky guy," Tom said, studying the pin. "I wish I was going north to try ice fishing, and it would have been fun to have someone stay at my house during your visit to Winnipeg."

Moses presented Dietmar with a small carving. "I made this for you," he said quietly. Then he stared at the terminal's high ceiling. Suspended far above was a single-seater biplane with yellow wings. "Man, this place is so huge. I can't believe my eyes."

Dietmar gave the twins souvenir pins of Winnipeg's famous Golden Boy statue. "Come on, I'll introduce you around."

People stood in groups, waiting for the luggage. Some talked and laughed; others were quiet. Tom was introduced to Constance and Frieda, two friendly teachers from Gjoa Haven. "Call us by our first names," Constance said with a smile. "We're very informal up north."

Someone touched Tom's shoulder. He saw a muscular little man with brown hair cropped close to the scalp and piercing green eyes. He was chewing gum. "I'm Luke Yates," the man said. "Call me Luke." He parked his gum behind an ear. "I'm a freelance writer. I'm on assignment for a newspaper called News/North. They're paying me to report on the visit of these northern kids to Winnipeg. It's good money, but a lousy assignment."

"Why's that?" Tom asked.

Yates glanced at the twins. "I'll tell you another time." He opened a notepad. "So, how's it feel being visited by a bunch of Eskimos?"

Before Tom could answer, they were joined by two more adults from the north. One was an Inuk with a strong face, large eyes, and black hair that gleamed under the airport lights. The second man looked unhealthy. Behind old-fashioned spectacles, he had watery blue eyes; his skin was very pale. A few days worth of blond bristles outlined his jaw and chin.

The blond man spoke to the writer. "I'm Sam White. Is there a problem here?"

"Not at all, mister. I'm on assignment for a newspaper, so I'm interviewing these Eskimos."

"A writer? Then why so ignorant?" Sam poked Luke Yates in the chest. "Let me tell you something, sir. The word Eskimo means eater of raw flesh, and is considered an insult. My friends appreciate being called Inuit, which simply means people. Now, leave them alone, okay, and leave me alone, too."

Shaking his head, Luke Yates walked away. As he did, Sam turned to the Inuk. "You okay, Junior?"

"I'm fine," Junior replied. "I've met people like him before."

"It's a poor start to our visit," Sam said. "That guy acts racist. He'd better not cause any trouble."

* * *

The next day, the sightseeing northerners and their hosts arrived at the University of Manitoba, just south of Winnipeg. The visitors had asked to see real farm animals, and they were also looking forward to Professor Dunbar's lecture about the Arctic. Several teachers were with them, and so was Luke Yates. The freelance writer carried a camera and his notepad.

The campus had many different buildings; students hurried between them, their breath turning white in the cold air. After taking some photos outside the administration building, the group walked across campus toward the Faculty of Agriculture. Tom was with Junior and Junior's father, who were both chaperons from the Arctic. Junior's father was taking a holiday from his duties as the Mountie in Gjoa Haven to be a volunteer on the trip south.

The group reached one of the barns where research was conducted to help farmers. It was filled with the cackles, bellows, and whinnies of many animals. Moses covered his nose. "That smell is so strong!"

"Look!" Rachel pointed across the barn. Her eyes were huge. "Look at that—a horse, a real horse!"

Dietmar smiled at her. "It seems amazing you've never seen farm animals before."

"I wish I could ride it. On TV, horses look like fun."

Soon after, they entered Tache Hall. The building was jammed with students. On one colourful wall, a poster proclaimed, *If you can read this, thank a teacher*. Listening in on conversations, Tom heard discussions about lectures and parties and movies and someone's missing wallet.

"I hated that course," one student said, "it was extreme torture."

"You did all that work? You keener, you."

"The prof had, like, all this curly, curly hair but he shaved it off."

"See that guy? He knows how to juggle. I mean, that's so cool."

Tom grinned at Dietmar. "What a bunch of characters! If a crime happened here, there'd be some great suspects."

Dietmar winked at Rachel. "I've suffered this detective nonsense since we were kids. Austen will never grow up."

"I hope not," she replied, favoring Tom with a pretty smile.

"Hey," Dietmar said, frowning. "I hope you don't *like* Austen, Rachel. His taste in music is the pits."

"What's wrong with Elvis?" Tom asked.

"Come on!" Dietmar groaned.

Inside a lecture hall, they found hundreds of seats rising all around in a horseshoe pattern. Students were reading textbooks, making notes, and gossiping together as they awaited the arrival of Professor Dunbar.

"So many people," Rachel said as they were directed to reserved seats.

Tom sat beside Sam and his girlfriend, Faith. Her hair and eyes were the same beautiful black as the other northerners. Faith was exceptionally quiet, and seemed on edge. City noises made her jump nervously.

"How'd you end up in the Arctic?" Tom asked Sam.

"I served with Junior in the same army unit. Later I went north to visit him, and fell in love with Faith." He smiled at her. "Since then, the Arctic has been home. It's paradise to me."

Faith kissed Sam's cheek. "I'm glad you decided to come on this trip."

"It was a last-minute decision," he said to Tom, "but I don't regret it. Winnipeg's a fun city." Sam wiped his watery eyes. "I wish you'd try a different perfume, Faith. My allergy's real bad today."

She looked at him, but said nothing.

Sam smiled at Tom. "I hope you'll enjoy our town, when your class visits."

"Unfortunately," Tom replied, "I'm not going north. I'm playing hockey instead."

"You're the lucky one," Dietmar said. "I'm dreading this trip. Snow and cold and frostbite—ugh."

At that moment, Professor Dunbar appeared on a small stage in his motorized wheelchair. Dark circles lined his tired eyes. "Did the prof sleep in that sweater?" Dietmar whispered. "He looks terrible."

Faith leaned close to them. "Guess what? The professor is going to die."

4

Sam smiled. "We're all going to die, sweetheart."

"No, I mean *soon*. Professor Dunbar is dying."

Tom was shocked by the news. "What do you mean?"

"See those students?" Faith glanced at a group of young women chatting together. "I just heard them talking. The professor has terminal lung cancer." She turned to Sam. "It proves what I've been saying, sweetheart. People with addictions are asking for trouble."

"Well . . ."

The professor switched on a microphone, and everyone fell silent. The students waited with their pens, ready to make notes.

"Today . . . " A hacking cough shook Professor Dunbar's body. "Today is special. Our guests are from the Arctic—please welcome them." As applause rang out, the northern visitors smiled with shy eyes.

The professor looked at some of the Winnipeg teens. "The Arctic is a fabulous land—the place of dreams and drama. Put away your video games, for this is the ultimate adventure." He then began a fascinating lecture on Arctic explorers; although racked by coughing, Professor Dunbar spoke for an hour while his students wrote busily.

"Finally," he said, "I want you to imagine today's astronauts disappearing without a trace while exploring the moon. You can guess what the uproar would be back home! Well, that's exactly what happened in the nineteenth century when the British explorer Sir James Franklin and 128 men vanished while attempting to become the first Europeans to travel across the top of Canada by sea. They were searching for the fabled Northwest Passage."

A severe bout of coughing shook Professor Dunbar's body. "Like many men, Franklin assumed he knew everything. While exploring the Arctic, he thought there was nothing to learn from the Inuit— even though they'd lived successfully for centuries in the harsh northern climate! His vessel carried china and silverware and over a thousand books, but precious little that could be of real help when the two British ships were trapped by ice."

Professor Dunbar looked around the lecture hall. "The Franklin expedition ended in tragedy. The British ignored the Inuit, who could have helped them survive. The sailors tried to walk to safety—without any snowshoes and wearing canvas coats instead of caribou skins.

Starving, they were forced to eat the flesh of their dead friends."

He paused. "Every man perished; 138 years later, anthropologist Owen Beattie from the University of Alberta discovered three coffins on Beechey Island. Inside were the bodies of young English sailors, perfectly preserved by the bitter cold."

The professor touched a switch. Projected on a screen was the face of a dead sailor. "Dr. Beattie took this picture of James Torrington. He was 20 years old when he died on New Year's Day, 1846."

The sailor's eyes stared from their sockets. His nose was black, and so were his lips. His mouth was frozen open; he wore a striped shirt with mother-of-pearl buttons. "This is beyond gross," Dietmar moaned, gazing in horror at the screen. "I'm never going to the Arctic. Never."

"Those young men needn't have suffered such a fate," cried the professor. "They died because their commander, the famous Sir James Franklin, did not respect the Inuit. Are we any different today? I hope so."

He looked at his northern guests. "We would do well to listen to your ancient civilization. We have much to learn from your wisdom."

As the university students applauded enthusiastically, the professor slumped back in his wheelchair, coughing horribly. After wiping a weary hand across his face, he left the stage.

Sam looked at his Rolex. "I'm hungry. Let's eat something."

Dietmar grinned at him. "You think like me—with your stomach."

After eating lunch in the cafeteria, the teens and adults sat talking at large tables. Alone in a corner, Luke Yates scribbled notes.

"What did you think of the lecture?" Tom called to the writer.

"It was garbage," snarled Yates, without looking up. "That prof is a fool."

Sam went in search of the washroom. The moment he was gone, Faith and Junior moved to another table and began talking in low voices. Tom couldn't hear their discussion.

"Okay if I take off for a few minutes?" he asked his teacher. "I'd like to find Professor Dunbar's office, and thank him. It was nice of him to invite us today."

"Good thinking, Tom. But hurry back, please. Don't start looking for some major villainy to investigate."

Tom smiled. "Crime at a university, sir? I doubt it!"

* * *

A student in a jaunty black beret directed Tom to a staircase. "You'll find Professor Dunbar's office on the second floor."

The hallway was lined with doors. On one, a nameplate read, *Professor Lionel Dunbar*. The door, like the Austens' refrigerator at home, was covered with witty cartoons and interesting items clipped from newspapers. Through a small window, Tom saw the professor's office. It was cluttered with books, books, and more books.

When Tom knocked, a voice called, "Enter!" Inside, Tom noticed that several news clippings had been thrown into the professor's waste basket. They were about his son, Prime Minister James Dunbar.

The office contained a sofa and easy chair, plus a large desk and high-tech work station. A door led to a small private washroom. The floor-to-ceiling bookcases contained many titles about the Arctic. Tom moved closer to the window, wishing the professor would open it; the air reeked of stale tobacco.

Outside, he could see Luke Yates standing under the bare branches of an elm. He was smoking a cigarette, and staring moodily into space. Tom looked at him briefly, and then said, "We all enjoyed the lecture, Professor Dunbar. I came to say thanks for the invitation."

The professor smiled, and for a moment the sadness left his eyes. "It's good to see you, Tom." He was shaken by terrible coughing. "Let me show you some interesting photos of the Arctic. You're going to love your visit to Gjoa Haven."

"Unfortunately," Tom replied, "I'm not going."

"What a shame."

Professor Dunbar went to his desk and eyed the red numerals on a small box. When the digits reached 00:00, a cigarette rolled out. "This box dispenses one an hour," the professor explained, grabbing the cigarette and a lighter. He dragged heavily, then his body was racked by appalling coughs and hacks.

Tom examined a picture on the wall. "Is this the *St. Roch*? We studied it in school."

The professor finished his cigarette and coughed again before replying. "Yes, that's the RCMP's famous schooner. Imagine the adventure, Tom Austen. Valiant

Mounties in a wooden boat, braving the Arctic ice. They were the first to circumnavigate North America. These days, cruise ships make the same journey—but the *St. Roch* was wooden-hulled, and tiny by comparison. It would almost fit into one of those ships' swimming pools."

Tom walked to the window. No one stood by the elm tree. Where had Luke Yates gone?

"Listen, Professor Dunbar, can you give me some inside information on Roald Amundsen? I'm writing a report on him for school."

The professor rolled to another picture. "This is Amundsen, the Norwegian who was the first European to get through the legendary passage. He trained hard before making the attempt. But it was worth it—his childhood dream came true." The professor glanced at the wastepaper basket, sighing. "I'm sure his father was proud."

"Is that his boat? It's so small."

"You're right, Tom. It was originally used to fish for herring. Amundsen wanted a craft that could sneak between drifting ice floes." Professor Dunbar leaned forward in his wheelchair, coughing painfully. "Roald Amundsen wasn't a snob like Franklin. He put on caribou skins, he travelled light. He learned from the Inuit."

"What was his boat called?" Tom asked.

"The *Gjoa*. During his voyage, Amundsen wintered on King William Island at Gjoa Haven. Hence the community's name." The professor's brown eyes turned longingly to the digital readout, but his next cigarette wouldn't arrive for 56 minutes.

"Professor Dunbar, may I use your washroom?"

"Of course."

Stepping into the washroom, Tom closed the door. There were no windows; a fluorescent light glared over the sink. He was drying his hands when he heard a knocking sound. "Enter!" cried the professor.

"Blake Decker?" Professor Dunbar sounded surprised. "You're here? But why—I don't understand. Is it about my dinner tonight with James? Surely my son hasn't cancelled!"

Tom stayed motionless. He heard the outside door close. "Nice office, professor," said the smooth voice of the Prime Minister's aide, Blake Decker. "It stinks of cigarettes, though."

"What do you want, Decker? And who's this?"

"You may call this person ZULU-1. I decided to bring some muscle, in case you get difficult."

"Why are you here, Decker?"

"What have you learned about CanSell, Professor?"

"CanSell is the code name for a secret plan to sell water from Canadian rivers." The professor sounded angry. "A good friend called me from Washington, D.C. He said James has been promised a fortune if he can advance CanSell's secret plans by getting Canada to join the USA. I'll demand answers when I see James tonight. If it's true, I'll go straight to the media. The Canadian people must know the truth about their Prime Minister."

"Your friend in Washington is correct," said Blake Decker. "It's all true about CanSell—and I should know. I'm involved myself."

"Just as I feared. So James is controlled by CanSell?"

"Yes."

"My son, my son! A traitor to his nation!" The professor hacked and coughed terribly. "My heart is broken. What will I say to the media?"

"Don't worry about that, Professor. You won't be talking to the media. You'll be dead." Blake Decker's voice was low and ominous. "Okay ZULU-1, it's time. Use the silencer."

"No," the professor cried. "You can't . . . "

A sharp SNAP of sound was followed by a terrible crash, and then moaning that made Tom's scalp creep. He leaned close to the door, terrified.

"A clean shot," Blake Decker said. "You got him through the heart. The professor is dead."

* * *

Tom stared into the washroom mirror. His skin was chalk-white, his eyes enormous. Inside his chest was a terrible pounding.

"I'll phone the Prime Minister on his private line," said Blake Decker. "He didn't like his father, but he'll still be shocked." He chuckled.

A few moments later, Decker said, "Prime Minister? Decker here." There was a brief pause. "I know you're entertaining VIPs, but I've got important news. Your father's been shot dead." The aide's voice had a sharp edge to it. "Now, listen. I arranged the hit, so you're involved. If I'm ever arrested, they'll get you, too."

A long silence. Then Decker said, "We must cover up the truth about your father's death. Otherwise, you're finished, U-SAC is finished, and CanSell is finished. We don't want that, correct?"

Tom was frozen. He was certain his heart could be heard through the door.

"A good decision, Prime Minister. I agree, let's cover it up. I'll take your father's wallet so the police will think a thief shot him. His death won't be connected to you."

A pause.

"Don't worry, Prime Minister. The truth won't come out. I'll be in touch soon. Goodbye."

Tom heard Decker hang up the phone. Then the man laughed. "See this micro-cassette, ZULU-1? I just used the telephone answering machine to record the Prime Minister ordering a cover-up. I'll edit out my voice, then play him the tape and threaten to release it to the media. He'll be terrified. This gives me absolute control over the Prime Minister. I can make him do anything—I'm going to be a very wealthy man."

Again a chuckle. "We'd better get moving. But first I'll use that washroom."

Tom was horrified. His eyes darted around, seeking escape, but he was trapped.

5

The doorknob rattled. "It's locked," said Blake Decker. "I wonder if there's someone . . ." Then he exclaimed, "Look—through the window! A campus police car, heading this way. Let's get out of here."

Tom remained paralyzed until he heard help arrive. Rushing out of hiding, he saw two university police officers kneeling over the professor. His body lay sprawled on the carpet next to the forlorn sight of the fallen wheelchair.

An officer stared at Tom. "Who are you?" she demanded.

"I heard everything," Tom exclaimed. "The Prime Minister is involved! Is the professor dead for sure?"

The second officer nodded. "He had a weak heart and was in danger of having a heart attack, so he wore a warning alert system linked to our headquarters. It triggered an alarm a few minutes ago, at the moment he was shot, I guess."

The officers called city police for emergency backup, and requested an APB for the arrest of Blake Decker. Then they began taking a witness statement from Tom. To his dismay, he learned that his evidence against James Dunbar could not be used in court.

"It's called hearsay," one officer explained. "There's no proof of what you heard. The Prime Minister would claim innocence."

"Also remember," the second officer told Tom, "you only heard Blake Decker on the phone. Maybe he was pretending to speak to the Prime Minister."

"I doubt it," Tom said grimly. "James Dunbar ordered a cover-up of his father's murder."

"That's a major accusation, young man. You need proof."

"It exists," Tom replied. "If that micro-cassette can be found, the Prime Minister is finished."

"There'll be a full investigation, of course. Now, tell us more about ZULU-1. Did you hear him speak?"

"Never. Which means the person could have been a woman."

"Good point. Now—think back to the hallway outside the professor's office. Did you notice anything suspicious?"

Tom shook his head. "The hallway was empty. I didn't see anyone there, but . . ."

Feet were heard in the hallway. "Someone's coming," an officer said, "running fast. I wonder who?" He went to the door. "Keep back. I'll deal with this."

The officer switched off the lights, and the room went dark. He stepped into the hallway. Through the window in the door, Tom saw Luke Yates come running up.

"Is there trouble here?" Yates demanded. "I was listening to police calls on my radio scanner, and I intercepted your request for backup. This is Professor Dunbar's office, right? He's the Prime Minister's father, right? So what's the story—what's going on?"

"No comment," replied the officer.

"Listen, I'm a freelance writer. I make money by finding important news. I smell a big story here, and that means big money. Let me in that office."

The officer blocked the door with his large body. "Not a chance, mister. There's a witness inside. His identity must be protected."

"A witness?" said Luke Yates. "A witness to what?"

"Murder."

"*What?* Who's dead—the professor?" Luke Yates stared at the officer. "I gotta find a phone! The media will pay huge for this story." He rushed away.

The officer returned inside. "We should move this kid away from here. He could be in danger."

"It was a mistake to mention a witness," the second officer pointed out. "If Blake Decker realizes he can be identified, he'll go into hiding."

"You're right. But it's too late now."

* * *

From the time of the murder, Tom slept uneasily. In his nightmares, he relived the professor's cry of horror. His evidence had been classified by the Winnipeg police, and his identity as a possible witness was also a secret, but he still felt nervous—especially when he thought about Blake Decker.

Unfortunately, the media had quickly spread the news about a witness to the murder, and Decker had disappeared. An extensive police investigation had failed to find his hiding place, to the outrage of news commentators. Some suggested that senior investigators like Inspector Ted Austen should be fired—making for gloomy faces at the Austen household.

On the final evening of the Arctic guests' visit, a farewell banquet was held at the James Bay Inn, a classic small hotel in a residential area of Winnipeg. Tom arrived with Dietmar and his guests, Rachel and Moses. They stood outside, under the hotel's cheerful lights, waiting for the others to arrive.

"The Prime Minister was on the news," Dietmar said. "At his father's funeral."

"I saw him," Tom said. "He was crying crocodile tears."

"What's that mean?" Rachel asked.

"When a crocodile is eating its prey, big tears roll from its eyes. But the croc's not crying for the victim—it's happy."

"How's that connected to Prime Minister Dunbar?"

"I can't tell you," Tom said unhappily. The PM's possible link to the murder remained a secret; the public only knew of the involvement of Blake Decker and ZULU-1.

"I felt sorry for Dunbar at the funeral," Dietmar said. "If I was old enough, I'd vote for U-SAC. It's a good deal for Canada. I hate those long, boring waits at the border crossing. They ruin trips to the States."

"Then stay home," Tom growled, "and spend your money here. It keeps Canadians working."

"Who cares about work?" Grinning, Dietmar put his arm around Rachel. "I just want to party."

When the others arrived, everyone went inside. The hotel's dining room was decorated with colourful balloons and large banners. Photos on one wall showed highlights of the visit by the Gjoa Haven teens.

"I like this one," Moses said to Tom. "It shows our volleyball game against your school."

"We didn't have a chance," Tom lamented. "Your serve is wicked, and so is Rachel's. How come you're so good?"

Moses shrugged. "In the middle of our winter, the sun never rises. It's eternal darkness, 24 hours. Some people hibernate, but not us kids. We play hockey, volleyball, basketball, hour after hour."

They sat down at a long table decorated with flowers. Rachel and Dietmar joined them, along with Joey and Stephanie Villeneuve from Tom's class.

"Still in the detective business, Tom?" Stephanie asked. "What's the latest?"

"I've developed a new message system. You send a sentence that makes no sense. But, secretly, the first letter of each word forms a message."

"For example," Dietmar interrupted, "a spy sends the mysterious message, TRAVEL ON MOST ICE SEES ANIMALS LITTLE OR SMALL ENJOYING RAINBOWS. What's the code's secret meaning?"

"Let's see," Stephanie said, writing on a paper napkin, "T . . . O . . ."

Dietmar grinned. "The code reads TOM IS A LOSER."

"Oban wasn't born," Tom commented, "he was hatched in a lab. Too bad the experiment failed."

Everyone laughed. Then Joey turned to Rachel. "I saw pictures of the carvings Moses has done. They're wonderful."

Rachel nodded. "I think Moses will be a famous artist."

Moses smiled proudly at his sister. "Rachel will lead our people," he said to the others. "She speaks three languages, and she's always studying."

"I am gathering the wisdom of our elders," Rachel said shyly. "So much has changed during their life-time. As children, the elders lived in snow houses and hunted on the land. Now our people live in settle-ments, with little hunting or other work. Many young people in the north kill themselves. I want to give hope to kids in despair."

Stephanie's eyes were solemn. "What will you do?"

"First, we must understand the system. That is why I stay in school. For many years, all decisions were made for us by government *kabloonas* from the south. Now my people control Nunavut, which is our home-land. This gives real hope for the future."

"What's a *kabloona*?" Tom asked.

"A white person—it means *man with bushy eyebrows*. There is a legend about my grandfather. As a little boy, he saw *kabloonas* arriving in a boat and ran away, think-ing they were ghosts because of their white skin."

"Homeland is a nice word," Dietmar said. "It sounds peaceful, just like a home should be."

"I wish I was going north," Tom said. "I feel like skipping that hockey tournament."

"I'm the opposite," Dietmar commented. "I'd give anything to miss the trip."

"But why? Don't you want to see Rachel again?"

"Of course I do, Austen. But I hate being cold, and Arctic winters are legendary. Up there people freeze solid, all the time."

Rachel giggled. "It's not *that* bad, Dietmar."

He shuddered. "I'll have ice in my underwear."

Moses laughed. "You're so paranoid."

"We studied a poem called 'The Cremation of Sam McGee.' That poor guy was *so* cold. I've never forgotten."

Sam and Faith approached their table, holding hands. Sam smiled. His eyes looked bad, and his nose was dribbling. "Okay to join you?"

"Sure," Tom replied. "Too bad you're leaving tomorrow. I'll miss you guys."

"You're not going to visit Gjoa Haven?" Sam asked.

Tom shook his head. "Unfortunately, no. Maybe I'll see the Arctic after I join the Canadian Security Intelligence Service. They've got agents everywhere."

"You're looking at CSIS for a career? Why's that?"

"Being a secret agent would be cool."

Sam smiled. "Well, if you're in CSIS, you'll see the country for sure."

Some other teens came over to the table, followed by the Inuk Mountie and his son, Junior. "Would you please explain something?" Tom asked the Mountie.

"Certainly, Tom."

"What's the difference between 'Inuk' and 'Inuit'?"

"I am glad you are interested." As the Mountie paused to think, Tom studied his brown skin. It was seared and wrinkled by countless hours in extreme weather conditions. "The word 'Inuit' refers to all the people. An 'Inuk' is only one person—or two."

"I'm confused," Dietmar said.

Tom smiled at his friend. "May I have that in writing?"

The Mountie looked at Tom. "I have spoken to your father on the telephone. We discussed his murder investigation."

"Dad's working on it around the clock."

"I saw the Prime Minister on television, at his father's funeral. His comments to the media about the Winnipeg City Police were not favorable."

Tom's temper flared. "That guy is such a hypocrite!"

"One thing is strange," the Mountie said. "The Prime Minister demands action from the police, yet he's stalling on a government inquiry into his father's death."

For the first time, Faith spoke. "Perhaps because his aide Blake Decker was involved."

"What I can't figure out," Sam said, "is why the cops can't locate Decker. He's got to be hiding somewhere."

Tom stared glumly at the table, wishing he could help his Dad by finding Blake Decker, or by identifying the contract killer code-named ZULU-1. Unfortunately, the list of possible suspects was large—anyone who was at the university that day could have been the killer.

Tom felt eyes on him, and saw Faith staring. Then she smiled. Her face was lovely, but troubled. "You were lost in thought, Tom."

Before he could respond, Tom saw Luke Yates enter the dining room. As usual, the muscular little man was full of energy. "Gimme a few quotes about your visit," he said to the Mountie. "I'm faxing my final story to News/North tonight."

"Please, join us for the banquet." The Mountie gestured at the table. "As my guest."

"Not a chance. I just ate." Luke Yates pulled out his notepad. "Now, give me some quotes. Make them good—I'm hoping for extra money from the paper. I've got a hunting trip coming up."

At the head table, the principal of Tom's school called for attention. As she welcomed the students and their chaperons to the event, Luke Yates sat down at another table and made notes.

Steaming food appeared from the kitchen, carried on large trays by young waiters. Tom recognized one of them; he was Liz's current boyfriend. "Hey, Zoltan," he waved, "good to see you!"

The boy gave him a friendly smile.

"He's so cute," Stephanie said. "Liz has all the luck."

Following the meal, the tables were cleared away for dancing. A student from Tom's school set up a music system, and before long an excellent party was in progress. As voices grew noisy and music pounded the air, Luke Yates prowled with his notebook in search of quotes.

Returning from the washroom, Tom stopped in the lobby to talk to Sam. Then he said good night to the Mountie, who was leaving the hotel, and chatted briefly with Junior. Back at the party, Tom found Dietmar picking his teeth with a book of matches.

"Where's Rachel?"

"In the washroom." Dietmar tossed the matches on a table. "That's cheaper than flossing."

Tom laughed. Then he glanced at the matches and his heart froze. On the package were the initials JBI.

"Hey!"

"What now, Austen?"

Picking up the matches, Tom read *Enjoy your stay at the JBI.* "Those initials mean the James Bay Inn."

"Good work, Sherlock."

Still staring at the matches, Tom walked slowly away from Dietmar. He remembered being at the Prime Minister's hotel suite when Blake Decker spoke on the phone to someone named Ashley. They'd agreed to meet at "JBI-306."

Tom broke into a sweat. What if Blake Decker was hiding upstairs, in Room 306 of the James Bay Inn?

* * *

Tom hurried to the kitchen. Zoltan was stacking clean dishes on a shelf. "I saw you dancing, Tom. I tried it once but I quit—I've got two left feet."

"Listen, Zoltan, I need help."

"No problem, my man. What can I do?"

Minutes later, Tom was dressed as a waiter. On his hand, he balanced a tray containing a silver coffee pot, cups, and cutlery. "How do I look?" he asked.

"Nervous, but okay. You'd pass as a room service waiter."

Zoltan led Tom to narrow stairs at the back of the hotel. "Follow these to the third floor. Good luck."

"Remember what I said, Zoltan. If I don't return soon, call 911. Tell Dad I may have located Blake Decker."

"Let's call him now, Tom. Let the police deal with it."

"It's only a theory, Zoltan, and I've got a bad reputation at police headquarters for some bogus suspicions I've had in the past. First, let me check upstairs. I'll pretend I'm delivering room service, and look for signs of Decker. If he's there, the cops can make the arrest."

"But Room 306 hasn't ordered anything."

"I'll say I got the number wrong. I'll ask to use their phone, to find out the correct room. If I spot any signs of Decker, he's finished."

"This could be a mistake."

Tom smiled bravely. "Not a chance."

* * *

Light from old-fashioned lamps shone on wooden doors along the hallway on the third floor. No one was around. Tom forced himself forward. Room 306 was at the far end. As he approached, Tom heard a voice through the door. A man was speaking. Tom crept closer, straining to hear.

"No," the man's voice said. "You can't take the micro north to Joe. The boat is fine for hiding low-level stuff, but this micro is worth a fortune in blackmail. It stays with me."

Tom leaned his head close to the door. The paint was a bright yellow. He'd heard that voice before; it sounded like Blake Decker.

"I said *no*, ZULU-1, and I meant it. Now, here's your final payment for the hit on the professor." Then, suddenly, the man exclaimed, "Hey! What's with the gun?"

A mumbled response.

"Sure!" Decker sounded terrified. "Okay, here—I'll give you the micro-cassette. Just don't shoot! Here—here's the micro. Now put that thing away, *please*."

Then Tom heard a dreadful SNAP, followed by a horrifying cry, and the thump of a body falling to the floor.

* * *

For a moment, Tom was frozen. Then he turned from the door and walked quickly along the hallway. His hand trembled under the heavy tray, and his legs were like rubber. The hallway seemed impossibly long, the service stairs too distant to reach.

Desperate for refuge, Tom knocked on the door of Room 303. From inside, the voice of an elderly woman called, "Be right there!"

Tom listened to footsteps inside 303—the woman was moving slowly toward the door. *Hurry*, he screamed silently. *Please, hurry!*

The door opened, and a friendly face smiled up at Tom. "Yes, young man?"

Somewhere behind him, a door creaked open. Tom glanced at the coffee pot—the hallway was reflected in its curved surface. The image was distorted, but Tom saw the shape of a person sneaking out of Room 306.

"Yes, young man?"

"Uh . . . " Tom glanced at the woman for a brief moment. "Uh, room service . . . "

When he looked at the coffee pot again, the killer was gone. "Ma'am," he said desperately, "call the front desk . . . call the cops . . . there's, there's . . . been a shooting."

"What?"

"Blake Decker's been shot! Please, get help fast!"

* * *

Within minutes, the hallway swarmed with people. The first sirens could be heard in the distance, wailing closer. The hotel manager had been the first person inside Room 306 and had discovered Blake Decker dead; now he was waiting for the police. Dozens of rumours swept along the crowded hallway—then, suddenly, all voices stopped.

Everyone turned to stare at a woman who'd stepped out of the elevator. She was carrying food from a grocery store in plastic bags. Her face registered surprise. "What's happened?"

"There's been a shooting," the manager said. "In your room, Miss Romero."

"Blake," she cried. The bags crashed to the floor as she covered her mouth with both hands. "Someone shot Blake?"

"Blake Decker was a fugitive from justice, Miss Romero. You let him hide in your room?"

"He threatened me!"

The police arrived at that moment, and the spectators lost interest in Miss Romero. Instead, all eyes were on the manager as he opened the door to 306. The victim could not be seen, but Tom glimpsed a homemade flag on the wall. It was the Stars and Stripes, modified slightly by the presence of a single red maple leaf among the stars.

Tom turned to Zoltan, who was one of the onlookers. "Blake Decker told me he'd designed a flag for U-SAC. I guess that's it." He paused. "Decker will never see it flying over Canada, but what about us?"

"It's a depressing thought," Zoltan replied. "Let's hope U-SAC never happens."

6

Two days later, Tom was at the Winnipeg airport with his classmates. They were checking in luggage tagged *Gjoa Haven*.

Everyone was excited. "This is *so* fantastic," Desmond Chan exclaimed. "Hey, it's great you're going with us, Tom."

"Thanks, Des. Deciding to skip the tournament wasn't easy, but now I'm really glad. I just couldn't miss seeing the Arctic."

Dietmar joined them, face gloomy. "I wrote my last will and testament last night. It's in my room. My collection of movies is yours, Austen. Enjoy them with your girlfriends, and think of me occasionally."

"Hey," Desmond said, "I wouldn't mind getting your silk shirts, Dietmar. What do you say?"

Tom glanced at the check-in counter. "See the guy with all the gear? That's Luke Yates, the freelance writer."

"He looks tough," Desmond said. "I bet he works out with weights."

"He's checking in a rifle. This must be the hunting trip he talked about." Tom frowned. "But I wonder— there's a media uproar about the two murders, so you'd think Yates would stay in town. Chase some stories, make some money."

"I'd holiday instead of working," Dietmar said. "Besides, look at you. Instead of staying home to meddle in the murder investigation, you're taking this trip."

"That's true."

Desmond looked at Dietmar. "Know what my Dad says about the north? It's so cold the fillings drop from your teeth. I couldn't tell if he was joking."

Dietmar whimpered.

"You shouldn't be so nervous," Tom said. "I'm not."

"What about the huskies? You're scared of dogs."

"Yeah, well . . . "

"We're going to sleep overnight in *igloos*, Austen! We won't survive, I guarantee it. Make one little mistake in the Arctic and you are toast."

"Correction," Tom said. "You're a polar bear's frozen TV dinner."

The students were herded together for a group picture, and then said goodbye to their families. Mrs. Austen and Liz were present, but Tom's father was busy investigating the murders.

Liz was watching the news on her tiny hand-held television set. Inspector Austen was at a press conference; he was sweating under the glare of lights as reporters yelled questions. "Just because ZULU-1 has vanished," Liz said, "the media's all over the police. It's not fair!"

Next on the news was the latest opinion poll on the referendum. With only ten days left until the vote, almost 70 percent had decided to say yes to union with the United States. Mrs. Austen sighed unhappily as the Prime Minister appeared, beaming at the poll results. "Liz, turn that thing off."

Tom shook his head. "I'm convinced the missing micro-cassette holds the truth about the Prime Minister. Now the killer has it—but who knows where?"

"You couldn't identify ZULU-1 for the police?" Mrs. Austen asked.

Tom shook his head. "I only saw a distorted reflection. ZULU-1 was disguised in a balaclava and overalls. The police found them later, abandoned in the hotel's cellar."

"Tell me again," Mrs. Austen said. "What did Blake Decker say to ZULU-1 in Room 306?"

Tom opened his notebook. "He said—'You can't take the micro north to Joe.' There was also something about hiding it in a boat."

"Finding Joe is the key," Liz said. She handed Tom some miniaturized binoculars. "Makiko gave me these, as a souvenir of St. Andrews. They may be useful up north."

"Thanks, sis."

"I wish you'd take my key ring with the rabbit's foot and four-leaf clover."

Tom smiled. "I'm not superstitious."

Liz hugged her brother goodbye. "Enjoy the meals,

but don't choke on the raw seal."

Tom kissed his mother. "Tell Dad to relax. He's so tense these days."

"He'll be okay, honey." Mrs. Austen smiled, but Tom knew she was worried.

* * *

After a smooth flight, their Canadian Airlines jet approached Yellowknife, the north's largest city. After passing hundreds of small lakes, they were descending over Great Slave Lake, which was enormous. The city stood beside it, surrounded by snow-covered trees.

"They've got high-rise buildings," Bonita Vanderveen reported from her window. "And I see a mall!"

Inside the terminal, they assembled for instructions from one of their teachers, Mr. Cousins. "Our next plane leaves in three hours," he announced. "So we'll go into town."

After shopping at the YK Centre, they toured a museum in the heart of the city. "Look at the teeth," Dietmar said, examining an enormous polar bear. "I hear these bears can run incredibly fast."

"Only if they're hungry for an Oban-burger," said Tom, who was studying another display. "Look at this—the saber-toothed cat once roamed the north. Camels, too, and woolly mammoths. They're all extinct, but the musk-oxen still survive up there. They go back two million years. Wouldn't it be something to actually see one?"

"Thrilling, I'm sure."

"Relax, Oban. You'll love the Arctic."

"Sure thing, Austen."

* * *

Back at the airport, they saw Luke Yates waiting for the next flight. Also in the lounge were some Inuit who would be going home to Gjoa Haven on the plane. Dressed in colourful parkas, they sat surrounded by shopping bags and large packages from Tim Hortons Donuts and McDonald's. Their children stopped playing to stare at the teenagers from the south.

Tom sat beside one of his teachers, Mr. Plantinga. "Why've they got all that food, sir?"

"You won't find the golden arches in Gjoa Haven, Tom. These people are returning with treats for their families."

"My Mom forced me to bring a pineapple for my hosts. I feel like an idiot, travelling with a pineapple!"

The teacher smiled. "Good for your mother. Fresh fruit is a delicacy in the Arctic."

Then a familiar person appeared. It was Constance, one of the teachers from Gjoa Haven. "Surprise! First Air kindly flew me down here to welcome you to the north. Everyone's very excited about your visit! You know my husband's an Inuk, eh? You'll be overnighting with him in igloos far from town. It's called going out on the land. The winds blow *really* cold out there!"

Dietmar moaned.

"The people in Gjoa are my family now," Constance said, as she smiled at the Inuit waiting for the flight. "I miss the city, but I'm staying north."

"Excuse me, Constance," Tom said. "Did you just say, 'the people in Joe'? What's that mean?"

"Gjoa is short for Gjoa Haven. Just like Spence means Spence Bay."

"But you pronounce it 'Joe'?" Tom jotted the information in his notebook. "That's really important!" Grabbing Dietmar, he led him away from the others. "I've got a theory."

Dietmar rolled his eyes.

At that moment, a voice announced, *First Air flight 842 now boarding for Gjoa Haven.* "On the plane," Tom promised, "I'll tell you all the details."

"What a thrill awaits me."

* * *

Outside the terminal, they hurried across the snow-blown tarmac toward a turbo-prop displaying the logo of First Air. The space inside was divided between seats for the passengers and a large area for cargo.

"What are you taking north?" Mr. Cousins asked the friendly flight attendant.

"Fresh eggs, new movies, snowmobile parts, a shortwave radio. All the essentials of life."

The Hawker-Siddley HS 748 bumped along the runway and then roared into the air. "So long, Yellowknife," Dietmar said mournfully, looking down from his window. "Farewell to civilization."

"Relax, Oban." Tom glanced across the aisle at Luke Yates, who sat alone, loudly chewing gum. The writer was studying an ad for high-power rifles in a magazine for hunters. "Listen to the noise he's making. Disgusting."

"You're so neurotic, Austen."

"He's got a bottle of rum hidden inside his coat. I saw him take a drink."

The flight attendant welcomed them on board. "As we will be flying over remote areas, this plane is equipped with emergency survival equipment."

The announcement produced another groan from Dietmar.

"You're so neurotic, Oban," Tom laughed.

"It's huge down there," Dietmar said, leaning close to the window. "There's nothing but snow."

Tom wrote some ideas in his notebook. "Here's what I figure," he whispered. "Remember I told you the secret about the hitman?"

"Don't worry, I haven't told anyone."

"I know that, Oban. Now listen up. ZULU-1 wanted to take the micro north to Joe, to hide in a boat. I thought Joe meant a person, but it's the place—Gjoa Haven."

"What use is the micro to anyone?"

"Blackmail! It could prove that the Prime Minister is part of a conspiracy. Dunbar would pay big money to keep that a secret."

"Why take the micro-cassette up north?"

"It's the perfect hiding place. Who'd ever look in Gjoa Haven for the micro?"

"No one except Tom Austen, the defective detective. You'll waste your entire visit searching for it—and you'll find nothing."

* * *

After serving a delicious lasagna, the flight attendant announced a contest. "Guess the combined age of me and the two pilots, and you can try flying this plane."

"I'll win this," Tom predicted, but he was wrong. Dietmar's guess of 90 years took the prize, and as he went forward, the other students requested permission to leave the plane.

"Fasten your seatbelts," Mr. Plantinga laughed. "We're in for a rough ride."

"I've got to watch this," Tom said, going to the cockpit with his camera. Dietmar sat in the co-pilot's seat, facing the instrument panel. Outside were vistas of endless snow, shadowed by low sunshine from the west.

"It's a white desert," Dietmar said over the droning roar of the engines. "Why aren't there any houses?"

"People live under the snow," the pilot replied. Then he grinned. "Hey, I'm kidding."

"Why no trees?"

"They don't grow this far north."

As the pilot demonstrated the controls, the plane swerved left, producing loud cries from the cabin. The co-pilot laughed. "You're ruining this kid's reputation with his friends."

The pilot pointed to a infinitesimal speck far away in the white landscape. "There's Gjoa, straight ahead. Franklin's men died on that island, Amundsen anchored the *Gjoa* in the harbour, and the Mounties on the *St. Roch* watched these same skies. This is real history, guys!" He grinned at them. "You'll like the people up here. Now, you'd better hustle back to your seats."

In the cabin, the teens with window seats were taking pictures and videos and calling out to their friends as the plane circled before beginning its descent.

"Boy, it's *tiny*!"

"Awesome. We're actually here."

"I'm scared."

"I don't have butterflies in my stomach, I have penguins."

"Look at the sunset!"

Pale shades of cloud covered the sky. The sun glowed red, just above the horizon. "Welcome to Gjoa Haven," said the flight attendant as the wheels bumped down on the frozen land.

Cheers rang out.

The adventure had begun.

7

Snow clung to the terminal building, which was the size of a portable classroom. Faces peered through windows, and a welcoming sign in bright colours hung on the wall. When the plane engines stopped, a crowd of people hurried outside, heads down into the wind. They wore heavy-duty parkas with fur-fringed hoods. Their breath blew away in clouds.

As the plane's door opened, the frigid wind rushed in. "Help," Dietmar yelped. "That's brutal!"

"Look," a boy cried, "they've come to the airport on snowmobiles. I want to ride one!"

Outside in the cold wind, the locals and their guests—happily reunited—mingled beside the plane while the luggage was unloaded. Far away across the ivory-coloured snow were the houses of the hamlet's one thousand people.

Junior was among the welcomers; he shook hands with a powerful grip. Faith was also present, clinging to her boyfriend Sam's arm. He no longer had the glasses and scraggly blond beard. But his eyes and nose remained runny.

"Tom," he said, shaking hands. "I'm surprised to see you."

"Austen's crazy," Dietmar said. He was shivering in the cold. "Can you believe it? He dropped out of his tournament to experience *this*."

Sam smiled at Tom. "Good for you."

"I'm excited to be here."

"As for me," Dietmar moaned, "I'll never be warm again."

Sam laughed. "I was like you, my first time north. Scared to death, but then I fell in love with the land and the way of life." He put his arm around Faith. "And with the people."

Constance approached Tom. At her side was the Inuk Mountie. "Good news," Constance said to Tom. "You'll be staying with the Mountie and his family. You can discuss police work together."

Tom enthusiastically shook the man's hand. "Thanks for your hospitality."

He smiled. "Your friend Dietmar Oban will be staying next door at the home of Moses and Rachel. You can visit each other."

"Not if he keeps complaining."

Sam looked at Tom. "I remember your interest in CSIS. You're into crime busting?"

Tom nodded.

"I guess the Mountie has probably mentioned that major crimes don't happen here. This airport is the only exit from town. Escaping would be impossible."

"Except," Junior said, "on the land." He looked at the white landscape that stretched away in all directions. "Out there, a person could hide forever."

* * *

Tom looked at Luke Yates, who was collecting his luggage. "That guy bothers me."

As if reading his mind, Yates snapped his eyes in their direction. Lifting his rifle and a bulky tote bag, he crossed the snow to them. "You're the Mountie here, right?"

"That is correct, sir."

Yates looked around, studying everything. The gum snapped and popped inside his mouth. "I'm here to shoot me an Arctic big white. Where are those polar bears?"

"You must request a hunting tag in advance, sir. You've come a long way for nothing."

Yates studied the Mountie's face. "We're in the middle of nowhere! I don't need a hunting tag up here—I pay my taxes, I've got rights. This trip is costing big bucks, so where are those bears? I'm here to kill one, and I don't need a tag."

"If you hunt illegally, sir, I will arrest you."

Sam gestured at the plane. "First Air is the only exit from Gjoa Haven. They'd never let you fly with an illegal trophy."

Yates looked at the plane, then at Sam and Faith, and then at the Mountie. His jaw moved energetically. "Okay," he said at last, "I'll buy a hunting tag. How much, Mountie?"

"This year's tags are all taken, sir."

"There's always a way." Yates pulled a wad of bills from his pocket, and peeled off several. "There's gotta be tags around. Get me one."

"Are you attempting to bribe a police officer, sir?"

"Ah, forget it." Yates snapped his fingers at a local parent. "You there! I want somewhere to stay."

"Try the Amundsen Hotel," she replied.

"I don't suppose this dump has a taxi service?"

She pointed at a snow-caked car. "That is our taxi."

Yates started walking toward it, then paused to stare at the Mountie. "I'm here to get me a polar bear, Eskimo. I won't fail."

* * *

Tom was upset by the man's behavior, but wasn't sure what to say. He helped his host carry his gear to a big snowmobile displaying the RCMP crest. As the Mountie roped the luggage on a wooden sled behind, he said, "We call this a *komatik*."

Climbing on the SnowCat behind the Mountie, Tom grabbed tight. "This is great," he yelled, head down against the bitter wind as the powerful machine roared along a frozen road into town. "I can't believe I'm actually in the Arctic!"

Kids were playing hockey in the streets of the hamlet; a lot of snowmobiles buzzed past, but Tom saw no cars and only a single pickup truck. Huskies on chains prowled outside many homes. Power lines were silhouetted against the sky, where a full moon was rising. The snow was blue under the evening light, which shone on the windows and wooden walls of the houses where smoke drifted away from chimneys.

"My office." The Mountie pointed at a small portable building.

Tom looked at an enormous metal tank that rose above the town. "What's that for?"

"Bulk storage for fuel. It holds more than 500,000 litres of gasoline. Barges bring the fuel up the Mackenzie from Hay River."

"That thing could be a target for terrorists. Blow it up, and you'd cause havoc."

"True," the Mountie replied, "but why terrorists in Gjoa Haven?"

Tom pictured the cold eyes of Luke Yates. Maybe not terrorists, he thought to himself, but how about armed thugs? Gjoa would be the perfect hideout for a contract killer.

* * *

At the Mountie's small, cozy house, an excited family was waiting to greet Tom. They watched with grinning faces as he pulled off his parka and boots. "Don't worry about the caribou," the Mountie said, gesturing at a bloody haunch of meat on a chunk of cardboard. "We've got fish and chips waiting for you."

"I wouldn't mind trying some caribou."

"Excellent." Using a small, crescent-shaped knife, the Mountie sliced meat from the haunch for Tom. "This knife is called an *ulu*. How do you like the caribou, Tom?"

"Not bad," Tom mumbled, forcing himself to swallow the raw meat. "I'll get used to it."

The Mountie led Tom to an elderly woman in a rocking chair; her brown face was creased by wrinkles. After he spoke to her in Inuktitut, she beamed at Tom. "*Qanuritpit.*"

"My mother says, how are you?"

Tom shyly handed her a pin showing Winnipeg's Golden Boy statue. "This is for you, ma'am."

"Aaah!" Eyes glowing, she displayed the pin to the others.

"My mother does not speak English." The Mountie smiled at Tom. "You're a big hit with her. It must be that hair, the colour of flames. It is unusual around here."

Next he introduced his wife and a mob of kids in T-shirts and jeans. "These are not all ours," the Mountie explained. "They are nieces, nephews, cousins, children of cousins. We are one big family in Gjoa Haven."

Digging in his luggage, Tom found the slightly battered pineapple. "Mom sent this."

"Wonderful," the Mountie exclaimed, and the kids whooped with joy. "Fresh fruit is a luxury to us."

Surprised and pleased, Tom pulled apples and oranges from his pack. "Here's more stuff."

"Your parents are kind," the Mountie said. "I enjoyed meeting them."

"They both say hi."

Tom glanced around. A western movie was on TV; it seemed strange to see trees. On the wall above, a poster featured the flashing blades of a hockey great. Outside the window, he saw huskies on chains patrolling their territory; beyond them, the snow went on forever.

"You are looking at the Arctic Ocean, Tom. Your home is straight south of here, more than 2,000 kilometres as the snowy owl flies. The huskies belong to my son, Junior." The Mountie beckoned him to the table. "Now you must eat."

Tom enjoyed a delicious Arctic char with potatoes as the youngest kids stood around the table, staring. "*Teagukpin*?" said the Mountie's mother, offering tea.

The Mountie smiled. "The children call my mother Tea-Granny. She drinks it all day."

"So does my Nan!"

While Tom ate, people kept arriving and leaving. He lost track of the names, but liked all their smiles. Kids ran in and out the front door, yelling in loud voices and rough-housing under people's feet. No one seemed to care.

"We believe that children are the reincarnation of our ancestors," the Mountie explained. "How can I discipline my son if he's really my grandfather?"

His wife nodded. "But do not worry, Tom. The children grow up strong. They have many aunts and uncles, many grandparents. Their wisdom becomes a part of each child."

As Tom helped wash the dishes, he listened to a CB radio crackling out messages. "What's this for?" he asked one of the kids.

"People send messages by CB. Most people in Gjoa have one. Few have telephones."

Junior arrived at the house. After respectfully greeting his grandmother and his parents, Junior chatted with Tom. Then someone knocked loudly on the outside door.

"Must be a *kabloona*," Junior commented. "My people just walk in—we have no secrets."

Several children ran to open the door; in the darkness outside, Tom saw a yellow Ski-Doo. Luke Yates pushed past the kids and advanced on the Mountie, who sat beside his mother watching *Coronation Street* on TV. "Okay, Eskimo—I'll tell you again. I want a hunting tag, and I want it *now*."

The Mountie's mother touched the teapot at her side. "*Teaqukpin*?" she said to Yates.

Ignoring her, Yates leaned over the Mountie. "Some locals have hunting tags, right?" He pointed at a computer in the corner. "The names are in that thing, right? So tell me who they are, and I'll buy a tag from someone."

"I cannot do that, sir. It's against the rules."

Eyes blazing with anger, Yates raised a hand as if to strike the Mountie. Tom expected Junior to defend his father, but the young Inuk didn't do anything.

After a tense moment, Yates lowered his hand, then spat a filthy word in the Mountie's face. Storming out of the house, Yates gave the door a mighty slam.

Junior immediately returned to his conversation with Tom, the soap opera commanded attention once again, and the children returned to their play. It seemed Yates had upset only one person—Tom was enraged.

* * *

"That racist scum," he stormed at Dietmar as they walked around town that night with Moses and Rachel. "I expected Junior to deck him, but he didn't even speak."

Moses nodded. "Junior is a man of strength."

Dietmar laughed. "Strength? You're joking."

Moses didn't react to Dietmar's sarcasm. "My people believe in peaceful coexistence—maybe it comes from living together in igloos. He who attacks another is weak."

"But Yates was so insulting," Tom said.

"All the more reason to show strength. Junior and his father demonstrated their maturity. Luke Yates revealed his weakness."

Although it was nighttime, children rode past on bicycles, giggling as they stared at Tom and Dietmar. A young woman stopped to greet them; on her back was a baby, peeking out from the folds of a brightly decorated packing-parka. The snow crunched underfoot as they continued on to the arena, listening to snowmobiles in the night. "Professor Dunbar was right," Tom said. "The Arctic is the ultimate."

* * *

At the arena, they exchanged smiles with the people of all ages who came in from the cold, wearing beautiful parkas and fur-fringed *kamiks* on their feet. After watching a hockey game, the teens joined the other visitors and their billets in wandering the hamlet under brilliant stars. Tom was warm inside a caribou parka loaned by the Mountie; the *kamiks* he wore on his feet had soles that were slippery on the snowy streets.

For hours, the teens visited house to house, meeting people, talking, staring at everything. Long after midnight, Tom left the home of a friendly boy named Silas Atkichok and crunched through the night, homeward bound.

Ahead loomed the black outline of the bulk storage tank. A wire fence provided security, but its gate stood open. Nearby was a yellow snowmobile that Tom recognized.

He'd seen it earlier when Luke Yates had arrived at the Mountie's house.

* * *

The Ski-Doo's engine was warm. Tom looked at a metal staircase that curved up the side of the tank. Had someone climbed up there?

Sliding silently in his *kamiks* along a frozen path, Tom reached the staircase. He started up, aware of his pounding heart. Somewhere in the night, a dog howled, and others joined in.

Tightly gripping the rail, Tom climbed further. All around were the roofs of houses in which people slept peacefully. The cries of the dogs died away, then rose to higher notes. Gulping air, Tom reached the top. A metal catwalk led to the centre of the tank, where someone in a dark parka knelt over large nozzles and other equipment.

The person's head was hidden inside a parka hood. Cautiously, Tom stepped on to the catwalk, hoping for a better view. But his *kamiks* slipped on the icy metal and he suddenly fell sideways.

Tom's hand tore loose from the railing. Landing heavily on the tank's sloped roof, he shouted in horror. His feet couldn't grip, and he was swiftly plunging toward the edge.

8

At the edge of the roof, Tom slammed into a wooden platform. Somehow he seized it, breaking his fall. But his feet went over the side, leaving him dangling in midair.

"Help," Tom yelled.

The person turned toward him, eyes hidden behind snowmobile goggles.

"Please!"

Hurrying along the catwalk, the person disappeared down the staircase. Using all his strength, Tom struggled to safety on the platform and lay gasping in shock. Then, getting to his knees, he crawled along to the staircase. Somewhere below, an engine roared, and moments later the yellow Ski-Doo disappeared into the night.

* * *

The next morning, Tom was awakened by a clock radio. "A cold front is moving along the Arctic coast," said the announcer, "and temperatures will continue to drop. Have a nice day, and be good to yourself."

As she began speaking in Inuktitut, Tom remembered a dream in which he'd played hockey at the Gjoa Haven arena, astounding everyone with his moves. He studied the Canadian flag on the wall above him, then his eyes travelled to a poster of a rock star and a framed award for perfect Sunday school attendance.

Showering under a nozzle shaped like Dracula, Tom thought about the storage tank. He could have died. Shivering, he added hot water. Later, he ate Rice Krispies in bright sunshine while writing in his notebook. Outside the window was the Mountie, feeding Junior's dogs.

After drinking some tea, Tom put on sunglasses and several layers of clothing before stepping into air so icy that it pinched his nostrils painfully. The Mountie's face beamed a greeting from inside his parka. "*Ublaqut*, Tom Austen. This means good morning."

"*Ub . . . la . . . qut*," Tom replied, struggling with the word.

"*Hila unaituq*. It is cold."

After hearing Tom's description of the events at the fuel storage depot, the Mountie promised to investigate immediately. Tom offered to help, but was politely reminded of the morning's special assembly at the school. "The mayor will welcome your class. You are special guests in our community."

"You're right. It's important that we all be present."

Tom eyed the huskies. They were securely chained, but he still kept his distance. Beyond them was the frozen sea; tiny diamonds of light reflected from the bright snow.

"It's beautiful here."

"Thank you." The Mountie looked toward the west. "Long ago, our ancestors came from Asia. This is a splendid place they found." He tapped the snow with his foot. "On this land, my grandparents walked, and their grandparents before them. It has long been so."

The Mountie and Tom returned to the front door, where they said goodbye. Dietmar was just leaving with the twins from their house, and Tom joined them.

"*Ublaqut*," he said. "*Hila unaituq*."

Rachel grinned. "Very good, Tom."

As they climbed a frozen slope, Dietmar yawned. "I've been awake for 37 hours straight, playing Nintendo and hanging out. The sunrise was cool to see, but I didn't eat breakfast. It was raw caribou."

Moses smiled. "Wait until we have ptarmigan heart, Dietmar. It is good and soft."

"Yech."

Reaching the top of the hill, they passed the bulk storage tank. True to his word, the Mountie had arrived to investigate, and waved to them from the metal stairs. A lot of kids and parents were walking through town toward the school, which was a large building painted a brilliant orange.

In the twins' classroom, they peeled off their outer clothing. The technology was typical of any well-equipped school, but the posters were unique, showing snow-swept vistas and the faces of northern celebrities like the singing star Susan Aglukark and her Arctic Rose Band.

In the hallway, posters gave instructions on building an igloo. "Look at the exit sign," said Adam Marx, joining them for the walk to the gym. "It's in their language. That's cool."

A large crowd had gathered in the gym. Students of all ages sat on the floor; seated around the walls were grandparents, parents, and babies. After the singing of *O Canada* in English and Inuktitut, a prayer was given. Then the mayor stepped to the microphone with words of welcome; he was young and wore jeans and a "Screaming Eagles" sweatshirt. As the visitors were introduced and gifts were exchanged, many people recorded the event on video, including Rachel and Moses, who had twin Sonys.

The assembly ended with a display of Arctic Games. "When our people lived on the land," the mayor explained, "we would gather in a *qaggi*, a large snow house where singing and games took place. Today, people from the polar nations gather every two years for Arctic Games to test our skills and renew friendships."

The school's gym teacher demonstrated the Alaska high kick. A bit of cloth was hung from the basketball hoop; with a mighty leap, he managed to kick the cloth and then land in the same precise spot. Huge applause rang out.

"That's amazing," Adam exclaimed.

"You should try it," Moses suggested.

"No, thanks!"

The teacher called for volunteers to attempt the knuckle-hop. "It's like doing push-ups, only on your knuckles and toes. You have to hop forward—our school record is one lap of the gym."

As the southern teens whimpered at the thought, Tom was astonished to see Dietmar raise his hand. "I'll try."

He managed to knuckle-hop for several metres before collapsing. As cheers broke out, Dietmar waved to the crowd and grinned. "That was fun," he exclaimed, returning to sit with the others.

"I'm impressed," Tom admitted.

Next, they toured the town. The first stop was the Northern store, where everything possible was for sale, from snowmobiles to CDs to frozen pizza. When the friendly manager showed them the storage area, they discovered pop in huge stacks that reached to the ceiling.

"Every summer, a barge arrives with a year's supply of this stuff." The manager smiled. "Folks here love soft drinks—maybe it's the caffeine."

Lots of people were in the store. Tom posed Dietmar and the twins against a display of northern clothes, then took a close-up of a solemn-eyed toddler in furs.

"Things are expensive here," Dietmar said, as they left the store.

Moses nodded. "Prices are 82 percent higher than in Yellowknife."

"Yet another reason," Dietmar said, "to avoid this place in future."

Mr. Cousins approached them. "Tom, someone just contacted me from the hotel. A fax has arrived for you."

"Hey," Tom exclaimed. "This could be from Dad, about the murders. Can I go get it, sir?"

"Sure. Our next stop is the town hall, for a visit with the mayor. Catch up with us there."

Rachel decided to accompany Tom. He took photos as they crunched along the snow-packed streets in their *kamiks*. "Sorry about Dietmar's sarcasm," Tom said to Rachel. "I hope you're not upset."

"Thanks, Tom, but I don't mind what Dietmar says. I understand him. He is an unhappy person."

"Yeah, it's true. His home life isn't much fun."

Dietmar came running to join them. "Let's have a hot chocolate at the hotel, okay?" He smiled at Rachel. "I'm buying."

The Amundsen was a small, single-storey building. Quite a few snowmobiles were parked outside; some were yellow, and had the words *Amundsen Hotel* on them.

Inside, Sam was working at a desk. On it, a large photograph of Faith was displayed in a silver frame. "I'm the hotel manager," he explained to Tom. "This fax arrived for you."

Quickly, Tom read it. "It's not about the murders. Liz wants me to find a carving for Zoltan's birthday."

"That's her boyfriend?" Rachel asked.

Tom nodded.

"Let's get that hot chocolate," Dietmar said.

They went into the small dining room. It was smoky, and filled with people. "Government workers," Rachel said, "on a coffee break."

Tom saw Faith and Junior together at an arborite table. She was speaking urgently and gesturing. "Are they civil servants?"

Rachel shook her head. "Faith and Junior own a business together. At night, they clean the town hall and places like that."

"Sam's eyes looked bad today," Tom commented. "He says it's an allergy, but I wonder . . . "

"Yes?"

"Look at Faith and Junior—that's an intense conversation they're having. Maybe Sam's love life is a mess, and he's been crying."

"I doubt it," Rachel said. "Junior would never betray Sam. They're close friends."

Tom shrugged. "Stranger things have happened."

The only available seats were at a table with Luke Yates. The writer smelled of a strong aftershave; he was staring moodily at the arborite. Tom remembered the storage tank, and his skin prickled. The man could not be trusted.

Luke Yates looked at Rachel. "Anyone in your family a hunter?"

"Yes."

"Great! Have they got a polar bear tag? I'll pay good money."

"We do not hunt polar bear," Rachel replied. "There is no such tag in my house."

Luke Yates swore, and angrily slapped the table. "I'll find one!"

Tom sipped the hot chocolate provided by Dietmar. "Thanks, Oban." He looked at Yates. "Why kill a polar bear? What's the big deal?"

"It's one of the supreme trophies," Yates explained. "Like a Siberian tiger, or a grizzly. Bag one of those, and you're acknowledged as a champion hunter."

"Aren't they endangered species?"

Luke Yates shook his head in disgust. "What's wrong with kids these days? All that garbage about animal rights—are you sick in the head, or what?"

Tom felt his skin glowing. "What about you," he said, struggling to control his temper. "What's wrong with *you*, killing defenceless animals! The government should take away your rifle."

Yates laughed. "That'll never happen. Especially when the referendum passes, and we join the United States. Down there, the gun laws make sense. It's written in their constitution—people have the right to bear arms. Once we're part of the States, I'll have that right, too. I'm thinking of opening a store in Winnipeg to sell handguns and ammo. The money will be good—every house will need weapons for self-defense." He stared at his coffee cup. "I'm sick of being a freelance writer. I'm good, but it's still hard to scratch up enough stories to make a buck."

Dietmar grinned at Rachel. "Austen's been talking recently about becoming a writer some day. That's as unrealistic as being a detective."

Luke Yates chuckled. "A kid detective, huh? Had any luck?"

"A bit," Tom replied.

Dietmar grinned. "Tell him your latest theory, Austen. About the hitman being loose in Gjoa Haven."

Tom groaned. "You fool, Oban! That's confidential information."

Luke Yates narrowed his eyes. "A contract killer, *here*? Give me the details."

Tom was saved from replying when Sam spoke.

He'd been standing by the table, listening to the conversation. "There's a phone call for you, Mr. Yates. It sounds important."

"Stay here," Yates warned Tom. "I've got questions to ask you."

As he walked away, Sam sat down. "Was that guy bothering you?" he asked Rachel.

She shook her head.

Within a minute, Yates was back. "There wasn't a phone call." He gave Sam a dirty look, then glanced across the noisy room at Faith and Junior. "That's your girlfriend, right? Well, mister, take my advice. Never trust an Eskimo."

"I've got a suggestion to make," Sam said to Yates. "Catch the next flight out. You won't find a hunting tag in Gjoa, and you're just causing trouble. If you continue to insult the Inuit, I'll throw you out of this hotel."

"I'm not a quitter, mister. When I want something, I get it." Yates pointed a finger at Tom. "I'll speak to you later."

As the writer walked out of the dining room, Sam shook his head. "What a loser," he sighed. "That guy actually believes the Inuit created all their problems, when in fact they lived in absolute balance with their world before the first *kabloonas* arrived and started killing everything in sight. We took away these people's rights, laughed at their traditions, herded them into settlements. What happened was a tragedy."

Changing the subject, Sam asked, "You enjoyed the assembly at school?"

"You bet," Dietmar said.

"I loved the Arctic Games," Tom said. "Can that teacher ever jump!"

"He's called Laser because of his volleyball serve. Don't get in front of it!" Sam waved at Faith and Junior. "Come join us."

As the pair crossed the dining room, Tom noticed Faith dabbing at her eyes with a Kleenex. She gave Junior an unhappy smile before sitting down.

"More trouble with that guy Yates?" Junior asked Sam.

"Yes. I keep hoping he'll go home to Winnipeg."

"I have a hunting tag," Junior said, "but that *kabloona* won't get it."

Sam turned to Faith. "We were discussing the Arctic Games, honey." He smiled proudly at the others. "Faith's a world champion. She took a gold and two bronzes at the last games in Alaska. The medals are shaped like *ulu* knives."

"Congratulations," Dietmar said. "I've had some experience with those games. They're brutal."

She smiled shyly. "The medals are not important. It is the sense of family, the unity of the people. We cheer all competitors, and help each other. To be there makes me happy." She looked at Sam. "You should tell them about your high school golds."

"I was pretty good with the javelin," Sam told them. "But sports down south are too competitive for me. Up here, nobody is made to feel like a loser."

"Guess what?" Tom said. "The Mountie is planning a trip out on the land for me. I can hardly wait! The other Mountie gets back from holidays on Sunday, so we're leaving right away. We'll overnight at the ice-fishing igloo, then push on to the Franklin Cairn and maybe Starvation Cove. Have you ever seen the cairn?"

Sam nodded. "It's just a pile of rocks with a small sign, but it's real history. That's where long-ago explorers found some bones and skulls of sailors from the Franklin expedition."

"Wow! I bet there are ghosts everywhere!"

Sam smiled. Then he turned to Faith, and asked about her family. As they spoke, Junior stood up and quickly walked away. He didn't say goodbye.

* * *

When they rejoined the others, the tour was just leaving the town hall. "They've got a small museum in there," Mr. Cousins reported. "It's worth seeing."

Through his sunglasses, Tom watched some little kids in parkas building a small igloo, while others played with dolls and toy trucks. Then he saw a yellow snowmobile approaching, and his heart beat rapidly. Was it Luke Yates, looking for trouble?

Faith was on the machine. "Tom," she said, "you're wanted back at the hotel."

"Another fax?"

Faith shook her head. "Jump on fast, okay? It's important."

Mr. Plantinga checked their schedule. "Meet us at the Coop, Tom. We're seeing a demonstration of carving."

Tom climbed on behind Faith, and the yellow snowmobile buzzed quickly through town to the Amundsen. Sam was behind the desk. "Thanks for coming, Tom."

He looked at Faith. "Would you run things for five minutes, sweetheart?"

In the hotel office, Sam motioned Tom into a chair and sat on the edge of the desk. "Tom, I've just spoken to your father at Winnipeg police HQ."

"Hey! Is there a break in the murder investigation?"

"It looks possible." Taking out his wallet, Sam handed Tom a white business card. In one corner was the Canadian flag, with the initials CSIS underneath. Printed in black letters was the name *Samuel G. White*.

Tom's eyes bulged in surprise. "You're with CSIS?"

Sam nodded. "Working at this hotel is a cover. My territory covers the entire western Arctic."

"Remember when we talked at the James Bay Inn? No wonder you knew about CSIS!"

Sam nodded. "I went to Winnipeg on an agency matter. My disguise included the beard and eyeglasses." He smiled briefly, then became serious. "I just called your father on a secure line. I asked his permission to tell you I'm CSIS, Tom, because your theory is absolutely right. Like you, we believe ZULU-1 is in Gjoa Haven."

9

For a moment, Tom was speechless. Then he said, "How can I help?"

"First, tell me who you suspect."

"Luke Yates."

Sam nodded. "That's not a surprise. Why him?"

"Yates has a rifle, so he understands weapons. He was nearby at the time of both murders and, in fact, I saw Yates outside the professor's office just before the shooting."

"Anything else?"

Tom described the events at the storage tank. "I'm sure Yates was responsible."

Sam wrote some notes. "I'll keep your Dad advised of developments, using the secure line. If you're phoning home, Tom, don't say *one word* about this. Anyone in town can listen to long distance calls being radioed south."

"I understand," Tom replied. "What about the Mountie—should I tell him about Yates?"

Sam shook his head. "Gjoa Haven is deep cover for me. Even the Mountie doesn't know the truth." He stood up. "I'll have my people in Ottawa check on Luke Yates. I'll advise you what we learn, and what action is planned." He shook Tom's hand. "Good work."

"Thanks! I hope something really exciting happens while I'm in Gjoa."

"Maybe it will."

* * *

Later that day, Tom decided to catch some of the annual Hamlet Days events. At the snow-packed harbour he saw a small boat which had been abandoned for the winter and hurried to it, remembering that the microcassette could be hidden in a boat. But drifting snow had filled the motorboat to the gunnels; it would be impossible to search.

A yellow Safari roared to a stop beside Tom. Faith was at the controls. "Want to try this thing, Tom?"

"You bet!"

Soon they were moving fast, cutting figure eights into the snow. Finally, Tom stopped the machine near the crowd that had gathered for the special events. "Thanks," he said with a grin at Faith, as they stepped off the machine.

"No problem."

The Mountie was there, and he smiled at Tom. "I have investigated the storage tanks. Nothing was tampered with, but the lock on the gate was picked by an expert."

"Thanks for letting me know." Tom looked across the harbour. "That big boat over there, with the cabin. What's its name?"

"*Netsilik*. It means seal."

"Okay to look inside?"

"I'm sure that would be fine. Any reason?"

Tom shrugged. "Just curiosity," he replied, feeling guilty about avoiding the question. As the Mountie began talking to someone else, Tom crossed the snow to the Ladies' Igloo-Building event. One of the competitors was Faith, and Sam was present to cheer her on.

Racing against the clock, each woman quickly traced the outline of an igloo and then began cutting large blocks of snow using *panas*, long knives that glittered in the sunlight. As the crowd rooted them on and video cameras rolled, the women lifted the blocks into place. Quickly the walls grew.

"I can't believe how fast they're working," Tom said to Sam, "and look at *that* woman go. She must be 80 years old!"

"Last year Elsie won with a time of 22 minutes," Sam replied, "and I think she's about to repeat her victory."

The woman dropped the last block into place, quickly smoothed the snow with her *pana*, then raised both hands and grinned as the audience cheered her success. Moments later, the Mountie's wife finished her snow house, followed by Faith. All three congratulated each other.

Sam hugged Faith as she joined them, gasping for air. Sweat poured down her face. "That Elsie, she's so good."

"What's next, honey?" Sam asked.

"The harpoon throw."

"No problem—that's your gold medal event from Fairbanks."

Tom crawled into Faith's igloo. It was beautiful inside, filled with an ethereal light. From the entrance, he took a picture of the full moon far above in the blue sky, and then he wriggled out. "I can't believe I'm in this amazing place," he exclaimed to Faith as he lined up a shot of the snow-swept harbour. "I keep thinking about Amundsen arriving here, or those Mounties in the *St. Roch*. Imagine—they were at this very spot."

Using Faith's *pana*, Tom began constructing an igloo. Within moments he was sweating hard, and he quit after making one crooked snow block. "I'm not cut out for this work," he joked to the others.

"Long ago," Sam said, "the *pana* was made from a caribou antler. Imagine cutting snow blocks with that." He wiped his runny nose. "They made enormous igloos back then, as large as 20 feet in diameter. Imagine sleeping on a bed made of snow! When their homes melted in the spring, people moved into tents."

Tom photographed a mother and her child affectionately brushing their faces together. After herding together the local teens and their visitors for a picture, he captured Dietmar on film with the twins. All three were very cheerful. "Look at this carving Moses gave me," Dietmar said. In his hand was an Inuk with a husky, carved from ivory. "This guy is living free.

Look at his happiness. Know what's nice here? People smile at you in the street, and they ask questions. They actually *care* about you. It's so amazing."

"You're getting to like this place," Tom said.

Dietmar nodded. "I phoned my Mom to say I love it here. She started crying, I don't know why."

"Because," Rachel said, smiling, "she's happy for you."

"Wasn't that igloo-building event something else?" Tom said.

Moses looked proudly at his sister. "Rachel is entered in the same event for teens. She's really good, but Sheena Kamookak is tops."

Faith looked across the harbour. Sam followed her eyes, and then frowned. The yipping and yapping of a dog team announced the arrival of Junior, cracking a long whip in the air. The huskies were magnificent, straining against their leads as steam rushed from their mouths and nostrils.

Junior grinned at the crowd. "You kids from the south," he called. "Who wants a dog team ride?"

Dietmar quickly raised his hand to volunteer, and bumped away on a *komatik* behind Junior and the team. There was a big smile on his face.

Sam left for the hotel. Tom was getting cold, but he stayed for Faith's final event. She was a champion at throwing the harpoon—a long pole with a sharpened point—and he wanted to watch.

"What an arm," he exclaimed, after Faith successfully took the event. "Congratulations."

"Thank you," she said. Then the happiness faded from Faith's face. Coming across the frozen harbour was Luke Yates on a yellow snowmobile. "That guy," she said. "He is trouble."

"You bet he is," Tom agreed. "In fact, Yates could easily be . . . "

Tom slammed his mouth shut. *Fool* he thought to himself—maybe Faith didn't know about Sam's link to CSIS. He'd almost released confidential information!

Faith's beautiful eyes were studying his face. "Yates could possibly be what?"

"Nothing," Tom mumbled.

Faith said nothing more. They both watched Luke Yates walking through the crowd, talking to people and waving around a wad of money. "He's desperate for a hunting tag," Tom remarked.

"He won't get one," Faith said.

Luke Yates approached them. "Listen, kid, what about that contract killer? Give me some information, okay? I could sell that story, and make big money. I'll give you a cut."

"No comment," Tom replied.

Faith said nothing. Her eyes darted between their faces.

Yates studied Tom through narrow eyes. "If you change your mind, contact me at the Amundsen. I'm offering good money."

Climbing on the snowmobile, he roared across the harbour. "He's heading for the *Netsilik*," Tom said. "Listen, Faith, may I borrow your Safari?"

"Sure thing."

Powering up the machine, Tom followed Luke Yates at a safe distance. He thought the man might be planning to hide something in the *Netsilik*, but Yates passed the snowed-in boat without stopping. Roaring up a hill, the yellow snowmobile disappeared over the crest.

Tom slowed his machine, and glanced back at the distant crowd. Hoping Faith didn't need her Safari in a hurry, he continued up the hill.

From the crest, Tom saw Luke Yates in the distance. He was travelling fast, heading away from town. Staying a good distance behind, Tom followed Yates until he reached the dump.

Leaving his snowmobile in hiding, Tom crept to the top of a hill. Using his binoculars, he watched Yates stare at the snow-covered mounds of rubbish. For a long time the man stood without moving; then he seemed to make a decision.

Yates walked to an abandoned snowmobile. The windshield was missing, and it was thick with snow. Suddenly Yates bent forward. His body blocked Tom's view but he seemed to reach for something, then put it inside his parka. After that, the man walked rapidly back to his snowmobile.

With a big smile on his face, Luke Yates headed for town.

* * *

Tom roared back to the harbour, where events were wrapping up. "Sorry I took off with your machine," he said to Faith.

"You followed that guy?"

Tom nodded.

"Why?"

Tom avoided Faith's eyes. "It was just—something to do."

Saying goodbye, Tom hurried to the hotel. Inside the dining room, Sam was sitting alone with a coffee. Joining him, Tom described the mysterious trip to the dump by Luke Yates.

Sam listened intently. "That's really valuable information." He stood up. "I'll check it out immediately. Excellent work, Tom!"

Glowing with pleasure, Tom walked home with the snow squeaking underfoot. When the Mountie returned, Tom went outside with him to feed Junior's dogs. The air was intensely cold. The snow was blue, and so was the sky. The sun was small in the west, glowing with an orange light.

Seeing their food approach, the huskies pawed the snow and strained against their long leads. Their ears pointed forward, their bushy tails straight up. "Each has a personality," the Mountie said, tossing frozen char to the huskies, who snatched it from the air. "Aqnaq is a hard worker. Kajuq is playful and Kumaq is lovable, but they are not good pullers."

The food was gone within moments. "I'm very happy here," Tom said, photographing the huskies from a safe distance.

"You are a welcome guest, Tom. Ah, here is my son."

Junior had approached from behind, moving silently. Tom was startled by his sudden appearance, but managed a smile. "*Qanuritpit*, Junior. *Hila unaituq*."

"It sure is cold! In February, we hit 80 below with the wind chill. I was alone on the land, but I survived. I love it out there."

"Do people ever get lost?"

"Many have died, Tom. Inuit, and people from elsewhere. One recent summer, three students from Japan drowned during a canoe expedition. The people of Cambridge Bay warned them of an approaching storm, but they journeyed on. Nothing was found except a Seiko watch on a severed arm."

"Wow—I'll put that in my notebook for sure. Have you ever seen a polar bear?"

"Yes. I have hunted them."

"That doesn't seem right."

"This land is our farm," Junior replied. "It is how we feed our people. You've seen the price of food from the south? After I kill an animal, I kneel to thank it, for the gift of nourishment. I pour water in the animal's mouth, to ease its journey to the spirit world."

The Mountie nodded solemnly. "Some of our hunters sell their game, to buy food for their families. These days, unhappily, people in Europe refuse to purchase anything that has been hunted. As a result, many people are hungry."

"We do not kill for trophies," Junior said quietly. "It would be against our beliefs."

"That guy Yates bugs me," Tom said. "I'm glad he hasn't found a polar bear tag."

"I've got one," Junior said, "but he can't have it."

The Mountie looked at his son with worried eyes. "Be cautious around that man. He carries evil in his soul."

"Don't worry, Father. He will not harm me."

* * *

After a supper of delicious Arctic char, radio bingo was played by those in the community who had CBs. Tom listened to the game for a while, then picked up the family scrapbook and flipped through it. One part was devoted to Junior's career in the army, where his unit had received special training on bomb disposal and demolitions. Tom also saw several pictures of Faith and Junior together.

Later in the evening, he was alone in the house when the CB radio spluttered out his name. *Tom Austen*, said a man's voice. *Report to the arena immediately*.

Surprised, Tom stared at the radio, but the message wasn't repeated. After a moment's thought, he wrote on a piece of paper ARTICLES RENTED END-LESSLY NEVER ARRIVE. "That's good backup," he said to himself, leaving the note on the table, "just in case I don't return. Rachel will figure it out."

Outside, Tom covered his cheeks and nose with his caribou mitts, worried about frostbite. The moon was huge in the black sky as he walked quickly through the bitter cold until he saw the arena ahead.

Lots of people were inside, watching fast-paced hockey. Tom walked slowly around, searching the faces. Had the message come from Sam? There was no sign of him, or Faith.

During a break in the hockey action, a woman's voice announced over the loudspeakers, "Message for Tom Austen at the concession stand."

When Tom reached the stand, he was handed an envelope. "This just arrived for you," said the friendly woman behind the counter.

Amundsen Hotel was printed in a corner of the envelope. "Who brought this?" Tom asked, tearing it open.

"The taxi driver. Someone paid him to drive it over."

Inside the envelope was a slip of paper. On it were the words, *Report to the cemetery. Tell no one.*

Quickly, Tom scribbled a note that read CALIFORNIA ELEPHANTS MEMORIZE ENTIRE TUNES ENDLESSLY ROWING YACHTS. "Please keep this," he asked the woman behind the counter. "Just in case I disappear."

She smiled. "Nobody disappears in Gjoa. This isn't the big city, like on TV."

Tom waved goodbye to her, and stepped into the empty night.

* * *

Burrowed down in his caribou parka, Tom walked resolutely toward the cemetery. His heart thumped heavily. Above, the black sky was lustrous with stars, but Tom couldn't pay attention. Who had sent the messages?

The cemetery was in the middle of town, near the huge fuel storage tank. A large white cross was surrounded by snow. In its shadow was a man. He waved Tom forward. It was Luke Yates.

The writer's head was bare, and his coat was open at the throat. "Thanks for coming, kid. I don't want anyone to know about this meeting—that's why the messages."

Tom kept his distance from Yates. "What's going on?"

"First, tell me about the hit man. Who's your suspect?"

Tom stepped back a pace, ready to leave. "I can't tell you anything about that. Sorry."

"I'll give you cash, up front." Yates patted his pocket. "I've got plenty."

Tom turned to go. "No, thanks."

"Wait, kid!" Yates stepped forward, out of the shadow of the cross. "One more thing, and for this I'm offering *real* money. Break into the Mountie's computer, and get me the names of people in town with a polar bear tag."

"Not a chance."

Yates pulled money out of his pocket. "Everyone's greedy," he said. "Here, take some."

Tom walked away. His back felt vulnerable, but instead of bullets, Luke Yates hurled insults. "You stupid little creep. Here's your chance, get some money! Stop playing the hero, you're just a nothing."

Rachel came running out of the night. "Tom! Are you okay?"

"Sure," he replied. "I'm fine."

From the cemetery, Luke Yates yelled, "Eskimo lover!"

"What's his problem?" Rachel asked.

"He just failed to bribe me." As they began walking home, Tom smiled. "You figured out my messages?"

"Sure—it was easy. I dropped by the Mountie's to say hi, and found your code. But what's going on?"

Tom could only shrug his shoulders and say, "Nothing much." He longed to discuss the case with Rachel, but he was sworn to secrecy. He could tell no one that a contract killer might be in Gjoa Haven, ready to strike again.

10

The next morning, Tom was awake early. The class would be overnighting in igloos, and he was both excited and apprehensive.

The students gathered outside the school with their gear. Everyone was dressed for ultimate cold. "Guess what I'm wearing," Rebecca Bowden said to Tom. "Three pairs of socks, caribou socks, liners, *kamiks*, tights, jeans, snowpants, caribou pants, T-shirt, flannel pj top, sweater, parka, caribou parka, gloves, caribou mitts, scarf, and sunglasses. And I am extremely, extremely hot."

Moses approached with his arm around Dietmar's shoulders. "Your buddy is becoming a real Inuk. Last night, he ate raw caribou with our family."

"It was okay stuff," Dietmar told Tom, "much better than that earthworm soup you served me in the Kootenays."

"That was just mushroom soup."

"So you claim, Austen, but I'll never believe you."

The teens helped the adults pack their gear on *komatiks* covered with caribou skins, then climbed on for the ride. Towed by snowmobiles, the big sleds bumped through town and entered the wilderness. The sky was clear above the frozen sea, with a yellow sun small in the south. Tom wore wolf-skin mitts against the wind, and thick wool across his face.

"This land is a good one," Moses said, as the caravan picked up speed.

"It sure is big," Tom replied, watching the sunlight reflect from a circle of ice. His teeth rattled together each time the *komatik* slammed over another wind-formed ridge.

"You could travel from here to Asia," Moses said, "and never cross a road."

"That would be a lonely journey."

"Junior loves it out here. This is his natural home, I think, far from anyone."

Eventually, they were waved to a stop by the leader of the expedition. "He has seen something," Moses whispered. "Look, there! Musk-oxen. We call them *oominqmaq*, meaning the animal with skin like a beard."

Their big bodies were covered with brown fur. Tom counted six adults, protectively encircling a young calf. The musk-oxen raised their shaggy heads to study the intruders, then suddenly broke and ran. Clouds of snow swirled from their hooves.

"Wow," Tom exclaimed. "Seeing them makes me feel like a time traveller! Musk-oxen have lived here *forever*."

As Tom put away his camera, Moses smiled. "You'll have lots of pictures of *oominqmaq*. I stopped counting after the first ten."

"I guess I got carried away."

Although Tom hoped to see a polar bear, they encountered no more animals on the journey to the igloos that had been constructed at the ice-fishing site. Groaning, Tom stood up from the *komatik*. "What a ride—I ache all over." Grabbing his gear, he dragged it into the nearest igloo. Light seeped between the blocks, shining on the snow where he would sleep that night.

Tom touched the chocolate bar in his pack, looking forward to a treat. Outside the igloo, he and the others kept warm by rolling down a hill and then playing Arctic Games. Someone found a harpoon inside an igloo, and they tried tossing it. "Are these permanent igloos?" Tom asked Moses.

He nodded. "There are supplies left here, for travellers, and a short-wave radio in case anyone needs help. I'll show you."

An aerial dangled from a pole near the biggest igloo. Inside, the radio crackled and spluttered. "There's another radio at the Amundsen Hotel," Moses explained.

They rode snowmobiles and played soccer and tried ice fishing, but caught only ice. When Tom unwrapped his chocolate bar, it was frozen, but he still ate it. He was very hungry. As the sky grew dark, the wind picked up, driving some people into igloos while others continued to play in the snow.

Finally, Tom went inside. Warmth came from a Coleman stove, which was vented through a small opening in the domed roof. He sat down, warming his hands. "I'm learning so much in the Arctic. I'll never be the same."

"Promises, promises," Dietmar responded.

"You know something amazing? The pattern of each snowflake is unique—no two are the same."

"Prove it."

Moses grinned. "You two are a laugh."

"Listen to the wind," Tom said, tilting his head.

An elder taught them a traditional string game called *ayarak*, then prepared musk-oxen stew on the stove. "It tastes like steak," Mr. Plantinga said, when the food was served. "You kids eat up, okay? Your bodies burn a lot of energy keeping warm."

"I'm glad I've eaten musk-oxen," Desmond Chan commented, "just to say I did." They celebrated his birthday with a frozen cake, then went outside to play under the stars. The igloos glowed with light, beautiful in the darkness.

Tom walked a short distance into the wilderness, and stood looking at the radiant stars. He was at peace with the world.

* * *

In the middle of the night, Tom awoke. The stove was out, and his toque had fallen off. His hair had frozen! For a moment, this seemed important, and then he drifted back into a dream in which a polar bear bounded across the dark night, pursued by Luke Yates. Tom stirred in his sleep, murmuring in fear.

With morning came the smell of tea brewing. Someone had put frozen pop beside the stove to thaw, but the bottle had exploded and pop was now frozen across the wall. Tom went outside to the biffy—a separate small igloo—and then hurried back for a breakfast of oatmeal and Mr. Noodles.

After breaking camp, they headed for Gjoa Haven. As the *komatik* bumped along the streets to the school, Tom felt good. "The sled dog race is this afternoon," Rachel said. "Come with us, okay?"

After agreeing on a time to meet, Tom hurried to the hotel. Fortunately, Sam wasn't busy and had time to talk. "I've had some feedback from CSIS headquarters," he told Tom. "Luke Yates has a criminal record for violence. We're doing further checks, and I'm expecting an arrest very soon."

"Excellent," Tom exclaimed. "Listen, have you talked to Dad lately?"

"I spoke to your parents an hour ago. They miss you, and send their love. Liz was still asleep—she went dancing last night with someone named Zoltan. Is that her boyfriend?"

Tom nodded.

"Anyway," Sam continued, "there's interesting news. Your Mom will be flying to Ottawa to join a television panel. A group of citizens will be debating U-SAC with the Prime Minister."

"Great!"

Sam handed him a daily newspaper from Edmonton. "This arrived on today's plane. The debate is a big story across the country." Photos of the panel members were on the front page. Tom's mother looked wonderful, and he glowed with pride. "The newspaper says the debate is tomorrow. I can't wait."

Tom described the meeting at the cemetery. "Yates is a weird guy."

Sam nodded. "Therefore, Tom, keep clear of him. Your parents say you're adventurous and a risk-taker. Not on my turf, okay?"

"Sure," Tom said, disappointed. "I understand. This is a matter for professionals, right? Amateurs need not apply."

"Don't be blue," Sam said, smiling. "Tell you what—the moment something breaks, I'll contact you. Maybe I'll need help in some way."

"Fabulous! That would be great."

* * *

Back at the house, Tom ate lunch while telling the family about his trip on the land. Then he left for the dog team races. "I hear Junior's a competitor," he called from the door to the Mountie's wife. "I'll be cheering for him!"

She waved goodbye from the kitchen window as Tom walked toward the ice with Dietmar and the twins. Dogs were howling all over town. "They're lonely," Moses explained. "Only the best pullers are chosen for the race. The others stay home."

"It's already started?"

"The teams left two hours ago. They travel out eleven kilometers, then head back to Gjoa."

"I'd get lost. There aren't any highway signs."

"Or billboards," Dietmar laughed.

"I see Luke Yates—I wonder why he's here?"

A crowd of all ages had arrived by snowmobile and on foot. The sunny air was festive with laughter and the sound of children playing. The only sullen face belonged to Yates, who sat on a yellow Ski-Doo away from everyone. In the distance, at the top of the hill, the fuel storage tank dominated the community. Tom photographed a boy playing with his husky pup, then chatted with the local teachers.

"The women raced this morning," Frieda said, "and there was a big crowd to cheer them home. People here celebrate each other so wonderfully."

"I'm glad you think so." Laser, the gym teacher, smiled. "I hope you and Constance will stay forever in our community."

"I certainly will," Constance replied. She bounced a baby in her arms; her husband, a handsome Inuk, was shooting the scene with his video camera. "This little fellow would miss his extended family."

"Everyone here has such respect for the elders," Tom said. "I like that."

"The old have overcome many difficulties," Laser commented. "Their wisdom helps us all."

A shout went up, and faces turned to the horizon. Clapping began as a tiny speck grew into an approaching shape, and then became a figure in a caribou parka urging on his dogs. "It's Junior," Moses cried. "Come on!"

The excited crowd ran forward to surround the victor. Junior was lifted high on his *komatik* as people cheered. Then he ran with the crowd to greet the next sled.

As Tom photographed Junior's huskies rolling in the snow, he saw Luke Yates climb off the Ski-Doo.

Approaching Junior, Yates pointed a finger in the other man's face. "I just found out. You've got a hunting tag. I want it."

"My tag is not for sale."

The crowd fell silent. Yates stepped closer to Junior. "*I want that tag*. Turn it over, or there'll be big trouble. For you—and your family. Got that?"

Junior said nothing.

"Say something," Yates yelled. "You stupid Eskimo!"

When Junior remained silent, Yates stormed to the Ski-Doo and powered it up. "I won't forget you," he shouted at Junior.

Tom watched the snowmobile roar away. "I wish that guy would leave town."

"He's an ugly *kabloona* for sure," Frieda observed. "I think he's a secret boozer. I smelled alcohol when he was shopping at the Northern."

"Junior's a big guy—I thought he'd plant a fist on Yates. Anyone else would have lost it by now."

"No chance," Laser said. "My people value emotional control. It's the ultimate maturity."

* * *

"Junior will snap eventually," Tom predicted, as he walked home later with Rachel.

"Know what happened in Winnipeg?" she said. "Those guys happened to be shopping in the same store, and Yates told the manager Junior was a shoplifter. Junior was kicked out."

"What a creep."

For hours Tom simmered, thinking about Luke

Yates's cruelty. He was still troubled as he walked to the community hall that night with his friends. The black air was crisp; kids played outside on their bikes, and snowmobiles buzzed past.

"It's so cold tonight," Dietmar said. "Even the marrow of my bones is frozen."

Moses laughed. "Is that why you're holding hands with my sister? To keep warm?"

Outside the community hall, they talked to Junior, who'd arrived on a yellow Safari. "This is Faith's machine," he explained, "but she's busy tonight." Inside, people sat facing a large floor. All ages were present for the drum dance in honour of the visitors. People in parkas and jeans sat around the walls, many holding babies; children chased each other everywhere.

Tom and his friends found chairs beside the teachers. In front of them, an older man in a baseball cap and parka was circling while pounding a large drum. On the stage, a woman chanted a song in Inuktitut.

Laser leaned toward Tom. "My people have always celebrated with feasts and drum dancing. It was our entertainment. These days, sadly, video games and satellite TV amuse the young. Few of them dance with the drum."

Finished, the old man walked to Tom and offered him the drum. Tom's face flared red; everyone was staring. He sat frozen until the man walked away. Someone else took the drum, and began dancing as the woman chanted.

Dietmar chuckled. "Way to be, Austen."

"I couldn't move, I couldn't think. Why did he do that?"

Laser smiled. "He honours you, Tom. The people know you are interested in how we live. They have seen you making notes. But don't worry—few *kabloonas* participate in our culture."

As others took a turn with the drum, Tom fidgeted. Was it too late to dance? Did he have the courage? Then, an outside door banged open, and cold air blew in. As it met the warmth in the community hall, the air turned into fog that billowed across the floor.

Tom glanced toward the open door, and his heart jumped. Standing there was Luke Yates, reeling back and forth. He was obviously drunk.

* * *

Yates stumbled onto the floor. "Stupid . . . Eskimos. I want . . ." He swayed, his red eyes searching the faces. "I want . . . *you*!"

Yates pointed at Junior, who sat near the stage. The singer had stopped her chant, and was looking at Yates with impassive eyes. The dancer laid down the drum and returned to his seat.

"*You* . . ." Yates weaved toward Junior. "Deny me . . . will you? I want a big white . . . Why don't you . . . ? I want . . ."

Pulling out a bottle of rum, Yates finished it off. After wiping his mouth, he threw the bottle against a wall. It shattered, and glass rained down.

The children had stopped their play. All eyes watched Yates.

"*Morons* . . . you're all morons . . . you're . . ."

Yates lurched toward the door.

"I hate . . . I hate . . . you . . ."

Then he was gone. For a moment, there was total silence, followed by the excited babbling of the southern teens. Tom looked at Junior, and then at the people in their colourful parkas. Sorrow was in their eyes.

Standing up, Tom walked on shaking legs toward the drum. Applause rang out from all sides. He saw faces suddenly grinning. The drum was decorated with the face of an Inuk; Tom picked it up, aware of his pulsating heart.

As the chant began from the stage, Tom danced. He felt awkward at first, pounding the drum, but soon his feet were moving faster and faster. When the song ended, he returned to his seat, grinning at the applause.

"Where's Junior?" he asked Mr. Cousins.

"He left." The teacher took a photo of the next dancer, and then said, "I feel sorry for that big guy, the way Yates insults his people. Junior must be steaming inside." He shook his head. "You've got to admire that Inuit self-control."

Tom stood up. "I think I'll head off, sir. Tomorrow I'm going on the land with the Mountie. We'll be out two nights."

"You're a lucky guy, Tom. I guess it's your Irish roots. Have fun, and stay out of trouble."

Outside the community hall, Tom looked for signs of Junior, but he was gone. Passing the hotel, he saw Luke Yates at the front desk, reading a message slip. Faith sat behind the desk, watching him.

Yates left the hotel. Keeping well behind, Tom followed him to the harbour. From the shelter of a house, he watched through his binoculars as Yates crossed the snow. He was walking toward the *Netsilik*.

Suddenly, Tom dashed from hiding and yelled, "Watch out!" Startled by the cry, Luke Yates turned to stare at him. "Run," Tom shouted. He pointed at the boat. "It's going to explode!"

* * *

Luke Yates stared at the *Netsilik*. Sparks were racing across the snow-bound deck of the boat. "It's a fuse," Tom yelled at Yates. "Run!"

The man took off fast. As he did, a massive explosion shook the night. The roof of the *Netsilik* blew straight up into the sky, and wood flew in every direction. Black smoke and orange flames billowed from the doomed vessel while the town echoed with the sound of the blast.

Knocked to the ground, Luke Yates lay motionless. Then he got slowly up, and staggered to Tom's side. He smelled of rum. "You saved my life, kid! I'd have been blown up."

"Why are you here?"

"I got a message about a hunting tag for sale. It said to meet at the boat. I figured the person didn't want to be seen."

"Was the message signed?"

Yates shook his head. "Anyway, kid, what's going on? Why are you here? Were you following me?"

"I was heading home," Tom replied. "It's lucky for you I saw the danger. Someone tried to kill you, and I'm not surprised. You've insulted everyone in town."

"So what?" Luke Yates spat on the ground. "They can't stop me, even with a bomb. I'll get a tag, and I'll kill a polar bear."

A large crowd quickly gathered to watch the remains

of the *Netsilik* burn. After being questioned by the Mountie, Tom walked to the hotel. But he was unable to report in person to Sam, who was not feeling well. Faith was working the desk for him, so Tom ripped a page from his notebook and wrote a description of the night's events.

"Please give this to Sam," he said, sealing his report inside an Amundsen Hotel envelope. "ASAP."

"Huh?"

"As soon as possible."

"What is it?"

Tom shrugged. "Just something. But it's private."

Faith looked at the envelope, then at Tom. "Okay," she said. "Sam's sleeping now, but he'll get this in the morning. I promise."

The moment Tom left the hotel, the lights went off. The lobby was plunged into darkness. He squinted his eyes, trying to see Faith. But she had disappeared.

11

In the morning, Tom went with Dietmar and the twins to the Anglican church. It was a small wooden building with a bell tower. Snowmobiles were parked outside, and the minister stood by the door greeting his congregation.

Many people sat inside in their beautiful parkas. They smiled a welcome as Tom and his friends joined other teens from Winnipeg. Above the altar was a large tapestry displaying the syllabics of Inuktitut.

"Have you wondered about my name?" Moses whispered to Tom. "It was chosen from the Bible by my parents. It is a good name."

A choir enthusiastically led the singing of a hymn, prayers were said in Inuktitut, and the minister gave his sermon. Tom didn't understand the words, but was moved by the tears that rolled down the man's face.

"He's talking about the future," Rachel whispered. "He hopes the visit of such fine young people will bring us all closer together. Let us forget the time of fear, when the southerners controlled our lives. Instead, let us build our culture, and our faith."

Tara and Nicole, from Tom's class, concluded the service by singing an anthem, and everyone hugged goodbye at the door. The wind had picked up, whipping the fur that fringed Tom's parka hood.

"The world's coldest breezes," a woman grinned, climbing on to her snowmobile. As she buzzed away into the blinding white landscape, Tom put on his sunglasses. "One hour until the U-SAC debate," he exclaimed to his friends. "Let's watch it together, at the Mountie's."

Soon they were gathered in front of the TV, clutching mugs of tea. The room was packed and everyone cheered when Mrs. Austen was shown, seated at a table beside five other citizens. Across from them were the Prime Minister and his advisers.

"Mom looks nervous." Tom smiled. "It's her first brush with fame."

"Look at that red hair," said the Mountie's wife. "Just like her son."

"Mom's a member of Lawyers for Social Responsibility. Maybe that's why she was chosen for this panel."

"Is she against U-SAC?"

Tom laughed. "I'll say! It's all we hear about."

Prime Minister Dunbar was a natural for television. The colour of his eyes was enhanced by the blue shirt he wore with a stylish suit. He spoke with confidence about the merits of U-SAC in an opening statement, then handled the panel's questions with skill. The studio audience applauded him enthusiastically.

Following the debate, the TV commentator said, "James Dunbar has earned the trust of Canadians. People seem prepared to follow this Prime Minister anywhere, even into union with the United States. The PM's performance tonight was brilliant, and our early polling indicates U-SAC has now gained huge support."

Tom groaned. He believed the Prime Minister's scheme could be stopped, but only if the micro-cassette were found.

"I'm impressed with Judith Austen," said the commentator. "This fiery criminal lawyer from Winnipeg is well spoken, and a natural leader."

"Yes, Mom!"

"The debate's strongest moment came when she clashed with the PM on the subject of handguns. Let's watch it again."

The commentator looked at a screen. On it, Tom's mother was arguing with the Prime Minister. "The fact is," she said, "citizens of the United States have the constitutional right to bear arms, which means the right to defend themselves with guns. Will the people of U-SAC *all* have this right? Will Canadians be able to purchase handguns at a corner store?"

The Prime Minister's soothing reply was cut off by an angry Mrs. Austen. "Don't pretend the Americans will change their constitution to suit us! We're the little country, so they'll make the rules."

"True, but . . ."

"If your referendum wins, and Canada joins the States, will our citizens have the constitutional right to purchase handguns? Please answer my question!"

Prime Minister Dunbar whispered with an adviser. Then he said, "My own father died of a gunshot wound, Mrs. Austen. In your hometown, in fact." He looked directly at the audience. "I know the pain. I know the suffering. I will protect our citizens, in every way I can."

The audience burst into huge applause. Some rose to their feet, clapping and smiling.

Facing the camera, the commentator held up a copy of *People* magazine. Prime Minister Dunbar was on the cover, looking good. "With this kind of success," she said, "our PM is becoming a big name in Washington. Some day, he could be the first president of U-SAC."

* * *

Outside the house, the Mountie and Tom roped their gear onto a *komatik*. Whipped up by the wind, snow blew around them. "Your mother is wise," the Mountie said quietly. "Who controls the land, controls the future. If the referendum passes, Americans will decide all matters for us. My people have experience of losing control to *kabloonas*. We were powerless, so our needs were ignored."

Tom stopped his work to listen. "Weren't you angry about it? Didn't you want to punch someone?"

The Mountie shook his head. "Violence leads only to more violence. That is how wars begin, bringing terrible pain."

"But don't you ever get upset about things?"

"Of course." The Mountie smiled. "I feel anger, then I let it go. I know there is good and bad in each person. No one is perfect, so I forgive. In this way, my heart is peaceful."

The Mountie studied the wind-swept landscape. "This land of ours is a good one, Tom. In Canada, people live in harmony. We show the world the meaning of peace. If our country disappears, it will be lamented. Just like the lost civilization of Atlantis, Canada will never return."

"I won't let that happen!"

"Good for you. Our country needs kind and caring leaders. We must work together, the young and the old, to cherish our land, and protect it. Canada was a gift to us at birth, and we must pass this benefaction on safely to future generations."

* * *

Powering up his black SnowCat, the Mountie waved goodbye to the little kids at the window. Tom smiled at them. Seated behind the Mountie, he was warm inside a caribou parka and wolf-skin leggings.

As they bounced through town, various people called hello. Faith and Junior were outside the hotel speaking together with great intensity. Neither paid attention to the Mountie's snowmobile as it passed by. Watching over his shoulder, Tom saw Junior put his arms around Faith.

He glanced at the Mountie, wondering if he'd seen. But the man was concentrating on the horizon as they left town. Banging over drift after drift, the big machine roared across the white landscape. At last they stopped for a tea break, and Tom was able to stretch his legs.

"What's happening about that explosion?" he asked.

"An RCMP expert is arriving tomorrow from Yellowknife to assist in the investigation. Like you, I think it was a bomb. Unfortunately, this means our trip on the land will be shorter."

"There must be dozens of suspects. Everyone dislikes Yates."

"I met with him this morning," the Mountie said. "He refuses to leave Gjoa Haven. Mr. Yates tells me he's investigating a story."

"About what?"

"He did not say." The Mountie cut strips of raw caribou with his *ulu*. "Mr. Yates was drinking last night, which is against the law. Gjoa Haven is a dry town. I am considering action against him."

"What's a dry town?"

"No alcohol allowed. The people have voted for this. Many of the settlements are dry towns. We do not have the same problem with suicides as those settlements where alcohol is allowed."

Eating the meat, Tom began to sweat. "I feel hot," he said. "As if I've got a furnace burning inside."

"Your body is burning energy to keep warm." Standing up, the Mountie pointed. "Look, Tom. Caribou."

The animals were some distance away. Their heads were bent forward to the snow. "They're like reindeer," Tom said. "What are they eating?"

"Mosses and lichens hidden beneath the snow. The

covering is not deep—we actually get very little snow here."

"Do you have blizzards?"

The Mountie nodded. "High winds pick up the snow, and swirl it around. Such a ground blizzard can last for days. Many hunters have died. When someone is lost on the land, people in town barely sleep. Inuit and *kabloona*, we join together as a family, waiting for news. We share our prayers for the missing person, and we share the joy of a cherished friend's safe return. Or, we share our sorrow, if the worst has happened."

Tom thought of Franklin's men, staggering through this same wilderness until they died. He felt lonely. "I've heard that those British sailors became cannibals. Yuck, what a thought. I'd rather be eaten by a polar bear."

"Not me, thank you. Polar bears are ferocious. They run very fast, and we cannot escape up a tree."

As the Mountie packed their gear, Tom looked at the distant horizon. The weak afternoon sun shone above the frozen sea. "It's so silent out here."

The man smiled. "No car alarms. Your father would like that."

"You're right—they're his pet peeve." Tom took a photo of the desolate beauty. "The sun never shines in winter, eh? What's that like?"

"People kind of hibernate. They slow down, and sleep a lot. It is a good feeling to see the sun again."

"What about summer? I hear you get eternal sunshine."

"Everyone is busy. At three a.m. the sun is bright. But we have no grass, only sand. It blows around, and bothers the eyes. I welcome the return of snow."

"Has your face ever been frozen?"

"Yes, and it was not pleasant. It felt like pliers, pinching my skin."

Travelling on, they reached the igloos at the ice-fishing site as the sky grew dark. Tom helped drag their gear into the biggest igloo, then watched the Mountie flick the short-wave radio's *on* switch.

"I like staying connected to the outside world," he explained. "Later tonight, we'll call Sam at the hotel. Just to say hello."

"Maybe tomorrow we can toss the harpoon, and do some ice fishing. Last time, the harpoon was kept in this igloo. I wonder where it's gone?"

The warmth of the Coleman stove made the igloo cosy as the Mountie cut caribou meat and dropped it into a boiling pot.

"I feel good," Tom said to the Mountie while writing in his notebook. "Earlier, I was kind of freaked. I got scared of the wilderness, or something. It was like a feeling of doom."

The Mountie nodded. "It gets lonely out here. But the spirits of my ancestors journey with us." He smiled gently at Tom. "You have eaten caribou with my family. Now you are a part of us."

Tom was very pleased. "Thank you," he said.

"Come outside. We will search for the Great Bear."

The black night was filled with stars. Moonlight glowed on the snow, which was silver, like a desert of the night. "Look directly above, Tom. There you see Ursa Major. The Greeks named this region *Arktikós*, meaning the land of the Great Bear." For long moments he was silent. "I am part of all that surrounds me—

every living thing. In the jungles, in the deserts, in the cities, the people are my people. Others may live far away, but we share this world. I protect it, for them and for future generations. We must owe the young no apology."

He raised a hand. "Listen."

Tom strained his ears, but heard nothing. "What is it?"

"Someone is coming."

The Mountie was motionless, listening intently. Then Tom heard the sound, a distant buzzing. It grew louder as the bouncing headlight of a snowmobile appeared. "It's Luke Yates," Tom warned the Mountie. "Be careful."

The Ski-Doo roared to a stop. Throwing back his parka hood, Yates stared at the Mountie. "Well, cop? Where is it?"

"What do you mean, sir?"

"Don't mess with me, mister. Where's that hunting tag? I came miles into this emptiness to get it."

"Would you explain, please?"

"You sent a message, saying to meet here. Saying you'd found a tag for me. I fly home in two days, so stop wasting time. Give me the tag."

"I did not send a message, sir. I have nothing for you."

For a moment, Yates could only stare. His mouth moved, but no words came out. The night was electric with tension. Then, suddenly, he swore furiously, and brandished his fist.

"This is your fault!"

The Mountie said nothing.

"You lousy, no-good Eskimo. You make my life a misery. You and your smug rules! My hunting trip cost big money, and I haven't killed anything." Yates stormed away, then swung around and advanced again on the Mountie. His face was red with fury.

"I should get my gun, and shoot *you*." Foul words poured from his mouth. "I hate this place," Yates screamed, "and I hate *you*!"

The Mountie showed no emotion, but Tom's heart was beating fast. Anything could happen! Desperate for help, he remembered the ham radio and ran to the igloo.

Slithering inside, he grabbed the microphone. "Hello, hotel! Sam, help us! Get someone here—the Mountie's in danger, and . . . "

A hideous cry sounded from the night. Dropping the microphone, Tom crawled out of the igloo to a terrible sight. Under the glow of the moon, a man lay face down in the snow.

Quivering in his back was a harpoon.

12

Before Tom could react, the roar of a snowmobile split the silence. Scrambling to his feet, he ran toward the sound. Tom was in time to see the bouncing lights of a snowmobile escaping into the night. The rider was a dark shape, leaning over the controls.

The dead man's arms were spread wide in the snow. Kneeling over him was the Mountie. "What happened?" Tom cried. "Is that Yates—*dead*?"

The Mountie nodded. "Yates was walking to his snowmobile. A harpoon came from the darkness, and took him down." He stood up from examining the body. "The harpoon was thrown from behind our igloo. The killer must have hidden there, listening to every word we said."

Frost was whitening the dead man's hair. "I wonder what he'll find in the next life," Tom said.

"Perhaps forgiveness. His was a troubled soul."

The Mountie used Tom's camera to photograph the scene, then made extensive notes as they sipped tea and ate caribou. He tried to reach Gjoa Haven on the ham radio, but failed. "There must be a wire loose."

"I probably wrecked something, trying to reach Sam for help." Tom looked around at the darkness. "I had a look at the harpoon. It's the same one as our first trip here."

"Thank you for that information," the Mountie said, making a note. Using ropes, he secured the murder weapon and the victim to the *komatik*. "You take my SnowCat," he said to Tom. "I will follow on the dead man's Ski-Doo."

Although shaken by the death of Luke Yates, Tom liked being at the controls of the big machine with the RCMP crest on its side. His head whirled with thoughts and theories about Yates, and he was anxious to see Sam. Reaching town, he followed the Mountie to the RCMP office. Almost immediately, people came running. Rachel was among them.

"What happened?" she asked breathlessly. Moses began filming the scene with his video camera as a crowd quickly gathered. "Is that *Yates*?"

The Mountie approached. "I will take the dead man to the morgue at the nursing station. Tom, the hour is late. Try to sleep, and in the morning I will take your formal statement about the murder."

As he rode away on the snowmobile, Moses ran behind with his camera. "Your brother's getting some good stuff." Tom smiled at Rachel. "He's got a future in TV." He told her about the night's events.

"Any idea who escaped on the snowmobile?"

Tom shook his head. "It was yellow, but that's a popular colour for those machines. The person was just a dark shape. It could have been anyone." He sighed unhappily. "With Yates dead, I'll never find that micro-cassette."

"What do you mean?"

"Sorry, Rachel, I can't reveal too much. I've been looking in Gjoa for a micro-cassette hidden in a boat. But all the boats are swamped with snow, or blown up."

"Hey," Rachel exclaimed. "I know another boat!"

"You do?"

"Yes, in the museum."

"What kind—big, small?"

"Come on," Rachel cried. "I'll show you!"

* * *

Minutes later, they reached the town hall. It was in darkness. All around, snow glistened under the bright moon. Like other places in Gjoa, the door wasn't locked. Stepping inside, Rachel flicked on a pencil flashlight. The tiny beam of light moved slowly up a staircase to a wide hallway. It glittered against the glass of a large display cabinet. Above it hung a harpoon and a kayak; inside the case was caribou clothing and an ancient photograph of long-ago elders.

A map on the wall traced the routes of Franklin and other famous Arctic explorers. Nearby were volleyball trophies, and a display of T-shirts and baseball caps with the words *The Hamlet of Gjoa Haven*.

"You think the micro's in that kayak?" Tom whispered.

"No." Putting a finger to her lips, Rachel led Tom up the stairs. The flashlight beam led them to the display cabinet. Inside was a scale-model of an old-fashioned fishing boat with full sails.

"That is the boat I mean," Rachel whispered. "It is a scale model of Amundsen's boat, the *Gjoa*."

Rachel stopped speaking, and her light snapped out. "What was that sound?"

"I didn't hear anything."

"Sssh." Rachel was motionless. "Tom, there is someone in this building. I hear movement."

Tom pushed back his parka hood. Now he could hear it, a faint scuffling sound. Crouching beside Rachel, he tried to see through the darkness.

A door handle squealed.

Then he heard feet, moving stealthily through the darkness.

"Got you," Rachel yelled, flicking on the flashlight. "Don't move!" The beam jumped through the darkness to show Faith, her mouth open in an *ooooh* of surprise.

"Faith," Rachel cried. "What are you doing here?"

"I was walking home and saw a flashlight inside. I wanted to make sure my cleaning materials weren't being tampered with, so I slipped in the back door. I wasn't taking any chances." She stared at them. "Now tell me—what are *you* doing here?"

Quickly, Tom explained about the death of Yates. When he was finished, Faith frowned. "But why are you here?" she demanded.

"I'm looking for a micro-cassette, and it may be hidden in the model of the Gjoa. That's all I can say."

Faith studied his face. "Okay," she said at last, "let's test your theory." Using her key, Faith opened the display cabinet and lifted out the green and yellow model. "The deck is hinged. Open it, Tom."

The sails tilted as Tom looked under the deck. "There *is* something in here," he whispered in excitement. "And guess what? It's a micro-cassette!"

* * *

At that moment, the outside door opened. Shocked by the sudden noise, Tom almost yelled in horror. Rachel swung the flashlight beam to the door, and for a moment they clearly saw Junior. Then he was gone, slamming the door behind him.

Tom and Rachel ran to open the door. "Look," Tom exclaimed. "Junior's escaping from town! He's got his dog team."

"What do you mean, escaping?"

"I think," Tom whispered, "that he's the one who killed Luke Yates."

"How horrible." Rachel looked at the night. "Junior could live on the land a long time. Unlike a snowmobile, his dog team won't run short of fuel. Junior may never return."

Faith was waiting for them beside the display case. The *Gjoa* was back in its place, and the glass door was closed. "I don't know why Junior ran away," Faith said. "That's very strange behavior. We work together cleaning this place."

"Where's the micro?" Tom asked.

Faith fished it from her jeans pocket. "There's no identifying information—it's probably just a blank tape. Anyway, I don't know why it's so important."

Pocketing the micro-cassette, Tom turned to Rachel. "Let's go, okay? Thanks for your help, Faith."

"No problem."

Tom and Rachel walked together through the snow-packed streets. The night was black, with some light from the windows of homes and the occasional passing snowmobile. Saying goodbye to Rachel, Tom went into the hotel. There was a lot to tell Sam.

The building was closed for the night, but the door was unlocked. At the front desk, Tom rang a bell. A few minutes later, Sam came from his living quarters. Looking sad, he glanced at the photograph of Faith.

Tom smiled. "She must be proud of you, eh?"

"I'm forbidden to tell Faith I'm CSIS, Tom. If she knew, the agency's secret northern operations would be vulnerable. My life could even be at risk."

"Could she have learned somehow, maybe from Junior? He's your best friend—does he know you're CSIS?"

Sam shook his head. "Anyway, Tom, I'm glad you're here. I appreciated your report about last night's explosion. I heard that Luke Yates has been murdered. What can you tell me?"

Tom gave Sam a full report on the night's horrifying events. He finished by saying, "Almost anyone could have killed Luke Yates, but unfortunately I think it was Junior—which is really sad."

"Why Junior?"

"Yates was incredibly cruel to Junior and his people. I mean, there's a limit to self-restraint. Junior finally blew his top, and killed Yates. Then he escaped from town—I saw him. He probably wanted that harpoon from the museum, to use for hunting."

Sam sighed. "I hope it's not true, Tom. He's my friend."

Tom remembered Junior putting his arms around Faith, but he didn't say anything.

"But," Sam said, "I'll get CSIS to run a check on Junior. While that's happening, I'll contact your Dad on the secure line. Get some sleep, and let's meet here in the morning."

"Is there anything more from CSIS on Yates?"

Sam nodded. "There's a top RCMP officer arriving on the morning flight. Luke Yates was about to be arrested."

"I wish I'd seen that happen." Unable to contain his excitement any longer, Tom proudly displayed his trophy. "Look, Sam! I've found the missing micro-cassette."

Sam was astonished. His mouth dropped open, and his eyes stared at Tom. "You are *brilliant*!"

Tom beamed.

"But wait a minute." Sam studied the micro. "Nothing's written on it. This could be any cassette."

Tom's eyes were bright with excitement. "It was hidden in a boat in Gjoa. It's *got* to be the missing micro!"

"Let's find out."

Sam quickly removed a tape from the hotel's answering machine, snapped in the tiny cassette and pushed *Play*. They heard nothing, and Tom's heart fell. It was blank.

Then a familiar baritone was heard from the machine. *What is it, Decker?* said the voice. *I'm entertaining important people.*

"Yes!" Tom punched the air. "That's the Prime Minister for sure. We've nailed James Dunbar!"

Grinning, Sam shook Tom's hand. "I'm signing you for CSIS," he joked. "You're an ace sleuth."

Together, they listened to the entire conversation. "The PM is finished," said Sam. "So is U-SAC, I'd say. He's betrayed the people."

"What'll we do now?"

"I'll contact CSIS headquarters immediately. Meet me here at 0700 hours, and I'll tell you what they've decided. In the meantime, not one word to anyone."

"You bet." Tom cracked the air with a huge yawn. "I've got some sleeping to do. Suddenly, I'm exhausted."

* * *

Inside his host's house, Tom peeled off layers of clothing. The Mountie's parka wasn't on its peg, so he was probably still at his office. Tea-Granny was watching the late-night news; the sound was off. Her wrinkled face broke into a warm smile. "*Teagukpin?*"

"Thanks, but no."

A picture of the Prime Minister appeared on the TV screen. "May I?" Tom asked, turning up the volume.

"With only days remaining until the referendum," the news announcer said, "union with the United States seems certain. A poll released today names James Dunbar the most trusted prime minister in the history of Canada. The same poll indicates that the referendum will pass easily. The Prime Minister is greatly admired, and has successfully silenced the critics of U-SAC."

"He won't be admired for much longer," Tom said with great satisfaction.

After the news, Tea-Granny climbed the stairs to bed, but Tom remained on the couch. Flipping through the family scrapbook, he studied the pages about Junior's army career.

Frowning, Tom closed his eyes to think. There was an important connection in the scrapbook, but he couldn't quite get it. He was *so* tired. He began to snore.

In his dreams, Tom drifted through a frozen landscape. Darkness and snow were everywhere. An ancient sailing ship was trapped forever by ice. Skeletons rose up from the frozen land, their skulls thick with frost. A bony finger beckoned Tom to join them. "It's too cold," he moaned. "Leave me alone."

Tom woke from the dream, shivering. He looked around—where was he? Shaking his head, he tried to concentrate. Had the Mountie come home?

At that moment, outside the house, the silent night was shattered by a terrible blast. Tom sat up on the couch, eyes wide. "What was that?" he cried.

Running to the door, he threw it open. At the top of the hill, fire raged. The storage tank had blown apart, filling the night with roaring flames.

13

Fire consumed the night. The walls of houses reflected the flames that leapt into the sky. Tom grabbed a jacket and ran outside. People were everywhere, yelling and pointing at the flames. Tom could see the Mountie near the fire, organizing help.

A Polaris snowmobile roared out from behind the twins' house. The rider called to Tom, and gestured urgently. It was Sam. He stopped the Polaris. "Listen carefully, Tom. Your life is in danger—we must act fast."

"What do you mean?"

"Junior is ZULU-1."

Tom was shocked. He couldn't speak.

"Get your parka, fast. Your Dad wants you in hiding. Junior has killed before, and he could kill again. He may figure you've got the micro-cassette."

"But where is it now?"

"With me." Sam showed Tom the micro, then returned it to his pocket. "At dawn, a planeload of reinforcements is arriving from Yellowknife. You and I can take refuge at the ice-fishing igloos, then return to Gjoa in the morning."

The thunder of the fire filled the night. Black smoke billowed toward the stars. "But why the explosion?" Tom asked.

"To create a diversion. With everyone focused on the fire, it's a lot easier to kill you."

"I'll get my parka."

Dashing inside, Tom grabbed some paper and scribbled FOR INTEREST SAY HI. IN GLOVES LIVE OILY OINKY SLOTHS. After wiggling into the big caribou parka, he pulled on his *kamiks* and ran to join Sam.

Out on the frozen sea, they stopped to look at Gjoa Haven. The houses of the tiny hamlet seemed defenceless, huddled together under the roaring flames. Sam shook his head. "What a disaster for these good people."

"I can't believe Junior would be so cruel."

"I made a big mistake," Sam admitted. "I should have realized my buddy could be ZULU-1. Like you, I wanted to believe the hitman was Luke Yates."

"Why did Junior kill him? Because of his racism?"

"Probably not. Yates was sniffing around Gjoa, looking for signs of a hitman. I think Junior got nervous, and killed to protect his secret." Sam cranked up the engine. "We'd better keep going."

As they travelled on, the wind roared past Tom's face. The night sky was beautiful, but he could only think about Junior. The killer could be anywhere, and probably he was armed.

"Junior may have that gun and the silencer," Tom called to Sam.

"No," the man yelled back. "Luke Yates found it, at the dump. He moved it to another hiding place."

"That's what I saw Yates find? The gun?"

"Yes. It belonged to ZULU-1."

"How do you know?"

"We're almost there," Sam called. "Then I'll tell you."

The ice-fishing igloos appeared ahead. They looked lost and unhappy, alone under the vast sky. When they stopped, Sam raised his face to the wind. "The weather is changing."

"For the better?"

"For the worse. Let's get settled in."

Before long, they had made themselves cosy in the largest igloo. There was warmth from a hissing Coleman stove, and good tea to drink. "I hope there isn't another harpoon around here," Tom said. "I keep hearing Yates scream, when he went down."

Sam didn't reply. He was concentrating on the ham radio, trying to get it fixed. "Remember at the James Bay Inn?" he asked. "When you were carrying that coffee pot? Did you see my reflection, when I left Room 306?"

Cold fear gripped Tom's throat. "What do you mean?"

Sam grinned. "When you listened at the door of Room 306, Tom, I was in there. I was the hitman." He chuckled, pleased with himself. "I'm ZULU-1."

* * *

Sam casually poured himself another mug of tea. "Want some?" he asked. "You're allowed a last meal before dying—any requests? Caribou stew?"

"I . . . You can't . . . "

"You shouldn't have snooped around, Tom. Your death will be a tragedy. I saw your Mom on TV—she's gorgeous. She'll be crying those beautiful eyes out."

"You'd never kill me."

"This is about money, Tom. You must die, to protect my secret."

Cold sweat soaked Tom's body. "You killed for that stupid micro-cassette. *Why?*"

"Blackmail. The Prime Minister doesn't want this tape released to the media. He'll pay me to keep it a secret." Sam chuckled. "We're talking big, big bucks."

"You kill for money? That's so disgusting."

Sam's face went red. "Watch your mouth."

"Why's the money so important? To buy that Rolex you wear? You'd kill someone for a watch?"

Sam laughed. "Don't be stupid, Tom. The cash is for cocaine." He wiped at his eyes. "Coke is so great. It makes me super powerful. Just give me a little snort of my friend and I rule the world. I'm number one—I can do anything."

"Is . . . " Tom could barely speak the words. "Does . . . Faith . . . ?"

"No." Sam shook his head. "Faith is the kindest person I ever met. Her people have become my family. She's a true innocent." He grinned. "Faith says cocaine is like a monkey on my back, and it won't let go. But she doesn't understand what coke gives me. With it, I can do anything. I'll get big money by blackmailing the Prime Minister, and then I'll have my power forever." He gestured at his pack. "I've got some with me. Want to try coke before you die? You might as well."

Tom ignored the suggestion. "Is that how you wrecked your eyes and nose? Snorting cocaine?"

Sam said nothing.

"I bet you framed Junior. Your friend!"

Sam shrugged. "I needed to protect myself. I created several false identities, including Samuel G. White, CSIS agent." Smiling, he poured more tea. "That's good," he said, smacking his lips. "As part of my protection I picked a fall guy, just in case. Junior was perfect."

Sam took another gulp. "Several years ago, Junior was framed for a murder. He spent a long time in prison, then was released when the true criminal confessed." Sam shook his head. "The poor guy, the experience left permanent scars. Junior is terrified of prison bars."

The killer casually studied his fingernails. "I told Junior he was suspected of murdering Luke Yates, and he panicked. As I'd expected, he decided to escape from town. I promised to meet him at the Franklin Cairn with supplies. Instead, I'll shoot Junior with my rifle and get rid of his body. The chief suspect in the Luke Yates harpooning will never return from the wilderness. That file will remain inactive, and life will go on."

"What about *my* death? It will be investigated."

"You're a kid from the south. You wandered away from the igloo and froze to death. It happens, what can I say? The Mountie may smell a rat, but so what?"

"It's stupid to kill me! I've never hurt you."

"You've got to die, Tom. You're the only person alive who knows the truth about this micro. I lied about talking to your father. He doesn't know a thing." Sam grinned. "Too bad, eh? You actually found ZULU-1 and the micro. You're a hero, but your family will never know."

"Why'd you pick the code name ZULU-1?"

"I didn't—it was Decker's choice. You'd better ask him, when you get to Heaven."

Outside the igloo, Tom saw snow blowing past the Polaris. The machine could easily carry him to safety, but how could he get to it? "Can I use the biffy? I'll come right back."

Sam chuckled. "Not a chance."

"I need to know something," Tom said, hoping to somehow reach the Polaris. "Was it you at the storage tank?"

The killer nodded. "When you arrived from Winnipeg, I got worried. You're a bright kid, but too snoopy. At the tank, I was confirming how I'd attach explosives, in case I needed to create a diversion. Which is exactly what happened tonight."

"I nearly fell to my death. You didn't even try to help me!"

Sam shrugged. "It was your choice to be there, Tom. I wasn't about to blow my cover by rescuing you."

"I remember that you and Junior were in the same army demolitions unit. That's where you learned about explosives."

Sam sighed. "This week's been a nightmare. You were after a hitman, and so was Yates. I tell you, I lost some sleep."

"Good!"

Sam ignored Tom's comment. "I shut you down by claiming to be CSIS. That was easy, but Yates remained a problem. I saw him snooping around the hotel, then checking other places in town. I knew he was looking for a hidden gun."

"Why wasn't it with the micro-cassette?"

"That model boat is too small to hide a gun."

"You used Faith's key to open the cabinet?"

Sam nodded. "Anyway, Yates eventually located my weapon at the dump. Smart reasoning, but that moment sealed his fate."

The man's watery eyes stared at Tom. "I lured Yates to the boat, expecting to blow him apart. But he escaped death," Sam said resentfully, "because of you."

Tom glanced longingly at the night, just outside. Escape was so near, yet so far. Then he was startled to see a movement. Desperate for time, Tom searched for another question. "You arrived at the igloos first, and disabled the radio?"

Sam nodded. "Then I waited in hiding. Yates had the pistol and the silencer, so I decided to use the harpoon. I've got a throwing arm—I won all those javelin golds. Knowing the Mountie planned to overnight at the igloos with you, I lured Yates here in search of a hunting tag."

"People will know you killed me."

"I'm a smart guy, Tom." Sam finished his tea. "I figure all the angles. I'll have a sad story to tell, when I return home with your body roped to my *komatik*. How you panicked after the explosion, and figured Junior wanted to kill you. How I reluctantly agreed to help you hide on the land. How you wandered away from the igloo, and perished tragically."

He smiled. "I'm leaving now with the Coleman stove. I'll ride to the Franklin Cairn and shoot Junior, then return here. Your body will resemble a large ice cube."

"The Mountie will get you!"

"He needs proof, Tom. But there isn't any."

A girl's voice was suddenly heard. "Want to bet on that?"

Tom and Sam both looked toward the sound. Someone knelt outside the entrance to the igloo holding a video camera. It was Rachel—and she was taping them.

"It's all on video," she told Sam. "Your whole scheme."

* * *

With a snarl, Sam scrambled out of the igloo. Quickly, Tom pulled on his parka and followed. The wind was harsh, the night black. Snow swirled around the igloos. Rachel dodged among them, trying to escape from Sam.

Racing across the snow, Tom threw himself at Sam's legs. They both went down hard. Rachel pulled Tom to his feet. "Hurry! We must get away."

Running from the igloos, they passed Moses. He was crouched on the snow, taping with his Sony. "My brother backed me up with his own camera," Rachel cried.

Dietmar waited at the controls of the twins' snowmobile. Tom glanced back at Sam—he was getting painfully to his feet. "He can't catch us."

"Not on foot," Rachel said, "but his Polaris is power-ful. Let's keep moving."

Rachel climbed on behind Dietmar, and Tom knelt on the *komatik* with Moses. The boy continued to shoot the scene as they escaped across the snow, feeling every bump.

"I saw you outside the igloo," Tom shouted to Rachel. "I tried to keep Sam talking."

"After the explosion," she called back, "I looked for you, but found only your code." She laughed. "Oily oinky sloths? Where'd you get *that*?"

Tom grinned. "I had to think fast."

"I talked to my brother and Dietmar, and we decided to follow. When we approached the igloos, I saw Sam's Polaris. I sneaked up on the igloo, just in case of trouble."

"Thank goodness for that," Tom replied. "But there's still a problem. Sam's got the micro-cassette." He looked at the distant igloos. "He's not chasing us. Let's see what happens."

Dietmar stopped the machine. The wind drove hard pellets of snow across the ridged landscape, stinging Tom's face like broken glass. Moses raised powerful binoculars to his eyes. "He's going northwest on the Polaris."

"Maybe he's heading for the Franklin Cairn," Tom said. "He wants to kill Junior."

"We've got to help Junior," Moses exclaimed. "Let's follow Sam at a distance. Keep the headlight out, Dietmar."

Staying well back, they followed the bouncing light on Sam's snowmobile across the frozen sea. Then, without warning, they were surrounded by snow. Lifted by the wind, it rose into their faces and swirled against their bodies. It was everywhere, swarming like white bees, sticking to the fur of Tom's parka, clogging his vision.

"Stop the machine," Moses yelled. "This is a ground blizzard! We must make an igloo, fast."

Fumbling under the snow-coated caribou skins on the *komatik*, Moses pulled out some large *panas*. He passed a knife to Rachel, and they began hacking out snow blocks. Their backs were to the wind, their parkas white with the coarse grains.

Working together, Tom and Dietmar lifted the blocks into place. Tom was shaking with the cold; he had to force his muscles to keep working. He felt bare to the wind, his parka defeated by its power. The snow hissed past, forming drifts that immediately blew into new shapes. The wind was a steady roar, high above.

With the last block in place, Rachel and Moses sliced out an entrance. Inside the igloo Tom and Dietmar helped block the entrance with snow, then spread out caribou robes from the *komatik*. Rachel lit candles, and the air began to warm.

"Good work, everyone," Moses said.

Tom wriggled his toes and banged his hands together, restoring the circulation. "Sam's out there somewhere. He's got a rifle."

"Sam will need more than a gun in this blizzard," Moses replied. "He needs a really good prayer."

"I'm hungry," Dietmar said. "There's a Coleman on the *komatik*. I'll get it, and some food." Punching a hole in the snow that blocked the entrance, he crawled out of the igloo and was lost in the blizzard.

"I hope he'll be okay," Rachel said.

Moses smiled fondly at his sister. "Dietmar will be fine."

The white shape of Dietmar wriggled into the igloo. He blocked the entrance with snow, then got the stove working. Before long they were ferociously devouring caribou strips and huge portions of Mr. Noodles. "I've never been so hungry," Tom said. "Is there more?"

Dietmar nodded. "Sure, I'll just . . ."

At that moment, a fist smashed through the snow blocking the entrance. As everyone yelled in shock, a man struggled into the igloo.

"It's Junior," Tom yelled. "Look out—he's got a harpoon!"

14

The friends cowered back, terrified by the sight of the weapon. Junior stared at them. "You guys? I thought I'd found Sam."

"Don't kill us," Dietmar cried.

"No chance of that," Junior laughed.

"But why are you here?" Tom asked.

"Just what I was about to ask you." He smiled. "Listen, I am so hungry."

"How about some Mr. Noodles?"

"Sounds good. But first I'll settle my dog team." After some time, Junior returned inside and blocked up the entrance with snow. Brushing back his parka hood, he made himself comfortable on a caribou skin. Outside, the huskies howled unhappily. "Sam said to meet at the Franklin Cairn, but he didn't show up. I was so nervous, back in Gjoa, that I was only half listening. I thought maybe I'd got the meeting place wrong, and we were supposed to meet at the ice-fishing site. I was travelling there when the blizzard struck. I tried to keep going, thinking I could reach the igloos. Then I found this one, and figured Sam was inside."

"Is that why you've got that harpoon?" Tom asked. "For self-protection?"

Junior nodded. "I've always wondered about Sam's mysterious trips south, and his expensive collection of laser discs. Hotel clerks don't make big money. I wasn't sure I trusted Sam, even though Faith did. But love is blind, right?"

"Not necessarily," Dietmar said, glancing at Rachel. She smiled shyly.

"Faith knew about Sam's addiction to coke," Junior said. "She turned to me for advice. I tried to help, but Sam was really hooked. Getting started was easy for him, but stopping was impossible."

"Sam was planning to kill you," Tom said. He told Junior about his own narrow escape from the killer. "Rachel and Moses have the proof of Sam's guilt on their video cameras."

Junior finished his Mr. Noodles, drank some tea, and then said, "I'm going to check my dogs. I won't be long."

After he'd left the igloo, Tom said, "I wonder what's happened to Sam? Could he build an igloo, by himself?"

"Possibly," Moses replied. "But he'd have trouble, working alone in this blizzard." He chewed thoughtfully on a caribou strip. "Sam will try to reach Gjoa on the Polaris."

"Unless he's doubled back," Rachel said. "He could have returned to the ice-fishing igloos for shelter."

"If Junior found this igloo," Tom said, "Sam could, too."

Dietmar's face turned pale. "Surely you're joking, Austen."

"Franklin's men died here. Anything's possible in this wilderness."

Moses smiled. "It's not wilderness to Rachel and me. It's our home."

Junior crawled into the igloo. "The dogs don't like this blizzard. But they're burrowed down. They'll be okay."

"I saw you at the museum," Tom said. "Were you after the harpoon?"

Junior nodded. "When I saw you, I got scared and took off fast. I already had one harpoon, but I wanted another. I figured I'd be hunting on the land a long time."

"Was it horrible in prison? It looks bad in movies."

For a moment, Junior closed his eyes. "It was the worst possible experience. But my spirit wouldn't die. I knew I was innocent, and I was determined to survive."

The teens listened quietly.

"When the real criminal confessed, I was released to freedom." Junior's voice shook with emotion. "I returned to Nunavut, to my people, but I have never forgotten that prison."

For many hours, the blizzard howled past outside. Tom slept poorly, his nightmares filled with weapons of death. Whenever he opened his eyes, the harpoon was close by in Junior's hand.

Eventually, the constant roaring stopped. The wind was gone. After a meal, they kicked their way outside. Drifts of snow were everywhere; the sky was gray. Nothing could be seen.

"Where's our Ski-Doo?" Dietmar said.

"Buried," Junior replied.

"What about the poor huskies?" Tom said. "I don't see them!"

Junior dug into the snow. "The dogs are used to this weather. They can breathe fine, even buried under snow." The black eyes and big muzzle of a husky appeared. Standing up from his little cave, the dog pressed its face against Junior, greeting him. Its tail wagged happily.

Junior dug out the remaining dogs. Standing up, they shook the snow from their bodies and yapped eagerly for food. Meanwhile, the teens had begun digging out the Ski-Doo and its *komatik*. They were still sweating from the task when everything was ready for the journey home.

A buzzing was heard in the misty distance. It grew louder, and Tom wondered if Sam was approaching on the Polaris. But it was the Mountie, who waved as he pulled up on his SnowCat.

"I've found you! We've been so worried." He stepped off the machine. "Several search parties are out."

Tom and the others described the night's events. When they'd finished, the Mountie smiled at his son. "Last night, Sam told me you'd confessed to killing Luke Yates. I didn't believe it was true."

"Thank you," Junior said quietly. He turned to the others. "Who's travelling with me to Gjoa? Tom Austen?"

"For sure!"

After Tom found a space on the *komatik*, Junior cracked a huge whip above the dogs. They took off running, yapping with excitement. Each was on a separate trace, spread out like a fan. "They love running," Junior called back to Tom. "*Hey—ho*," he cried to the dogs. "*Hey—ho!*"

Holding tight, feeling each drift they crossed, Tom looked at Dietmar and Moses on the nearby *komatik* being towed by Rachel on the Ski-Doo. Above their heads, a snowy owl glided past, then beat its short wings and was gone. The land was white and the sky was gray; Tom was amazed that Junior could travel with such confidence in a landscape without any signposts to guide the way.

Junior pointed toward a distant, ivory-coloured shape. Puzzled, Tom squinted his eyes. The figure was moving across the landscape, running on powerful legs. "It's a polar bear," he cried. "I can't believe my eyes!"

As though hearing Tom's voice, the polar bear paused. Its big head turned in their direction. Through his binoculars, Tom saw ferocious teeth in the bear's blue-black mouth. It snuffled the wind, then bounded away.

"I'm glad you've seen *nanook*," Junior said. "Those bears move fast, up to 25 miles per hour when they're chasing prey."

Tom was amazed at his good fortune in seeing the polar bear. If only he hadn't lost control of the micro-cassette, life would have been perfect.

Again, Junior pointed at a distant shape. Wishing he'd brought his camera, Tom waited for a beautiful bear to bound gracefully across the frozen barrens. But as they approached the shape, it remained motionless—a white shadow on the white land.

"What is it?" Rachel called, as Junior stopped his dog team. Everyone stood up, knocking snow from their caribou parkas. They stared at the drift-covered mound, wondering what it could be.

Junior brushed away snow, and they saw black metal. Then the name *Polaris* became visible. Next they saw Sam's face. He lay beside his snowmobile, frozen to death.

* * *

"He tried to outrun the blizzard," Junior commented.

Searching in Sam's pockets, the Mountie found the micro-cassette. "The cocaine made him take foolish chances."

"Did you know he was using that stuff?" Tom asked.

"No," the Mountie replied. "I guess Sam was clever at hiding his secret."

"I knew about it," Junior said, "because Faith asked for my help in getting Sam off cocaine. I talked to him about my experiences with coke, but it didn't help."

Dietmar looked at Junior. "You've done cocaine?"

"When I went down south a few years ago, people told me cocaine would make me feel like a god, in total control of everything and everyone, so I did some. It's true, you do think you're the coolest person alive—until you come down again. Then you just feel rotten."

Tom glanced at the Mountie. He was listening attentively to his son.

"When I did coke," Junior said, "I felt like a big success story, but the feeling lasted only a short time. The exhilaration was followed by this dead, flat emptiness. That's why it's addictive—you ache to feel the power again."

Junior looked at Sam's dead face. "Finally, I realized that cocaine is for losers. There's no good way forward, it's just a downward spiral. I don't judge others for what they do, but I made a personal choice to give up coke. I told this to Sam, but he wouldn't listen. When he died, he was probably high on cocaine, in the middle of a nightmare, but still thinking he was a god."

* * *

Journeying home on the *komatik*, Tom did his best to ignore Sam's frozen body at his side. Smoke was rising into the pale sky as they approached Gjoa Haven; the ruins of the storage tank still smouldered.

A giant plane descended loudly into the airport. "What's with the army transport?" Tom asked.

"The Armed Forces got the fire under control," the Mountie explained. "Those tankers are bringing in fuel. The government is providing emergency supplies until the storage tank can be rebuilt."

"Was anyone hurt in the explosion?"

"Happily, no."

"Then things are turning out okay," Tom said, "and there's more excitement to come. Just wait until that micro-cassette is public knowledge."

* * *

Late the next day, Tom and Tea-Granny were watching television together. As usual, the house was crowded with visiting relatives. On the screen, a news announcer suddenly appeared.

"I have a bulletin," she said. Looking excited, she quickly put a radio receiver into her ear. Somewhere off camera, a voice yelled, *This is political dynamite!*

Ignoring this interruption, the announcer breathlessly said, "There's been a major breakthrough in the investigations into the murders of Blake Decker and Professor Dunbar. We believe the Prime Minister may be involved."

She listened to the radio receiver.

"We're going live to Winnipeg, where the police have begun a press conference."

Tom's father was seen, surrounded by reporters. Dozens of microphones were in his face. "A warrant has been issued for the arrest of Prime Minister James Dunbar," said Inspector Austen. "He will be charged in connection with his father's death."

The reporters all shouted questions. The loudest was, "Can you prove it?"

Inspector Austen held up a micro-cassette. "Thanks to some courageous people up north, proof now exists. The Prime Minister must answer for his actions."

The announcer appeared on camera. "We take you live to Ottawa. Carys Evans is standing by."

The network's chief political correspondent appeared. Behind her were the Parliament Buildings, spotlit as evening came to the nation's capital. The Peace Tower was framed by sunset colours.

"This is an amazing story," Carys Evans said. "I've

just learned the Prime Minister has resigned. He'll be leaving the Parliament Buildings any minute now."

Television lights glared on a waiting police car. It was surrounded by hordes of reporters, all shouting questions as James Dunbar was rushed to the vehicle.

"He looks scared," Tom said.

As the car struggled away from the reporters, Carys Evans said, "I've never seen anything like this! Prime Minister Dunbar has fallen, the victim of arrogance, the victim of overweening pride."

The Mountie shook hands with Tom. "You have accomplished a great deal, Tom. Perhaps you have even changed history."

* * *

The next day, Tom was packing for the trip to Winnipeg. He was feeling sad; he would really miss his new friends.

Downstairs, Tea-Granny waited with a gift for Tom. It was a ring, carved from ivory, showing a snowy owl with its wings spread wide. "Thank you," Tom said, hugging her frail body. Tears were streaming down her face, and he was also crying. "Thank you!"

Outside, Tom and the Mountie roped his gear to the *komatik*. "You must return, Tom," the man said quietly. "You have become part of us."

Tom nodded, a lump in his throat. "I'll be back."

As they roared through town, he looked at the houses and thought about the good times he had enjoyed in Gjoa Haven. "I know what keeps this place warm," he called to the Mountie. "The people."

Lots of snowmobiles were parked outside the airport terminal. The tiny departure lounge was jammed. Rachel was crying as she hugged Dietmar goodbye. There were tears on many faces.

"Guess what, Austen?" Dietmar grinned. "Mom phoned last night. If I want to return here when I've finished school, she'll pay for the plane fare. She's glad I'm so happy."

"That's wonderful news."

Moses put his arm around Dietmar. "This is my brother. He is an Inuk now."

Dietmar beamed with pride.

Tom saw Faith enter the building, and went to say goodbye. "I'm sorry you lost your boyfriend," he said.

"Thank you," Faith replied, smiling sadly. "But I lost Sam long ago. The cocaine drained away his life, and then it killed him."

The Mountie beckoned to Tom, and they went outside together. The air was crisp and clear. Sunshine sparkled on the snow. The Mountie looked at the scene for a moment, then spoke.

"In our language, Tom, there is no word for goodbye. We are always a part of those we know and love. Your spirit has joined with all of ours." He shook Tom's hand. "Until we meet again."

"Thank you," Tom said, gripping the Mountie's hand. "I'm very proud to know you."

* * *

A week later, Tom was back at the Winnipeg Convention Centre. Instead of slaving over dirty pots, he was on stage. With him were Dietmar and the twins, who'd come south for the occasion. The friends were smiling and waving as a huge crowd cheered and whistled.

U-SAC was dead, and Canada would not be joining the United States. The referendum had been defeated by voters outraged at James Dunbar's betrayal of their trust. The capacity crowd at the convention centre had just seen the referendum result announced on the giant television screens, and they were applauding the young heroes, whose recovery of the micro-cassette had led to the end of the corrupt Prime Minister and his sinister plans.

As news cameras lit their faces, Dietmar grinned at Tom. "So this is fame. I could get used to it."

* * *

When the fantastic evening ended, Tom drove home with his family. Everyone was in a good mood—especially his Dad. Liz was humming a tune as their car approached River Heights. "I can't wait to phone Zoltan, and tell him about tonight."

"Will you go dancing on the weekend?" Tom asked.

"I doubt it! Zoltan can't dance."

"I know," Tom said. "He told me about his two left feet, but I'd forgotten when Sam said you'd been out dancing together. I should have realized he was lying about phoning my family."

"How'd he know Zoltan's name?"

"He heard me mention it at the Amundsen Hotel."

Liz turned to her mother. "Were the rumours true about CanSell?"

Passing lights shone on Mrs. Austen's face. "Yes," she replied. "James Dunbar was secretly involved with the scheme. Now that U-SAC is defeated, CanSell hasn't a chance. Our rivers are safe."

Mr. Austen glanced at her. "The world needs political leaders like you, sweetheart. People who want to help others. You're so compassionate, you'd make a wonderful Prime Minister."

Liz and Tom beamed at her. "That's a great idea," Tom said. "Go for it, Mom."

When Mrs. Austen didn't reply, Liz smiled. "We'll convince you, Mom. Just wait and see."

* * *

Arriving home, Tom climbed the stairs to his attic office. On the door, a faded sign warned KEEP OUT! THIS MEANS YOU. A slip of paper remained wedged in the door frame, so there'd been no intruders.

The ceiling seemed lower these days. Tom studied the faces of Canada's Most Wanted Criminals, then sat at his trusty computer. Opening a file, he began a letter to his cousin Duncan in Newfoundland.

I can't wait to tell you, he wrote, *about what happened in the Arctic. I think this story should be called THE INUK MOUNTIE ADVENTURE, in honour of the people I met up there. Anyway, it all began when I got this terrible job at the convention centre . . .*